FOOTSTEPS IN TIME

ARCHANA PATHAK

Leadstart
INKSTATE

ISBN 978-93-90463-75-6
Copyright © Archana Pathak, 2020

First published in India 2020 by Inkstate Books
An imprint of Leadstart Publishing Pvt Ltd

Sales Office:
Unit No.25/26, Building No.A/1,
Near Wadala RTO,
Wadala (East), Mumbai – 400037 India
Phone: +91 969933000
Email: info@leadstartcorp.com
www.leadstartcorp.com

Disclaimer: The views expressed in this book are those of the Author and do not pertain to be held by the Publisher.

Editor: Mannat Lumba
Cover: Swapnil Behere
Layouts: Victor Patali

To my parents,

Krishna and Shanti,
For raising me to believe in myself.

About the Author

Archana Pathak is based in Pune. She has done her Master's in English Literature and has taught English to senior classes, for almost a decade and a half.

She is a voracious reader and has read a large number of books by authors of various genre, but her preferred genre is mystery fiction. Her favourite authors are Victoria Holt, Daphne du Maurier, Dorothy Eden, Phyllis A. Whitney, Mary Stewart and present day authors like Kate Morton, Lucinda Riley, Jojo Moyes and so on. She is an ardent traveller and has a keen ear for music.

She has always been passionate about writing. She has been writing blogs on and off. She writes short stories on her Instagram handle a_tale_so_arcane. 'Footsteps in Time' is her debut novel. She is already working on her second novel and aims to be a full time writer.

Name - Archana Pathak

E mail Id – pathakarchana15@gmail.com

- awordtoadd.blogspot.in, : a_tale_so_arcane.

ACKNOWLEDGEMENTS

Special thanks,

To my husband for making this book possible,
To my children for their faith in me.

CONTENTS

"What's the earth
With all its art, verse, music worth –
Compared with love, found, gained, and kept?"

- Robert Browning

PROLOGUE

The moon was in its full glory. Everything looked ethereal in its silvery glow. The cool breeze picked a sweet scent from *raat ki rani* and sprinkled it over the mango and neem trees. The trees swayed as if inhaling the heady and intoxicating perfume. It was not midnight yet, but the world seemed to be submerged in deep slumber. It looked as if the moon had cast a spell over the landscape, adding a certain mystique to the already mysterious night.

And then, the tinkling sound of an anklet broke the quiet like a pebble breaking the ripples of a tranquil pond. It was soft and sweet and musical, penetrating softly with its lilting rhythm. The bearer of the sound slowed her pace and walked softly, as if trying to float in the air. Clearly, she did not want to break the quiet. Her bangles jingled as she tried to wrap her shawl tightly around her shoulders. She tried to walk as fast as she could, putting her feet softly on the path. The dirt road she was walking on was familiar to her, as she had travelled it many times. The landscape that looked so familiar in the daylight looked different and impersonal at this late hour. It was like an acquaintance that appeared known at times and vaguely familiar at others.

Another few yards and she would reach her destination. Every few steps she would turn her head and look over her shoulders. She heaved a sigh of relief when she heard the light splash of water. She quickened her pace. Now she was almost there. As she reached the banks of the river, she walked a few more steps and started climbing the marble stairs. A gust of breeze made her shawl fall off her shoulders and her long and dark hair came undone. She looked ethereal; not belonging to this world.

It was a beautiful garden lined with mango, neem and gulmohar trees. The flower beds were laden with roses and jasmine, and the *raat ki rani* bushes were in full bloom. The place did justice to its name; '*Phulwari*'. She moved with confidence, as if she knew the place well. She stood when she reached, her gaze wandering. A look of uncertainty mixed with annoyance reflected on her stunning face. Her eyes started brimming. Her chest was heaving and her perfect breasts moved up and down with every breath. She stood there for some time, and as she turned to probably go back, two strong arms held her.

She buried her head in his chest, as relief and joy washed over her. A few moments passed then she pushed him away.

'Why were you not here?' she hissed.

'I was very much here. I just wanted to look at you as you climbed the stairs. You looked like an *apsara* descended from the heavens,' he said and pulled her in his arms. 'You are more beautiful than ever,' he murmured.

This time she stayed in his arms inhaling his manly scent. He kissed her forehead, her cheeks and then he started kissing her lips. She responded passionately, clinging to him. He stopped, took her hand, and they moved towards a hut that was built to house gardening tools, some tin watering cans and a temporary shelter for the gardener to take refuge in, during the rains or any such inclement weather.

But today it did not look as ram-shackled as it generally did. The floor was swept clean. There was a clean sheet spread over the ground. Some candles were flickering in the corner, and the quivering and soft glow of the flames made the place look a little romantic.

'Someone has been busy,' she said, looking at him with utmost affection.

'I had to pass time somehow waiting for you. So I cleaned up a bit.'

'How long did you wait?'

'Say, about an hour.'

'How did you come? What did you tell the boatman?'

'There is no boatman. I rowed the boat myself.'

'What? You do know it's quite a distance.' Her expression was troubled.

'I have come rowing and I will go the same way. Now if you stop interrogating me, there is so much I want to talk about. And yes, before you ask any more questions, everyone back home thinks that I have gone for some fresh village air, and to accompany my friend on his hunting trip.'

'And what does your friend think?' she asked softly.

'He knows, obviously,' he said in a calm voice.

She stared ahead.

He took her hand in his hands and said, 'he would not breathe a word. I can trust him with my life. I would not have managed to come here, had it not been for him. Have faith in me. These few hours are all we have got. You can't even imagine how long I've waited for this opportunity. I had decided not to tell you, but just so you know how desperately I want to be with you, I have come despite the fact that father is unwell but thankfully he is recovering now. When my friend suggested that I should spend couple of days with him, before I left for England, father insisted on sending me. So I owe this opportunity to my father and my friend Deepak. I am leaving tomorrow morning.'

There was a solemn look on his face and she thought she saw a tear glimmering. She threw her arms around him.

'I don't care if the world comes to know. I love you with all my heart and that's what matters. I will love you till the time I breathe my last.' Her voice was quivering.

They were kissing again and clinging to each other, as if they would melt and become one.

She disengaged herself and sat down on the sheet, and when he sat next to her, she took his face in her hands. Her heart filled with such love looking at his beautiful face that she thought it would burst. And then she started crying clinging to him. Her body shook with sobs.

'Why, my darling? What's wrong? Please tell me. I can't bear to see you like this.' He was kissing her tear-streaked face.

She stayed in his arms for some time till the storm passed.

'I want a life with you. I can never be anyone else's but yours,' she said, her head resting on his shoulder.

She did not see his eyes brimming and two tears rolling off his cheek. He wiped them quickly before she could see them. He was not ashamed of crying in front of her, but he did not want to make her weak. He knew they both needed a lot of courage for the paths life had chosen for them.

He took her in his arms and lay her down gently on the sheet. He kissed her forehead, her eyes, and traced the outline of her swan-like neck with his soft lips, and then as he looked at her face, he played with the stray locks on her face. She started unbuttoning his *kurta*. He looked at her questioningly.

'What kind of a man are you?' she asked with a mischievous glint in her eyes. 'A woman is lying in your arms and you are just staring at her.'

He caught her hand.

'It wouldn't be right. You know I have no right over you,' he said.

'But I have a right over you and a right over myself. I have wanted nothing but to be yours, body and soul, from the day I first saw you. My life begins with you and ends with you. Why shouldn't I be given the choice of what I want to do with my body and soul? This is my body, my existence. I am going to bear the joy and sufferings that come with this mortal form, no one else is going to share it, so why shouldn't I decide what I want to do with myself? I am the master of my own body and soul; I will act according to my will.'

'But...,' he murmured.

'Shhhh...' she hushed him and took his hand, keeping it over her heaving chest.

'There is nothing in this world that I want more than to drown myself in your beauty, but I want you to know that I will always love you, you alone, and on one else. I might not see you for years but my heart will beat only for you. And if there is another life, another birth, I will find you and love you again.'

She was oblivious of the tears that were rolling down her cheeks. She was kissing him with all the fervour her body could allow. Time stood still. They were in another world, another dimension. The joy she felt surrendering herself to him was indescribable. She revelled in his love, relished every touch of his body and thanked the universe again and again for bringing them together.

They walked to the bank holding hands. The moon had risen very high and its light had dimmed. Soon, it would be dawn. The wind had picked up pace, as if to bid farewell to the moon. The river looked inky and silent. They reached the spot where the boat was anchored. She embraced him with the intensity of a woman possessed. She was crying uncontrollably. He held her tightly in his arms, tears rolling down.

'Don't go! Please don't go! I cannot live without you!' she beseeched.

He kissed her forehead and said, 'I have to go, darling. We both have to go. We have to think of the others. Just remember my love for you will increase, every passing day. I consider myself extremely lucky to have found you, to have found such happiness. The moments I have spent with you will last me a lifetime.'

'Promise me you will meet me again. I will only go if you promise to meet me again.'

There was the same determination in her eyes he knew so well. He knew she meant every word of it. And suddenly it became easier for him. He felt as if he had found the will to live again. He would come and meet her, whatever it took. He was sacrificing enough for the sake of others. He would not sacrifice the little happiness they both would get by meeting again.

He looked into her eyes and said, 'I will come and we will meet again. That's a promise, sweetheart.'

The sky had started turning red in the horizon. Somewhere, a bird tweeted.

He disengaged himself gently from her. They both knew it was dangerous to stay any longer. Soon, people would start coming from the village for their morning rituals.

He untied the rope from the iron rod and pushed the boat into the water. He sat on it, took the oars and started rowing backwards, looking at her. The pain in his heart grew with every inch the boat moved away from her. He kept looking at her. He allowed his tears to flow. She looked like a vision standing at the bank. Her beautiful face smeared with tears, started blurring. She looked like a nymph who had just emerged from somewhere. With her long hair falling below her hips, her sensuous figure looked like an artist's sketch.

He could not hear her but he knew she was saying, 'Please don't go' again and again.

She was shouting, 'Don't go please! I can't live without you!' The pain in her chest was unbearable.

Someone else was also there, calling someone. But she didn't care. She kept calling his name.

Someone was dragging her.

There were voices.

She felt numb. Her body was wet and she felt cold.

'Lift her gently.'

'I should have given him my shawl. It's cold,' she was murmuring.

'Wrap two three blankets around her... gently, gently.'

She felt being lifted and then drifted into the darkness.

CHAPTER 1

PRESENT DAY

I looked out of the tall French windows in the receding sunlight, as dark clouds started gathering from the north east. The wind had already picked up and the trees were swaying wildly, as if possessed by a great energy. I could see the pedestrians quickening their steps to reach the safety of their transport or homes, before the storm struck. I turned back from the window and pressed the buzzer. Cathy, my assistant–cum-secretary was at the door.

'Cathy! Why don't you leave before the storm comes? It looks menacing.'

'What about you Dr Chat? We are finished for the day.'

'I wanted to go through the case files for today's patients before I leave. But I think I will carry them home.'

'That sounds like a good idea. Let me keep your stuff in the car.'

'You know that's not necessary. I can keep the stuff in the car myself. Don't spoil me,' I said with a hint of affection in my fake rebuke.

'You can! Can't you?' She flashed her charming smile.

She took my leather case and a thick folder of notes that I'd made during the sessions today. She stopped at the door, remembering something.

'I forgot to mention, there was a letter for you from India in the post today. I will just get it for you.' She exited with that.

I knew where the letter came from. My mother still believed in letters and preferred them to phone calls. I could picture her sitting in her armchair, dictating the contents to Kamla, who would sit down on the floor and write slowly. My mother would ask her to repeat the lines she had spoken aloud and Kamla would do that dutifully. The letter would contain a discourse of the afflictions of old age, though she was still fit and healthy at seventy-two, gave people sound advice and helped them in any way she could. And then, again, how worried she was about me. She would close her eyes happily when I found a life partner. Though she was extremely proud of me and my profession, she wanted me to have marital happiness. 'A woman is not complete without a man, *Bitia*', was the constant advice in one form or the other.

I had tried many a time to bring her to England but had failed every time.

'I will not drink the water of a foreign country in my lifetime,' she had told me time and again. And her one and only complaint was of my singlehood. She had agonised at the fact that I had had a perfect marriage, but had thrown it away for some small misunderstanding. It had hurt me in the beginning that my own mother held me responsible for my failed marriage. But I got over it as time went by. It was really difficult to make her see that one did not have to pay a price for being a woman, that a woman was also made of flesh and blood and had an equal right to happiness. But then, she was from a different era where a woman made lots of compromises and sacrifices. What she did not understand, that one did not balk at the idea of compromising, as marriage was not easy, but the sacrifices and compromises worked when there was mutual love. There was no point trying to make a marriage work when there was no love. She had not understood why I would do something like this, because girls from the decent families did not behave in this fashion. Divorces were not so common in our community at the time Ashok and I decided to part ways. She had constantly blamed my education for this despicable act of mine. The fact that Ashok had kept in touch with her and made a phone call to ask about her health every now and then, had made her feel more antagonised towards me. She simply could not fathom why I would ever let go a thorough gentleman like Ashok, and live a lonely life devoid of any pleasures that marriage brought.

The fact that nothing very drastic had happened between Ashok and I, made things even more difficult to explain. There was no such reason that was generally common between couples who sought divorce. There were no affairs, fights or any such compelling circumstances that made us part ways. It was just that we found that what had looked like love in the beginning was just mild attraction. It was the fondness for each other that had brought us together. It was a folly of young hearts. We had not really given much thought to what we had between us. We were both young, good looking, devoted to our dreams, and everyone thought that it was more than enough for two people to fall in love. In fact, it was more of our friends who were responsible for making us think that we were ideally suited for each other. Their constant cajoling and admiration of us made us believe that we were made for each other.

Ashok was not a romantic person. He was barely aware of his good looks. For him it was the beauty of the mind that mattered. He saw me in the same light. Whereas my good looks were a source of envy and admiration for women and men alike, Ashok hardly seemed to notice it. I did not attach too much importance to it. There were too many people reminding me how beautiful I was. But his indifference towards everything started getting to me. I understood his devotion to his career, I myself was concentrating on mine. But life for me was a little more than that. I wanted to indulge in the small pleasures of life, like any other young girl who thought she had found her prince charming. I wanted to seek comfort in the small things, like sitting in bed together a little longer and sharing a cup of tea while talking about just anything. Or taking a walk or escaping to some place away from the hustle bustle of our busy lives for a couple of days, just enjoying each other's company.

But Ashok laughed at my suggestions and made me feel like a hopeless romantic. What he did not realise, that his banal practicality was smothering the very spark of our relationship. His pragmatic approach to life was extinguishing the flames of our already tepid love. We both had come to realise that we had very little in common except our ambitions. Our friends advised us to work a little harder on our marriage. As far as they were concerned, we were a star couple right from our medical college days.

Ashok was a year senior and part of the gang that had come to rag the newcomers. But he was silent during the process, and looked a little disconnected. In the end it was he who had put a stop to the whole process, and we fled to our respective classrooms. I had bumped into him a couple of weeks later, and he casually asked whether any senior had troubled me. That was the beginning of our friendship. I had already come to know that besides possessing good looks, he was a star student and the heartthrob of all the girls in the campus of the King George Medical College. But I had also come to know that though he was socially affable, he was totally devoted to his studies. I was surprised to know that despite so many girls vying for his attention, he mostly kept to himself, and was even more surprised when he made excuses to meet me. Soon I earned the title of 'the enchantress' and we became a couple. When Ashok left for England to pursue his PhD in Genetics, I missed him, but then I was happy for him. We both kept in touch constantly and when he returned after two years for a short period and proposed, it only looked like the right thing to do. I had to stay back for a year to complete my MD, so we got engaged and tied the knot after a year. I moved to England with him and applied for a PhD in the Science of Behavioural Studies. The initial months as a newly married couple were pleasant, if not blissful, though the picture that I had created in my mind of our newly married life was different than reality. I had some time before my course started, but Ashok was not able to take out time from his busy schedule. He was now working as a research scientist and also writing a paper on Genealogy.

We both did not want to start a family for some time, so going our separate ways became easier. I used to often wonder how things would have turned out, had both of us not been so ambitious, and added to the family. I still think of the same when I see a family buying groceries at the supermarket or taking a stroll in the park.

They seem to be happy enough with their lives, doing the predictable things a family does. In the initial years, I would feel a flicker of remorse seeing the 'joie de vivre' illuminating their faces.

But then, as some time passed, I became sanguine that it was not love that I had felt for him. Time went by and I immersed myself in my work. I came to realise that though my vocation gave me all the contentment I needed, yet there were times when I felt that I was waiting for the right man to come along, and this time I wanted to experience love in its full intensity. I guess our separation caused more grief to our friends than it did to us. But then, we'd both discussed and decided that we were better suited as friends than a married couple. And this time we were very right. We went on to become good friends. We had the same set of friends, and met each other as and when our busy schedules allowed us.

After our separation, I met some men who wanted to take things seriously, but none of them could match the image I had in my mind. I knew that I would never find this dream man of mine, yet I was waiting for someone like him. So I found the whole dating thing hopeless as I was not going to settle for anyone who didn't fit that picture. Meanwhile, my work was the most important thing, and I was ready to live my life dedicated to my profession.

I thought of the letter as I parked my car in the garage. I did not open it till after I had a hot shower and made myself a cup of ginger tea. There were some habits I could not let go of, even after staying in England for almost fifteen years. Making myself ginger tea was one of those. I sat down on the couch in the warm and cheery glow of the tall lamps and opened the letter. Outside, the storm was in its full fury, and the rain was pattering on the shutters of the windows.

I opened the letter and saw Kamla's neat writing become the voice of my mother. I expected the usual tit bits of news of the neighbours. But as I started reading I was surprised to learn that this letter was not a usual one, but had a subject that made me feel a little unsettled. My mother wanted to go to her village and sell the ancestral house. She had finally decided to sell all the land and the house as she knew that it would be of no use to me after her. *Mukhia Chacha* had been working on it for some time and he had a buyer for the house and the land. Though it would be difficult for her to sever ties with the place that held so many memories for her, but it had to be done sooner or later. So, in order to carry out the task, she would have to go to the village and stay there till the time the formalities were done. Kamla and Urmila *Chachi*, Kamla's mother, would accompany her. And also, she would get a chance to meet all those people she hadn't met for a long time. Though, she had talked about selling the house every now and then, she had never actually considered it seriously. There was a sense of finality in the tone of the letter that made me think about it. At the end of the letter there were the usual instructions for me to not neglect my health and not to work too hard etc. I started folding the letter when I saw a PS on the other side of the paper.

'Please come to India if you can manage, Didi. It would be good for Dadi (as Kamla addressed my mother affectionately). There is nothing to get alarmed but ever since she has decided to go to the village to sell the house, she has been a bit restless and at times she gets up in the night scared. I thought I must tell you about this though Dadi and Amma did not want me to mention it to you, because they think we should not bother you with such small issues. But personally I feel that you need to be with her, and who can understand the mind better than you?

That was all. I got worried. It was very unlike Kamla to write a 'PS' at the back of the letter. Clearly, my mother did not know about this message. I looked at my watch. It was past midnight in India. I decided to call home first thing in the morning.

We had shifted to Lucknow when I turned three and had not gone to the village after that. I had very few relatives from my father's side. My mother was an only child; therefore she didn't have any blood relatives of her own, as her mother had also been an only child. My mother's father had a reasonably large piece of land and it made good income. He had also renovated his ancestral house and made it bigger. It was passed down to my mother after his demise. My father had a sizable chunk of land and a big house in Lalgarh, and he had bought a nice and spacious house in Lucknow later and moved us to Lucknow when I was three years old. He was a very progressive and intelligent man, and though he could only study till intermediate, he wanted me to gain higher education, and hence Lucknow became our home.

Though my father went to the village periodically as to see to the lands, as well as the ancestral house, my mother never accompanied him. *Mukhia Chacha* and the neighbours took care of the house, and the land was given on contract. Distant relatives or neighbours often came to Lucknow for some work or to seek some medical help, and my parents hosted them and looked after them. But we never went to our ancestral house as a family. In fact, once I had asked mother if we could go to the village with some of my friends from college, as I had heard it was a pretty place, she had flatly refused. I did not insist as it was just a random idea. After that I'd got busy with my life and the village became a speck in the bigger spectrum of things, and gradually dwindled from memory. The only people from the village who I remembered well and fondly were Chandu *Kaka* and *Kaki* and their daughter Dulari. The reason behind it was that they came to Lucknow regularly, and deeply cared for my parents. And then later, Dulari got married and stayed with her in-laws in Lucknow. That was the only connection I had with the village.

My thoughts went back to the contents of the letter. I was planning to go to India sometime in October, but it looked like I would have to make some changes. It was early July and I would see how fast I could manage to leave. I would have to reschedule my calendar and that was a very tricky job. I would assign some cases to Jason. I could not let mother go to the village alone, knowing that there was no good medical care centre in the village. Though Kamla and Urmila *Chachi* would accompany her, and I had the support of Rajat's staff who would be by my mother's side in no time if need be, yet I felt a little uncomfortable. She would be away for days there, and what if she fell ill and required good medical help? Also, the house in the village must be in a bad condition. Though my mother kept giving money to *Mukhia Chacha* for the upkeep of it, I was quite sceptical of the condition of it. All these thoughts assailed me and I found that I could not go through my notes. I went to the kitchen, poured myself some wine and put the music on. The comfort of the warm kitchen and wine relaxed me a bit and I started making dinner. I grilled two breast pieces of chicken and sautéed mushrooms, baby corns, carrots and broccoli. I added some boiled baby potatoes and sautéed them over a high flame in a little butter, sprinkled some dry spices till they turned golden brown. I carried my dinner to the study with another generous draught of wine and started going through the notes as I ate. The storm had abated but the rain was in full frenzy. After about an hour I felt drowsy and retired to bed. The last thought on my mind was the village as I closed my eyes and drifted into sleep.

After a few rings, Kamla picked up the phone.

'Hello!' she said panting.

'Kamla is everything alright? Why are you panting?'

'*Didi, Namaste*! *Dadi* wanted to sit in the veranda so I was taking her there.'

'How is *Amma*?'

'*Dadi* is doing fine at the moment but there are times when...,' she hesitated.

'When what?' I felt worry creeping in my heart. I hoped that it was not the beginning of Alzheimer's.

'*Didi, Dadi* has started talking to herself. And at times she gets quite agitated. It started with her mumbling in her dreams at night. I thought she was having some bad dreams but then, for the last few nights, I found her saying something,' she said, lowering her voice.

'What does she say?'

'I cannot make out much but I have heard her saying something like she is asking someone; why did you do it? I asked her casually who she was talking to. But she said she wasn't talking to anyone and told me that I have an active imagination. *Didi*, at times she just sits and stares ahead, and she is not her old self.'

I knew what Kamla meant by saying that mother was not her old self. My mother was a good person but she had a temper. Though it was only short-lived and she would go out of her way to help people, but if things did not go her way, she would scold the person there and then. But Kamla, her mother, and Mahesh, the driver who also tended to the small lawn and was the handyman for all the odd jobs, did not mind her bickering, and were extremely loyal to her. So were the neighbours.

As I drove to my office, I admired the remnants of the fading summers. Though the scattered leaves bore evidence of the fury of last evening's storm, the colourful flowers in the baskets that were hung on the entrance of pubs and boutiques were still in bloom, albeit their vibrancy and the lustre somewhat subdued. The trees looked solemn, as if quietly waiting for the oncoming winters. I loved English summers no matter how short-lived these were. I had read somewhere that the summers in England made the winters tolerable, and I was in agreement. It had taken me quite some time to get used to the winters and I had complained and whined in the beginning, but as time went by, I had grown rather fond of the country. There were a few reasons, but they were enough to keep me staying on, and it had become my home.

When I reached, Cathy had already organised the appointments and put the kettle on.

'Morning Dr Chat! Your first appointment is at 9.45 and these are the hard copies of the yesterday's cases A1 and B1. Is Dr Jason coming today?'

'Yes he is coming around lunch time. Thank you Cathy!'

Jason was my prodigy. That's what I liked to call him. I had met him during a seminar and was impressed with the deep knowledge and understanding he had of his profession. He told me later that he always wanted to meet me after reading my papers, and he had let a family commitment go in order to attend the seminar so he could meet me. I had liked him instantly. Despite the fact that he had achieved a lot at a very young age, he had this insatiable hunger to learn more. Also the fact that he was very down-to-earth with a witty sense of humour made him even more endearing. Though we had hit a snag when I noticed that something was not very right, and one day I decided to ask him. It turned out that he had a crush on me. I knew I had to tread gently and make sure he did not get hurt in the process. I asked him to say aloud what he felt about me. We sat down till late and sorted things out. I knew it would take some time for him to let the attraction go completely, but a long chat and discussion of human emotions in their most rudimentary form, and the fact that we both had a deep understanding of the human mind and psyche, helped us remove any awkwardness that would have been there in the first place.

I knew Cathy liked him a lot, but Jason couldn't see it. He was always so engrossed in his work. He handled my cases when I went to India because that was the longest I stayed away from my work. And today again I had requested him for the same. I decided to go to India and help mother with the sale of the ancestral house in the village, and bring her back to Lucknow. I decided to leave in a fortnight. I always felt a little ill at ease whenever I went back to my native country. One of the reasons was, though my mother loved me a lot, yet for the last few years she had become a little withdrawn, especially after my father's demise. If she wanted me to move back to India she did not say so, but I hated to see her a little forlorn when I would return to England. She would not come to England with me and I could not move back to India. So I would feel guilty and often find myself in a quandary.

I came out of the Indira Gandhi International airport and saw a driver holding a placard with my name on it. He wished me good morning and took the luggage trolley from me. I looked out of the window as the Mercedes started moving towards Rajat's luxurious bungalow in South Delhi. Rajat was Ashok's family friend, and both the boys had grown into the closest of friends. Though they both had chosen different paths in their careers, it had not dulled the spark of brotherly love they had for each other.

During our days in medical college, Rajat would try to spend as much time with us as possible, whenever he came from America, where he was pursuing an MBA, in order to take over the family business. He had been as close a friend to me as he was to Ashok. His wife, Alice, who was an American, was a sweet-natured and cheerful woman who was very much in love with her husband and his country. It was an unwritten rule that whenever I came to India I would stay with Rajat for a couple of days, and even if he was travelling abroad, I would stay with Alice. I liked to spend time with them as they'd become quite close like an extended family to me. Rajat was like a brother I never had. So I always looked forward to spending time with him. I considered myself very lucky to have someone like him in my life. I could talk to Rajat about things I could not talk to Ashok. Ashok had a very clinical view about life. He saw life through a microscope of logic. He did not realise that there were certain matters that needed to be seen as they were; raw and naked. They did not require the opaque garb of logic. Life could not always be measured by some parameters; it could not be contained within a given set of rules. It was like a river flowing constantly and taking the path and curves it desired. Ashok was brilliant in his field of profession, but not so cognizant in matters of the heart and soul.

CHAPTER 2

The car snaked out of the traffic in the busy streets of Lucknow. I had stayed with Rajat and Alice for two days, and had enjoyed every moment of it.

The car came to a halt and I realised I had reached home. I had always felt a connection with the place, because it held the memories of my father. There are some memories that become the core of our existence. One can define one's whole life based on them, and they stay as fresh as the dew drops in the morning; never fading, never drying up. And though life is constituted of thousands of moments, it's that one portion of our life where our heart and mind escape to, whenever they need the cocoon of warm security. My childhood and adolescence years constituted that part of my life. Those years, when I had spent most of my time with my parents, were the best years of my life. I had treasured those memories like a parched person would treasure tiny droplets of water. Those were the years when I had seen my mother happy. Though there were times when she would get a little withdrawn and speculative, but then, my father's sunny disposition would expel the darkness, and his affectionate behaviour would bring her back.

Mahesh opened the door of the car and as I came out, a jubilant Kamla came running.

'*Didi*! I am so happy you are here,' she said hugging me.

'I am too Kamla. How is *Amma*?'

'She has been so excited that she couldn't sleep. I had to give her that pill doctor has prescribed. Hey children! Don't touch the car,' she chided the children who were trying to open the door of the car.

'Who are these children?'

'They are the children of the neighbour's servants.'

'I will get the luggage inside, madam,' Mahesh said.

'Yes, thank you Mahesh.'

I looked at the house where I had spent the formative years of my life. It always evoked a feeling of sweet nostalgia in me. It brought back my childhood and along with it, a warmth of the cosy security I had felt. Though I was the only child, I had never felt the need of a sibling. My parents had never let any void creep into my life. They were there with me, for me, all the time.

The house looked frozen in time; there were very few changes that my mother had allowed to be done. She liked it the way it was. There were more open spaces in terms of 'Angans', verandas and rooftops terraces than the rooms. But this was the way it was built some seventy years back. It was already twenty five years old when my father bought it from a family who were shifting to Delhi for good. But it was built solidly and still looked pretty strong.

I crossed the threshold and the courtyard. Amma was sitting in the veranda in her easy chair with Urmila *Chachi* sitting beside her. Her face lit up the moment her eyes rested on me. She tried to get up but I stopped her. I hugged her and inhaled the familiar scent of her body. I noticed that she had lost weight since I saw her last. I sat down in the empty chair that was probably kept for me. As we sat talking, the neighbours came to meet me. I had lived in two different parts of the world and had visited a considerably large part of it, but the genuine love and affection of the people of this neighbourhood had always restored my faith in love for mankind. I was not the daughter of just one family here, but I was a bit of a family to all the people who had seen me growing up. The evening turned into dusk and Kamla switched the lights on. After some time, the neighbours left, but not before inviting me to their respective homes, and we were finally alone.

Later that evening, after taking a refreshing bath, we all assembled in my mother's room and I gave them the gifts I had brought for them. I decided to speak to mother the next day as I just wanted to enjoy their company. I had not told mother about the letter, the reason I was here. Instead I had simply informed a week back that I had decided to visit her as I had some break from my work. She looked very happy. We sat down to dinner and my mouth watered as I saw that Urmila *Chachi* had cooked my favourite dishes. Urmila *Chachi* had been with us for nearly sixteen years. She was a distant relative, and my mother had taken her and an infant Kamla in, when she had lost her husband and her in-laws had refused to keep her with them. She was a soft spoken and gentle woman who cared for *Amma* like her own mother. So she and Kamla were like my family and I was very close to them.

I sat down to a delicious meal of *vadi aloo*, rice, *arhar daal* with a tempering of garlic and chillies and potatoes cut into the finger chips style and cooked in mustard oil till crispy. Though I intended on eating only rice, but *Chachi* insisted on giving me hot *chapattis,* smeared with pure ghee. It was here in this *chauka* that I had taken my meals with my father sitting next to me and Ramia *Kaki*, an old lady from the village who cooked and helped in other household chores, cooking over the *chulha*, while my mother supervised the meals, during my childhood. He would always narrate an interesting anecdote and I would feel content and secure with my small family. During summers we ate in the veranda, but it was during winters that I loved to sit in the cosy *chauka*, enjoying the warmth emanating from the chulha, and felt very happy. Later, when the gas stove came, *Amma* did not let the *chulha* go, and it was used occasionally for making *Daal* because she insisted that the food tasted good only when it was cooked slowly over the fire of wood and coals.

Once dinner was over, I tucked mother in and went to my room. I was changing into my pyjamas when there was a knock on the door. I found *Chachi* standing with a hot glass of milk.

'Oh *Chachi*! You shouldn't have. I am so full,' I said, protesting.

'Drink it after some time. You are way too thin,' she said affectionately. '*Bitia,* we are relieved that you have come. We both had started to get worried for *Jiji.*'

'Why *Chachi*? Has anything unusual happened? Kamla said something about *Amma* talking in her sleep and phasing out at times.'

'Parni, (she called me by my nickname), after all she is getting old. But yes, I think she has been a bit upset ever since she decided to sell the house in the village. At times, she gets agitated and Kamla says that she often shouts in her sleep. I have never known *Jiji* to have a weak or confused mind, but now she often mistakes the present with the past. But then, you know that she stayed in that house with her parents, and then with you and your father. In fact, you were born there. So I think she has a deep emotional and sentimental connection with that house, and that might have stirred some old memories. She has not gone to the village for almost thirty seven years. So selling the house and the land might be a bit too much for her to handle.'

Kamla came and sat down at the edge of the bed.

'But why did she decide to sell it all of a sudden? I mean, she used to talk about it, but I was surprised to learn that she was finally going to sell it.'

'Well! It was about a month back when Chandu *Bhaiya* had come and told her that the Haveli in the village was being sold. That evening she was alright but that very night she started shouting in her sleep and Kamla got scared and called me. I woke her up and gave her some water but she looked very confused and disturbed. I had to give her the sleeping pill. And she has been getting restless sometimes in her sleep since then. A few days back, she got up and started walking to the door. Thankfully Kamla is a light sleeper so she heard the movement and got up.'

'When and what exactly happened, Kamla? You said she talks in her sleep. Could you make out what she says?'

'Generally she just mumbles but once I heard her saying '*Amma* why?' and then at times she takes your name. Rest is difficult to make out.' Kamla added.

We all were quiet for some time. I was quite puzzled to hear this account of events. My mother had been in sound health, mentally and physically, when I had visited her eight months back. She possessed a sharp mind and her memory was still very good. Except for the age related ailments like Osteoarthritis which had affected her knees, she seemed to be doing fine for her age. She had always been mentally agile and had never shown any signs of deterioration. What had triggered this then? *Chachi* said that it all started when Chandu *Kaka* brought the news of the Haveli being sold.

'*Chachi*, you said that when she came to know about the Haveli being sold, she decided to sell her property as well. But why would she get disturbed with the news of the Haveli being sold?'

Chachi was quiet, as if thinking of something. So at least it was not the Alzheimer I was worried about. This had started all of a sudden. But I still couldn't see the connection between the sale of the Haveli and my mother's sudden distressed mental condition, and her decision to sell her property too. I would have to find out what was wrong, but for now I was glad that I had decided to come. At least I would finish off this business of the village and then persuade mother once again to come with me to England. It was time she moved and stayed with me.

CHAPTER 3

As the cars moved on National Highway 25 towards Rae Bareli, the landscape was changing rapidly. I noticed the change that was taking place, replacing the quaint and old world charm of the countryside with the garishness of the so-called modernity. I was expecting to see pretty mud wall cottages surrounded by trees, but was a bit disappointed to see the small houses made with bricks and tin roofs. There were very few stretches of fields. Mostly, the road was lined with small shops and some brick and mortar houses scattered in a haphazard way.

I felt sad at the ugliness of these small towns that had robbed the villages and landscapes of their beauty, and could not help but compare them with the untouched and pristine beauty of the villages in England. I only hoped that the village that was my destination was something like that; serene, beautiful and with a dreamlike quality.

The car stopped when we reached the town that lay between Rae Bareli and Shivgarh. The driver got down to buy bottled water as I had instructed him, since I was a little apprehensive about the water in the village. I stepped out of the car to stretch my legs and as I was taking in the hustle bustle of the small town, my eyes rested on a shop that looked quite familiar. It looked brighter and neater in the image that popped up in my mind, and housed colourful items like ribbons and bangles but it looked old and shabby now. I remembered it as being a neat and newer shop. I must have come to this shop with *Amma* and *Baba,* I smiled at the memory and looked inside the car to ask *Amma*, but she was sound asleep. Everything around me looked distantly familiar.

After an hour, the landscape changed and the road, though narrow, was flanked by big trees and they sort of created a vista. We entered the village and it looked suspended in time. I was glad to see that the vices of the modern world had not taken over it completely. The village was very old and had a quaint quality. I hoped it stayed the same and did not ape its neighbouring town that had lost its identity; being neither old nor modern, hanging somewhere in between. The legend went that the village was established by the descendants of the sage Bharadwaj, whose offspring continued to live here. I had heard the story from my grandfather when I was a child, of how we were the direct descendants of the learned sage. And the most important features of the village were the river Ganges and a very old temple of Lord Shiva, which the village derived its name from.

The car stopped in front of the house I was born in, and as I looked at the house, a sense of familiarity dawned upon me. The earthy smell of the dirt tracks and the clean air knocked at my mind trying to bring the hidden memories out from its deep recesses. I tried remembering more but everything was shrouded in obscurity. The house looked older than I remembered. But as I crossed the threshold, I felt a warm rush of emotions. The house welcomed me as if asking, 'Where were you all these years?' There was an elderly man who I presumed was *Mukhia Chacha* with some other people who welcomed us into our own house. There were some neighbours and children looking at us intently, though the children ran out to see the cars that both the drivers were parking. The kitchen was active and a couple of women were already working there. They had *ghoonghats* over their faces and they looked quite young. I caught them looking at me lifting their *ghoonghats* a couple of times. I smiled, but the *ghoonghat* was quickly in place again. The colourful bangles on their hands jingled as they made tea and refreshments. There was a *takht* in the veranda, covered with a mattress and a white sheet. It had some bolsters thrown on it. And some chairs were kept around it for all of us to sit.

'*Bhabhi*, I hope you find the house to your satisfaction. I tried to make it as comfortable as I could,' *Mukhia Chacha* said, addressing my mother.

'*Bhaiya*, I am so grateful to you. I really put you through a lot of trouble. The house looks very nice and comfortable. Thank you so much for your help,' my mother replied.

'The bedrooms downstairs are for you and Urmila *Behen*. I have prepared the big room on the first floor for Aparna *Bitia*. I hope she feels comfortable there.'

'I certainly will. Thank you so much,' I said.

He filled my mother with news of the village, while his sons, who I presumed were the husbands of the young women cooking in the kitchen, served us tea with some sweets and savouries. After about an hour the neighbours left, telling us that we should not hesitate in asking for anything that we'd need.

'*Bhabhi*, do you know the Haveli is being sold?' *Mukhia Chacha* said.

There was silence. My mother didn't say anything. I thought that probably she had not heard. She seemed a bit lost.

'*Amma! Mukhia Chacha* is saying something,' I said gently.

She came out of her reverie.

'But who is selling and who is buying?'

'*Baba Saheb* is selling it. I believe buyers are going to turn it into some sort of hotel. What is it called Gopal?' he asked one of his sons who had been sitting quietly until now.

'They are making a resort,' Gopal said.

'*Baba Saheb* had come last week. Chandu will be able to tell you more since he stays there only as you know.'

Mother nodded again, deep in her thoughts. I felt that she was probably tired. Though the drive was only two hours, it had taken longer because the condition of the roads was bad in some places. It was seven in the evening but the sky was overcast and the late July evening was already melting into night.

I did not remember my parents talking about the Haveli in the village but I felt as if I had seen the Haveli a long time back, and now an image of it appeared in my mind. I must have seen it before we left the village, I thought to myself. And then there was this urge to go and see the Haveli. But that was nothing new. I always liked to visit the past, unravel it and try to trace the footsteps that were lost in time. My love for the old and antique was beckoning me in the form of the Haveli.

Mukhia Chacha took my mother's silence as a sign of fatigue and he got up to leave.

'*Bhabhi,* you must be tired. You take rest now,' he said. 'Ask your wife whether dinner is ready,' he told one of his sons in an authoritative voice. His son went to the kitchen; spoke to one of the women, who was supposedly his wife.

'It's almost ready *Baba.*'

'Alright! Just see that the drivers are comfortable. Take food for them and escort your wife and sister-in-law home. You can wait outside till then,' he instructed his son.

I felt a little uncomfortable with all the work being done by them. I looked at Kamla and she understood what I wanted. She told *Mukhia Chacha* that there was no need for any of them to wait and she would take it from there. They had already done everything. He probably would have insisted but my mother intervened and said that everything was done and now they must go home. The cabbie left after he had dinner, and Mahesh settled down in his room that used to be a store for grains, but had then been converted into a small yet neat room by my father, a long time back. It was always given to the driver when my father visited the village.

After they left, we sat down to dinner. It was a simple meal of *chapattis, daal*, vegetables and rice but everything was mouth-watering. The fresh produce and the vegetables from the village made the meal exceptionally delicious. The *daal* was tempered with pure cow ghee and it was heavenly. We summed the dinner up with *kheer* that was loaded with dry fruits. We settled *Amma* in her room and I saw to it that *Chachi* and Kamla were comfortable in their room, and then finally headed up to my room. There were two rooms that were built on the first floor. One of them was prepared for me. It was a simple but spacious room and had a huge window that opened into the courtyard below. The furniture consisted of a queen sized wooden bed with four carved posts, two small wooden nightstands, a big wooden almirah and a simple writing table with a chair. There was a rocking chair that I remembered had belonged to my grandfather, and was kept next to the window. It was a neat room. *Mukhia Chacha* and his family had done lots of work to make the entire house pleasant and liveable. My suitcases had already been kept in the room.

I walked to the window and looked at the moon bathing everything in its silvery light. The large neem tree's branches on my left almost reached the window. This neem was very old. There was a cemented bench that went around its huge trunk and I remembered sitting on it playing with my dolls. Out of the four mango trees in the courtyard of our house, the biggest one was on the right side of the house and bore the sweetest fruits. The *raat ki rani* below my window emitted a sweet scent. As the cool breeze caressed my face I felt a strange sense of déjà vu as if I had felt this breeze and inhaled the scent of *raat ki rani* in this very village before, and there was a vague memory that sent a pleasurable wave down my body. I closed my eyes and sighed. When the feeling passed I wondered what had triggered the sensation. I had never come to the village as an adult, and what I had felt just now was definitely not a memory of a three year old child.

I woke up with a start. I was still sitting in the rocking chair. I had sat down just to gaze at the stars and to breathe in the silky solitude, and had probably dozed off. I thought of the delicious feeling that was still coursing through my veins. Was it a dream? It definitely was but then I had never felt any dream so vivid.

When I got up in the morning, I lay awake, confused about my bearings for a few seconds. There was a chatter of birds that sounded very different to my ears, and then I realised I was home; well, in my childhood home. The bright rays of the sun filtering through the branches of the neem, were making a zig-zag pattern on the floor and the walls. It was so different from England where most of the mornings, this time of the year, would be dull, as the sky would be overcast if it was not already raining. I stretched my body languorously. I looked at my watch. It was 9 am.

'Ahh... The luxuries of a holiday!' I said to myself. I became fully awake shaking the cobwebs of sleep, and then I remembered the dream I had had last night. It had left me with a feeling I had not had for a long time. And then I suddenly remembered that there was someone else with me in the dream. I tried catching fragments but the dream was already fading.

I lay for some time, thinking of this new day. There had been a feeling that kept peeping from the recesses of my mind. It was difficult to explain the very nature of it. It had surfaced ever since I had started my journey to the village. I felt this slight nagging feeling when you feel a memory lurking in the depth of your mind but are not able to recall it. I felt happy yet a little forlorn; happy that I was fulfilling my mother's wish by bringing her here; forlorn because I did not know how this was going to go further. I had not thought of the village for a very long time. In fact, I hardly remembered it. But now it seemed that I had a deep connection with it. A vague sense of familiarity had started peeking from somewhere in my mind when I stopped in the town short of the village, and then again while entering the village. It was growing with every passing hour. In my mind's picture, it was a little different than what it was now, but the difference was quite small and I kept thinking that it was amazing to remember the village with such clarity, considering my memories were of a three year old child. And then there was this dream.

My thoughts turned to my work. I had spoken to Jason from Lucknow. He had filled me up about the cases, and we had discussed some of them. I had told him that I was going to the village and it would probably not be possible to speak with him. He had assured me that I need not worry as he would take care of everything. I had no doubt that he would. I wondered how Cathy was managing working with Jason. I only hoped that her feelings for Jason did not deepen as she was likely to get hurt. I sighed and turned on the bed, looking towards the window and then there was a soft knock on the door bringing me out of my reverie.

'*Didi*!' It was Kamla.

'Please come in Kamla,' I said.

She entered with a hot cup of tea.

'Oh! You are an angel. This is such a luxury.'

'What *Didi*?'

'Getting a hot cup of tea in bed. Thank you Kamla!' I said, sipping the tea infused with ginger and jaggery.

'I hope you like it. *Dadi* said to put jaggery instead of sugar. She said you would love it. Though *Amma* had her doubts,' she said smiling.

'Oh! This is heavenly. So what is the plan today? Has *Amma* said anything?'

'*Mukhia Chacha* had come in the morning. He has requested *Dadi* to ask you if you could see some people with some medical problems.'

'Oh! What kind of medical problems? Did he say?'

'No, but I guess you are going to have a busy morning, but before that *Amma* wants you to have breakfast. She is making *poori aaloo* for breakfast.'

'*Arey* Urmila! *Bitia* is up. Is there hot water in the *ghusal khana* for her bath?' mother called out, the moment she saw me descending the stairs. She looked at me with pure affection and though she still looked tired, she looked much better.

I had to sit and give some solutions to the various health problems of the neighbours who always visited when I came home to Lucknow. The problem was that in spite of my reiterated explanations that I was not a general physician, they kept asking me for treatment for their ailments. I gave up after some time and helped them just the same, at times depending upon my general knowledge, at others, calling my colleagues and asking them for solutions. As Ashok had said light-heartedly, as far as they were concerned, I was a doctor; whether I treated the mind or the body, it didn't matter to them. For them I held all the answers. But it still had been a bit easier in Lucknow because they could show me prescriptions, and that helped to a certain extent. But I wondered how I was going to help the people here. I braced myself to go through the rigmarole of explaining that I could not treat physical problems, albeit could help with the rudimentary ones.

After a delicious breakfast of *poori aaloo*, I prepared myself to see 'the patients.'

The day turned into afternoon, and I felt the same nagging feeling when everyone had left. I suddenly had this urge to go and see the Haveli. I was in a way happy to have been occupied, finding solutions to the medical problems of the neighbours, but now I felt a little unsettled. For some strange reason my mind kept going back to the Haveli. The urge to go and see it was persistent. So after having some fruits for lunch, I decided to take a walk towards the Haveli.

'*Amma*! I am going for a walk,' I said.

'Don't go alone. Take Kamla with you.'

'It's alright *Amma*! I am not a small child,' I said.

'*Didi*, I want to come if you don't mind.' Kamla was by my side.

'Of course! It would be nice to have you with me. Come along then.'

The weather was lovely. The July sun was playing hide and seek with the clouds and the breeze was deliciously cool. It had rained a couple of days before our arrival and though the clouds had scattered, the possibility of rains could not be ruled out. I breathed deep, filling my lungs with clean air. The breeze carried a whiff of the wet soil that it picked from the banks of the river. I was told that one could see the river through the thick curtains of the trees when my mother was a child. But now the river had shifted and the banks had become wider. I had heard *Mukhia Chacha* bemoaning the atrocities of the poachers and the timber merchants cutting the trees ruthlessly, thus stripping the forest in and around the village and all over the district. But this was happening everywhere in India and the population explosion had made things worse. But this year the monsoons had come at the right time and they were hoping to get good rains. The Haveli was situated at the other end of the village. In fact, it was supposed to be a kilometre or so away from the boundary of the village. I did not know whether the village had expanded and swallowed the distance between its boundary and the Haveli. I was going to find out soon.

I was enjoying the walk listening to Kamla's conversation when suddenly I stopped in my tracks. The Haveli loomed up partially hidden by the thick cover of trees, challenging time. Something stirred inside me. As I reached closer to the Haveli I felt a tug in the pit of my stomach. The cool breeze blowing over the Ganges made the trees sway.

I felt a shiver run down my spine. There was a faint recognition mixed with something else; a kind of magnetic pull. And then there was this mixed emotion; I wanted to look at it but at the same time wanted to tear my gaze off it. There was a feeling of longing yet a feeling of evasion. I felt rooted to the spot. I felt as if I had visited the Haveli just yesterday. The feeling of familiarity was acute and sudden.

'*Didi*! Is something the matter?' Kamla asked.

'No! Nothing really. Let's keep walking.' I shook off the feeling and attributed it to my love for the old and forgotten.

I always had a thing for the past. I always went exploring old monuments; I visited castles and forts in the UK, whenever I took a break from my busy work schedule. The lives of the people, who had lived in those places in the past, intrigued me. As the guide would narrate the history of those places, I would picture the occupants coming to life. I would get transported to that era walking with them, observing them, feeling them. And this place was no different, and was having the same effect on me. I turned to take the path that would lead me to the Haveli. The gulmohar trees formed a vista and after walking some five hundred meters, the dirt road ended at the huge wrought iron gate. Kamla undid the iron latch by putting her hand through the bars of the gate and we both pushed it open. After walking another hundred metres or so, on the cobbled path, the drive in, which was flanked by tall bottle palms, the Haveli came into full view. The Haveli seemed to be on the banks of the Ganges, with its back to the river. I felt different emotions churning inside me. It invited and challenged me at the same time. The feelings were so strong that I again felt a little dazed. But now as I started walking on the cobbled path, the distance of the years had evaporated. I felt I had walked that path as recently as yesterday. There was a sense of nostalgia. I had often read and found the theory quite correct that we tend to romanticise our memories by making them spectacular. As time passes, more beauty gets added to them making them larger than life. Memories become like old photographs that turned sepia with time, adding a sense of mystery to its occupants, therefore making the past more and more enigmatic. And the places visited in the childhood, when revisited as an adult, lose some of its glamour because the childhood memory is always grander than the reality. But in my case, the Haveli was as enigmatic as it was in my mind's eyes, although a bit lustreless.

The garden right in front of the Haveli was in need of care and attention. The grass was unkempt and in need of a trim. Only the huge bottle palm trees that lined the garden still stood as tall and green. It was evident that the garden was in acute need of gardeners. But then, the whole place looked like it needed care and love in order to gain its erstwhile glory.

'Let's go and meet Chandu *Kaka*,' I said tearing my gaze from the big fountain that looked strangely familiar but in a state of disrepair.

We walked towards the rear of the Haveli, where I assumed the staff quarters would be. We passed through another garden on the right side of the Haveli. The staff quarters were towards the left side but a little away, in a grove, so as not to disturb the view of the river from the Haveli. Chandu *Kaka*'s quarters were a little away from the rest of the staff quarters. There were a total of four quarters including *Kaka*'s. But three of them had fallen into disrepair and looked unfit for lodging. *Kaki* saw me first. She was sitting on a cot under the neem tree. I had met the couple some eight years back when they had come to Lucknow for *Kaki*'s treatment. She looked frail and older now. A big smile broke on her face.

'Aparna *Bitia*! Is it really you? *Arey* come out! Look who is here!' she shouted.

I marvelled at her memory.

'How are you *Kaki*?' I asked sitting on the cot.

'Just counting the days *Bitia*, till the time comes. When did you arrive?'

'Arey Aparna *Bitia*! How nice to see you!' Chandu *Kaka* walked towards me as fast as his arthritic knees would carry him. I got up and hugged him.

'Yesterday only. How are your knees *Kaka*?'

'Arey *Bitia*, these are the gifts of the old age. The body has to weaken then only it would perish.'

'He cannot sleep in the night because of the pain *Bitia*,' *Kaki* said.

'*Kaka* I think you have to go for a check-up. You and *Kaki* come with me when we leave for Lucknow.'

'*Bitia*, I cannot leave this place. There is no one to look after it. And now *Baba Saheb* is coming. So I have to keep the place clean and running.'

'I am here for a few days *Kaka*. So there is some time to decide.

I think you should see a doctor. Let me know if you change your mind. How is Dulari?' I enquired after their daughter who was married and lived in Lucknow with her husband and his family. Her husband's family had a decent chunk of land and livestock and were adequately well off. Dulari's husband was a nice fellow and he kept her happy. I had not met her for quite some time, but *Amma* had always filled me in about the people from the village.

'Dulari has been blessed with a daughter *Bitia*,' *Kaki* informed me with an affectionate smile on her face.

'Congratulations to both of you!'

We talked a bit about the village and its inhabitants. *Kaka* was respected and loved by everyone in the village. He was a selfless person, always trying to help everyone. I did not have much of an idea what he did for the Haveli earlier but it was evident now that he was the care taker of the Haveli.

Kaki brought a plate of the homemade *laddoos*, made with wheat flour, dry fruits and pure ghee, I so loved. There was also a plate of homemade freshly fried potato chips. 'We came to know that you and your mother were coming. That's why I made *laddoos*. Your *Kaka* was supposed to come to your house with *laddoos* today but you beat him to it,' she said smiling.

'*Kaki* I had lunch not very long ago. But I will have this laddoo.'

'*Bitia*, you must eat. God knows what you get to eat in Chiristaan (slang for England used in the villages). You are so thin you look like a seventeen year old.'

'Don't force her just because you want to hear her praise your *laddoos*,' *Kaka* said in an affectionate tone.

'*Kaka*, can I see the Haveli from inside, if it's not too much of a bother?'

'Yes, why not! You must see it in its original form and shape. Who knows what changes would be done once it's sold,' *Kaka* said in a lugubrious tone.

I felt a small flutter in my stomach as we started walking towards the Haveli. Kamla stayed back to help *Kaki* clean the glasses and plates and take the stuff inside.

'So *Kaka* I am hearing this talk of Haveli being sold?'

'Yes *Bitia*! *Baba Saheb* has finally decided to sell it. After all, how long can you keep a place just because of its sentimental value? Also it's reaching a derelict state. It wouldn't be long before it starts falling apart. *Baba Saheb* and his family are mostly living abroad. He does come to Delhi and lives in his bungalow there but what use does he have of this place?'

I could detect dismal resignation in *Kaka*'s voice.

'So how long has the Haveli been lying vacant? When did the occupants shift from here?'

'It's been almost five decades since anyone has stayed here for more than a few days. After Barrister Saheb passed away some fifty years back, the Haveli has been lying vacant except for a couple of short visits by *Choti* Baby *Saheb*, Barrister *Saheb's* daughter, but those visits were a long time back and were very short. For a long time no one visited until around three years back when *Baba Saheb*, Barrister *Saheb's* grandson, came to see the condition of the Haveli. After that he has been coming for two or three days whenever he comes to India. Apparently his mother had asked him to look after the Haveli for as long as he could. But now it seems *Baba Saheb* has made up his mind to sell it. He must be having his reasons,' *Kaka* said gravely.

We walked around the Haveli to reach the front side, this time from its left flank. Being a shorter route, we passed through another garden, which was on the left side of the Haveli.

'So, the Haveli has three gardens, what a luxury!' I mused. But how does it seem I already knew that? I wondered.

I wanted to ask more about this family but held myself. We had reached the porch in front of the building and climbed the marble steps that led to a veranda. The veranda seemed to be running all around the building. There was a massive door that still looked grand with brass knockers. This was the main entrance to the Haveli. The door was flanked by a series of bay windows, extending till the end of the veranda, on both sides. As we approached the main door, suddenly, I had this flash as if I knew the Haveli inside out. I could see its rooms, corridors beyond the heavy wooden door. I must have come with my parents here as a child and clearly, the Haveli had worked as a stimuli and my brain was reproducing the long forgotten memories of the past. There was a big brass lock on the brass bolt, which *Kaka* opened with a big key from a bunch of rattling keys.

It was early evening, the sun was low on the horizon and the light had become weak as the clouds had started building up. As we stepped inside I stopped, looking at the familiar room that was for visitors. There were two Victorian style wooden sofa sets placed in a circular manner with small teapoys kept in front. In the centre of the room, there was a big circular table with an equally big porcelain flower vase. About eight feet above the table, hanging from the ceiling was a crystal chandelier. There were no curtains on the windows. Apparently they were not required as it was meant for the visitors to look out and admire the beauty of the fountain and the garden. At the far side of the room; in the centre, there was a door, which was open, leading to a dark lobby as wide as the visitors' room, probably running to the far end of the building.

Kaka led me around the centre table to the door and switched on the lights of the lobby.

I could now admire the full glory of the lobby. It had a shining granite marble floor and wood panelled walls, fixed with a number of antique crystal lamp shades glittering like diamonds. At the far side of the lobby there was an elegant wooden staircase leading to the first floor. Right ahead, on the wall, where the staircase ended, there was a huge alcove with a vacant flower vase. Five intricately carved wooden doors were opening into the lobby, two on the left side and three on the right side.

'On the left side, the first door leads to the morning room and the second door to the dining room. On the right, we have the drawing room first, then the library and a wash room at the end. There is a gun room also on this side which opens into the rear veranda. There is a door leading to the rear veranda under the staircase, which is used by staff to enter or exit the Haveli,' explained *Kaka*.

'Let's see the Drawing room first,' said *Kaka*, leading me to its door.

It was a huge room with a carpeted floor and fully wood panelled walls. There were five bay windows on the far side, opening towards the garden on the left of the Haveli and three bay windows on the right hand side wall, offering a beautiful view of the front gardens. The room had some elegant pieces of furniture but not as much as were probably there earlier, I thought. There was a huge, spectacularly coloured crystal chandelier hanging from the centre of the ceiling. As I turned left, I saw a big fireplace with two big candelabra placed on either side on its ledge, but it was the huge life-like canvas above it that captured my attention. I was pulled towards it as if in a trance. It was a painting of a couple. But I noticed the man first. And my heart thudded inside my chest. I felt a longing so acute that it brought tears to my eyes. I wanted to touch him, to feel him in flesh and bones.

'That is the image of Barrister *Saheb, Baba Saheb's* grandfather,' *Kaka*'s voice brought me back from the faraway place I had slipped into.

I thought anyone who would have looked at the painting, would have had the same reaction. The man was handsome beyond words. He was standing erect and looking directly at the painter. He was a tall man with the kind of a physique that would make many women sigh in anticipated pleasure. His thick dark hair was swept back, showing his broad forehead. There was an aristocracy in the Greek nose and firm jaw. But it was his eyes that stirred something inside me. Those were the kind of eyes that made promises only to keep. Those were the eyes that peeped into your soul and I felt a sensation going down my spine. I always thought that Ashok was a very handsome man but after looking at this man, I couldn't help thinking that no woman could help falling in love with him.

'And that is *Mem Saheb*, Barrister *Saheb's* wife and the mistress of the Haveli.'

My trance was broken once again by Chandu *Kaka's* voice.

I dragged my eyes from him to the woman who was sitting on an ornate chair. I had a feeling of unease and I had this overwhelming sense of discomfiture as I looked at her. She was pretty in a delicate sense. She wore a pale pink frock with small motifs. There was a string of pearls adorning her neck and pearl studs in her ears. She was wearing a diamond and pearl bracelet on one of her wrists. On the whole she looked very western and sophisticated. Her features were delicate and her figure was slim. Her hair was cut in a smart bob and she looked very chic. She seemed to be looking straight at me. There was a resigned look in her eyes. And then it struck me that both the man and the woman were not smiling. They both looked as if they were going through a commission of being painted without any actual enthusiasm. Why were they like this? Did they love each other? The question just popped into my head from nowhere. I was a bit surprised at the randomness of it. It was just a painting. Why was I interested in the relationship between them?

I still could not understand the tumultuous onslaught of emotions that I had felt looking at the painting. I looked at the man once again, filling my heart with a sweet sense that one gets after looking at something pleasant and equanimous.

'*Mem Saheb* and Barrister Saheb had studied in Britain. My father used to tell me that *Mem Saheb's* father was British and hailed from a very rich family. Though he had joined the British Army, he had taken retirement after receiving an injury in the leg. *Mem Saheb's* mother was Indian and was a daughter of a rich *Taluqdar*. *Mem Saheb* was in many ways like a British lady. Her clothes and perfumes and shoes used to come from Paris. *Mem Saheb* used to throw big parties in Lucknow and Delhi and my father used to tell me that all the rich and important people were invited. The *khansama* and the housekeeper were trained in cooking English dishes and running the house like a British *Saheb's* house. But though *Mem Saheb* did not talk to the staff much, she was very kind to the staff. That's what my father used to tell us. The Haveli saw some very good times when the barrister Saheb and *Mem Saheb* used to come here. There was always a festive kind of atmosphere when their friends visited and there were lots of revelries and merriments during those times.'

Kaka's voice was cut off by the sound of thunder and it grew dark inside. I looked at the painting and had this disturbing feeling that the mistress of the Haveli was staring right at me.

'Shall we continue the tour *Bitia*? It looks like it's going to pour; you will have to wait till the time rain stops. You have come walking I presume?' *Kaka* was asking.

'I will make a move now. *Amma* would get worried,' I said turning my head away from the boring eyes of the mistress. 'I shall come again in a day or two.'

'Alright *Bitia*. I would suggest that you should wait till the storm passes.'

'I must go *Kaka*. We will make it home before it starts raining.'

As we walked back home I kept thinking about the suave couple in the painting. They both must have loved each other. After all, they both were perfect for each other, yet there was something in the expressions on their faces that belied the cosy concept of deep love. It was only when I exited the wrought iron gate that I stopped dead in my tracks. Looking at the portrait of the '*Mem Saheb*' as *Kaka* had addressed her, I thought that I had known her. How was that possible? She had died much before I was born.

Chapter 4

It had started raining by the time we reached home. We both got wet and found a worried *Chachi* waiting at the door. The car was not in its usual place.

'Thank God! You both are here. *Jiji* was getting worried.'

'Where is Mahesh? The car is not here.'

'I sent him to go looking for you. He will be back soon. The village is not very big.'

'Where did you both go?'

I looked at Kamla and she held her tongue.

'We just went for a walk and ended up at the Haveli,' I said.

There was an expression on *Chachi's* face that looked like she didn't approve of what we had done. But it was gone as soon as it had come.

'Please don't mention it to your mother; that you went to the Haveli,' she said.

'Why, *Chachi*? Is there a particular reason for *Amma's* dislike for the Haveli?

'Let's just say that she probably has some unpleasant memory attached to it, that she does not want to relive. Now you must change into dry clothes while I make some ginger tea for both of you.'

The rest of the evening passed pleasantly as we sat in *Amma's* room and chatted, but the painting kept jumping into my mind. The storm had passed but it was still raining. There was a delicious petrichor emanating from the earth. The neighbours had sent dinner that consisted of a dish called 'Rasaje' that was basically made with the steamed and fried strips of gram floor that floated in a delicious curry, and a dry veggie made with jackfruit and potatoes. There were *chapattis* smeared with pure ghee and steamed rice to be eaten with the curry. I had often heard people say that vegetarian food was not as exciting as non-vegetarian. They probably should have eaten the food we were eating; it was heavenly. Every family in the village wanted to invite us over. But when we politely asked them not to take the trouble, they insisted on sending food home. This was the bonhomie that was so missing in the big cities.

When I came to my room I found my mind stubbornly going back to the Haveli. There was a restlessness that was difficult to suppress. Images of the painting kept floating in front of my eyes. One particular image filled my mind with an unexplained longing that was pleasant to the core of my being, while the other filled me with a kind of unrest and foreboding that made me feel depressed. I could not understand these kinds of emotions churning inside my heart. I felt a kind of connection with the people in the painting and I felt the Haveli beckoning me, as if it wanted to tell me something. I tried reading but found myself too distracted to concentrate. After tossing and turning in bed for almost half the night, I finally fell into a light sleep.

After a quick breakfast and attending to some more 'patients', I decided to go to the Haveli. The more I thought about it the more it became clear that my interest in this majestic and imposing structure, sitting on the banks of the river Ganges like a shining gem in that small yet pretty hamlet, was not just confined to my love for the past and bygones. There was something more that I could not yet define. I wanted to know more about the people who once lived and had a life there. I wanted to see the rooms where they had slept, the library where they had sat reading. For some strange reason I wanted to bring them back to life.

I told *Amma* I was going for a run and declined Kamla's offer to accompany me. I did run up to the narrow road that ran parallel to the river, and stopped at the wrought iron gate. I caught my breath and walked inside.

I found Chandu *Kaka* in the front garden.

'Ah! Parni *Bitia!* I was wondering when you would come again! But before we start the tour of the Haveli, let me inform your *Kaki* that you are here. She would kill me if you go without eating something. And then we can start the tour that would enhance your appetite also,' *Kaka* said in his good humoured way.

I will have to fight a battle to lose kilos, I thought to myself. It was not only *Chachi* and *Amma* who were hell bent on fattening me, but the entire village had joined in the conspiracy. Every day there was some mouth-watering delicacy cooked by some neighbour or the other. Cathy would probably have a heart attack if she came to know I had thrown all caution to the wind, and was indulging without any remorse. I was a poor eater and Cathy had often admonished me for eating so little. But the fresh air of the village or the aroma and taste of the dishes that I could never get to eat in England, made me devour them.

We started the tour. We walked into the lobby and *Kaka* stopped in front of the first room on the left and opened it.

'This was *Mem Saheb's* room,' he said. I wondered why *Kaka* was addressing the mistress of the house as 'Mem Saheb', a form of address only used for the colonial ladies. But then that was appropriate in her case too, as she had spent a great part of her life in England and lived like a true *Mem Saheb*, hence she must have been addressed like that by the staff.

The room had three big bay windows, like the drawing room, opening towards the front gardens, and two on the adjacent wall offering a view of the garden to the right side of the Haveli. The curtains must have been baby pink and off white, but now they looked a dirty cream. There was an ornate writing table with lots of small drawers. In the centre of the room was a king Edward recliner flanked by two Queen Ann's chairs. There was a centre table with a big bone china bowl and some small figurines placed at the one of the corners. On the right hand side wall was a door, probably connecting to the dining room, I thought.

'This was called 'The Morning Room',' *Kaka* said. For a few moments I forgot I was in India. It was so similar to those old British castles boasting of morning rooms, card rooms, ante rooms, gun rooms and all.

'Apparently, as my father used to mention, there were more valuable items like silver bowls, crystal vases and paintings, but those were removed and transported to the house in Delhi,' *Kaka* said.

I looked at the dainty Queen Ann chairs and suddenly there was a flash that came to my mind, and I saw the room in its previous glory. I could swear I saw the mistress sitting on one of the chairs, holding a dainty cup of china in her hand. The flash passed as soon it came.

'This is the Dining room,' *Kaka's* voice seemed to be coming from afar but it brought me to the present nevertheless. I silently followed him, still a bit unsettled. We had moved through the connecting door to the dining room.

There was a huge eighteen seat wooden dining table placed along the length of the room, with a glass-like polished top, and beautifully carved legs. It appeared to be as old as the Haveli. There was a red runner in the centre along the length, with four silver candelabra of intricate designs placed on it at equal distance. Each candelabrum could hold five candles. Dining chairs were equally impressive, intricately carved and with red tapestry woven with golden 'Fleur-de-Lis'. To add to the whole grand spectacle, was a huge crystal chandelier hanging from the roof. I could imagine how breath-taking it must have looked during formal dinners, with bone china plates, silver cutlery, crystal water goblets and wine glasses laid out and all the candles of the candelabra and chandelier lit.

'The kitchen is beyond that door on the far side, with a door opening into the rear veranda for the staff. Actually, the kitchen was not inside the house first. It was a little farther away. There was a big pantry where the present kitchen is, where the food was brought from the kitchen and organised before serving at the dining table. But *Mem Saheb* got the kitchen made in the pantry itself. You see Bitia, this Haveli was made by Barrister *Saheb's* friend's father, for his 'Firangi' friends. It was called 'Hunting Lodge'. Barrister *Saheb* had come here a couple of times with his friend, and when his friend asked him whether he would like to buy it, he happily agreed,' said *Kaka*.

'Let's go upstairs first and then we will finish the tour with the library and the kitchen.'

'So why did his friend sell it?' I asked.

'He moved to Britain and settled there.'

We climbed the elegant wooden stairs. On reaching the top, in front of the alcove, I noticed that there were passages turning to both sides in an inverted 'L' shape, to the corridors leading towards the front of Haveli.

Kaka led the way to the left side first. Inside the corridor, I could see two doors on the right side, and three doors on the left. There was a bay window at the end of the corridor opening to the front gardens.

'This is the 'East Wing'. There are two bedrooms on the right and a sitting room and two wash rooms on the opposite side, in this wing. The 'West Wing' on the other side, also has a similar setup, which we would see later,' *Kaka* said.

He stopped at the first door on the right and opened the lock with a key out of his big bunch of keys.

'This is the Master Bedroom,' he said.

The door was wide and carved elegantly but the moment I stepped inside the room I gasped in surprise. The bedroom was huge, adorned with a king-sized four poster bed with a canopy, set against the opposite wall in the centre of the room. There was one bay window on each side of the bed looking onto the garden on the right side of Haveli. But it was the view from the room towards the rear of Haveli that was the most mesmerising. The whole right wall of the room was covered with French windows, end to end, opening to a huge terrace overlooking the river. There were light lace curtains and as *Kaka* opened one of the French windows, a gust of wind disturbed the curtains, blowing through them. I walked to the end of the terrace and looked at the calm waters of the river. There was a kind of tranquillity that transports a person to another realm, a serenity that was though engaging, yet a little upsetting. It felt as if fragments of some moments of a bygone era were still floating in the air. As if the time from long ago on a calendar, was still standing still. I didn't know why, but I felt I could still breathe those moments. It was like a picture that held the promise of beauty along with a hint of melancholy.

'This was the favourite place of Barrister *Saheb*. So my father used to say,' *Kaka* said.

'So did they spend lot of time in Haveli?'

'They used to come two-three times a year just for a week or a fortnight.'

I could see boats in the horizon. It was an engaging picture. I would have stood there for some more time but *Kaka* asked me if I wanted to see the other rooms. As I was following him, I noticed that the bedroom of the other wing also had similar French windows and terrace, overlooking the river.

There was another door in the Master Bedroom, on the left wall, that connected to the adjoining bedroom. *Kaka* opened it. The room was as big as the master bedroom and quite similar to it, but for the three bay windows, on the wall on the far side, in symmetry to windows of the morning room below it, offering a grand view of the front gardens. However, everything in that room indicated that it was the room of a woman. The four poster bed was queen-sized, with a canopy that must have been pale pink. The two bay windows astride the bed, providing a beautiful view of the garden to the right of the

Haveli, were draped prettily. The dresser was a beautifully carved piece with a stool done in pink cushion with tassels. As I turned left, my eyes rested on the full-sized painting of the mistress of the house, on the wall opposite the bed. But there was a difference in this one. This was probably made during her younger days. She looked happier in this painting than in the one that was in the drawing room. She was wearing a powder blue frock with blue sapphires shining on her neck. One side of her hair was swept with a sapphire hair pin exposing one ear that was adorned with the same gem. But it was her smile and light in her eyes that made her look stunning. It was the kind of smile that could light up a room with its dazzle. Her eyes were shining as if filled with an undulated joy. As I looked at the portrait I felt a memory stirring again, but couldn't recall what it was about.

'Come! I will show you the other rooms.'

The Sitting Room opposite the Master Bedroom was small but had four Queen Ann chairs and a small coffee table. The curtains were velvet and dark maroon.

'Let's go and see Baby *Saheb's* bedroom, in the West Wing,' *Kaka* said, walking in the opposite direction.

The room was an exact replica of the Master Bedroom, including the French windows and the terrace, but I was surprised to see that this room was done up in a more modern and utilitarian way.

'This room used to be of Baby *Saheb*, Barrister *Saheb's* daughter. *Baba Saheb* now stays in this room whenever he comes here,' *Kaka* said.

The connecting door to the second bedroom was locked and *Kaka* did not offer to show that one to me.

'What about this door *Kaka*? Is this the adjoining bedroom?' I asked.

Kaka stopped in his tracks.

'It's a guest room Bitia. But it's not in use.'

'Oh! Is there any particular reason?' I asked, unable to suppress my curiosity.

Kaka cleared his throat before replying. 'It is said that *Mem Saheb* had become quite ill before she moved to England. And she spent most of her time in this room. I guess this room did not hold pleasant memories for Barrister *Saheb* and his daughter. So this was locked and never used. So I was told.'

I couldn't take my eyes off the room. I looked at the locked door and had a pressing urge to go inside but thought better of it. I did not want to make a request that would make *Kaka* feel uncomfortable.

As I turned my back to go downstairs, there was a change in the atmosphere. I felt heavy and dejected. I looked at the locked door and thought of the illness of the mistress. Maybe it was just a feeling of her sufferance or something else. Whatever it was, it made me feel unsettled.

Once downstairs, *Kaka* led me to the library. It had wood panelled walls and there were bookcases lined with hardbound books, but some of the shelves were empty. There was a big Edwardian desk, near the bay window, with an elegant chair, a bigger replica of the one that I had seen in the morning room. The elegant marble lamp along with the heavy brass penholders indicated that it must have been where the Master would have sat and worked, writing letters or going through account books. There were some comfortable leather chairs with a coffee table for reading pleasures. The air smelled of old books and wood.

'Let me show you the kitchen and then we will go and see what your *Kaki* has cooked for you.'

I wanted to have a quick peek in the wash room also, but out of politeness, followed *Kaka* to the kitchen through the dining room.

The kitchen was spacious and had a whole lot of shelves, but it had been upgraded with modern day appliances. In place of the old earthen oven, that must have been used in the past, was a four burner stove, and there was an electric oven kept on the polished counter flanked by a food processor and a toaster. There was a big refrigerator in one corner. A huge glass cupboard was placed in one corner, which had bone china dinner sets, silver cutlery and a whole lot of crystal glasses of different types. The lower shelves were full of Scotch, Single Malt Whiskies and expensive wine bottles.

'The changes were made in the kitchen by *Baba Saheb's* mother and then some of the new items were added by *Baba Saheb*. He brings his own *khansama* and butler from Delhi whenever he comes here.'

We found Kamla sitting with *Kaki* when we reached the cottage.

'*Dadi* was getting a bit worried *Didi*. It's lunch time and you hadn't come,' Kamla explained her presence.

'But how did you know where to find me?' I asked Kamla.

'Mahesh had seen you running towards this side. He wanted to ask you whether he should get the car out but since you were running he thought you had simply gone for a jog.'

'I did come jogging.'

Kamla and I had our fill of the delicious food *Kaki* had prepared, and then I took my leave and walked back home with Kamla. All that food was making me a bit drowsy but the picture of the *Mem Saheb* kept crowding my mind. What had happened to diminish the sunny smile from her countenance? I wondered. The psychiatrist in me had read more in the different expressions in both paintings than anyone else would have cared to notice.

By the time we'd said our farewells, the clouds were building up in the late July sky, making the sunlight weak. This had become a pattern with the rain falling almost every day in the evening. I was constantly thinking of the '*Mem Saheb*' and on an impulse I turned back to look at the Haveli, thinking of the times when there was life and love in this forlorn looking abode. I was about to turn my head back towards the gate when I felt I saw a figure standing in the window of the '*Mem Saheb's*' bed room. I blinked to peer at the window but there was nothing.

'What is it *Didi*?' Kamla asked.

I realised I had stopped walking.

'Nothing! I was just taking a look at the Haveli. '

I started walking and this time did not look back. I knew it was a trick of my mind. I had been thinking of the mistress ever since I had come to the Haveli a day prior, and it had become an obsession. And now, I was imagining things.

After dinner we were all sitting and talking in general. *Amma* and *Chachi* were regaling us with interesting titbits of the happenings in the village.

'*Amma*! I met Chandu *Kaka* today as I was jogging.'

I looked at Kamla and she understood that I did not want to tell mother yet that I had gone to the Haveli.

'He was saying that the owner is coming soon to sell off the Haveli.'

A shadow came over my mother's face. It was subtle but I saw it nevertheless.

'Anand is coming?' mother asked.

'Who?' I enquired.

'Barrister *Saheb's* grandson Anand is the owner of the Haveli.'

'Then it must be him. Do you know him?'

'I haven't seen him for ages. But as a kid he was a very nice boy. He saved you once from falling into the river.'

'He saved me? You never told me this.'

'I must have. You were very young. I had gone to the Haveli as I was summoned by Baby *Saheb*, Anand's mother. We were sitting in the garden and you must have wandered off and reached the bank of the river. You were standing at the edge when Anand saw you. He ran and caught you just in time and brought you back to the garden.'

Amma was silent after narrating this little anecdote, which I was very sure she had never told me before. A little later she said that she was tired and wanted to go to bed. The wall had again come up and I decided not to probe too much. She had talked about the occupants of the Haveli and that was a good start.

Later that night, when I went to my room, I felt as if there were layers about my mother's past that I was completely oblivious of. Something kept tugging at my mind but when I tried catching it, it slipped like sand from my fingers. I had a restless night and when I finally fell asleep, I kept dreaming of the Haveli.

The next morning, I decided to go for a jog in the opposite direction. I needed a little break from the Haveli and the effect it was having on me.

I walked a little distance in order to cross some houses and took the dirt road along the river and the dense foliage. After running a couple of miles, the foliage became sparse and I could see the river through the shrubs. I slowed down and started moving towards the river. I was still a few meters away from it; I felt a sense of panic. I was on higher ground and the river was some five feet below. I felt a bit dizzy and clutched the branch of a small tree. I was in good health and this kind of run was a very normal activity for me. I took deep breaths to steady myself. On a sudden impulse I turned back and walked a few paces back till I reached a huge neem tree. I put my body against the thick trunk and tried to control the feeling.

'Are you alright?'

I jumped out of my skin hearing the deep voice.

'Oh I am so sorry. I had no intention of startling you.'

I blinked and my heart missed some beats. I was facing a man in his mid forties with an envious physique. He was tall and looked very attractive in his running gear. His handsome face looked familiar and then I realised with a jolt that he looked like the man in the painting in the Haveli; the deliciously handsome Barrister *Saheb*. I was nonplussed. I couldn't understand whether I was dreaming or this was real, whether this was a ghost or a live man standing and looking at me with some concern on his face. It was a bit too much for me. I blinked again, thinking the image would vanish. I was definitely having some sort of an episode which I couldn't explain. But when I opened my eyes again, I found him standing at the same spot. I was not dreaming then.

'I am fine. Thank you!' My own voice sounded strange to my ears.

'You look pale. Here! I have some water. Please drink some.'

He offered a small water bottle. I gulped it down. I felt slightly better but was still reeling with the effect of the likeness of the man with the Master of the Haveli. As if reading my thoughts, he proffered his hand.

'Hi! I am Anand. And you are Aparna if I am not mistaken,' he said with a smile that lit up his handsome face. I felt a quickening of my pulse.

'Hello! I am Aparna. But how did you guess?'

'Well it's a small village. And the comings and goings of distinguished people like you can hardly be a secret. Right?' he said with a twinkle in his eyes.

'So, Chandu *Kaka* told you about me,' I said, feeling a bit better.

'There you are... the 'Mind Doctor' as they call you.'

'You seem to know a lot about me,' I said.

'Not a lot, just that you have come with your mother a few days back and visited Chandu *Kaka*.'

If he knew that I had gone inside the Haveli, he didn't mention it. I decided not to say anything that would put Chandu *Kaka* in an awkward position.

'Are you feeling better? Would you like to continue with your run or walk, whatever it was, or head back home?' he asked.

'I think I will go home now.'

'In that case let's walk together. That is, if you don't mind my company,' he said flashing the same captivating smile.

In response I just smiled. I was still trying to control my feelings that this surprise encounter had sprung on me. Till yesterday, the Master of the Haveli was just a picture in the painting; he had lived in the past, in another era. But today he was very much alive, bringing the past to the present and merging the thin line between them. We started walking.

'How is your mother doing?' he asked, keeping the conversation going.

'She is doing well considering she is in her early-seventies.'

'That's good to know.'

'So when did you come to India?'

'Last week.'

I was again a bit puzzled at the easy manner he had acquired while talking to me. It seemed that he knew more about me than I did about him.

'When did you arrive here?' I asked, keeping the flow of conversation going.

'Last night. Actually, I had no plans until next week but the buyers wanted to come and take a look at the property this weekend so I had to cancel some plans and come here. Chandu *Kaka* was in a bit of a fit. He felt that he hadn't got enough time to do up the place. So have you come to the village before, or is it the first time since you left for Lucknow?' he asked.

'I have come for the first time after we left for Lucknow. Though my father kept coming but I somehow couldn't make it then,' I said thinking that once or twice I had wanted to accompany him to the village, but every time my parents had dissuaded me. They felt that I was too used to the city life, therefore, I would not be able to adjust even for a short period of time. And then gradually the small village was lost into oblivion.

'So what brings you here now?'

'My mother has decided to sell the house and the land. So I have accompanied her to help her out.'

'Oh! Looks like we both have the same mission. So how long are you here?'

'A couple of weeks,' I said. 'And what about you? Have you visited this place often?'

'I used to, when mother was alive. But have not been able to come very often for quite some time now. Last I visited was about three years back.'

'Oh, I didn't know that…,'

'It's alright; it's been five years now.'

Our conversation was interrupted as we gave space to a passing bullock cart. We talked a bit about the village and the fresh air and soon we were at the door of my house.

'It was really nice to meet you. I do hope to see you again,' he said with that charming smile I was noticing a lot.

'Yes! Of course!' I said a little too eagerly and cursed myself.

And with that he turned and walked away briskly. I stood there watching his retreating back and then I suddenly felt lonely. It was as if the clouds had obscured a cheerful sun and everything lost some of its sheen. After standing there for a few moments, I jerked my head slightly in order to bring myself back to reality. I walked towards the small garden and sat down on the cemented circular bench of the neem tree. I tried to figure out what had just happened. Why did I feel the way I felt? I was used to meeting a lot of people in my profession. In other words, meeting new people was a part of my profession and it was just that. I'd attended lots of conferences in different countries, and in the process met many men. And though I always got hints and signals, and at times direct proposals for a date, I steered clear of them. It was not that I wanted to live a life of celibacy; it was just that I compared every male with Ashok. I had accepted dinner dates a couple of times, thinking that it might work out but Ashok had always won. It was as if he was always present, smiling tauntingly just to see how far I would go. Once he'd asked me why I wasn't moving on. Was he the reason? And I was so angry at his superciliousness that I had told him that he was mistaken, I had long gotten over him. He was a bit surprised at my acrimonious tone. I had repented the words the moment they were out of my mouth. I could have handled it with more dignity. I had only shown my weakness by acting like that. I knew Ashok was in and out of relationships. He was far too self-absorbed to give a piece of himself to anyone for long. Probably he felt guilty, and that was the reason he wanted me to move on and rekindle the romance in my life. And I would have, had someone stirred the feelings inside me like today. I realised with a sinking feeling that I had never felt like this with Ashok. This was definitely not something I was prepared for. And then, suddenly, I was angry at myself. What was wrong with me? I had met a complete stranger for a few minutes and was letting my imagination run riot. I was a mature, grown up woman with a lot of dignity, not a teenager wearing my heart on my sleeve.

The cool breeze seemed to calm the irk I was feeling. Why was I fretting? It was not as if I was going to meet him anytime soon. Also, I was here just for a few weeks and then I would go back to my quiet yet busy life. That thought seemed to calm me a bit more and I got up and entered the house. I had succeeded in regaining my composure as I sat down to eat breakfast in the cosy confines of the kitchen, or so I thought.

CHAPTER 5

The sky was overcast. Dark grey clouds had been gathering for some time now, with a cool breeze giving the indication of rainfall somewhere earlier. It was ripe with petrichor that never failed to fill the atmosphere with a cool, pleasant sensation. The trees were swaying as if engaged in frolic, depicting their joyous celebration at the advent of the monsoons. A cuckoo perched on the mango tree joined in the celebration, singing enthusiastically, welcoming the clouds.

She looked out from the window of her room. A squirrel came running down a tree to collect enough food before it started raining.

A zephyr gently stirred her hair and her locks came loose, falling on her cheeks. She closed her eyes, savouring the moment. She felt that all-familiar rapture that bathed her soul. She wanted to sing with the cuckoo, dance with the trees, mingle with the clouds floating weightlessly. She felt that inexplicable joy that always came with this season. She floated like a wisp of cloud.

She was lying under the fragrant plumeria tree. The pregnant clouds were about to burst any moment. Something brushed her lips gently. She smiled parting her lips slightly in anticipation. A shiver ran down her body to the innermost sanctum of her desire. And it was just then that the clouds opened up, pouring down with an impregnable urgency.

Someone was calling her name from afar. She ignored it. She did not want to leave her cocoon, her blissful existence; not when she was going to receive her gift. She was called again. The voice was close, very close. She fought to stay where she was.

And then her whole body shook like a leaf in a storm.

I woke up with a start. There was a stirring in my body. I wanted to be kissed deeply; but by whom? It was a dream. But all my senses seemed to be engaged with the delicious desire that was still coursing through my veins. I was surprised at the vividness of the dream. I could still smell the petrichor and the notes of the cuckoo's songs were still ringing in my ears.

For a few moments, I felt the coolness of the rain. I lay confused for some time and then looked at my watch. It was around three in the morning. I wrapped the blanket around myself and closed my eyes. I wanted to be there again... in my dream. As I was slipping into the haze of slumber, I opened my eyes with a start. I was being called in the dream; but was I, because it was not my name that I had heard? I tried recalling it but it slipped into the labyrinths of my mind.

I overslept, and this time it was the soft voice of Kamla that woke me. I yawned and stretched deliciously. I looked out of the window, at the neem tree. The breeze was cool as a result of last night's rains. I breathed deeply. I felt happy as I thought of the dream, and it was the face of Anand with that disarming smile of his that flashed in front of my eyes, and I felt warmth filling my whole body.

We had just finished breakfast and I was checking the papers of the property as the buyers were coming to meet us and finalise things, when Chandu *Kaka* came.

'*Kaka*! How did you come? Hope you did not walk all the distance.'

'No *Bitia*! I have come in *Baba Saheb's* car. Actually Peter and I are going to Lalgarh to buy some provisions so I thought I would meet *Bhabhi* and bring these *laddoos* that your *Kaki* has sent for you,' he said, handing over a brass container to Kamla.

'*Kaka*, please tell Kaki not to take so much trouble.'

After sitting for ten minutes or so *Kaka* took his leave saying that he should get going. I walked him to the door.

'I was hoping that you would walk me to the door *Bitia*. Actually

I had to give you this.' He took out an envelope from his bag and handed it to me.

'*Baba Saheb* has sent this for you,' he added seeing the question on my face.

'He wants a reply. I will come after a couple of hours or so,' he said without adding anything. He looked at me with an expression that said something without putting words to it. There was hope mingled with a hint of joy in his insightful eyes. I stood there with the envelope in my hand. There was a tumult of emotions raging inside me. I felt elated like a sixteen year old girl and then I realised that I had been waiting to hear from him, though I had been telling myself otherwise. I went straight to my room and opened the envelope. Inside was a single sheet of heavy and expensive stationery with Anand written in curling letters.

Hi,

I am hoping to turn a dull evening into a pleasurable one by adding your gracious presence to it if you would accede to do so. Please forgive my forwardness, but then, the prospect of meeting you and catching up is all I have been thinking of since yesterday.

So may I request the pleasure of your company for dinner at the Haveli? I shall pick you up at eight in the evening?

Regards,

Anand

His name was signed with a flourish.

It was a direct request. In fact there was a hint of complacence in the tone of the message. He was aware of his effect on people, more so on the opposite sex. I wanted to know whether he was conceited or just confident. I liked men who knew their minds and were straightforward. In any case, the truth was that I wanted to go to the Haveli. I had thought of nothing else but him since meeting him. Also, this was the perfect opportunity to know about his grandparents. But I did not know how to broach this to mother. I did not know what her reaction would be, but then I decided to take my chances.

Mother was surprised when I told her about the invitation. She was quiet for a couple of moments. I saw her exchange glances with *Chachi* and a look had come over her face, but then after a pause she acquiesced, albeit reluctantly. The nagging feeling of misgiving had again started nudging me. I was more determined to find out what it was about the Haveli that brought this change in mother. I sent back my acceptance of the invitation.

After the buyers left after checking the papers and promising to come back as soon as possible to seal the deal, I went up to my room and opened the cupboard to decide what to wear. I generally wore slacks or a pair of jeans with shirts in the village and had brought very few dresses. I chose a monochrome, A-line dress that I had picked up in New York during my recent visit there. I decided to don a pair of pearl studs and black pumps to accessorise my dress. I found myself waiting for the evening which I knew was a sign of trouble. I was allowing myself to be swept away by this gale of unexpected events. To spend a pleasant evening over dinner was one thing, but to attach something more to it was another. Why was I letting my heart play this trick on me? I felt a wave of annoyance at behaving like a complete fool. There were still a few hours to go before Anand came to pick me up. I tried reading a book but couldn't concentrate. Finally, I decided to take a stroll to divert my mind from the evening.

Anand came right at eight o'clock. I found him sitting with *Amma* as I came down the stairs. *Chachi* and Kamla were also there.

'*Didi*! You look so beautiful! Kamla said the moment she saw me. Anand turned back and stood up. He smiled at me and there was a twinkle in his eyes. Our eyes met and my heart stopped for a moment. He looked very handsome in a light blue shirt and dark slacks. He did not say anything but his eyes said it all.

'I came to introduce myself to *Chachi* but she remembered me,' he said, breaking the moment.

I really liked the way he addressed my mother as '*Chachi*'. It showed that he was very familiar with the simple traditions of the village where one always addressed the elders as *Chacha*, *Chachi* or *Kaka*, Kaki. He may have spent a major part of his life in USA, but he didn't let his roots go.

He took his leave of *Amma* and escorted me to his Mercedes.

'Thank you for accepting the invitation,' he said opening the door for me.

'You are being formal. And in that case I should be thanking you for extending the invitation.'

He laughed. It was an honest laugh.

'Touché! By the way, you look stunning. No wonder they talk about your beauty.'

I looked at him questioningly.

'We might have some common friends in Delhi, or acquaintances you might say,' he said keeping his gaze on the road this time.

'And who are these friends that we have in common, pray tell me?'

'All in good time! We have an entire evening to talk. Don't we?'

It was a short drive. We were received by *Kaka* and another man I had not seen earlier. He was Ramesh, Anand's butler, as I came to know later.

The Haveli had a different look today. It looked like a woman, dressed in her finery to greet her lover, who was coming to meet her after a long time. Gone was the sullen air that it had earlier worn when I had visited. There were lanterns lit and hung in the branches of the trees. There were big glass lamps lit and kept in the veranda. I drew a breath, as in that soft and warm quivering light, the place wore a magical look.

Anand escorted me to the terrace through his bedroom, in the West wing. And again I had to stop in admiration. There were two comfortable leather sofas flanked by the tall wrought iron candle stands with thick flickering candles. The fresh flower arrangement on the centre table looked elegant. There was a big earthen pot with tea lights and fresh flowers floating over the water. And in the far corner was a small round table laid with a setting for two. It was all so dreamlike and romantic that I couldn't help but let a sigh escape. It was just the kind of setting that I loved.

'I hope you like it. It's not much but I tried bringing a little life to this place. Come, let me take you to the far end you can see the river from,' he said.

We both stood looking down at the river that was midnight blue. The breeze was cool and sweet with a faint scent of roses that it must have picked up from somewhere. It swayed the trees and somewhere a bird flapped its wings. The moon was not full but it was casting its silvery moonlight making the already perfect picture even more perfect.

'I have always loved this place. I often lose myself in the serenity and solitude it has to offer,' Anand said.

'It's very serene and peaceful here.'

'*Baba Saheb*!' Our trance was broken and we both turned back. *Kaka* and Ramesh were standing there with a trolley.

'Thank you *Kaka* and Ramesh. I will let you know if we require anything more,' Anand said taking the trolley from him. Ramesh placed a platter of cheese, olives, crackers and some hors d'oeuvres on the centre table.

As we both sat there with our drinks in our hands; red wine for me and a single malt whiskey for him, we both waited for each other to speak. And then, the silence was broken by Anand.

'So how is life in England? I know you are a very accomplished psychiatrist. So besides your devotion to your job, what else are you passionate about?'

'Life is as good as it can be. As for your other question, I don't get much time for anything else, but yes, I do have a passion for something other than my job. I like to read about the past. I love visiting places that are hundreds of years old. I feel this connection with the yesteryear. The history of places attracts me to an extent that I just want to touch and feel what was there, eons back. I want to know the stories of the people who lived their lives in the bygone eras. The human mind always remains the same. It goes through the same tumultuous emotions; love, joy, sorrow, etc., only time and the fabric of society change. A man and a woman must have laughed, loved, cried, and must have felt all the emotions we feel today, ever since humankind came into existence.'

I didn't know what was responsible for such a detailed answer to Anand's question. Probably sitting on that terrace of the Haveli that was a link to the past had betrayed my emotions.

'Sorry! I just got carried away.'

'No! I really admire your devotion to your passion. To feel for something this deeply is the true essence of life.'

He looked at his glass, tilting it a bit so that the ice cubes made a tinkling sound.

'I wish I could find something I could lose myself in,' he said.

'How is your life in America?' I said in order to change the solemn mood he had slipped into.

'Well I have... what should I say... not a bad life. Work keeps me busy and I have some good friends who are dependable and fun to be with. But it's my son I like to spend my time with. That is, when he comes to spend some time with me.'

I wanted to ask more but waited for him to speak. He was quiet for some time.

'I met Anjana in Oxford. We fell in love, or that was what it felt like at that time. We both were young and life looked like a dream. It was only after a few years that we started drifting apart. It's strange that two people who feel so close at one time can grow so far apart at another. Anyway, there was no point carrying on and living the pretence, especially when our son was growing up. We did not want him to suffer because we both couldn't stand to be with each other. Anjana wanted the sole custody of Shourya and I let her have it. Shourya is a good boy. He never sulked or blamed us for our separation. He is a loving soul and divides his time between me and his mother, whenever he can manage, now that he is in college. This is the sum of my life. Let me refill your glass,' he said reaching for the bottle of wine.

'So, any progress on the sale of the house?' he asked.

'The people who want to buy the house and the land came today. They checked the papers and said that they would come next week to finalise the deal. So once that is done we will go back to Lucknow and after a couple of days I will go to Delhi and fly from there to England. That's the plan at the moment. What about you?'

'The buyers are coming day after tomorrow to see the property. I guess I would also head back next week.'

'So do you go back to the States?' I asked.

'I have some business to wrap up in Delhi. And also fulfil the formalities if this Haveli is sold. I am not sure about the exact date yet. So I will be in Delhi for a few more days.'

'How old is this Haveli?' I asked.

'This is about a hundred and thirty years old. This was built in the year 1885 by a Taluqdar who owned quite a substantial piece of land in the Rae Bareli District. He basically built this as a hunting lodge for the highly placed British officers, to please them, I think. If you have noticed, the architecture is quite similar to that of the Victorian era. It resembles a villa in a typical British countryside. After the death of the Taluqdar, his son also continued to use it as a Hunting Lodge. My grandfather and the Taluqdar's son were close friends and my grandfather came here a couple of times with him, and as word goes, he fell in love with this place. So when his friend offered to sell this to him he readily bought it. And it has been in the family ever since.'

Anand was quiet as if he was still in the past.

'I don't want to intrude but I can't help asking; why are you selling it? It's a perfect getaway from the madding crowd,' I said.

'Yes! I know that, but I don't think my son would be interested in this faraway place. He is too used to the American life. He would find this place dull and lifeless. We used to come with friends in the early years of our marriage, and of course, whenever mother wanted to visit, but I don't come very often now. Moreover, it's falling into disrepair. Also, Chandu *Kaka* is getting old and I don't think I can find anyone as reliable as him, as his replacement. So I guess it's the best thing to do, under the circumstances. I wanted to shift *Kaka* and Kaki to my bungalow in Delhi but he is not keen to leave his birthplace so I did not push. Though I have told him that he and Kaki are my responsibility and I will keep taking care of them.'

I wanted to ask more about his grandparents but before I could speak, he suddenly said, 'May I ask something?'

'Please go ahead.' The wine had relaxed me and the breeze was adding magic to the ambience. Probably, that was the reason that I did not mind him asking anything.

'I take it that you are... as they say... single?' he said with a nervous smile that made him look very boyish. 'So is there someone in the scene or are you ... single?'

I was a bit surprised at the directness of the question but his evident discomfort made it sound innocent enough.

'No! There is no one. I am as they say... single.'

And with that we both started laughing. The awkwardness of the previous moments was forgotten.

The conversation took a different turn and the remainder of the evening was spent in general talks of music, theatre and books.

The food was elegant but sumptuous, followed by rich chocolate pudding. And when Anand offered some Cognac it only looked appropriate, as the evening was giving way to night, the chill in the air had increased, and sitting there wrapped in my Pashmina stole in the golden light of the candles, sipping Cognac listening to Anand's deep and soothing voice, I wished for the evening to never come to an end.

When I got up the next morning, my first thought was of Anand and it brought a smile to my lips. I lay in bed, reminiscing the details of the evening. I had felt tipsy by the time I had finished my cognac and then I remembered Anand opening the door of the car and driving me home. I had thrown my head back, closed my eyes and just relished the beautiful night. I remembered Kamla opening the door and after wishing Anand good night, I had come tip toeing to my room.

I came down and saw *Amma* and *Chachi* sitting in the angan, chatting amicably.

'*Bitia*! I have made *aaloo ki sabzi* and would make some hot *pooris*,' *Chachi* said.

'*Chachi*, please don't work so hard. I could have eaten *dalia*. Also I need to switch over to *khichdi*; otherwise I am going to get indigestion.'

Chachi started laughing.

'Alright! I will make *khichdi* for dinner. I don't want you to get indigestion.'

'I am sure even the *khichdi* made by you would be heavenly,' I said, hugging her. I was a bit surprised seeing mother looking relaxed. I was a bit apprehensive thinking that she might not have liked my coming back late from the Haveli.

As I went about the day, my thoughts kept turning to Anand. I was wondering whether I would be able to see him again sometime soon. I did not have to wait very long. Anand came and asked if I cared to go to town, where he was going to pick some fresh fruits and other provisions, for the buyers who were coming the next day.

'I thought you might have some work there too,' he added, again wearing the same boyish look.

'Sounds like a good idea. I will ask *Chachi* if she requires anything for the house,' I said smiling. Once again we fell into a kind of chatter that comes after easy familiarity. This was the third time I was meeting him but it felt as if we had known each other all along.

'Aparna, why don't you join me and the buyers for dinner tomorrow? It would be nice to have you there.'

'But this is a kind of business dinner. What would I do with you all?'

'It would just feel nice to have you by my side as my friend. After all, who can be so lucky to have a friend who is internationally renowned?' he said looking at me with his honest smile.

'You are pulling my leg.'

'No! I am just stating a fact.'

I looked at him. He was looking earnestly at me.

'Alright! I will come. Anything else I can do to help?' I asked.

'Please come a little early, at about 6:30, so that I can brief you about the deal they are offering. I would like to have your input on the same,' he said.

Ever since I had met Anand, the thought of his grandparents and my mother's connection with the Haveli had slipped to a corner of my mind. I was basking in the warm glow of this new feeling that had become a part of my life. Everything looked beautiful and there was this new energy and hope within me that I had not felt for a long time. My world revolved around him, when I was with him. I could think of nothing but him. And I just wanted to feel like that forever.

I wore a golden satin blouse with deep burgundy trousers. I chose to wear dull gold stilettos. I thanked myself silently for bringing some good pieces to the village, though I was sure I was not going to require these kinds of clothes in the village. But clothes were my weakness and I was one of those people who couldn't bear the idea of getting caught in a situation where they didn't have suitable clothes to wear. I always carried more clothes and shoes than I ever wore during a vacation. But my obsession was paying off in a way I had never thought it would.

The Haveli had lost its look of neglect and had started looking habitable and charming to some extent. There were two gleaming Mercedes SUVs parked in the porch giving the indication of Anand's perspective buyers. Anand was standing at the porch to receive me. I drew a breath as I looked at him. He was wearing a black shirt with steel grey slacks and a jacket. He had an air of easy confidence that added more to his killing looks.

'Wow! I wonder whether my guests would be able to concentrate on anything but you. And that is so going to work in my favour,' he said with a mischievous glint in his eyes as he helped me out of the car.

'Oh! So now I know the reason behind this invitation,' I said smiling. 'By the way, you yourself look divine,' I said, meaning every word.

'Thank you!' he said smiling.

He escorted me to the terrace which looked even more beautiful than it had looked the other night. There were candles lit in glass jars and flower arrangements done on the dining table. I looked at it wondering who would have done the arrangements. And I did not see any florist who could have kept such beautiful blossoms in the small town.

'I had a guy driven from Lucknow. I have to make the place look presentable,' Anand said as if reading my thoughts. 'They will be joining us shortly. They reached around four and then after light refreshment, wanted to see the area around. So I delayed the dinner a bit. Hope it's not an inconvenience to you,' he asked.

'No! It's perfectly alright. I love the place so I am glad I will get to spend more time here.'

He looked at me as if wanting to say something but then thought better of it.

'Come! Let me get you a drink. What would you like to have?'

'Some wine would be good,' I said taking in the beauty of the place. The breeze had acquired a delicious nip coming from the river and the flickering light of the candles wavered and drew patterns on the floor.

Anand handed me a crystal wine glass and fixed himself a drink. He sat down in the opposite chair and we both clinked our glasses.

'*Saheb*! Peter needs to speak with you,' Ramesh was standing at the door.

'Could you excuse me for few minutes? I am sure he wants to clarify something related to the dinner.'

'Sure! Please see to it. I am very comfortable here.'

I got up from the chair and walked to the extreme edge of the terrace hoping to see some boats, if there were any, of the fishermen returning home or someone crossing the river to go to the village on the other side. The river looked inky in the darkness but as I peered I saw two dots of lights floating very slowly on its bosom. It was a beautiful sight to behold. I stood there for some time and poured some more wine. I was enjoying the solitude and looking at the dots that seemed to come closer. I was so engrossed looking at the horizon that I jumped a little as I heard a rustling of clothes. I turned back sharply but there was no one there. The terrace was as vacant of anyone else as it was before. I was a bit perplexed because the sound was as close as someone standing just next to me. It was probably some bird that woke up from its slumber and disturbed the leaves. I looked back at the door that opened into the terrace, hoping Anand would come any moment. In order to occupy myself I turned and walked to the corner of the terrace and stood looking at the similar terrace, of the East wing, that was in front of the Master Bedroom.

The mistress and the master would have spent so many evenings together on the terrace, I thought to myself. I looked at the big French windows that were dark and looked a bit menacing. I felt an overwhelming sense of melancholy. I wanted to tear my gaze away, yet found myself rooted there. After a little while I could stand it no longer and I turned and started walking towards the chair I had sat in earlier. I closed my eyes. And then I heard the same sound... the rustling of clothes and this time I felt as if it was enveloping me. I had never felt any fear while going to the most abandoned and old buildings or castles, but the hair on my neck stood and I felt someone very close to me. I froze, and then there was this whiff that carried a faint fragrance of flowers. I had a feeling that if I looked back, I would find someone standing right behind me. I took deep breaths and turned sharply. There was no one. The mood of the terrace had changed from romantic and cosy to melancholic and disquieting. Suddenly, I didn't want to stay there alone and was contemplating going down when Anand entered with his guests and I let my breath out. I hadn't realised I'd been holding it.

'Aparna!' Anand started saying something and stopped mid-sentence. 'Are you ok?' he asked.

'I am fine!' I managed a weak smile.

'Let me introduce you to...,' and he went on to introduce me to the gentlemen, who all proceeded to exchange pleasantries with me, in the most gracious way. I went along the motions, but I was still not able to concentrate fully on the proceedings of the evening. My mind was elsewhere and it seemed as if I were on autopilot. When I finished my third glass of wine I felt a little relaxed, but my gaze kept going to the spot in the extreme end of the terrace, where I had stood. Anand kept me involved in the conversation and every time I looked at him I saw concern in his eyes, but it was his dazzling smile that was reassuring and warmed my heart. During dinner, there was light conversation in the beginning and then it switched over to the history of the Haveli and the village. I listened to Anand talking about the Haveli and its owners and occupants in his rich and clear voice. I hoped to hear something more about his grandparents but it was only what I already knew.

The evening came to an end and we saw the guests off together. I was glad for it as I just wanted to go home, but at the same time the thought of being away from Anand was depressing. Suddenly, I had this feeling of resting my head on his shoulder and falling asleep in the protective shield of his presence.

I was a bit surprised at how quickly I was advancing towards him. Maybe it was the effect of the strange happenings of the evening, or all that good wine that I had downed.

'A night cap?' Anand asked me.

'I think I will go home now,' I said though I was tempted to stay.

'I have not been able to talk to you the entire evening. But if you are tired then wouldn't keep you,' he said.

'I will have a small draught but can we sit here in the veranda?' I said looking at the two wicker chairs.

'Of course!' He looked happy. 'Aparna, hope you don't mind my probing, but you looked distracted most of the evening. Did you find the company boring?'

'No! Not at all! I am sorry. I guess that I was feeling a bit more relaxed with all that wine. I didn't realise I was making it that obvious.'

We had some liqueur as I did not want to have more wine and then he dropped me home. We both kept our conversation casual because I for one, was definitely on my guard, as I was feeling a bit tipsy and I think he realised that, and kept it light, though I caught him looking at me with a smile that again made me feel light headed. We bid each other good night as Kamla opened the door.

'Did Anand say how long he is going to be here?' Mother asked me when we all sat down for breakfast next day.

I was a bit taken aback at the question as mother and I had not really discussed anything about Anand or the Haveli. She had kept away from the topic and I was comfortable that way. I still did not know what to say if she asked about my growing friendship with him. Also, he had not mentioned anything about meeting again and I could hardly stop thinking about him and was feeling a bit low.

'A week probably, but then, I am not sure. It all depends on the sale of the Haveli I guess.'

'Hmmm! I hope the buyers decide fast for our deal as well because it would be nice to go back to Lucknow,' she said.

'But I thought you were enjoying your stay here meeting everyone and catching up,' I said looking at her. I could not understand her sudden longing to go back to Lucknow. Was it something to do with Anand?

'It is nice to meet everyone but then we should not overstay our welcome. Moreover, my home is in Lucknow now. I have met everyone and have visited this house where I came as a new bride and I am happy to have come here, but now I am ready to say goodbye to everyone and this house.' There was a note of resignation in her voice and though I was happy to know that she did not attach any sentiments to the house, I had a feeling that it had something to do with my increasing friendship with Anand.

'Would you call those people, Parni, and ask how long they would take to finalise everything? We will have to inform our lawyer as well to come here.'

'I will go to the post office and call them from there,' I said.

Chachi looked at me little nervously. And then I understood. Mother wanted me to be away from Anand. But why, I couldn't understand. She had been after my life all these years to find someone and settle down. And now she disliked the idea. Though, I did not know anything about how Anand felt about me, and it was preposterous to think about a future with him, but ever since I had met him I hadn't thought of anything but him. I felt as if I had known him all my life. I would watch him secretly when he wouldn't be looking at me. The way he spoke, his smile enhancing the cleft in his chin, his deep and expressive eyes speaking volumes; everything was so familiar, as if I knew each and every expression of his face.

There was something going on in my mother's mind, and I had a feeling she was not being candid with me. I decided to have a conversation with her in the night when *Chachi* and Kamla would retire to bed.

While I was immersed in these thoughts, there was a knock at the door and Kamla went to answer it. She came back with a white envelop in her hand and my heart skipped a beat.

'*Didi*, Anand *Bhaiya's* driver has brought this for you. He is waiting for a reply,' she said smiling.

As I took the envelope from her hands, I looked at mother but she simply averted her eyes. Some of the jubilation that I had felt went out of me. It was a note from Anand asking me if I could join him for lunch.

'*I have missed seeing you and there is so much I want to talk about,'* he had written.

Gone was the formal stance that he had used in his previous invitation. He sounded like a boy who couldn't wait to meet his friend. In spite of mother's consternation my heart filled with pure joy and I smiled.

'Kamla, please tell him I would join his master for lunch,' I said and then I asked mother.

'Hope you don't mind my going out for lunch *Amma*. Also I will make the phone call from Haveli,' I said with an easy smile hoping that she would not object.

'It is only fine that *Bitia* has a friend here *Jiji*, even if it is for a short time. She would have got bored otherwise. She is not used to this kind of a dull village life,' *Chachi* said. They exchanged a glance that confused me a little more, but then Mother said that *Chachi* was right and I should go and have lunch with Anand.

I chose a white linen shirt and a pair of denims, and wore nude wedges, completing the look with a swipe of mascara and a baby pink lipstick. But as I dressed, my mind kept going back to my mother and *Chachi*. There was something going on between them and I had to find out what it was. I did not want to be kept in the dark.

I sat in the car that was waiting for me and reached the Haveli. Ramesh asked me whether I would like to go upstairs or wait in the drawing room as *Saheb* had gone out but would be back soon. I told him that I would like to wait in the drawing room.

'Please make yourself comfortable. What should I get for you, tea or coffee?'

'Nothing now, maybe later. Thank you!'

The moment I was alone I walked up to the far end where the life-like painting was hanging. I again got that feeling in the pit of my stomach the moment I rested my eyes on the master of the Haveli. But this time the feeling grew pleasant with a tickle as I noticed the resemblance between Anand and his grandfather, the same intense eyes, the Greek nose and the strong jaw line. I looked at the mistress trying to see some resemblance with Anand but couldn't find any. She seemed to be looking at me directly. There was something like reproach in her eyes, as if she had found me staring at her husband and had not liked it. I averted my eyes and chided myself for being fanciful. I started looking around the room. As my gaze ran across the room I noticed an outline of a small door cut in the wood panelling in the corner, next to the Edwardian console table. I walked towards it and after a moment's hesitation pushed it. It was indeed a door. It creaked a little but opened inwards. The room was dark. I was deciding whether to enter or not but then on impulse, I entered the room and pushed the door ajar so that some of the light could seep through. I waited a bit, and as my eyes got used to the dark I looked for a switch and found one next to the door. I switched on the light and the room was bathed in the yellow glow of a bulb. It looked like a small store room. There was a door on the opposite wall that I guessed must open into the library. There were two almirahs with glass doors on either side of the door. I walked to take a closer look at the almirah on the right side. There were some books and albums stacked over each other. I was tempted to take those albums out but stopped myself. I could not pry into someone's private albums. As I was about to turn my back, I caught a glimpse of a framed photograph lying buried under the albums. I could take a look at the photograph at least, I thought. Maybe it was another photograph of the couple whose painting was in the drawing room. I opened the almirah. There was no lock, just a simple latch. I heaved the albums and pulled out the framed photograph. It was an old photograph and there was a film of dust over it. I looked around for something to wipe the dust with, but didn't find anything, so I just blew the dust and coughed a bit as I inhaled it. The dust seemed to have entered from the wooden frame that was chipped from couple of places and it had made the already sepia photograph even hazier.

It seemed to have been taken on some occasion, as along with the master and the mistress, there were also others in the photograph. It looked like it was taken in the front garden. The mistress of the house sat in the centre with another woman, the master and another man sat on either side of the women. There was a small girl sitting on lap of Anand's grandfather. He had wrapped his arm around her and there was a smile on his face that was full of contentment and happiness. But my gaze settled at the woman sitting next to Anand's grandmother. I felt as if my eyes were playing a trick. I brought the photograph closer to my eyes and then I ran out of the dimly lit room and threw open the curtains in order to get more light.

I was rooted to the spot. My eyes were not playing any tricks. And at that moment as I felt a little surreal, I knew that the photograph was going to change my life forever. The woman in the photograph resembled me.

If there is any measure of limitless beauty, the measure itself would have been insufficient. The woman in the photograph was an example of how exalted beauty could be. I have often been told that I have been bestowed with good looks and I have been grateful to

God for making me pleasant to the eyes, but there was something magnetic about the beauty of the woman in the photograph. Her beauty was bewitching yet pure, sensuous yet graceful, ethereal yet earthly. She was a juxtaposition of the two opposites and that was the most engaging quality of her beauty. Her face was oval with a broad forehead. The eyes were large and deeply set with long lashes, and they were the kind of eyes one could never tire looking into. Her nose was straight and small and her lips were full and luscious. Her figure clad in a *sari* and a jumper, was proportionate and very delicately built. Her hands lay crossed on her lap, bejewelled with glass and gold bangles and rings, and she wore a necklace and small teardrop earrings in her ears. Her hair was arranged in a bun and her head was covered with the gossamer material of the *sari*. The more I looked at the photograph the more it stared back with a likeness of me, that was so real that I could have easily been the person in the picture if I were dressed like her, and my hair were done in a bun.

Who was she? What was her connection to me? These were the questions that assailed my mind. And then I looked at the child, sitting on Barrister *Saheb's* lap, as Anand's grandfather was called by everyone. Was she Anand's mother? I looked closely and found the resemblance between the child and the woman sitting next to the mistress, undisputable. And as I was peering at the photograph closely, I noticed something else. Anand's grandmother was wearing a dress and I could make out a bulge on her stomach. Was she pregnant at the time the photograph was taken? That seemed the only plausible explanation because her figure was as slender as in the painting in the hall except that tiny bump. The man sitting next to the woman must be her husband, I presumed. He was though, not as strikingly handsome as Anand's grandfather, but was good looking in a simple and modest way. He was wearing a suit and looked respectable. He had kind eyes and a full head of dark and rich hair. He was the kind of man who would embrace life in whichever form it was presented to him.

It's strange how moments are frozen in a photograph. These people were alive and living their lives at that moment, not worrying about the future that would wipe them and leave behind just a moment frozen in time, as proof of their existence. Their lives would become stories in the footsteps in time.

CHAPTER 6

1930

The house was big and it had three wings. It was built by Pt. Shiv Prasad Pandey, who'd migrated from his native village to obtain education and get a job in Lucknow. Though his family had acres of land in the village, and while his cousins were happy living there, he'd decided to come to the city. He was hungry for knowledge. So in spite of the resistance put up by his father he moved to the city. After acquiring a graduate degree he landed himself the respectable job of a lecturer. His salary would have been adequate, had he stopped after producing a couple of offspring. But as the tradition was, he went on to have a healthy and boisterous houseful of ten. The division was done by Mother Nature herself, five sons and an equal number of daughters. He was a proud man and did not want to reach out to his father for any kind of help, so he started 'guiding' the students and started writing books in his spare time. His books were published and money was no longer a major issue. After a couple of years, his father passed away and he got his share of land which added to his already healthy financial state.

His eldest son, Kanti Prasad, who was a brilliant student, majored in English Literature and followed his father's footsteps to become a lecturer in Lucknow University. He was a thorough gentleman, and was a very responsible and obedient son. He idolised his father and listened to his every word, absorbing them like a piece of sponge.

So when his father asked him to get married and told him about a marriage proposal that had come for him, he just agreed. Later, when his parents went to see the girl and finalised everything, all he did was nod quietly when he was told about it. There was nothing to say about the matter, for such matters were settled by parents and they would only act in his interest.

The house soon filled up with relatives, and there were a whole lot of them. Because it was the first wedding in the family, each and every one was invited. Amidst the hustle bustle and gaiety of the wedding preparations, Kanti Prasad couldn't help but overhear about his betrothed and the wealthy family she was coming from. He was not interested in the dowry that she was bringing with her, but when he heard about her astonishing beauty, he felt intimidated and surprised. He couldn't understand why anyone with money and a daughter as beautiful as her would want someone like him as their son-in-law.

Kanti Prasad was not a matinee idol but he had a pleasing personality. He was of medium height with regular features. He was on the thinner side, and had the kind of sophistication that comes with intelligence and knowledge. His most attractive features were his big, expressive eyes and dark, curly hair.

So when the big day arrived and he tried taking a good look at his soon-to-be bride during the ceremonies, all he could manage was a peek at the very fair, delicate and beautiful pair of hands. When she stood up for *pheras* he could see a tiny waist. Everything else was hidden in a heavily embellished Banarasi *lehnga* and *chunni*. Her feet were small and shapely.

This was enough to confirm what he had heard about her beauty. Though he again wondered why her father would choose him when he could get a prince for his daughter.

After staying for three days and enjoying the grand hospitality of the girl's family, the wedding procession returned with the bride, who was laden with gold and brought a big fat dowry along with her. Kanti Prasad did not get a glimpse of his bride during the journey as she was hidden behind her jewellery and heavy bridal gear. He contended himself with the thought that sooner or later he would get a chance to see her. So he occupied himself in answering the politics related questions that his uncles posed to him. Kanti Prasad was a voracious reader and he watched and read everything about his country's political situation. The struggle for freedom was gaining momentum and the atmosphere was charged with pulsating tension. Though Kanti Prasad loved literature, and there was nothing closer to his heart than a book of poetry by Browning or Wordsworth, yet he was equally well versed in other fields too.

A week went by, and Kanti Prasad still did not get a chance to spend some moments alone with his wife. There were unending ceremonies. The first day, by the time they reached home, was already half over. So by the time the ceremonies to welcome the bride were done, it was already evening. After an early dinner, his wife, along with her *Dai Ma*, were escorted to the other part of the house, where the sleeping arrangements had been made for her and her escort. That portion of the house was forbidden for Kanti Prasad, as he was not supposed to meet his wife till a proper pooja was performed. During the various ceremonies he did get a few glimpses of her face through the transparent Banarasi Organza that covered her face, and he was mesmerised. Already the house was abuzz with the talk of her stunning beauty and the gifts that she had brought. Everyone was talking about the good luck of the Pandey family for getting such an alliance for their son.

Though Kanti Prasad was a patient man, he started wondering whether he would ever get a chance to meet his wife alone. The teasing and taunting by his friends made it even worse. Then one afternoon, when everyone had settled after eating a delicious meal and a special dessert cooked by the new bride, the neighbour's daughter in law, who was also his friend's wife came giggling to his room, holding the hand of his bride.

'*Lala Ji*! Give me a gift as I have brought your wife to you. You have half an hour to see her face. So don't just keep standing and wasting time. No one knows that I have brought her here. I will make sure no one comes this way,' she said and closed the door behind her.

Now that he was alone with his wife, he did not know what to do. He felt nervous. He had never communicated with a girl. He admired beautiful girls like any other normal boy of his age and had gone a couple of times with his friends to take a glimpse of this girl from the neighbouring college, who was driving everyone crazy with her beauty and was every boy's dream, but then that was it. He felt very shy in the presence of the opposite sex. Even when his friend's wife would apply *gulal* to his cheeks on the festival of Holi, he would shyly bend his head.

Some time elapsed and he realised that the new bride was standing there. He cleared his throat and said, 'Why don't you sit down here?' He quickly removed his clothes from the chair where he had piled them up. In the process of doing so, he knocked off a glass and water jug that was kept on a teapoy. There was a jingling sound of metal as the bronze glass and jug hit the ground.

He smiled nervously while picking up the jug and glass and said, 'Please sit.'

Her anklets and bangles made a musical sound as she slowly walked to the chair. She sat down with her head bent. She was wearing a light mauve georgette *sari* with a purple embellished border. Her face was partially covered with her *sari* but visible through the transparent material. Kanti Prasad stole a glance and was again enraptured by her beauty. Till now he had been only able to see her delicate hands with long tapering fingers during the ceremonies, as they both performed pooja, or when she cooked the first meal and served it to everyone. He had never dared looking at her because of the presence of elders. But now he felt something else too. He felt intimidated. He was suddenly aware of his wheatish complexion and thin frame. He felt more nervous and found himself at a loss for words. He was debating whether to call her by her proper name or the nickname she was addressed by her folks. Even his mother had started calling her '*Mishthi*'. It was such a sweet name but he felt that he should probably wait for some more time and get to know her a little more before he called her by her nickname.

'*Amma* was saying that your brothers are coming to fetch you this weekend.'

He did not know what else to say. There was a slight nod from her.

'Good, good! It would be nice for you to go to your parents' place.' He bit his tongue as soon as the words were out. Here he was, dying to spend some time with her and wanting so desperately to tell her that, but all he could say that he wanted her to go home as if he was not interested in her. What would she think of him? There was no response from her. Not even a nod.

Kanti Prasad did not know what to say next. So some more time elapsed. He quietly wished he was not alone with her and as if God granted him his wish, the door was thrown open at that very instant and his two younger sisters entered the room with his friend's wife in their wake.

'*Bhabhi,* you are sitting here and we have been looking for you everywhere.'

They chimed and held the bride's hand, 'Come let's go.'

'Wait, you two!!' said the friend's wife but the bride had already stood up and quietly followed the girls out of the room.

Kanti Prasad watched them leave the room and felt instantly dejected. Somehow he knew that he was not going to get another chance to see her before she left for Kanpur. Dejection was followed by anger. Why didn't he hold her hand? Why was his tongue tied? And when the anger subsided a revelation emerged like a creature in a tranquil lake... he would always feel inferior to her. He would never ever feel her equal.

After two days, the bride left for her parents' place. He didn't get a chance to meet her. He consoled himself that it was a matter of a few months and time would pass, and then they would be together. Meanwhile, he would feel proud when there would be talk of her beauty and her fine upbringing. Also, he heard his elders say that though she came from a rich family, she was respectful to her elders and affectionate to the youngsters. He felt even happier when his friends repeatedly told him how lucky he was. Though sometimes, he felt that they were jealous of him because some of them often hinted that his bride had got a raw deal in him. This disturbed him because his doubts about their pairing took a tangible form. One day, he confided in his best friend, voicing his doubts and apprehensions. His friend waved his misgivings by saying that they were all jealous and he should not pay any heed to their taunting, but Kanti Prasad, though he nodded solemnly, was not convinced.

Chapter 7

Sharmishtha put her feet on the berth of their first class carriage and turned her face towards the window. It was late October and the breeze was cool. She felt free and relaxed as she did not have to cover her face and keep her head bent. In a pink Japanese georgette *sari* with a silver border, she looked a vision. Her long and lustrous hair was pleated and lay coiled in her lap. The diamonds that she wore in her ears and neck twinkled with the light, adding a soft hue to her porcelain complexion. When she lifted her hand to brush away the stray locks from her face, her beautifully carved pink glass and gold bangles made a jingling sound. But even her radiant beauty could not conceal the sorrow in her eyes. Sharmishtha was heartbroken. The future looked meaningless. Her brother had tried engaging her in conversation by narrating anecdotes that otherwise would have had her in splits, but could only elicit a few smiles from her, before she turned and looked out of the window. Her younger brother looked at *Dai Ma* silently asking what was wrong. *Dai Ma*, who had brought her up, knew very well the reason for Sharmishtha's silence, and told the brother that it was nothing but fatigue. After all, Sharmishtha was now married and she had to fulfil her role of a daughter-in-law, and it was not an easy job. She had seen her beautiful eyes brimming with tears and her attempt at hiding them. During the three hours journey, Sharmishtha hardly turned her face from the window.

As the train rolled on the platform, Sharmishtha's spirits lifted, and when she saw her father standing with *Munim Ji,* her face broke into a smile. When she reached home, she felt as if she'd never left. Her younger siblings came running to her. She embraced them one by one.

'*Didi*, tell us about your new home,' asked the youngest brother.

'*Didi*, you will stay with us now. Don't go back again,' said her younger sister who was very close to her.

'What nonsense are you talking? Let *Didi* relax a bit and change her clothes. You can ask her later. Now go play,' her paternal grandmother, who she called *Ajoo* lovingly, chided them. Sharmishtha embraced her grandmother who caressed her back affectionately. She then hugged her mother.

'You must be tired,' said her mother, disengaging from her. 'There is a new *sari* in your almirah, change into that.'

Sharmishtha nodded. There was always a little awkwardness between them.

After washing her face and hands, Sharmishtha changed into another *sari*. She looked at her frocks longingly, kept in her sister's cupboard. Now, all her frocks belonged to her sister. She was supposed to wear only *sari*s as she was married now. She looked at herself in the full length mirror. She looked so young and vulnerable. The *sari* could not make her look mature or older than her seventeen years. As she was closing the door of her cupboard, something caught her eye. It was a book of poetry. Her heart lurched and her eyes filled with tears. So much had changed in so little time. Her life had changed so drastically in just six months. It seemed just yesterday when she flitted in the house like a butterfly weaving the dreams for a future she was so sure of. When and how did all that change?

Chapter 8

1929

Sharmishtha was going through her maths lessons when she was interrupted by *Nanoo*, her maternal grandmother.

'*Mishthi*! Have this *halwa* first otherwise it will get cold.'

Sharmishtha looked at her granny lovingly. She shared a special bond with her. In fact she loved her more than her mother, but then, her mother had never shown as deep affection to her as her *Nanoo* did. Sharmishtha could never bond with her mother as her daughter. Once, when she had let out her angst towards her mother's indifference, her grandmother had explained the reason. She'd told her that her mother was not ready for motherhood when she was born. She was all of sixteen when she conceived Sharmishtha. Moreover, she was the only child of rich parents and was pampered to the extent that motherhood looked a burden to her. She wanted to carry on living life adorning herself with pretty clothes and jewellery, and go out to markets and fetes with her friends. She had put on weight after the birth of her daughter and that had made her even more cranky and short tempered, as she used to take pride in her beautiful looks and sensuous figure. To make matters worse, Sharmishtha's father was a very handsome and stylish man and got a lot of attention from the opposite sex, which then constantly worried his wife - she feared that he might lose interest in her. However Pt. Girja Shankar was a well-bred gentleman, and was very much in love with his wife and children.

But Sharmishtha did not miss much when it came to love, because her *Nanoo* doted on her and pampered her. Sharmishtha's maternal grandfather was a businessman and his work kept him busy, and he travelled a lot. He doted on Sharmishtha, but then tragedy struck and her grandfather passed away when Sharmishtha was just five, she missed him terribly. Sharmishtha was given whatever she wanted and had her grandmother's and servants' undivided attention. As a result she liked to live with her *Nanoo* in her big and spacious house with a beautifully tended garden, situated in a beautiful village, Asanpur. Also, the house was situated on the banks of river Ganges and that made it even more beautiful. It was some hundred kilometres away from Kanpur. When she turned six, her father enrolled her in a school and she had to come back to her parents' place, against her wishes. And to her chagrin, she realised that her mother was even busier with her younger offspring, as two more were added since Sharmishtha was born. So Sharmishtha waited for any holidays, as she had made her *Nanoo* promise that she would get her to Asanpur as many times as possible. Every day at her grandmother's home was like a dream and she never wanted to come back to Kanpur. She had beautiful Japanese dolls, which she adorned with gold jewellery. The almirahs were full of frocks that were made of georgette and silks, with beautiful lace work. But as she turned ten, her mother started depending a lot on her, seeking her assistance in looking after the young ones and as a result her visits to Asanpur became less frequent.

Though she missed her *Nanoo* and the carefree environment of Asanpur, she felt it was her responsibility to take care of her siblings. There were servants to do the chores, but there was always something that needed her attention as her mother was either in bed, or not keeping too well. Luckily for Sharmishtha, *Ajoo* supervised the kitchen and other associated chores. She also oiled, washed and braided Sharmishtha's long tresses.

Sharmishtha was a diligent student and paid good attention to her studies. She dreamt of becoming a lecturer. Now she was turning sixteen and was like a beautiful flower in full bloom. She was never sent anywhere alone and was getting a little tired of the overprotective attitude of her family. So she was very happy to have escaped to Asanpur for her summer vacation. Here, she would flitter in the garden or sit under her favourite shady tree and play with her dolls. Sharmishtha never outgrew her dolls. She became a child again and glowed under the pampering of her maternal grandmother. She loved to sit in the boat that her granny owned and go across the river along with other girls who considered it a privilege to be in her company.

When the time came for her to leave Asanpur, she was teary eyed. She hugged her grandmother and asked her to come with her to Kanpur. Her grandmother laughed and said that she was not supposed to visit her daughter's place. But she would definitely come to look her up when she came to the city for her estate's work.

As Sharmishtha left Asanpur, looking lovingly at the familiar garden, temple and other places she so loved, she had no inkling that next time she would come to Asanpur, a changed person.

Pt. Girja Shankar Mishra, who was a businessman, was revered by everyone in his neighbourhood, because of his honest and compassionate nature. But he was very close to his immediate neighbour, despite the professional and cultural differences between them. His neighbour, Nandan Mathur was a renowned lawyer, who had acquired his degree from Britain, and his wife Anuradha Mathur was a lecturer who taught English in a reputed college in Kanpur. Also, she was a talented painter, and her paintings were always in demand and sold off within no time. She was very fond of Sharmishtha and Sharmishtha saw her as a role model. She called her *Kaki*. She always watched the way Anuradha dressed and conducted herself, and would later try to imbibe that. Though her mother was very beautiful, she lacked something that Anuradha had. Much later Sharmishtha came to understand that it was the confidence and sophistication that came with education.

'*Mishthi*! Come home! I have to show you something.' Sharmishtha turned towards the familiar soft voice of Anuradha. She was standing on the other side of the common wall they shared.

'I will tell *Amma* and come.'

She was at Anuradha's door in a jiffy. She pushed the door open and half-ran inside. As she was turning the corridor she collided with someone. And then she felt a number of emotions trigger at the same time; anger at the person who did not see her coming and something else she had never felt before. By the time she'd collected herself the person was already picking up his fallen books. As he straightened himself, his expression of irritation changed into bemusement and he stared at her. They both looked at each other for a couple of moments and then the silence was broken by Anuradha.

'*Mishthi*! You are here? This is my nephew, Kailash. He has come here to study for his exams. Kailash! *Mishthi* is the daughter of Pt. Girja Shankar, our next door neighbour. Isn't she beautiful?'

'Sorry, I didn't see you coming,' Kailash said smiling. '*Bua*, I will be in my room,' he added and left.

'Come *Mishthi*!! I will show you my new painting,' Anuradha led her to her studio holding her hand.

Though Sharmishtha followed her quietly into the studio, she was still a little unsettled and her heart thudded in her chest. Anuradha unveiled the painting and waited for her reaction. When she did not hear anything from her she turned back to see Sharmishtha lost in her thoughts.

'*Mishthi*! Where are you? You seem to be far away,' Anuradha said a little louder than she'd meant to.

'Sorry *Kaki*! I was... Oh my God! Is that me?'

Sharmishtha was staring at the girl in the painting. There was a likeness to her in the facial features but there was something different about her. The girl in the painting looked as if she had the whole world under her feet. Her eyes seemed to laugh at some merriment. Her lips curving beautifully in a smile, showed the contentment of the heart. Her long black tresses framed her face in soft curls. Her long and slender neck slightly tilted as if inviting attention. Sharmishtha blushed when her eyes rested on the swell of the breast under the thin *malmal chunni*. She unconsciously adjusted her *chunni*.

'She looks a bit different,' she said softly, almost murmuring to herself.

'No! She doesn't. She is a replica of you. *Mishthi* you probably haven't seen yourself like this because you are not in front of the mirror all the time. But believe me, this is you, with your free spirit, and in your element. I have painted you exactly the way you are... well I have tried painting you the way you are but then your beauty cannot be caught on canvas. It's so vivacious and lively that it's impossible to do justice to it.'

'Oh *Kaki*! You are exaggerating now,' Sharmishtha said, a little abashed.

'No, my child! What I said is true. I always wanted a daughter like you,' said Anuradha wistfully.

Later, when Sharmishtha came home she was in a slight daze. She was somewhat quiet and her *Ajoo* noticed that.

'*Mishthi*! Child! Are you all right?' she asked.

'I'm fine *Ajoo*!' she said and tried to be her garrulous self, but it wasn't until night, when she retired to bed that she allowed herself to think of her visit to Mathur's place. She felt a tickling in her heart when she thought of Kailash.

What did happen? Why was she so flustered? Why couldn't she take him out of her mind? Though the entire episode had taken less than a few minutes, it seemed to her as if time had stopped and his face was now etched in her memory forever. She tried recalling his entire face but it was only his eyes she could remember. They were intelligent, compassionate, kind, and had a twinkle that was probably the result of their somewhat unusual meeting.

The next morning, as she got dressed for school, she was still thinking of him and then she felt irritated. Why was she thinking of him as if she didn't have anything else to do? He did not even talk to her and probably would have already forgotten her. Since when had she become like this? He was *Kaki*'s nephew, so what? She did not allow herself to think of him in school and busied herself with her studies and friends.

But when she reached home, a surprise was waiting for her. There was a hustle bustle in the house and the *baithak* was being prepared. The covers of the *diwan* and the table cloth of the centre table were being changed. *Masnads* were being fluffed up. Sharmishtha knew that though the *baithak* was cleaned every day, this type of preparation was only done when they were expecting guests. And before she could ask anyone, she heard her father's voice.

'My sweet *Mishthi*! Come here!'

'*Baba*! How come you are home?' She was surprised to see her father home at this time of the day. Pt Girja Shankar used to leave home in the morning and come for half an hour for lunch, and after that, he would come back in the late evenings. He used to leave before Sharmishtha came back from school.

'How was your day, child?' he asked.

'Nice *Baba*! Who is coming home?'

'Don't tell me *Mishthi*, you have forgotten what day it is tomorrow?' Her mother said in a slightly reprimanding tone.

And then she remembered, 'Of course! It's *Baba*'s birthday tomorrow!!'

'See my *Mishthi* never forgets. I came home early to discuss the arrangements for the *Brahma Bhoj* with *Amma* and your mother,' Pt. Girja Shankar said patting her back lovingly.

'I will wear my red frock tomorrow,' she said excitedly.

'And she would look like a princess. Wouldn't she *Amma*?' asked Pt. Girja Shankar looking at his mother.

'Our *Mishthi* is a princess. But now you have to start looking for a prince for her,' *Ajoo* added stitching sequins on a small piece of silk cloth that she would turn into a scarf for her *Thakur Ji*.

Normally, Sharmishtha always remembered her father's birthday and quite looked forward to it, but somehow it slipped her mind just a day prior. How did this happen? She felt ashamed as she realised that her mind was occupied with the incident that took place at *Kaki*'s place. And then suddenly she felt a tingling in the pit of her stomach as she realised that Kailash would also come with *Kaki* and *Kaka*. She knew that she would not be able to act normally in front of him. Now the excitement of her father's birthday was tinged with something else; a kind of nervousness, and she felt distracted. She half hoped that he would not come but at the same time she knew she couldn't wait to see him again.

Both the neighbours invited each other's families on their birthdays. This was a tradition they had been following since as long as Sharmishtha remembered. But before that, there was a *Brahma Bhoj* in the afternoon. After that several people came to wish Pt. Girja Shankar and there was an array of sweets, savouries and dry fruits bought only from the best and most famous shops of the city. These were served with tea, buttermilk and juices as people came to wish him. Dinner was a special and private affair and only one family was invited, the family of Nandan Mathur, as both the families were very close and were always there for each other.

She could not quite control the butterflies in her stomach the entire day. The whole day went by as if she were watching a motion film, without actually being there. Luckily her family members were too busy looking after the guests to notice her distraction.

And then came the evening. The aroma of the various dishes that were being cooked wafted in the air. There were several dishes, all vegetarian, to be served with aromatic basmati rice from Dehradun, hot *purees* and *kachories*. Sharmishtha's family had a sweet tooth as common with all brahmins, so sweet dish was always a gala affair with a variety of dishes that included *kheer, kulfi, almond halwa* and many sweetmeats. Everyone sat down with a cup of tea to relax before the neighbour's family came for dinner. It was a nice family evening and everyone was cozying up to it. Normally Sharmishtha loved this time with the family, because these evenings had become a rarity since her father kept busy, looking after the business. She always enjoyed her father's company and found him intelligent with a superb sense of humour.

But today, though she sat listening to the interesting anecdotes he was narrating, her mind was not quite there. Every few minutes her eyes would go to the grandfather clock and she would feel something in the pit of her stomach. Pt. Girja Shankar noticed her distraction.

'What's wrong Princess? You are not your cheerful self today. Are you tired?'

'No *Baba*! I am fine,' she said, flashing a big smile. After that she did not let her attention wander and participated in the conversation. She was laughing her lungs out at a comment her *Ajoo* had made, when the servant informed them of Barrister *Saheb's* arrival. Sharmishtha's mirth stopped mid-way and she excused herself.

'Where are you going *Mishthi*? *Kaki* would expect to see you,' her father said.

'I will join you in a minute *Baba*.'

'Don't take long,' her mother added and they all left to greet them.

She could hear the warm welcome by their parents and *Kaka's* rich booming voice as he wished and hugged her father. She strained her ears to listen to some other voice but couldn't. She sat down trying to calm her nerves. A few minutes later, Kumari came looking for her. Kumari was the granddaughter of *Dai Ma* and stayed with Sharmishtha's family as they had taken over the responsibility of her education and marriage. She was of Sharmishtha's age and they'd played together as kids. She was more of a family member and helped Sharmishtha's mother in looking after the young ones. She also helped her *Ajoo* in organising her religious functions.

'*Didi! Amma* is calling you.'

'Who all are there?'

'Everyone, *Baba, Amma...*'

'Who all have come?' Sharmishtha asked cutting her off mid-sentence.

'*Kaka* and *Kaki*.'

'Only them?' asked Sharmishtha.

'Yes *Didi*! Who else?' Kumari looked a little puzzled.

Sharmishtha felt a wave of disappointment washing over her. She sat down.

'*Didi*, are you all right?'

'Yes, you go. I will follow you in a bit,' she said with a hint of irritation in her voice.

What was this? Why did she feel as if she was robbed of something? Why was she waiting so eagerly to see him? Was this kind of behaviour normal? And then she realised that her eyes were brimming. She felt cheated, as if a promise was broken. She would have kept sitting but then she heard footsteps, and quickly wiped her eyes with the back of her hand.

'*Mishthi*, what are you doing here? Go and sit with *Kaki*. I have come to see to the refreshments,' her mother said, a note of reproach in her voice.

'There you are! We were wondering where our sweet *Mishthi* was!' Anuradha said taking her hands in her own.

'You look beautiful,' she added.

'So sweetheart, how are *studies* coming along?' Nandan Mathur addressed her.

'Studies are going fine *Kaka*.'

'Good! *Pundit Ji*, let *Mishthi* take on law when she completes her graduation. I will guide her and make her a lawyer,' Nandan Mathur said looking affectionately at her. *Ajoo* gave him a look that Sharmishtha knew only too well. Any other time she would have loved *Kaka*'s comment and would have chatted with him regarding her studies, but today she just wanted to know whether Kailash was still with them and if he was, why hadn't he come?

'*Kaki*, have you completed the painting you were doing?'

'No sugar! It's still incomplete.'

'Oh! You must show it to me when it's complete. How long will it take?'

'Let's see! I would have finished it but I am busy preparing for a seminar. I will show you the moment it's ready.'

Sharmishtha had a sinking feeling. It was not any time soon that she would get a chance to go to *Kaki*'s place. Though normally she could go as and when she wanted to, but now she did not want to do that, lest Kailash thought she had come to see him. She tried making conversation that would somehow bring his name up but it didn't happen. Why didn't anyone talk about him? And when she was about to give up, suddenly *Kaka* mentioned his name.

'Anuradha's nephew Kailash is here these days. He has come to spend some time with us before he leavs for Britain. A bright chap he is.'

'Oh!! Anuradha, why didn't you bring him? Is he going to study in Britain?' Pt. Girja Shankar asked.

'Yes! He wants to get a degree in law and then can either join me or work on his own. You know *Pundit Ji*, Kailash is like a son to us. It's very magnanimous of Anuradha's brother and his wife to have given him to us. We are ever so in their debt. He would have joined us for dinner but he has to complete the essay that he has to send to his future college.'

'But *Didi* is sending dinner for him and he is quite looking forward to it,' Anuradha said smiling.

Sharmishtha felt depressed. She was hoping that Kailash would stay in Kanpur forever. She willed them to talk more about him but the conversation steered towards something else.

As she lay down that night, she tried reasoning with herself. Why was she so awestruck by him? She had only seen him for a few moments. How could anyone leave such an impression within that span of time? Sharmishtha had seen admiring glances from the opposite sex. In fact, there was no one who wasn't struck by her beauty. Did it have any effect on Kailash? She did not think so. He had hurried to his room without even a backward glance in her direction. And those eyes; there was something she couldn't quite comprehend. Was it admiration or mockery? She fell asleep thinking of it.

Chapter 9

Kailash lay awake in his room. It was past one but sleep was miles away from him. The face of Sharmishtha was as fresh in his memory as if she were just there in front of his eyes at that very moment. He had never seen beauty so ethereal, so divine. Her face was perfect with a porcelain complexion. She looked like she had walked out of a sculptor's imagination. And that hair; dark and shining and going past her waist, touching her derriere was enough to drive anyone crazy. He had been thinking about her ever since he had collided with her in the lobby. He wanted to stay and look at her for some time but then *Bua* had come and he had to hurry back to his room, which he repented later. He should have stayed back and tried making some conversation. From that day onwards, he hoped fervently that she would come home or he would get to meet her somehow. But that had not happened. He had tried asking *Bua* about her, making it sound casual. But *Bua* had looked at him with a glint in her eyes, so he had retreated quickly.

Kailash, like any other nineteen year old, had wondered about girls and listened to his friends talking about them, but he was too involved in his studies to pay much attention to any girl. True, he had listened to the anecdotes his friends often narrated, and had laughed when some of his friends made a fool of themselves falling in love with some girl only to realise that the girl wasn't even aware of it. He was always listening to their conversation, never participating in it, when girls were discussed. His friends respected him for his brilliance in academia and his unending knowledge on various subjects, and thus, found him far too reserved and serious to get involved in frivolities like love. Somehow, he made it look like that, and his friends were happy that way, because had he been interested in girls, they wouldn't have stood a chance. With his looks and intelligence, any girl would have fallen in love with him. They had noticed girls looking at him from the corner of their eyes when they went to college. But Kailash either did not notice or ignored them deliberately. When they teased him about it, he just looked surprised. That was not the era of open friendships between a boy and a girl. Co-education only started at the college level, and there were strict boundaries for both the sexes. Nevertheless, love stories happened. Some of them resulting in marriages and happily-ever-afters, but most of them ending in heartbreaks. Yet, the game of romance went on. The elite class was a little more tolerant of romance, provided the girl or boy chose the partner keeping their family's status in mind. Upper-middle-class and middle-class were stringent when it came to love and romance.

There was no question of a boy or girl choosing a partner. It was a matter decided completely by the parents. There were almost none, or only a few exceptions. So while cupid kept striking; most love stories remained only stories; a sweet memory that would tickle one's heart and bring a smile in the years to come.

Kailash found himself thinking how it would feel to marry a girl like Sharmishtha. She was exceptionally beautiful and devoid of the artificiality of makeup and fashion that other girls were crazy for. She was like a flower that had just blossomed, and was as pure and fresh as the morning dew. His parents were educated, quite open minded and ahead of their time. And then, Anuradha *Bua* was his father's only sister and he doted on her. This was the reason he had given her his own son when they came to know that she could not conceive. So there was a strong chance that it could work. Also, Sharmishtha's parents were very close to his uncle and aunt. So they might agree. Besides, he would work hard and try getting a gold medal, and then he would be eligible for her because she deserved only the best.

But as he thought of this, he also felt foolish at the same time. He did not have even the slightest idea whether Sharmishtha had even noticed him, leave aside liking him. She looked so young. Did she know anything about love? He doubted it. Was he also acting like his friends whom he used to laugh at? What was wrong with him? He had seen the girl only for a few moments and had decided the course of his life. He was just being plain stupid. He realised that he was distracted and wasn't able to concentrate on the paper he was writing. He had to send it to his future college in a week's time. So when Anuradha *Bua* asked him to go to Sharmishtha's house, he declined, though that was the only thing he wanted to do. But as he was rational, he chided himself for his foolhardiness and tried concentrating on his paper. He did not know that he was going to see Sharmishtha in a couple of days, and this time, all his doubts would vaporise and he would realise that he had fallen in love, and that he would never love anyone but her.

Chapter 10

There was a festive fever on, as it was *Dussehra*. Sharmishtha was dressing her younger siblings with the help of Kumari. She herself was wearing a mauve coloured *lehnga choli* with delicate lace work. They were all going to see the procession that had beautiful *Jhankis,* as they were popularly known, chariots carrying legendary characters depicting famous scenes from the epic Ramayana. People were dressed in colourful costumes, and many other delightful appurtenances. The procession passed through the road where Pt. Girja Shankar had his shops and office. It was a three storeyed building, and his friends and family always saw the procession from the rooftop, while they were served beverages and delicious snacks. It was a tradition for every year. The building was very close to their house and the rear gate was just four hundred metres away, so they walked.

As Sharmishtha climbed the stairs and reached the rooftop, catching her breath, she almost froze. Kailash was standing with his aunt, looking down from the balcony at the hustle bustle in the street below. Before she could collect herself, her younger sister ran towards Anuradha and that made Kailash and Anuradha turn back. Kailash looked at her and their eyes met. Sharmishtha felt her cheeks burning. She felt awkward.

'Finally! I was wondering when you all would come,' Anuradha said.

'*Amma* and *Ajoo* are coming soon,' Sharmishtha said, not knowing what else to say. Normally she would have chatted with Anuradha talking about how the *Jhankis* were going to be. But today her tongue had stuck to her palate. She couldn't look at Kailash.

'I asked Kailash to come and see the procession,' Anuradha said. Sharmishtha just smiled and looked away. She knew that she was behaving weirdly but just couldn't help it. She was saved as her father and mother arrived with some other friends. *Ajoo* couldn't climb the stairs so she remained on the ground floor with Kumari's mother.

The procession started. Sharmishtha stood at the farthest end. She did not want to be anywhere close to Kailash. But though she kept laughing and commenting at the Jhankis and the dancers dressed as half-humans and half-horses, her heart was thumping and she tried looking at him when no one was looking. He caught her looking at him, and her heart skipped a beat. She quickly looked away and cursed silently. What was she doing? But somewhere, she was ecstatic that he was looking at her too. She wanted to keep looking at him but could not gather the courage. She realised that he was more handsome than she remembered him to be. He was standing next to her father, and her father was a tall man, but Kailash was taller than him. She tried looking at him from the corner of her eye and found him nodding and looking at her father as he was explaining the history of the procession and how it had evolved and become bigger since he was a child. He was talking to her father reverently. Kailash was not very fair and not wheatish either. His complexion was smooth and even. His forehead was broad and his hair jet black and thick. His nose was straight and his lips full. But it was his eyes that mesmerised her. He talked through his eyes. When he looked at her she felt as if he were peeping into her soul. She felt she would never be able to hide anything from him if she ever got a chance to get close to him. She was still looking at him when suddenly he looked at her for a couple of moments with a hint of smile on his lips, as if saying 'Caught you!'. Sharmishtha went crimson and did not make an attempt to meet his eyes for the remainder of the evening. Kailash's face kept swimming in front of her eyes and her heart would beat faster when she would remember meeting his eyes.

After dinner she went to the rooftop terrace that had a common wall with Mathur residence. She wanted to relive the evening in her thoughts. It was a full moon night and the breeze was cool and fragrant, with the jasmine in bloom. Sharmishtha felt as if she were in a dream. She just wanted to look at the moon for the rest of the night. She realised that she was humming a song. She did not know how long she was sitting there humming, when she heard a deep voice that startled her. She jumped and stood up. Kailash was standing on the other side of the wall looking at her.

'I said you sing very well.'

She could not speak. She just lowered her head and kept looking at her feet.

'Mishthi! Can I call you Mishthi?' he asked.

She nodded.

'The procession was really nice. I am glad I got to see it. Do you go every year to see it?'

Sharmishtha nodded again.

'That must be nice.' He waited for some kind of response from her but as she kept standing with her head bowed, he knew he was not going to get one. He sighed to himself and then said, '*Bua's* painting is about to get completed. She was saying that you wanted to see it. So why don't you come to see it?'

Sharmishtha looked up and smiled at him, then turned and ran down the stairs. Kailash kept standing there looking at her retreating back. Her plait swayed over her beautiful figure and soon she was out of sight. In the moonlight she had looked a vision. Her complexion glowed and her pink lips quivered as he'd tried to make conversation. Her small and round bosom heaved slightly, and those eyes, when she looked at him, cast a spell on him. Kailash had seen pictures of beautiful girls and seen many good looking girls from the girls' college next to his, but this kind of beauty he had only read in books. Also, it was not only beauty that Sharmishtha was blessed with; there was a swan-like grace about her. Kailash came from a background that was considered elite. His grandfather was one of the wealthiest businessmen in Delhi and his father had followed in his father's footsteps. They lived in one of the poshest addresses of the capital and moved around in the high society of Delhi. So Kailash moved around in a society where he had come in contact with girls who were well groomed and fashionable. But none of them could boast of beauty and grace as unique as Sharmishtha's. He had come on the terrace to get some quiet as he couldn't take his mind off Sharmishtha. He couldn't believe his luck when he saw her there too. Was it providence? He asked himself. Back in his room he tried reading a book, but couldn't concentrate, gave up and lay awake till the wee hours, and finally fell asleep thinking of her.

Chapter 11

'Kailash *Babu*, Captain *Saheb* and his family are here. *Bibi Ji* is calling you.' Kailash was pulled out of his book.

'I will join them in a bit, Hari *Chacha*,' he said.

He was quite enjoying the tranquillity. It was a beautiful spot. He was sitting on the banks of the Ganges. The breeze was cool and slightly crisp. He was trying not to think about Sharmishtha. After that evening on the rooftop terrace two days back, he had hoped for her to show up, but she had not come. He had felt dejected and then this doubt crept in his mind that she probably did not think of him the way he was thinking of her. And probably, she was too young to know anything about attraction or love. Bua had mentioned in passing that she was all of sixteen. He had seen her only thrice and she had not made any effort to show that she was even remotely interested in him. But then, why did she look at him repeatedly, when they were watching the procession? Why did her cheeks turn crimson when he caught her looking at him? And the other day on the terrace, when she looked at him there was a twinkle in her eyes. Was he misreading everything? Maybe what he was mistaking as a sign of attraction was purely her shyness. A girl of her values ought to feel shy in the presence of a male. The more he thought about this, the more the answers eluded him. So when Anuradha asked him to come along for this picnic with their very close friends, he agreed. After the picnic they were going to his Uncle's ancestral villa that was some seventy miles away. Though Kailash was not very keen to be away for the night, he could not find an excuse to stay back. He had gone to the terrace every evening for the last two days, hoping to catch a glimpse of Sharmishtha, but after waiting for an hour or so, had come down.

What if she came looking for him and he was sitting miles away from her? He sighed and got up, walking towards the mango grove where his aunt, uncle and their friends were sitting.

'Come Kailash! Meet Capt. Alcott Langley, my dearest friend. Al! Meet our nephew Kailash,' Nandan Mathur said, introducing him to Capt. Alcott Langley. Capt. Langley was every inch British, and though he had an undeniable love for his country, he'd come to like India when he got a posting in the country. He had apprehensions when he got the posting, but he started liking the country eventually, and his liking and attachment increased manifold when he fell in love with an Indian girl. His father was Lord Alton Langley, and he was a Baron. Capt. Langley met Nandan Mathur in a club many years back when he had just come to India. Both had struck a connection as Nandan Mathur had studied in England and they found that they shared many similar interests, and so became bosom friends. Capt. Langley had participated in the First World War and had received an injury on his left leg, due to which he had to take premature retirement. Also, the reason behind his retirement was partially on the behest of his father who wanted him to come back to England and look after the estate. Capt. Langley and his wife had still not made up their minds to go to England, adding to the irk of Lord Alton. Capt. Langley's wife, Bina, was the daughter of a rich Taluqdar and had studied in England as well. She was a pretty woman with high society breeding and a pleasant demeanour.

'A fine lad you have here Nandan!' Capt. Langley said.

'Hello Kailash! This is my wife Bina, my naughty son Somendra, and my daughter Suchitra. We call her Sue.'

Kailash greeted them and made polite conversation. Capt. Langley went on asking about his future plans and discussed the college he was going to join in England.

The daughter was wearing a frock that was fashionable. She was fair and had a heart shaped face with delicate features. Her lips were pink with an enhanced cupid's bow. She was tall and had a narrow waist. Her hair was shoulder length and wavy, again, in sync with the latest fashion. She looked like a delicate doll. She had this kind of attractive vulnerability that would make anyone feel protective towards her. In short, she could make any boy's heart beat faster. She looked a little older than Sharmishtha. Kailash smiled inwardly as he realised he was comparing her with Sharmishtha. She smiled as they shook hands and her gaze lingered on Kailash's face a little longer.

Capt. Langley's son, Somendra, who they called Sam in short, had taken his parents' fair colouring, but had not got any of his sister's good looks. He shook hands with Kailash looking a bit grumpy. He was much younger and kept close to his sister who obviously doted on him.

Kailash made polite conversation with Suchitra as their Khansama laid out the food a little away from them. They all got up to eat. The spread was good and varied. Anuradha had got Indian food prepared and there was *shahi paneer, malai koftas* and dry stir fried potatoes in their jackets, that Kailash absolutely loved, with *boondi raita, kheer and gulab jamun*, whereas, Mrs. Langley had got sandwiches, cutlets, two different kinds of fruit cakes and a variety of fresh fruits.

'I say old chap! This food can feed an entire army,' Captain Langley said, serving himself a little of everything.

The elders sat sipping coffee for some time that was made by the Khansama on the makeshift clay stove that they used for heating up the food, while Kailash, Suchitra and Somendra had some fruit juices. Then it was time to start the journey towards their next destination. It was decided that the elders will travel in one car so Kailash, Suchitra, Somendra travelled in another with Khansama sitting in the front seat, next to the driver.

The drive was pleasant. The road was lined with big shady trees and there was an expanse of fields on both sides. They crossed small hamlets and saw farmers hurrying back to their homes, where cheerful hearths and simple yet heartening meals would greet them. Also, it was time for them to sit with their families after spending a gruelling day in the fields. Kailash saw plumes of smoke coming out of the huts, giving an indication of the evening meal being prepared. Children were playing in the backyards. Cattle were being given fodder. He found the whole scene very comforting. He was reminded of Wordsworth's 'Michael'.

And from their occupation out of doors

The son and father were come home, even then,

Their labour did not cease, unless when all

Turn'd to their cleanly supper board and there

Each with a mess of pottage and skimm'd milk

Sate round their basket pil'd with oaten cakes,

And their plain homemade cheese. Yet when their meal

Was ended. Luke (for so the son was nam'd)

And his old father, both betook themselves

To such convenient work, as might employ

Their hands by the fire-side; perhaps to card

Wool for the house wife's spindle or repair

Some injury done to sickle, flail or scythe'

Or other implement of house or field.

'These lines are so pictorial. They fit the scenery so well,' he thought.

Kailash was born and brought up in Delhi. His parents had taken him to their native village when he was a child and all he remembered was running after butterflies or wild rabbits as the elders sat in the veranda sipping their morning tea. Sometimes, he was allowed to go with the gardener's son to the mango orchard that was some five hundred metres away from their house. This was actual India. A major chunk of the population lived in the villages. There was a sharp contrast between the city and village life.

'How little do I know of my country?' he mused.

And then his thoughts kept returning to Sharmishtha. He kept thinking how different this trip would have been had Sharmishtha been sitting next to him instead of Suchitra. He would have told her everything about this place they were visiting. He would have smelled the perfume of her body sitting close to her. The proximity would have been heavenly. His reverie was broken by Suchitra's sweet voice.

'How much farther do we have to go?' She broke the silence in the car. Kailash realised that they had not talked much ever since the journey had started, but they had run out of small talk and didn't know what to talk about except answering Somendra's questions about the cows or hens that he watched from the window of the car.

'One more hour at the most, *Missi Baba*,' the driver replied.

By the time they reached, dusk had already fallen. As they parked the cars, the gardener and the housekeeper came out running. They entered the bungalow. It was a colonial bungalow sitting on five acres of land. Nandan Mathur's grandfather had bought it from a British Officer as he had moved to his native land. They entered the hall. It was a big room with old and bulky furniture. There were big oil paintings of Nandan Mathur's father and grandfather. There were some more paintings depicting the kills from their hunting trips. There was yet another painting depicting a British family. Nandan Mathur told them that it was the family of the original owner. As they sat there having a cup of tea in the soft and comforting light of Petromax lantern and the candles in the candelabra, the whole place wore a look of intrigue. Kailash looked at Suchitra and he sensed a little discomfort on her part. Her brother was whispering something to her and she was turning a little pale. Her soft face looked troubled and she looked very vulnerable. Kailash knew that she was absolutely a city girl as she had told him during the journey, and that she was quite excited at the prospect of visiting a village. But now her excitement had vanished and was replaced by discomfort, or probably, fear. Kailash felt sorry for her. He wanted to say something to her but then Nandan Mathur got up saying that they would go to their rooms to freshen up and rest a little before coming down for dinner. Capt. Langley and his family were escorted to the rooms on the ground floor, whereas Kailash, his uncle and aunt, took the rooms on the first floor.

Kailash's room was not very big but comfortable. There was a four poster bed with a mosquito net around it, flanked by two small night stands. There was a big wooden almirah and a table and chair. An easy chair next to the fireplace completed the furniture. A big painting, depicting two Englishmen on horses and some locals walking in front of them, carrying a drum and an instrument resembling a trumpet, only it was smaller than a trumpet, adorned the opposite wall. It looked like a hunting trip. The bed was next to a big window. The door on the left side of the room opened into a dresser and bathroom. Kailash walked up to the window. It was a clear, moonlit night, and a slow breeze was rustling the leaves of the big neem and mango trees. He was reminded of the evening he had seen Sharmishtha. It was just a few days back but he felt as if an eon had gone by without seeing her. Everything looked so dreamy and romantic and he wished that she was there, standing next to him. He would have cupped her stunning face in his hands and kissed those divinely beautiful pink lips. He would have put his hands around her narrow waist and drawn her towards him. He would have buried his head in those long black tresses. He would have...

'Kailash *Babu*, *Saheb* is calling you. Dinner is served.'

Hari *Chacha's* voice brought him back from his dream.

'Already? But I just came,' he thought to himself. He looked at his watch and was surprised to see that more than half an hour had passed.

After a quick wash and change into a fresh shirt he came down to find everyone sitting at the dining table.

'Come Kailash!' Anuradha called him to the chair next to her.

He sat down next to Anuradha facing Suchitra. She had changed into a red frock with black lace. It complemented her pale complexion. The soft light from the candles was making her look angelic. Soup was served and they started eating. Nandan Mathur had got accustomed to a certain lifestyle when he was studying in England. Also, he had worked as an apprentice under a reputed British lawyer who was very fond of him and considered him his prodigy. He had asked him to live with him as he had lost his wife and was alone in a four bedroom house. They became close, and Nandan Mathur attributed his success to his mentoring. So, in the process, he had acquired certain habits of an Englishman.

There was light-hearted talk. It was a pleasant evening. The windows were open and the slight breeze made the candles in the heavy silver candelabra quiver. There were two Petromax lanterns in the corners of the room but the light not quite reaching the dining table. The main course was served. Capt. Langley was narrating some interesting anecdotes and everyone was listening to him in rapt attention. Suddenly, the wind picked up and a gust of air made the candles blow out.

'Blimey!' exclaimed Nandan Mathur.

Hari *Chacha* ran to the kitchen to get the matchbox. This interrupted Capt. Langley's narrative briefly. Suddenly, there was a clattering sound. Suchitra had dropped her fork. Everyone looked at her. She was looking at the window. She seemed oblivious to the clattering sound fork had made. Everyone's gaze turned at the window but there was nothing there except trees swaying and casting shadows.

'Sue! Is anything the matter?' her mother asked.

'Sue?' Mrs. Langley repeated.

'Huh?? No! I am alright.' There was a small tremor in her voice. Hari *Chacha* had come back and lit the candles. Suchitra's fork was replaced and Capt. Langley picked up his narrative from where he had left it.

Sweet dish was served. After dinner they all came out to sit in the Veranda. The ladies sat talking to each other while the gentlemen had some cognac as a night cap. Kailash excused himself from the group and got up to take a walk. He wanted to be alone with his thoughts.

'Kailash, do you mind taking Suchitra for a walk with you?' Anuradha asked.

'How do you like this place?' he asked, just to start the conversation.

'It's nice.'

'You have been awfully quiet ever since we came here.'

'It's nothing. Really,' she said.

Kailash had a feeling she was hiding something. He didn't want to probe so he let it go at that.

'I have also come here after a long time.'

'When did you come here last?' she asked.

'I think almost fifteen years back. But not much has changed, save some renovation in the washrooms. I used to come to *Bua's* place for a short time and somehow we could not make this trip. Also, Uncle's mother did not like to come here, so there were no trips when she was alive.'

'Why didn't she like the place? Her husband bought this place, right?' Suchitra asked.

'Well, she was a little rigid in her outlook, or you can say she was compassionate because she wanted her husband to donate the money to a good cause that could benefit their own countrymen rather than buying a place from a foreigner.'

'Oh! But he bought it nevertheless.'

'He loved nature. He wanted a place in the country. The owner of the house needed the money since he was going back to his country. So you see, he, in a way, helped him out because he wasn't getting any buyer. Do you see that pond there?'

'Yes!'

'I fell into that once.'

'Oh! How?'

'Come, I will show you. Actually it's not a pond. More of a big tank to store water for watering the lawns. But since we were small, it looked like a pond. Do you see those three stairs there? That is where I hid one day while playing Hide and Seek with local friends, not realising that it was slippery because of the moss. I slipped and fell into the water. I did not yet know how to swim and the water was deep enough for a five year old. I screamed for help. It was quite some time before the gardener heard my shouts and rescued me. After the incident, uncle's mother forbade him from bringing me here.'

'Thank God you were saved!' said Suchitra, stopping and looking at him. For a moment he thought he saw something flicker in her eyes. But then the moment passed and she started walking.

'Mother was saying that you are going to England for further studies.'

'Yes, I am!'

'Why don't you study here?'

'It's actually more of my uncle's decision. He thinks I will get good education there.'

'Oh!'

'What are your plans? I mean, what do you plan to study?

'Literature. My parents are also planning to send me to England for further studies.'

'That sounds nice.'

There was a rustling sound and Suchitra stopped dead in her tracks. The sound grew louder and it came closer. Suchitra held

Kailash's arm firmly. Kailash stopped.

'There is something there,' she said in a whisper.

'Wait, I will go and see. It may be an animal; a mongoose or something.'

'No, don't go,' she said clutching his arm.

'Don't worry I am not going far. I will just go behind the hedge and see if there is something,' Kailash said gently.

'No let's go back. I don't want to stay out.'

Kailash wanted to say something but her expression stopped him short. She had turned pale and there was fear in her eyes. He had noticed it twice that evening. She was still holding his arm in a way that her nails dug into his skin.

'All right! Let's go.' He looked at his arm and then she quickly let it go. She lowered her eyes as if trying to hide her embarrassment.

They started walking back. She did not say anything and Kailash kept quiet as he was thinking of Sharmishtha. Somehow Suchitra's hand on his arm made him wonder how he would have felt if it had been Sharmishtha holding his hand, walking beside him. He missed her. She was always in his thoughts but there were times when he felt this desperate need of being with her. He had never felt like this ever before. He was going to be twenty soon and he had never felt any of these emotions as he was experiencing now. Was this love? Had he fallen in love with Sharmishtha? He was quite excited to go abroad and study but now the thought of going out of the country and away from Sharmishtha made him melancholic. When Suchitra asked him why he couldn't study here, he had answered mechanically and ever since, the thought was nagging him. Why did he have to go abroad? He could study here. They walked back in silence.

'You both are back already?' Mrs. Langley asked.

'I was feeling a little tired. Can I go to bed?' Suchitra asked.

'Ok sweetheart! Sam, please go with your sister.'

'But I am not sleepy,' Sam whined.

'It's already beyond your bedtime. Good night!' Capt. Langley said emphatically.

Somendra got up reluctantly. They both bid goodnight and went to their rooms. Kailash also excused himself and went up to his room. He changed into his pyjamas and stood at the window. He liked the tranquillity; it was required as he wanted to organise his thoughts. He started thinking about whether he should speak to his uncle about staying back in India. He could study in Delhi and keep visiting Kanpur. As it is, he was officially adopted by his aunt and her husband. But his father and uncle both really wanted him to go to England. So he was not sure about their reactions. It was not going to be easy, yet he would try it. He felt a weight lifting from his heart. But then as soon as the thought brought him comfort it brought a kind of uncertainty also. How could he alter his entire future based on a couple of short meetings with a girl he hardly knew? She was young and he had no idea what she was like. Could she understand the complexities and complications of love? Also, did she even know what love was? They had hardly met and she had not said a word to him. She had not even come to the terrace after that evening. He realised with a sinking feeling that if she had any interest in him, she would have definitely made an effort to see him. He felt a little dismayed. Then a question sprang to his mind; supposing Sharmishtha did not reciprocate his feelings, what was he going to do? Would he ever be able to forget her? What was this? He had seen her only a few times and had hardly spoken to her, yet he felt as if he had known her all his life. Was this love? He surprised himself with that notion.

So, was he going through the same thing his friends so often talked about? With a sigh he walked back to the bed and lay down. He closed his eyes and fell asleep thinking of Sharmishtha.

He got up with a start. He felt as if he'd heard a scream. He tried listening and heard some commotion down in the hall. He threw the covers and hurried to the door. When he reached the hall he saw his aunt and uncle hurrying to Suchitra's room. He joined them.

'What happened *Bua*?'

'Don't know, child. We heard Suchitra scream.'

They entered the room. Mrs. Langley had wrapped her arms around a sobbing Suchitra. Somendra was sitting in his bed looking frightened. Their father was not there.

'What happened?' Anuradha asked hurrying to the bed side.

'Sue says she saw someone standing outside the window.'

'Outside the window? When?'

Mrs. Langley looked at Suchitra, worried, and said, 'Suchitra was asleep. Some noise woke her up. She heard it again and she felt it was coming from the window. She thought that a cat or some animal was trying to come inside. So she got up to shut the window and then she saw someone standing at the window. She... she got scared and screamed. By the time we came here, the person was gone.'

'But there was someone outside. My daughter saw him with her own eyes.' They heard Captain Langley's voice in the hall.

Anuradha and Kailash came out in the hall. Capt. Langley looked a little agitated.

'But *Saheb*, we have seen everywhere outside. There was no one,' Hari *Chacha* said. The gardener and the driver also nodded in agreement.

'Did you see everywhere? And how long did you take to go out?' asked Nandan Mathur.

'*Babu Saheb*, I had fallen asleep just an hour back after cleaning the kitchen and then was woken up by *Missi Baba's* screams. I came running here to ask *Missi Baba* what was wrong. In the meantime Capt. *Saheb* and *Mem Sahib* also came running. When I heard *Missi Baba* saying that she had seen someone outside the window I went running out. There was no one there so I went to see if the gate was open because if someone had to run out he would have opened the gate, but the gate was bolted. Then I went and woke Murari,

Shyamlal and Ram Sevak. Together we searched the entire property but couldn't find anyone,' he added.

'If someone was there, it would have given him enough time to jump the gate, but it's a tall gate. The gate is always locked with a padlock and they found it intact,' mused Nandan Mathur.

'But you see, the person did not have to run out. He could have easily hidden in the hedges. They are pretty tall and thick. Maybe he is still hiding there.'

'Did you carry a torch when you went out?' Capt. Langley asked Hari *Chacha*.

'*Saheb* first time I ran without a torch because I didn't have one and I did not want to waste time going to the quarter and get one. Later we carried torches. We looked behind the hedges too.'

'Strange! Who would have come and what did he want? If it was a thief, then he should have tried entering the hall or kitchen because the locals know that since we don't stay here, we don't keep any money or valuables here. Agreed that the paintings and the silverware are of a considerable value, but why should a thief choose a night when there are people in the house? It would be easier for him to burgle the house when there is only the gardener staying here. The housekeeper too goes to his village in the evening,' said Nandan Mathur.

'But Sue saw someone and she is scared to death, so there...'

'Would you come inside for a minute?' Capt. Langley was stopped mid sentence as his wife called him.

'Excuse me! He got up and went inside.'

Nandan Mathur and Kailash stayed in the hall.

'What do you make of this Kailash?' Nandan asked.

Then he lowered his voice, 'Do you think Suchitra imagined this, because somehow I had a feeling she is not very comfortable here, considering that she is a city girl.'

Kailash thought for a moment. So he was not the only one to have noticed Suchitra's discomfiture, and then he remembered how skittish she was in the garden when they were taking a walk.

'But uncle, the way she screamed, I don't think she imagined it. Something must have happened to stir up that kind of fear. I do agree with you though that she is not very comfortable here.'

'Now, I don't know how to deal with this. I think the girl is hallucinating though she is not running any fever,' Capt. Langley said, throwing himself in the chair.

'What happened?'

Capt. Langley opened his mouth and then looked at the servants still standing.

'Hari! Make tea for everyone and you both help him,' Nandan said dismissing the servants.

He looked at Capt. Langley and waited but did not prompt him.

'Ahh! This sounds so foolish. I don't know how to even mention this.' Capt. Langley looked a bit exasperated. He leaned towards Nandan and said in a low voice.

'Suchitra says the person she saw at the window was dressed up like a British Officer.'

'You think anyone would take the trouble to don a British uniform for the purpose of stealing? Moreover, she says he was not a native, but British. Now there is no cantonment in the vicinity, and since she says the man was British, it rules out the possibility of him visiting the village. Even if we, for a moment, apply this theory that a British officer is visiting someone in the village, the village is some two miles away from here. Why would anyone walk all the distance to come here just for a peep? I really don't know what to make of all this.'

Kailash and Nandan exchanged glances as if saying that they also felt the same.

Nandan cleared his throat and said, 'Al! Is it possible that Suchitra had a bad dream?'

'I would have thought the same but the girl is totally shaken. She says that he just kept standing there staring at her. Even her screams did not make him move. Finally, she just closed her eyes and only opened them when we reached her room.'

'Sir, what does Somendra say? He must have been woken up by Suchitra's screams. Did he see any one?' Kailash asked.

'The boy is scared out of his wits but he says he did not see anything or anyone. But it just doesn't end here. Sue says she saw someone standing outside the hall window during dinner but it was only fleetingly, so she thought she had imagined it. Did you notice anything when you both went out for a walk?' Capt. Langley asked Kailash.

'She did look little uncomfortable and I asked her also, but she said she just wanted to go inside the house.'

'Hmmm!'

They sat for some time, lost in their own thoughts. Each trying to reach a conclusion. Hari *Chacha* came with tea tray. They took the cups and he carried the tray to Suchitra's room. After a while, Mrs. Langley came out.

'Kailash, do you mind sitting with Suchitra for some time? She will feel better speaking to someone her age,' she said smiling. Kailash understood that Mrs. Langley was worried for her daughter and she wanted to give her a break from all the questions she was being asked.

'Sure ma'am!' Kailash got up and went to Suchitra's room.

'How are you feeling?' he asked her once inside.

'Much better,' she said forcing a smile. 'I spoilt everyone's weekend. Didn't I?'

'No you didn't. In fact it was getting a little boring,' Kailash said smiling.

'Was it? I thought we all were having a good time until I screamed,' she again smiled. This time her smile looked genuine. Kailash looked at her. She looked very pretty in her pink night gown but also very vulnerable. He somehow felt protective of her. He took her hand in his hands, on an impulse.

'We are going to carry on having a good time. Tomorrow we will go back home and let's go to the movies next weekend,' he found himself saying and felt surprised. He had just met her.

'Really! That would be great.' This time her smile was even more radiant. 'And will you show me your collection of stamps?' she asked.

'Of course!'

'Would you also come to the club to play badminton?'

'Yes! Why not!' Some colour had come to her cheeks. They talked a little more about this and that, and they both avoided the incident that had taken place earlier in the night.

'Kailash!' Nandan said entering the room. He looked at Suchitra and gave her a big smile.

'So how are we doing?' he asked, looking affectionately at Suchitra.

'I am feeling better.'

'All right! Then let's all just get some rest and tomorrow after breakfast we head back home. Hari! Come inside.'

Kailash noticed a shadow crossing Suchitra's face. Hari *Chacha* came inside and shut the window and bolted it. Suchitra avoided looking at the window, as if she was scared to look at it.

'Uncle, Suchitra and Mrs. Langley can sleep in my room. I will sleep here.'

'Yes, why not? I think that's a good idea.'

Suchitra looked at Kailash, silently thanking him. After a little while, her mother came and Suchitra went with her to Kailash's room while Somendra slept in his father's room. Kailash sat down on the bed. He looked at the window. He sat for some time lost in his thoughts, and then he got up, and peered inside the hall. Everyone had retired to their rooms and a quiet had descended the house. He shut the doors of his room, walked up to the window, unbolted it and then threw it open. He peered outside. It took his eyes a while to get adjusted, especially against the light of the Petromax in the room. The moon was quite up in the sky, and the moonlight was adequate to make the outdoors visible. The garden looked exactly the same as he had seen it earlier that evening. There was a breeze blowing and Kailash realised it had a slight nip now. There was a big banyan tree just outside the window and its foliage cast shadows and the branches danced and swayed with the breeze. The garden was on both sides of the porch. It was surrounded by a tall hedge, made of mehendi bushes. There were big old mango, neem and banyan trees all around the garden. There was a sweet fragrance of roses in the air.

What did Suchitra see? Did she really see something or someone? The swaying branches cast shadows that could be mistaken for a human form if your mind was muddled with sleep. Or maybe she just dreamt the whole thing. He remembered her being a little jumpy in the evening. Or someone had really sneaked into the property? But how can one explain the British Officer? Her father said that she was sure it was an Englishman wearing an officer's uniform. Was it possible to imagine the whole thing? The mind did play tricks at times. But the fear in her eyes was disturbing. Also the colour of her cheeks had gone from peachy to pale. Whatever it was, it really scared her. Kailash kept standing for some time, trying to make something out of this whole thing, but as a gust of breeze made him shiver, he stepped back and went to the bed and fell asleep the moment his head touched the pillow.

132

CHAPTER 12

Kailash was woken up by a soft knock accompanied by Hari *Chacha's* gentle voice.

'Please come in *Chacha*!'

Hari *Chacha* entered the room with a tray with tea.

'*Chote Babu, Missi Baba* and *Bibi Ji* have come downstairs. You can go to your room to freshen up.'

'Ok *Chacha*! Thank you!'

Kailash finished his tea and came out of the room. He heard voices of his *Bua* and Mrs. Langley. He presumed they were in the veranda outside. He came down after twenty minutes for breakfast. Everybody was already seated and having breakfast. Some light conversation was going on. As he wished everyone good morning, he noticed Suchitra wearing a light mauve coloured shirt over dark slacks. She had gathered her hair in a high ponytail that made her look younger than her age. Despite the dark circles under her eyes that gave the indication that she had not slept well, she looked pretty. Everyone had seemed to recover from last night's episode, or they were deliberately trying to put it behind them. Suchitra, though smiling at the anecdotes being narrated by her father, was not succeeding in hiding her discomfort. Even Somendra looked a little subdued.

'Nandie, I haven't seen your library,' Capt. Langley addressed Nandan Mathur.

'Let's have our tea in the library then.'

Everyone got up to go to the library. Capt. Langley and Nandan

Mathur walked to the library that was across the hall. Anuradha started giving instructions to Hari *Chacha* for lunch basket. Initially, the plan was to go to the village as they had been invited by the local landlord for lunch, as was the ritual every time the Mathurs visited the village, but Nandan Mathur had changed the programme, deciding to start for Kanpur after breakfast and have a picnic lunch en route. Kailash noticed the Langley family's reluctance to stay there any longer.

Kailash and Suchitra entered the library. It was a room that ran parallel to the hall. There were wooden shelves lining the wall, painted in rich and shiny mahogany, filled with hardbound books. There was a big fireplace and a beautiful gilded mirror that was mounted a few inches over the mantelpiece, flanked by candelabra on either side. The bookshelves ran the length of two thirds of the room, and then there were some portraits on the wall. Nandan Mathur had told Kailash that these were the owner's relatives' portraits. He'd wanted to take them with him but had changed his mind at the last minute, asking Nandan Mathur's father if he could let them be there till he made arrangements to get them shipped. The senior Mathur had left them on the wall and they had been there ever since. The owner had not bothered to collect them. There were some reading chairs in the room, and though the previous owner had taken most of the books with him to England, he had left the remaining in the loving care of the senior Mathur. Mr. Mathur had added many more to the collection as he was an avid reader, and collecting rare books was his hobby.

'Some of the books are first editions,' Nandan Mathur was saying.

'But I think you should make some security arrangements. You have a treasure here,' Capt. Langley looked bemused.

'Don't worry! These two chaps are here and the Zamindar makes sure that my property is kept safe.'

'Well! He is not doing a very good job then,' Capt. Langley said. Silence hung in the air for a few moments and everyone looked uncomfortable.

'Another round of tea, before we leave?' Anuradha asked, changing the subject.

'Yes, why not! And a cigar. Thank you Anu!'

'Where is Sam?' asked Capt. Langley.

'He is outside with the driver,' his wife replied.

They settled down in the chairs and the conversation steered towards the current political and sociological situation in the country.

'Hope you slept well?' Kailash asked, walking up to Suchitra who was looking at a portrait. She did not answer.

'Suchitra!' called Kailash. He looked at her and was shocked to see her face. Her eyes were fixed on the portrait and her face was drained of colour. She seemed to be oblivious to anything around her. Kailash looked at the portrait. It was the picture of a British officer in his uniform. It was a handsome face with a pair of intense blue eyes, and he seemed to be directly looking at her. The plaque under the portrait read; 'Second Lieutenant Edmund Brightmore, 1st (King's) Dragoon's Guards.'

And then it struck him. Suchitra had mentioned that the person she saw was a British officer in uniform. The incident was still very fresh in everyone's memory.

'Sue!' he called out her name loudly and shook her slightly. Suddenly Suchitra looked at him and started shaking uncontrollably.

'What is it Kailash?' Anuradha asked. Kailash's firm and loud voice had caught everyone's attention.

'*Bua*! Suchitra...! He couldn't complete the sentence as he caught Suchitra's limp body in his arms. Suddenly, there was commotion.

'Sue!' called out Mrs. Langley as she rushed towards them. 'What happened to my darling?'

Everyone was beside her.

'Anu! Tell Hari to get some water and ask him if there is a doctor nearby,' Nandan Mathur said.

Capt. Langley had picked up Suchitra and brought her to the bedroom where he laid her on the bed. Mrs. Langley was beside herself with worry. She kept calling Suchitra's name softly. Anuradha sprinkled some water on her face and to everyone's relief she opened her eyes. Mrs. Langley kissed her forehead gently and asked her to drink some water. She gulped some.

'What happened? My sweet Sue! How did you faint?' Mrs. Langley asked holding Suchitra's hands.

'When are we leaving Mummy?'

Mrs. Langley looked at her husband questioningly.

'Depends on how you are feeling sweetheart. Can you take the journey?'

'Yes Papa! I want to go. I don't want to stay here another moment.'

Kailash was a little surprised to hear the emphatic tone of her voice. Till now he had only known Suchitra as a shy and quiet girl, but then, he had only known her for a few hours.

'*Babu Saheb*, there is no doctor in the village but I can call Vaidya Ji if you say,' Hari *Chacha* was asking.

'What do you say Al?' Nandan Mathur asked.

'I think we will leave for the city. I plan to take Sue to my family physician.'

After thirty minutes they started for Kanpur. Suchitra and Somendra were travelling with their parents in their car and Kailash and his uncle and *Bua* travelled in theirs. Suchitra's mother wanted to be with her so they decided to travel in their respective cars.

'I hope Suchitra recovers fast. Kailash what do you think happened there in the library?' Anuradha asked.

'I don't know *Bua*, she was looking at this portrait of a British

Officer and then she fainted. Remember she had said that she had seen a British Officer last night? I think she just got spooked. But this whole thing is really baffling. If she had dreamt the whole thing, you think the reaction would have been so intense? Did she really see someone?'

'Come on Kailash! You are a modern chap with progressive thoughts. You certainly don't believe in this supernatural nonsense,' Nandan Mathur said with a touch of reproach in his voice.

'No I don't! But can a dream have this kind of effect? *Bua*! You should have seen her face. She looked as if she had literally seen a ghost.'

'I really don't know what to make of this whole thing. All I know is that Suchitra has been of weak constitution ever since she was born. And I really feel bad that poor girl got so spooked,' Anuradha said sounding worried.

'That explains the whole thing. She must have seen the portrait of this Officer earlier in the evening without really registering it. At times, the things that we see at a cursory glance are often forgotten by our conscious mind but they stay in our subconscious mind. She must have dreamt of him and when she saw the portrait, she freaked out. By the way, I think her brother was also trying to feed some stories to her in the evening when we were having dinner. And as Anu says, the girl is of weak constitution and it was a bit too much for her to take in. Anyway, all's well that ends well. Thankfully, she is feeling better and I am sure she would forget the incident soon enough.' Nandan Mathur concluded.

Kailash wasn't so sure. Much as he wanted to believe his uncle's theory, he could not bring himself to dismiss the whole thing as a trivial incident. The kind of fear that he had seen in her eyes was not borne out of ordinary fear. It was much more than that.

They stopped at the same place for lunch where they had on their way to the village, but things were not the same. Suchitra said that she was feeling better but her eyes lacked lustre. They had lunch making light conversation but everyone seemed a little distracted. They decided to meet in Kanpur when Suchitra was feeling better. Anuradha hugged Suchitra and asked her mother to keep her informed about her well-being. Kailash walked up to the car and opened the door for her. When he said bye to Suchitra she smiled and there was softness in her eyes that he did not see.

The moment they entered Kanpur, Kailash felt a nervous excitement. He had been away for twenty-four hours and for most of the time, Sharmishtha had occupied his thoughts, till he had heard Suchitra scream. Now that he was back, the expectation of seeing Sharmishtha filled his heart with heady excitement. Did she miss him? Would she be waiting for him? And then he chided himself for making castles in the air. After having a cup of tea with the family he went to his room. He lay down for some time but got up and went to the terrace. It was late October, so the sun had set and a pleasant breeze was blowing. He peered into the terrace next to his house hoping to see Sharmishtha but there was no one there. He laughed inwardly at his foolishness but had a warm feeling of hope that felt wonderful. He was going to see her sooner or later. He was determined to speak to her and make her talk to him. He would beseech her, beg her to say something. After all, time was running out and he wanted to hear her talk, share her life with him. Oh! There was so much he wanted to do. He wanted to hold her hand, take her in his arms and kiss her eyelids. He stayed on the terrace till Hari came and told him that dinner was served. He felt disappointed. After dinner he tried reading a book but his eyelids felt heavy and soon he fell into a deep and dreamless sleep, only to be woken up by Hari's gentle knocking on the door.

'What time is it *Chacha*?'

'It's nine o'clock *Chote Babu! Bibi Ji* said not to wake you before nine. If you could freshen up and come for breakfast in half an hour, *Babu Saheb* wants to see you before he leaves for court.'

'Kailash, would you accompany your *Bua* to the District Magistrate's party? I would have gone but I have to work on this case and the hearing is tomorrow,' Nandan Mathur said the moment

Kailash sat down for breakfast.

'Sure uncle!'

'Wear your dark blue pinstriped suit. I suppose it's a formal party like always. And son! Meet lovely girls. Have fun,' Nandan said smiling and got up.

Kailash smiled and left the room after breakfast. He was a little disappointed. He did not want to go anywhere except the terrace where he hoped to see Sharmishtha. He would miss seeing her today also if she came there.

Evening came and he dressed up reluctantly. He looked at himself in the mirror. He looked breathtakingly handsome in a powder blue shirt and dark blue suit and a neck tie.

What's the point! The person I want to impress is not even remotely interested. He thought to himself. There was some commotion and he could hear some female voices in the corridor. He took a last look at himself and hurried out, thinking that *Bua* had already dressed, and he didn't want to keep her waiting. He stopped in his tracks the moment he reached the foyer. Standing there was Sharmishtha looking stunning in a candy pink georgette *sari*. Her long hair was plaited. Her ears and neck were adorned with gems. *Bua* was pinning her *sari* on her shoulder. And then Sharmishtha looked at him. Their eyes met and it was as if the universe stopped. She would remember this moment for years to come because this was the moment when she fell hopelessly in love with Kailash. Kailash, who had already fallen in love with her, knew that very instant that he would never ever love another woman. It is said that you fall in love only once and this can be experienced only by the people who have been lucky to have found love. He was looking at her kohl-lined eyes, her pink lips and her figure that looked like a statue of Ajanta, her curves accentuated by the *sari*. He had not seen her bedecked like this in a *sari* before, and the effect was mesmerising.

'Kailash! You look handsome! And see! Sharmishtha is looking so beautiful!' Anuradha said, smiling affectionately. '*Pundit Ji* and

Sharmishtha are coming with us.'

'I will see if Shyam *Chacha* has brought the car out,' Kailash escaped his *Bua*'s quizzical smile.

They were greeted by the host and his wife warmly. Pt. Girja Shankar introduced his daughter to them.

'What a beautiful daughter you have *Pundit Ji*! Where have you been hiding her?' The hostess said.

Sharmishtha got a lot of glances, from admiring men and envious women. Heads turned as she walked with her father, meeting people.

'There they are! Kailash, let's meet the Langleys. Suchitra is looking much better. Suchitra, how are you feeling sweetheart?' Anuradha asked hugging Suchitra.

'Suchitra, this is Sharmishtha. She is Pt. Girja Shankar's daughter. They are our neighbours.'

Both the girls greeted each other. They both assessed each other as it always happens when two beautiful women meet for the first time. Sharmishtha saw a delicate, pretty girl, who looked fashionable in her deep blue frock trimmed with delicate white lace. Her mannerisms reflected that she had gained her education from those upper class convent schools. The pearls in her ears and neck completed the picture of an English *Mem Saheb*. Sharmishtha suddenly felt dowdy in her *sari*. She felt angry at not being able to wear one of her frocks. This was all Ajoo's fault. It was her idea that she should wear a *sari* as she was going to be sixteen, and in a year or two would get married. Why did she agree? But it was of no use now. She would complain to her father later about Ajoo's insistence.

As Sharmishtha's gaze wandered looking for her father, she was oblivious of the effect she was having on Suchitra. Suchitra was mesmerised. She had never seen anyone so beautiful in her life. She was awestruck by Sharmishtha's beauty.

'Anuradha! Kailash! Could you come over here please?' Capt. Langley was calling them.

'Girls, you keep each other company. We will join you in a bit. Suchitra, don't leave Sharmishtha alone. She doesn't know many people here,' Anuradha said as she walked away.

Suchitra looked at Sharmishtha and smiled. 'Should we go and sit under that tree?' she asked.

Sharmishtha nodded and they walked to a cluster of cast iron chairs that were placed under a neem tree.

'So which school do you go to?' Suchitra asked to break the ice between them.

'Saraswati Gyan Mandir,' Sharmishtha said after a pause.

'You are very beautiful.'

'Thank you! You yourself are so very pretty! I like your frock. I was also planning to wear one but my grandmother insisted that I wear a *sari*,' Sharmishtha said making a face.

'I am sure you look as pretty in frocks too.' There was admiration in her voice.

'Anuradha Kaki said that you were looking better now. Were you unwell?'

'It was nothing much, but I am fine now. Aunt Anuradha is very caring and so is Kailash.'

The mention of Kailash's name brought a change in Sharmishtha's face. She wanted to ask her how well she knew Kailash. Or how well Kailash knew her but she thought it would be impolite and a little out of line as they had just met. But she looked at Suchitra with different eyes now. Did she detect softness in Suchitra's voice as she took Kailash's name? Was Kailash fond of her too? Was she more beautiful than her? When she had met her earlier in the evening, she had come across as a delicately pretty girl, but then it was just that. She was not turning heads as she had done. She was aware of hundreds of pairs of eyes on her. She had caught Kailash looking at her with pride in his eyes. But she said 'caring'. What did that imply? What did

Kailash do to her that was 'caring'?

And a small seed of envy took root in her heart that was going to grow into a big tree.

'Would you like to eat something?' Suchitra prompted as she noticed that Sharmishtha had gone quiet and looked preoccupied.

'I will eat with *Kaki*.'

Suchitra tried making conversation but it was obvious that Sharmishtha was distracted. She felt a little surprised and a little miffed, and was debating whether to make an excuse and get up, when she saw Kailash walking towards them, she felt happy and relieved.

'The dinner is served and *Bua* has asked me to escort you ladies to the dining area,' Kailash said smiling with a glint in his eyes, looking very suave in his suit, and his mannerisms were absolutely gentlemanly. Sharmishtha felt her heart beating a little faster. He was so handsome, so perfect. They started walking.

'How is Sam?' Kailash asked.

'He is fine but has sobered down a little. He has been finding excuses to be with me. I find that really sweet. But at the same time I am a little concerned as I feel he blames himself for that incident,' Suchitra said.

'But why is that?'

'Oh! It was just that he had been telling me that he thought there was something spooky in that house ever since we had reached there.'

'What? Did he also feel or notice something?' Kailash asked, surprised.

'No no! You know Sam is very possessive of me and he was feeling a little neglected that day as we two were talking most of the time. So this was his way of getting even with me,' she said smiling.

'By scaring the hell out of you?'

'By teasing me. He is just a child Kailash.'

Kailash did not say anything.

Sharmishtha heard the conversation and felt left out and ignored. Her suspicion became stronger. Kailash and Suchitra were talking animatedly of some incident and clearly Kailash was concerned for Suchitra. She suddenly felt deflated and miserable. She just wanted to leave them and go home.

'Where is my father?' she asked.

'He is with some gentlemen. They are deep into a discussion. *Bua* said that we should eat with her and Mrs. Langley.'

'Mishthi! Come sweetheart! Hope you did not get bored.'

'No *Kaki*!' Sharmishtha said in a small voice.

'Is anything the matter?' Anuradha asked her.

'No! *Kaki*, I am tired and want to go home.'

'Alright! Then we shall leave as soon as *Pundit Ji* finishes dinner.'

Kailash looked at Sharmishtha feeling that something was amiss.

The food was being served by the liveried waiters. There were beautiful flower arrangements and elegant candelabra on each table. There were at least sixty tables like that and the city's who's who were sitting there. Sharmishtha spotted her father sitting with other people. He caught her eyes and smiled affectionately. But amidst the soft chatter and beautiful dresses, Sharmishtha felt out of place. And her mind went back again to the conversation she had heard between Kailash and Suchitra. She felt a void in her heart. It was clear from their conversation that they not only knew each other well, but had spent some time together. Suchitra had referred to some incident. Was that the time when Kailash had taken 'care' of her? They both had talked to each other in a way that confirmed that they were close. They had forgotten that she was there too. And all this time she thought that there was a spark between her and Kailash. She felt angry at her naiveté. What was she thinking? Though *Baba* and

Kaka were good friends and neighbours, but there was a difference in their culture. While *Kaka* had had his education abroad and believed in western culture to quite an extent, her father was traditional in every respect. He believed strongly in his culture and values. He did not smoke or drink and loved Indian food. However these differences had never come in the way of their friendship. But Suchitra, with her anglicised manners and background, would fit in their household better. Maybe the Mathurs were thinking of an alliance between Kailash and Suchitra. Otherwise, how do you explain their closeness and an air of ease between them?

'Mishthi, you have hardly eaten anything!' She was brought out of her reverie by Anuradha's voice.

Farewells were said and they started for home. As both the girls bid farewell, there was heaviness in their hearts. Little did they know that their lives were going to be entwined with each other. Sharmishtha stayed quiet through their journey back home and avoided looking at Kailash.

Chapter 13

Two days had gone by and Kailash had not seen Sharmishtha. He kept going back to that evening when they had gone for the party. She had looked so astonishingly beautiful. All eyes were on her and Kailash had felt so proud. Proud of the fact that he had fallen in love with the most beautiful girl in town. And now he knew that he was hopelessly in love with her because not a single moment passed without him thinking of her. But, at the same time, he was not able to understand the change in her attitude. She had looked happy to see him that evening and he had seen a glint in her eyes. Normally, it would have amounted to something, but when she went quiet and avoided looking at him towards the latter part of the evening, he was confused.

'Kailash! Can I come in?' Anuradha was at the door.

'Please come in *Bua*!'

'I just got a phone call from Bina. Suchitra has got another fit.'

'Fit?'

'I don't know what else to call it. She got up screaming in the middle of the night. She said she had seen... err... the same British Officer. This time he was standing next to her bed looking down at her.'

'Oh God! What do you think it is *Bua*? Did she ever have a medical condition of that sort? You have known her ever since she was a child.'

'That's the problem. I am finding this so difficult to believe. Suchitra, though a gentle soul, has always been a happy and contended child. Both her parents and grandparents dote on her. She has everything she wishes for, so there is no question of any insecurity that might have triggered this condition. Frankly, I am as puzzled as you are. Anyway I am going to look her up. Would you like to come?'

'Yes, of course.'

Sharmishtha was trying to concentrate on her history lesson, as her half yearly exams were just round the corner. But it was proving very difficult as her mind was occupied with thoughts of Kailash. The more she tried not to think about him, the more he was there in front of her eyes. His handsome and kind face, smiling. She rebuked herself by reminding herself that he did not belong to her. Why her heart couldn't understand that? She had read in one of the romantic novels, while hiding in her room or under the quilt, that there was often a tussle between the mind and the heart when one was in love. In her case, her mind and heart were both ditching her. Her entire being craved for his love. Though there was a small voice telling her that she should be cautious. She might get her heart broken. Oh! It was so frustrating. She hit her forehead with the thick book.

'*Didi*, why are you hitting yourself?'

She had forgotten that she was guiding her siblings in their lessons.

'It's nothing,' she said smiling. 'Why don't you go and see if *Baba* has come home?'

They both ran out of the room. She just closed her eyes. She wanted to be alone. These days she either wanted to be with Kailash or with thoughts of him.

Kumari came and informed that *Baba* had come and lunch was being served.

'Mishthi, I was telling your mother and *Ajoo* how everyone was besotted with you. I felt very proud.'

'That's why I burnt chillies to ward off the evil eye,' *Ajoo* said feeling happy with herself.

'But *Amma*, Mathur *Saheb's* nephew is a very well brought up boy. He really knows how to respect elders. I am happy that Mathur *Saheb* has adopted him. He will prove to be a good son to them,' Pt. Girja Shankar said.

Ajoo murmured something about God always looking after his children. But Sharmishtha's heart was beating fast. She felt a little intoxicated. Ah! How sweet *Baba's* words sounded to her ears. She wanted to keep on hearing Kailash's praises, but then the topic changed to something else. She wanted to run to *Kaki's* house and see him. She waited for lunch to get over and *Baba* to return to his shop.

'*Amma*! Can I go to *Kaki's* house for ten minutes? I need some help in my English lesson.'

'Go! And carry the *ladoos* that Kumari's mother made this morning. Anuradha loves them.'

Clutching the brass container that contained ladoos, Sharmishtha half ran to Anuradha's house. Hari *Chacha* opened the door.

'*Mishthi Bitia*! Come inside.'

'*Chacha*, *Amma* has sent *ladoos* for *Kaki*. Where is *Kaki*?'

'*Bibi Ji* and *Kailash Babu* have gone to Capt *Saheb's* place. Suchitra *Bitia* is not feeling well.'

Sharmishtha felt a stab in her heart. Disappointment was soon taken over by anger.

'*Chacha*! Please tell *Kaki* I came to give *ladoos*.'

'I will *Bitia*! I have made *badam halwa* you like so much...'

'I am in a hurry *Chacha*. Some other time.' She cut him short.

She came home and went to her room. Her younger brother came running to her. She snapped at him. She told herself she was not going to see Kailash. He could go to Suchitra. She was not interested in him. She pictured many scenarios where she would ignore Kailash if they came face to face. Or if he tried talking to her, she would tell him that she was not interested in him. She decided not to think of him. Instead, she busied herself deciding the menu for the next day's lunch and dinner with her mother and *Ajoo*, as a day prior to *karwa chouth* her father's cousins' wives would come to their house. They would wear new bangles and apply *mehendi* and sing songs.

The next day started with hustle and bustle of the festival. Sharmishtha was adding finishing touches to her sister's hair when she heard Kumari calling her.

'*Didi*! *Aseeman Chachi* has come. She has the latest collection of bangles,' Kumari said excitedly.

Sharmishtha came down. Aseeman *Chachi* and her daughter were sitting in the *angan*. There were two wicker baskets full of beautiful multi-coloured bangles. Aseeman *Chachi*, had a shop in the bazaar and came personally to sell bangles to the household. This was every year's ritual.

'Come *Bitia*! Select your bangles. I have brought the latest ones. No one in bazaar has got them yet. See these red ones with cut work! Gauhar wore these in that new *saleema*.' She flashed a big smile showing her tobacco sainted teeth.

'*Arey Amma*! It's called cinema not *saleema*.' Her daughter Nazma corrected her.

'So you have seen the latest cinema Aseeman?' Sharmishtha's mother asked.

'*Arey Bahu Ji*! A woman has to look for some happiness in life. God knows I work day and night to feed these children while their father only eats and smokes *hukka*.'

'So *Bitia*! Which one do you like? I want you to wear them first, like every time.'

'I will wear the red ones with the green lines, *Chachi*.'

'*Bahu Ji*! Find a *shahezada* for Mishthi *Bitia* because only a *shahezada* deserves her.'

She cracked her knuckles and placed them astride her head, which was a common gesture to ward off the evil eye.

The afternoon slipped away as the relatives started coming. Nazma applied *mehendi* while Aseeman put bangles on the wrists of the women. Sharmishtha kept busy with Kumari fetching and supervising tea and snacks. Dinner was being cooked in the kitchen, and soon it would be time to serve everyone. In spite of the distraction, Sharmishtha kept thinking of Kailash. When she wore the bangles, she thought of him. When the women talked of the fast they were going to keep the next day, she wished she could keep one for him. Her anger had evaporated but her pride was intact, so when her mother asked her to go and call Anuradha to come and wear her bangles, she sent Kumari instead. Anuradha was in the college, so her bangles were kept aside and she came to wear them in the evening.

'Mishthi, go to bed sweetheart! You look so tired,' her father said.

She peeped into her brother's room and found him asleep. And then she went to her room. She put her arm around her sister and fell asleep, thinking of Kailash.

There was the sound of a conch shell coming from the temple.

'*Amma*! Moon is out,' shouted Madhav, her younger brother.

Sharmishtha accompanied her mother to the terrace, carrying the silver *pooja thali*. She watched her mother perform the *pooja* and tried not to look at the neighbouring terrace.

'Mishthi! Anuradha has not come up as yet. Just go and see why she hasn't come?' her mother said.

'She must be coming *Amma*! *Baba* is waiting to give you water. You go downstairs I will bring the *thali*.'

She looked at the neighbouring terrace when her mother left. Where is *Kaki*? She thought to herself. She was tempted to cross the short wall and run downstairs but stopped herself from doing that. She was wearing a pink *ghaghra choli* and she knew that she looked good. She wanted Kailash to see her. After meeting Suchitra, she wanted him to see her even more and realise that Suchitra was nowhere close to her, in terms of beauty. Maybe she had the advantage of her anglicised background, but Sharmishtha knew that she was a quick learner and she would learn things fast if need be. Moreover, her *Baba* was a well-respected businessman in the city, so that was also not an issue. But as she told herself these things, she knew in her heart that there was a very major issue that may come in between them, and that was the difference in their caste. She felt her heart sinking every time she thought of that. She looked at the moon and wished with all her heart for Kailash to be her husband. And at that moment she realised that she could never remain angry with him. That she would always love him whether he loved her or not, whether he married her or not. She would look at the moon every Karwa Chouth and see his face. She quietly wiped the tears from her face and picked up the silver plate.

'Mishthi!!'

She turned back and her heart leapt with joy. He was standing on the other side of wall, dressed in an embroidered Kurta, and looking so handsome that she wanted to run into his arms.

'Mishthi, would you come after fifteen minutes? I want to talk to you. Please!'

She nodded and went downstairs. It took her half an hour to make an excuse. He was waiting for her. The moon had gone up and was casting a silver glow. The evening looked magical. Kailash hopped over the wall.

'You look so beautiful. I can never tire of looking at you. Where have you been hiding? You haven't come to the house for so many days.'

'Why should I come?'

Her pride was back.

'Why not? Don't you want to meet me?'

She lowered her eyes.

'Tell me something. He took her hand in his. Do you feel something for me?'

'I don't know.'

'What kind of answer is that? Either it's a yes or a no. Tell me. I want to know.'

'You tell me first.'

He looked at her with a smile playing on his lips.

'All right! Sharmishtha! I am in love with you and want to spend my entire life with you.'

Those were the sweetest words that she would cherish for the years to come. This evening was going to stay with her, her entire life.

'But you keep going to meet Suchitra.'

He looked at her for a moment, and then he started laughing as he understood the reason behind her aloofness.

'Shhhh...!' She put her hand on his mouth. She was afraid that someone might hear.

'So that is the reason. You silly girl! Suchitra is just a friend. Her parents are very close to *Bua* and Uncle. And we went to her house because she is not well.'

'What happened to her?'

'Umm... It's difficult to explain.'

'If you don't want to tell, I will understand.'

'Of course I want to tell.' He paused for a moment and then narrated the whole incident including the latest one.

Sharmishtha was wide-eyed.

'What do you think it is? I keep thinking but can't find a rational explanation.'

'What can be more rational than the fact that she actually saw this err... ghost?'

'What! No! There is no such thing. I think there is some kind of fear that has manifested itself in this form. I was reading this book in the library yesterday and it says that our subconscious mind is capable of conjuring up certain images, and at times, when our conscious mind is asleep; it plays those images in the form of dreams. These dreams are so vivid and life-like that the person thinks he was awake and takes the whole thing as real. I think Suchitra's dream was based on her fear. She was not very comfortable in the bungalow in the village and Somendra's teasing made it worse. But what I find weird is what she told me yesterday, that she had seen the same person in the lawns when we were having dinner. I remember her dropping her fork. And this time the person was standing next to her bed. I really cannot make head nor tail of it.'

He looked a little exasperated.

'What do her parents have to say?'

'I think Mrs Langley believes in what her daughter is saying but Capt. Langley doesn't believe in the theory of ghosts. Anyway, let's not waste time discussing this. Mishthi, I want to ask you something.'

He looked at her. She was looking at the floor. He took her hands in his.

'Do you like me? I mean do you have feelings for me?'

She kept sitting with her eyes downcast.

'We don't have much time. Someone might come looking for us. Please look at me and tell me.'

She looked at him and nodded. He put his arms around her.

'Thank you! He whispered in her ears. You have made me so happy.'

'Do you like her?'

'Like who?'

'Suchitra.'

'I like her as a friend. Why are you asking this?'

She did not respond.

'Mishthi, I am in love with you and only you. I could never ever love another girl. I want to spend my entire life with you. When I came to Kanpur to spend some time with uncle and *Bua*, I had never thought I would meet someone like you and fall in love. But here we are.'

'*Ajoo* and *Baba* will never agree to this,' she said her eyes brimming with tears.

'I know, and I have to find a way to convince your father. That is the biggest challenge for me. Mishthi, will you wait for me?' he asked, looking at her with such earnestness that her heart filled with pure undying love for him.

CHAPTER 14

Kailash stayed in Kanpur, in spite of his parents asking him to spend some time with them. He went to Delhi only for five days as he had to complete the formalities for his visa, and told Sharmishtha that he couldn't stop thinking of her even for a few minutes. Sharmishtha felt love so deep that it hurt. She was living in bliss. They tried meeting as many times as they could, and what they couldn't communicate in person, they did through long letters that they would give to each other secretly. Sharmishtha had found a perfect place to hide them and when her sister would fall asleep, she would read them again and again. But she felt depressed when Kailash told her that he would leave in early April. He told her that he was going to take Anuradha *Bua* in confidence and going to tell her that he wanted to marry Sharmishtha. That would make things easier as they would be able to write letters to each other. At the same time, he would ask *Bua* to talk to Sharmishtha's parents about her marriage, and if need be, then they could be told about their decision to marry each other.

He told her that once he got admission in a college and settled down a bit, he would look for a part time job. By then Sharmishtha would have turned eighteen, and he, twenty-one. Then they could get married and she would go to England with him. She promised to wait for him for as long as it would take.

Sharmishtha was mesmerised by Kailash's intelligence and knowledge. He knew so much about everything. He had explained the world's history and geography to her. He had an answer for everything. He introduced her to poetry. She always had a love for reading but he refined it. The only disagreement they had was relating to Suchitra's illness. Kailash refused to believe that it had something to do with the supernatural, whereas Sharmishtha insisted on it. She had heard a lot of such stories from *Ajoo* and believed in them. They argued over it many a time.

A change had taken place; Sharmishtha did not feel envious of Suchitra whenever Kailash showed his concern for her, but instead felt sympathetic towards her. She always went to meet her whenever Suchitra visited Anuradha and Kailash. Though she never asked her anything directly, she showed her concern over it. And then, when Kailash told her that Suchitra was going to England for her treatment and was to continue her studies there, she had had mixed feelings. She had started liking Suchitra's gentle and pleasing demeanour, her soft voice and sophistication, and her down-to-earth attitude. Sharmishtha had not realised that she had established some sort of a bond with her. But just when she started thinking that she and Suchitra could be friends, the news of her going to England unsettled her. Suchitra was going to England, and so was Kailash. The jealousy that had died some time back raised its ugly head again. Her mind tried reasoning that Kailash loved only her, yet the mere thought of Suchitra being in close proximity to Kailash was disturbing.

But when Suchitra left and Kailash did not show any signs of missing her, her happiness was back. She tried bringing up Suchitra in their conversations, but Kailash, except mentioning once that he was happy she had gone to another country and how a change of place would do her good, did not talk much about her. Days were flying. Every day was a bliss, but she did not know that love was like a fragrance; it could not be kept hidden. So one day when she was about to go to Anuradha's house, her mother called her.

'Mishthi! These days I don't see you studying and you are not even combing your sister's hair. Kumari braided her hair yesterday. Anuradha must be in college. So why are you going there?'

Sharmishtha withered under her mother's stern gaze but she had to come up with something.

'*Amma*, I am having some difficulty understanding geography and maths so *Kaki* asked me to take Kailash's help.' It was not a complete lie.

'Call him Kailash *Bhaiya*. He is elder to you Mishthi,' added *Ajoo*.

'But you never needed help before.' Her mother was not letting it go.

'*Arey*! Let her take his help. Exams are round the corner. Kumari can look after the young ones,' *Ajoo* said.

Sharmishtha breathed again. Though she kept telling herself that she was imagining it, but something in her mother's eyes told her that she knew. When she told Kailash of her fears, he dismissed them saying she was imagining everything.

'But my mother never stopped me from coming here. In fact, if I missed a day meeting *Kaki*, she would question me. She said that I was like a daughter to *Kaki*.'

'It's nothing. Don't worry unnecessarily. Tell me; is your new dress for Holi ready?'

The month of March was flying. Kailash's departure day was approaching fast. She had tried spending as much time with him as possible, but there was always a shadow lurking to mar her happiness, as she thought of Kailash leaving in a few days. There was tension between them when they met. She had already made an excuse of learning painting from Anuradha, though it meant she could only go in the afternoons, as Anuradha would come home from college by then. But she was fine with it. One, it would give Kailash time to study as she did not want him to neglect his studies because of her. He was brilliant and she wanted him to get admission in the college of his choice in England. Two, it would look appropriate if she went when Anuradha was there. She knew that her mother was already suspicious.

Sharmishtha woke up to the sound of *Phalgun* songs being sung by *tolees*. She got up feeling excited. She kept humming as she dressed her siblings in the clothes they were supposed to play Holi in. There were baskets laden with *gujhia*, *ladoos* and a whole lot of savouries to be given to the *tolees*, and also to her father's employees, and the household help. Pt. Girja Shankar looked majestic in his pristine white *kurta* and *dhoti* and was giving away sweets and cash to his staff. Soon, people would start coming to greet him and apply *gulal*. Silver *thalis* were kept laden with sweets, savouries and *gulal* in bright, cheerful colours. *Bhang* was kept ready in silver glasses.

But Sharmishtha's eyes would go to the door and her heart would miss a beat every time people came, expecting Kailash to be there with *Kaka* and *Kaki*. And finally they came. Both the families greeted each other warmly. *Gulal* was applied on each other and while Pt. Girja Shankar and Nandan Mathur settled down with a glass of *bhang* each, Kailash and Anuradha ate *gujhias*.

'You know Kailash! How I wait for this day every year! *Didi* forbade me to make *gujhias* when she saw me struggling with it, and ever since she has been making our share also every year. I would have never been able to make these so delicious.'

'These are really very nice. Though mother gets *gujhias* made every year but those are nowhere close,' Kailash said.

He tried catching Sharmishtha's eyes but she avoided looking at him. She did not want to arouse her mother's suspicions. Kailash applied a little colour on her forehead and she did the same. So when her siblings dragged her out to play Holi, she joined them. The girls from the neighbourhood came running and applied colour on her cheeks. Normally, she would have run away because she was not a big fan of being smeared with colours but today she didn't resist.

'Don't take it off. You look so beautiful with red colour on your cheeks.'

She swung back. Kailash was standing with his hands full with colour and a mischievous look in his eyes. She started to run but her siblings caught hold of her. Kailash had conspired with them while her eyes were closed. He touched her cheeks with his fingers, smearing *gulal* all over them, and then he touched her neck. She felt a strange sensation coursing down her entire body. She closed her eyes without realising it.

'*Didi*! You should also put colour on him.' Her younger sister prompted. She took the colour in her palms and as she tried applying it to Kailash's cheeks, he held her hand. He had a challenging look in his eyes and a playful smile on his face. And then Sharmishtha's demeanour changed. Gone was the shy expression. Instead, there was determination and tenacity on her beautiful face. She fought like a tigress and freed herself, and smeared Kailash with as much colour as she could fill her hands with. Her siblings and their friends joined her, and then started a Holi that Sharmishtha and Kailash would remember all their lives.

Sharmishtha's cheeks had a rosy glow and it was not because of the *gulal*. *Ajoo* had applied *ubtan* on her and washed her hair, and now as she wore a turquoise georgette sari with a silver border, she looked stunning. *Ajoo* put a black dot on the nape of her neck, to ward off the evil eye. The turquoise stone earrings with a matching pendent added a glow to her eyes. It was a gift from her father. But Sharmishtha was in another world. There was a slight sway in her steps. She would smile from time to time. She kept greeting people as they came to their house to meet and embrace each other as the tradition was. She also helped Kumari serving *gujhias* and savouries, but her heart and mind were elsewhere. And when Kailash came along with his Bua and uncle, dressed in a silk *kurta pyjama*, looking breathtakingly handsome, her heart skipped a beat. Their eyes met and she went crimson. She did not notice her mother raising eyebrows when she entreated *Kaki* to stay for dinner. When the Mathurs started declining, her father insisted.

Sharmishtha was euphoric. Luck was on her side. She looked up at the sky, silently thanking God. This was a positive sign. God approved of their love. That's why *Baba* had intervened and asked the Mathurs to stay. The evening passed as a dream. Though Kailash did not look at her frequently as he was busy making conversation with his uncle and her father, but just having him sitting there was enough for her.

Chapter 15

'Why didn't you look at me yesterday?' Sharmishtha asked Kailash the next day.

'How could I? Everyone was there. Moreover, I was busy impressing your *Baba*. He should not think his daughter has selected some nincompoop as her life partner,' he said, smiling.

'Yes! *Baba* would marry his princess only to a prince,' she said with a twinkle in her eye.

'Is it? Then I think you should look for a prince.'

'I can find a prince anytime, but what will happen to you? Will you find a girl like me?' she asked, acquiring a regal look and a challenging smile.

'Mmmm! Let me see. I will find a *gori* in England. She will be as fair as you.'

'Oh! Is it? Then you go and marry a *gori*. Why are you wasting my time?' she said, sulking. Gone was the amusement from her eyes. Instead, there was hurt and anger that was turning her face red. She got up to go. He caught her hand.

'Where are you going?'

'I have some work.'

'No, you are annoyed.'

'Why should I be? You go and marry whosoever you want to. What is it to me?'

'Would it be nothing to you if I marry someone else?'

'No! Why should it be? Leave my hand. I have to go.'

He pulled her and she was in his arms. He started kissing her. First gently and then passionately. She went limp in his arms. Her whole body was tense initially, and then there was fire carousing in her veins. She did not know how long it lasted but when he stopped, she was still limp in his arms. Her eyes closed. He held her in his arms and just then Anuradha came into the room. They disengaged quickly and Mishthi ran out of the room. Anuradha was rooted to the spot. She looked at Kailash.

'*Bua*, I was about to tell you.'

'Tell me what Kailash?

He looked at her with determination on his face.

'I love Sharmishtha and want to spend the rest of my life with her.'

'Kailash! You know this is not possible.'

'Why not? She loves me too. So what can be the problem?

'You are very young to start talking of love and what about your studies and career?'

'*Bua*, I am aware of my responsibility. I am going to study and make a career. I am not going to let you, uncle or my parents down.'

'It's not only that, we would want Mishthi as our daughter-in-law. I am sure I will be able to convince your parents as well, but Pt. Girja Shankar would never approve of this. He very firmly believes in the caste system.'

'You have to convince him somehow! I am sure he will come round. Please *Bua*. I cannot imagine a life without Mishthi.' There were tears in his eyes.

Anuradha looked at his handsome face, at his beseeching eyes. Her heart went out to him. But how could she make him understand the rigidity of traditions, the age-old shackles that were unbreakable? How could she make his love filled heart see the norms of society, that were stronger than the bonds of love? She could feel his desperation. As she herself had experienced the beauty and purity of love before she'd got married to Nandan Mathur.

She broached the subject to her husband after dinner in the privacy of their bedroom. He listened to her quietly. Though he had not expected for things to take this turn, he wasn't very surprised to hear this.

'But Anuradha, you do realise that this is impossible. You will have to explain it to both the children. You know Pt. Girja Shankar is a hardcore *brahmin*. He would never ever agree to marry his daughter into a *kayastha* household. No matter how good Kailash or our family might be. There is no point even mentioning it to him. This will only spoil our relations with him.'

'Should we at least try once? Pundit Ji dotes on his daughter, he may relent. After all, this is a question of his daughter's happiness.' Anuradha said in a pleading voice. Her heart bled every time she thought of Kailash's face, pleading her.

'What is wrong with you Anu? Your affection for Kailash is clouding your reasoning abilities. Pundit Ji is a good person but he is too staunch when it comes to such matters. He might love his daughter to bits, but he would never compromise his status and good reputation in the society, and in his *brahmin* community. You have to put an end to this fanciful wish of Kailash's. Also I don't want him to be distracted by any of this when he is about to embark on a promising future.'

But when she tried telling Kailash about her husband's decision, he insisted on talking to his uncle. He went and knocked at the door of the study.

Nandan Mathur looked at him and gestured at him to take a seat.

'Uncle, *Bua* must have told you about Mishthi and I.'

'Kailash, how could you even think in your wildest dreams that

Pt. Girja Shankar would marry his daughter to you?' Nandan Mathur asked unable to hide his irk.

'Why not? I will keep her very happy. I will tell her father that I would give her all the comforts of this world.'

'It is not a question of love or comfort.'

'Then what is it? I thought you and *Bua* liked Sharmishtha.'

'Kailash! Son! We love Mishthi like our daughter. Nothing would give us more pleasure than to see you both as husband and wife. But Pt. Girja Shankar is a very traditional man. He would never allow an inter-caste marriage. There is no point even bringing this up with him. It would not serve any purpose and it would only spoil our relations.' Nandan Mathur reasoned.

'*Bua* and you have given up without even trying. If you permit, then I will speak to Mishthi's father. Please understand this is very important for me. I cannot imagine a life without her. I promise that I would go to England, do well and only then ask for her hand in marriage. Mishthi has promised that she would wait.'

'Son, do you think *Pundit Ji* would keep his daughter unmarried for the next four to five years? It is considered blasphemy in his community to keep a daughter unmarried after she turns sixteen. We may be good neighbours and friends but we are as apart from each other as day and night when it comes to our outlook towards such things.'

Kailash tried convincing him but he did not relent. He told Kailash that it would be better for him to stop thinking along those lines. He would only hurt himself by believing that this was possible. And he should, under no circumstances, try to speak to Pt. Girja Shankar. He would only put Mishthi in trouble by doing so.

Kailash had then gone to his room declining dinner, and Anuradha thought it best to leave him alone. She knew her husband was right. But then, she somehow felt responsible for this situation. Though she had not encouraged Kailash directly in meeting and liking

Sharmishtha, but then, neither had she prevented him from having any such ideas either. She loved Sharmishtha like her daughter. She had watched her grow and had always wished she had a daughter like her. In an era when everyone wanted a son, Anuradha had craved for a daughter. And probably, it was this desire that had made her somewhat oblivious to the reality.

Kailash did not tell Sharmishtha about the conversation he had had with his Uncle. He was determined to marry her. He was convinced that he would make them change their minds. He did not want to put fears into her heart. So they kept meeting. He told her about his determination to convince her parents in the time to come.

And thus, those beautiful days flew by. Kailash tried very hard not to cry as he held a sobbing Sharmishtha in his arms. He had beseeched his *Bua* to arrange a last meeting with her. He told Sharmishtha that he had resolved to marry her and nothing would keep him from that. He asked her to be patient and have faith in him. Meanwhile he would write letters to her, addressed to Anuradha.

Chapter 16

A month had passed since Kailash left for England. Sharmishtha felt listless. She went about doing her chores mechanically. This shift in her mood did not go unnoticed by her mother. But she just watched silently. One morning, as she was giving her sister a bath, *Munim Ji* came announcing that Rajeshwari Devi had arrived and was sitting in the temple.

'*Nanoo* is here? Nobody told me she was coming. *Amma*! I am going to meet *Nanoo*.'

'*Arey! Bitia* I am also coming,' *Ajoo* said, picking up her walking stick.

Rajeshwari Devi kept coming to Kanpur for the court cases she was fighting with her husband's relatives, who had grabbed a major portion of the property illegally after her husband had passed away, after succumbing to a short illness. She never came to her daughter's home as it was customary for the girl's parents to not even drink water at their daughter's home. So she stayed in a hotel and came to a nearby temple, where her daughter and her family would meet her.

'Mishthi, my child! How I missed you,' Rajeshwari Devi said embracing her.

'I missed you too *Nanoo*!' Sharmishtha said, not really knowing why she was crying.

'*Arey Bitia*! I have come to take you with me.'

In a couple of hours, Sharmishtha was packed and went to meet Anuradha. She did not stay there long as it was difficult to hold her tears; everything in that house reminded her of Kailash. Pt. Girja

Shankar had come to meet his mother-in-law and he hugged his daughter as she got ready to leave. Sharmishtha noticed tears in her father's eyes which she found unsettling. Her mother gave her a red silk pouch.

'What is it *Amma*?' Sharmishtha asked.

'Open up and see.'

As she opened the pouch and took out the contents, she gasped. On her palm lay two exotic earrings with diamonds and rubies. Though her mother had boxes of beautiful jewellery, this pair had always enticed Sharmishtha, and on several occasions she had expressed her desire to wear them, but somehow, though she was given various pieces of jewellery on the smallest of the occasions that were specially made in her father's shop, her mother had never offered these to her. When the initial joy and surprise wore off, an uneasy feeling settled that she couldn't quite shake off. Why was everyone behaving as if she were going for good? She asked herself but couldn't get an answer. After reaching her *Nanoo's* village, she gradually forgot about it as she met her childhood friends, and then being with *Nanoo* was what she loved most... Well, now there was someone else she loved to be with.

A month went by and Sharmishtha regained her cheerfulness... almost. Though she thought of Kailash all the time, but now his memory brought a smile to her face instead of tears. Somehow, she had started believing that Kailash would convince her parents. Time had dulled the sharpness of the doubts and apprehensions she had had. Reality always seems a little distant when it's not immediate. So now, she had started weaving dreams. Was it not a fact that her father loved her and would do anything to keep her happy? He had always said that only a prince was befitting for her. And there could not be a better prince than Kailash. It would be difficult to make *Ajoo* and *Amma* agree, but then *Baba* and *Nanoo* would tackle them. *Amma* and *Ajoo* always listened to *Baba*. So she enjoyed every day in Asanpur, and when *Nanoo* told her that Pt. Girja Shankar was coming to take her back to Kanpur, she was surprised. Normally,

Nanoo would accompany her to Kanpur or *Munim Ji* would come with Kumari to fetch her. Her father hardly had time to spare, as he was busy planning to open a hotel.

'But *Nanoo*, why is *Baba* coming? He could have sent *Munim Ji*.'

She was further confused when *Nanoo* started showing her the jewellery she had got made for her wedding.

'*Nanoo*! Everything is very beautiful but I am not getting married any time soon. Please tell *Baba* that I want to study. I want to be a graduate.' A barrister's wife should at least be a graduate. She thought smiling, and didn't hear *Nanoo's* mumbled response.

Back home she was given a warm welcome. Her siblings came running to her and clung to her. She hugged them and cuddled them. She had missed them.

'The house has come alive with Mishthi's presence,' a beaming *Ajoo* said.

Even her mother gave her a warm smile.

Sharmishtha was happy, though she loved her *Nanoo's* home, she had missed her family. If only *Nanoo* could stay with them in Kanpur. She often wished.

Amongst the hustle bustle of family and neighbourhood friends, Sharmishtha couldn't wait to go to Anuradha's place. So after lunch she told her mother that she would go and meet *Kaki*, as she would have come back from college. She was a little surprised when her mother told her that she should not disturb Anuradha as she might be resting. This was very unusual because they all knew that Anuradha always worked on her paintings in the afternoons, and Sharmishtha had always gone to her then, as Nandan Mathur would be in his office. It was the perfect time to sit and watch *Kaki* paint. Afterwards, they would have tea and chat. This was a routine that she had followed as far back as she remembered, and *Amma* had never stopped her. In fact, she herself had told her many a time to spend time with Anuradha. She looked at *Ajoo* for support but *Ajoo* kept murmuring, moving her fingers on her *Rudraksh Mala*.

Evening came, and Sharmishtha could not contain herself. She wanted to meet Anuradha because she loved to be with her, and was dying to talk about Kailash. She had waited patiently for a month to hear something about him and now her patience was running out. So she did not ask her mother's permission and went to Anuradha's place. She ran into her arms the moment she saw her.

'Oh! Mishthi! I really missed you, child.'

'*Kaki*, how is he?' she asked without any preliminaries.

'You are looking so pretty. How have you been? You must have enjoyed yourself in Asanpur. How is *Mausi*? I couldn't meet her last time. Is she coming to Kanpur in the near future?'

'*Kaki*, *Nanoo* is fine and she is coming next month. Have you got a letter from Kailash? Has he settled there? How is he finding his college? Is it very cold there?' Now it was her turn to ask all those questions she wanted to know the answers to. She only wanted to talk about him and nothing else.

'He is fine Mishthi,' Anuradha said in a small voice.

'*Kaki*, is something wrong?' She held Anuradha's hand and looked at her directly. She could see tears brimming in her eyes.

'He misses you a lot Mishthi. Though he is concentrating on his studies, he says he is only able to do it because of you. He wants to excel so your parents won't be able to say no to him, but he just does not want to believe that this will never happen.' And she burst into tears.

Sharmishtha just stood there for some time, frozen. And then she sat down next to Anuradha.

'*Kaki*! Why are you crying? I am sure *Baba* would agree to Kailash's proposal. He has never ever denied anything to me. He loves me more than any such stupid superficial customs.'

Anuradha looked at her through her tears, not knowing whether to tell her the truth and squash her hopes forever, or let her learn it through her parents. And then looking at her expectant face she decided to tell her. She somehow felt responsible for encouraging Sharmishtha and Kailash in believing that they could be together. She should have nipped it in the bud. She should have told Kailash that it was foolhardy, and that probably would have saved them this heartache, but instead she had watched their love bloom silently. Probably she did this for her own sake. Probably she had some hope tucked in a tiny corner of her heart for them. She wanted their love to culminate into a lifetime of togetherness. Probably she saw her salvation through them. A failed love had left a gaping hole in her heart that could never be healed. Their union could have worked like a salve.

'Mishthi, my child! Your parents are looking for a groom for you. Your mother told me herself.'

Sharmishtha looked at her stupefied for some moments, and then snatched her hand from her.

'You didn't tell *Amma* about Kailash?'

'I did. But she wouldn't hear of it. And you probably don't know but she has not been talking to me ever since. I am surprised that she allowed you to come here.'

'*Amma* cannot do this to me. I am going to talk to *Baba*.' She started towards the door.

'Mishthi wait!' Anuradha caught her hand. This is your *Baba's* decision too. Sit for a while. Please listen to me. Your mother had some suspicions about you and Kailash. As they say, love and fragrance can never be kept hidden. But on the night of Holi she saw you both together. She told your father and your *Ajoo*. Your *Ajoo* apparently told your father that she would end her life by fasting if he ever thought of mixing their high caste blood with an inferior one. She also told him of the consequences that would follow. No one would marry your sister from your caste and your brothers would not get their brides from their own caste. They would become the laughing stock of the society. Mishthi, they have made up their minds. I don't think they are going to change it.'

'If *Ajoo* can give up her life, so can I,' she said with a cold determination. 'I am her granddaughter after all.'

'And what would you achieve out of that? You would give immense sorrow to those who love you. You would finish Kailash's life before it even started. What kind of love is this Mishthi? Life doesn't always give you what you want.'

'So what are you suggesting; that I should marry someone who I would hate all my life? Do you think I can ever stop loving Kailash? *Kaki*, I can't live without him. I would rather die than live a life without him.'

She started crying. Anuradha cradled her in her arms.

'Mishthi, I am going to tell you something I have not told anyone. Probably this will help you getting through this. Like you, I was also in love with someone. I also wove dreams with him. But life is not always fair. I can tell you only this, that time heals the wounds of a broken heart. I love your *Kaka* and I made my memories my strength. I have them tucked away in a corner of my heart and I celebrate the fact that I got a chance at love. And that love taught me to perform my duties as a daughter and a wife. I feel my love is immortalised because I did not get married to him. Who knows how long it would have lasted had we got married. You yearn for something or someone till the time you own them, and then familiarity and closeness dulls the frenzy you once felt. But no one can take your memories from you. Your love will always be with you. You will never be alone.'

'I will not give up like this. I will not marry anyone.' There was a fierce stubbornness in her voice.

'Mishthi!' Anuradha started but she was already at the door and then she stopped and turned back.

'Does Kailash know about this?'

'Yes, he does,' Anuradha said quietly.

'And what did he say?'

'He is heartbroken. He feels that he can probably make them change their mind. But I know this is not possible.'

'*Kaki*, why are you doing this to us? I thought you loved me and Kailash, or you think I don't deserve him.' There was bitterness in her voice.

'Mishthi, I always saw a daughter in you. I love you as my own. I would not want anyone but you as Kailash's wife. But I know your parents. They are good people but they are also very traditional. They would never do anything that would tarnish their family's name.'

CHAPTER 17

'Mishthi! *Bitia* eat something,' *Dai Ma* urged her. They had all taken their turn; *Ajoo*, Kumari, even her mother who was the last to come, tried convincing her to eat. She had turned everyone away, saying she was not hungry. She had locked herself up in her room. Her anger had numbed everything inside her. She was not cattle who could be tied with just anyone. She was a human being with a heart and feelings. It was not her fault that she had fallen in love with a person who did not belong to the so-called 'upper caste'. There were hundreds of people belonging to the upper caste, but they did not come even remotely close to Kailash in terms of looks, intelligence and background. Above all, Kailash had a heart of gold, and he was a thorough gentleman. Why couldn't they see that it was impossible to find anyone like him in the entire world? Why were they getting blinded by their stupid customs? And what happened to their promise to marry her only to a prince? Now when she had found her prince, why were they opposing it?

She was furious at her *Ajoo*. How dare she blackmail everyone with the threat of taking her life? How ironic it was that the very people she always thought would do anything for her happiness had turned against her. Now they were strangers with cold hearts and colder intentions. She had made a promise to Kailash and she had to keep it. She would prove it to them that she was as steadfast as them. If she could not have a life with Kailash, she would not have a life at all.

She got up in the wee hours of the morning. It was still dark outside. She looked at her sister sleeping next to her and her heart and eyes filled with an indescribable sorrow. She bent down and kissed her sister's forehead, and before she could change her mind, she got down the bed and wrapped a shawl around her. She tiptoed down the stairs and as she reached the door she heard *Ajoo* calling God's name, as she did every day before opening her eyes. She undid the latch and slipped out. All this while her heart was beating so fast that she worried someone might hear it.

She hurried towards the massive gate that opened into the city. The city was waking up slowly. The cattle were being taken out for milking, some early risers were starting the hearth, and a plume of smoke was rising from their kitchens. She walked with determination. The river Ganges was not very far from her home. She got curious glances from some people who were starting their chores. She had covered her face and kept her head bent. Her heart kept thudding all this while. Finally, she reached her destination. She had to look for a place that was isolated. Some early bathers were already taking dips. She saw a spot that was closest to the bank and hurried towards it. She stood there and looked down. This was the moment for her.

'Forgive me Kailash! I couldn't keep my promise to you. But I shall meet you in my next incarnation. That is a promise,' she murmured. She took her shawl and dropped it. The breeze stirred her hair. She took a step, and then two, and leapt downwards. For a second she felt she was frozen mid-air. And then everything went dark.

The sting of the slap was still ringing in her ears when she opened her eyes. She was held tightly by a man who was dressed in orange clothes and looked like a *Sadhu*.

'Forgive me child! But I had to bring you to your senses. I do not know what it is that has propelled you towards taking this step. But the moment of unclarity has gone. And now you can see clearly. So open your eyes and look around. Along with this universe you are a creation of that Almighty and you have no right to destroy his creation. There is always hope, and more chances in life. But you can only avail them if you are alive. So go home and find hope and learn to live for others, not only for yourself.'

With that he released her arm and walked off. Sharmishtha stood there for a while and then she started walking back home.

What was she doing? If she thought that killing herself was going to resolve everything, then she was mistaken. It would have finished Kailash and she would have created a scandal. People would have talked about several theories and that would have brought shame along with loss to her family.

That sage was right. Hope was everything, and there was hope of seeing Kailash, and the mere thought that they co-existed in the same world, was a comfortable one. What she wouldn't give to get a glimpse of him! Her love for him was meant to make her strong, not weak. They had each other's love and that was enough for her to go through life. There was another way to defy her parents and her grandmother. And she would do just that. They could not win because she would always be Kailash's; body and soul.

A tonga went past her just inches away, and the driver shouted a warning. She came out of her reverie and realised that daylight had broken and the city was awake. Now she had the challenge of entering her house without anyone noticing. But that seemed impossible as the servants would be up, and so would the household. She felt panic rising. She covered her face even more tightly and kept her head bent, yet she saw people giving her a look from the corner of her eyes.

She reached the lane that would take her to her house. There was a big wood apple tree in front of the house that was two houses away from hers. She hid behind it and waited to see if she could sneak inside without being seen. But she was disappointed as she saw servants coming out and going to the barn to milk the cows. Even if she made a dash for it, chances were they would see her, and what if *Ajoo* was sitting in the courtyard doing her *jaap*? It wouldn't be long before her sister woke up and found her missing. She was twisting the ends of her shawl in her fingers nervously when she saw Anuradha's door being opened and Hari *Chaha* coming out. He walked towards her hiding place and went past it. He must have been going to the bakery to fetch fresh bread. She could go to *Kaki's* and climb back to her own rooftop terrace. The stairs in Anuradha's house were in a smaller courtyard that was not part of the main house.

What if *Kaki* or *Kaka* saw her? She decided that it would be easier to make them understand the reason for her being out at this hour, than her own parents. So she made a dash towards their house. Both the servants had their backs towards her, and were busy milking the cows. She entered Anuradha's courtyard, waited for some sort of sound and sneaked towards the stairs.

She was panting when she reached her room. It was just then that her sister opened her eyes. Sharmishtha smiled at her.

'Go back to sleep,' she said, catching her breath.

Her father finally came to her later that evening. He sat down and looked at her with such emotions that her heart lurched. She noticed that he had tears in his eyes.

'Mishthi, I know we are not being fair to you. I have always wanted to make you happy. I wanted to give you anything that you desired. But I am failing to give you the utmost happiness that you would have found with Kailash. *Bitia*, you did not choose wrong. Kailash is the kind of boy anyone would find suitable for his daughter. But unfortunately we live in a society where a person's virtue is decided by his caste, and to be a part of this society, we cannot go against its norms. I probably would have done that, had you been my only child. But you know you have one more sister and five brothers. Moreover, it's your *Ajoo* I cannot go against. She worked very hard and sacrificed a lot in making me who I am today. As you know my father was a rich man but he spent all his money on his relatives, helping them out. And then well... err... he had some mistresses as well. So when he died, those very people who had fleeced him of his fortune, turned their backs on me, my brother and mother.

'*Amma* had to work day and night to bring us food and my brother died for lack of medicine. I worked very hard to make this fortune that I have today. People respect me and I have wealth and a name in the society. So I cannot make mother unhappy, especially at her age. I just cannot change the way she thinks. So I beg you sweetheart, to forget Kailash and marry a boy from our community. I will be eternally grateful to you. I know it's not my right to ask for such a big sacrifice from you, but I wouldn't have if it were not absolutely necessary,' he paused.

Sharmishtha was quiet, sitting with her head bent. Pt. Girja Shankar got up and came and sat next to her. He held her hand.

'Mishthi, I have already seen a boy for you,' he said in a gentle voice.

Sharmishtha looked up sharply. She felt as if she had been stabbed in the heart. This was too soon, too sudden.

'But *Baba*! Why? Why can't I complete my studies at least? Why are you throwing me out?' With that the dam broke and she cried her heart out. Pt. Girja Shankar waited silently for the storm to pass.

'Mishthi, Kanti Prasad is a very well brought up boy. He is intelligent, kind and humble. He has topped his college and is a graduate. His father Pt. Shiv Prasad Pandey is a respectable and learned man. They have lots of land and are financially very comfortable, but what I like about the family is that they are well-read and well-bred people. You have always liked educated people and that was what impressed me the most. Kanti is going to pursue his Master's in literature and a doctorate in the same. He has been offered a post as a junior lecturer in the university and he will take that on along with his studies. Mishthi, I can promise you one thing that Kanti would keep you very happy. I have seen the world and I do have some insight into people. And Mishthi *Bitia*, you know that you are the apple of my eye. How can I throw you out? But you are going to be seventeen and in our community that is the right age to get married. As far as your studies are concerned, I can speak to Pt. Shiv Prasad and Kanti Prasad to let you continue. I am sure they would agree to that because they are very progressive people.

'Now *Bitia*, I request you to let the past go and concentrate on the future. I am asking you to do this at least for my and your siblings' sakes.' With that he folded his hands and two fat tears fell off his cheeks.

Sharmishtha's heart broke. She had never seen her father as

weak as this, in her life. He was a strong man and had weathered many storms without showing any weakness ever. Yet she could not find the words to assure him because what he had asked of her was beyond her daughterly love or generosity. She only nodded and he left the room. She felt cheated. She knew that they had planned all this and that was the reason she was sent to Asanpur. He had gone and met the boy and no one had told her. She had become a stranger in her own home. How fast the equations had changed. The flimsiness of love and affection was a painful reality. She had grown basking in the gentle care and blissful love of her near and dear ones, feeling secure, and now she felt as if she had been stripped off the warmth of her cocoon. They had taken the biggest decision of her life without involving her, as if she were an object. She felt betrayed by the two people who she loved most; *Baba* and *Nanoo*. They were quick to abandon her in order to safeguard their prestige. In the inky blackness of the night she cried till her tears dried. In the wee hours, she made a promise to herself that she would never love anyone unconditionally... except Kailash.

Chapter 18

A month had gone by, and the wedding preparations were well underway. Some relatives had already come from the village to help create various items, by lacing and embroidering items of clothing and linen. The patterns and designs of the jewellery were being discussed, and goldsmiths from Pt Girja Shankar's own shop had started creating the exquisite jewellery. Sharmishtha was going to be laden in jewellery from head to toe. Reputed shopkeepers from Banaras had come, and orders of various *saris* and *lehngas* were placed. Sharmishtha was to be given fifty-one *saris*, which comprised the finest silks and organza. She was also being given ten Banarasi *lehngas*. The *saris* and *lehngas* had zardozi work on them, and the patterns were to be woven with real gold and silver threads. But among this entire hustle bustle, she remained listless. She was fond of good clothes and jewellery, but now all those items held no interest for her. She went through the selection process mechanically, just to keep everyone happy. The house was filling with relatives. She often escaped to the terrace to find some peace. She was spending more and more time at Anuradha's, and kept waiting for Kailash's letter. Anuradha had told her that she had written a letter to Kailash telling him everything. Sharmishtha got up every day with the hope of receiving a letter, but it had not come yet. She was assailed with doubts and negative thoughts. Had Kailash forgotten her already? Had he fallen in love with Suchitra? Why was he taking so long to answer to *Kaki*'s letter? Or was he angry with her for not keeping her promise? The thoughts gnawed at her soul and she let herself drown in misery.

Notes of the wedding songs floated in the air, as women sang while carrying out the preparations. Sharmishtha became quite a stranger in her own house. Everyone was so busy with the forthcoming wedding that they hardly talked to her. Even *Baba* could not find the time. This was the first wedding in their family. He had to make sure it was the best. Ajoo had given a long list of ceremonies that had to be carried out. The Barat would stay with them for three days. Sharmishtha sat at the extended cornice of the terrace, which was her favourite spot. It was actually a nook where she could sit hidden from the world. It was also the place where she and Kailash had sat sometimes, weaving dreams. She had cried for hours sitting there, touching the walls, placing her hand where Kailash used to sit, willing him to be there somehow.

Everyone is happy at the cost of my happiness, she thought to herself. She was heartbroken to think that her father, who had always given importance to her happiness, could so easily sacrifice her at the altar of hollow traditions. She felt alone and she knew that there was a hairline crack in the solid foundation of love she had for her father.

'Mishthi! I knew I would find you here. Come with me, I want to spend some time with you.' She was startled out of her thoughts by Anuradha's voice.

'You look tired child. Aren't you getting enough sleep?' Anuradha asked, handing her a cup of tea.

'I am fine *Kaki*,' she said managing a smile.

'Mishthi, this is for you. I know you have been waiting for it,' she said handing her the light blue envelope with a British stamp.

She looked at it, not believing that she actually held a letter from Kailash. She brought it to her lips and kissed it. She felt so many emotions churning in her heart that she became oblivious of everything. She did not notice when Anuradha had left the room. She opened it carefully, not wanting to damage the letter inside. Her heart thudded in her chest as if wanting to come out of the cage of her ribs. The first words in his beautiful handwriting that were so familiar, brought all her emotions rushing back. The time gap evaporated and the thin layer of resignation cracked open, oozing out emotions. She returned to the same place she had been in, a few months back, and she knew that Kailash was her second soul and she would never be able to part with him. His words were like nectar to her soul.

My dear Mishthi,

It's one o'clock in the night and I am writing this letter to you after much debating with my mind. Forgive me for taking so much time. I just couldn't accept that you were being taken away from me forever. I believed so much in the power of my love that I thought I could change everything, make people see that love was above everything. Make them realise that by wrenching two hearts apart they were committing the most heinous crime, and to make them admit that they had no right to destroy the lives of two people by asserting their useless views and dead traditions. But, I think if there is anyone who is to be blamed, that's me. I should have never come here. I should have stayed there in Kanpur or Delhi and put my foot down. We should have eloped to some place far.

But I know that these words are meaningless as I am writing them. The hammer has fallen and both our souls have been crushed. But I want to tell you that no matter where you are and who you are with; you will always be my first and only love. I will love you till the time I breathe my last and if there is a second life, I will find you and love you. No one can take that from me. Though destiny has played a cruel role and has resulted in our separation for life, yet it cannot separate our souls.

But I have a wish, and I request and implore you to grant it to me. I want you to go ahead in life and accept it as it is, and find happiness in your new life. I know it's too much to ask for, but it will give me immense joy to know that you are happy, and I promise you that I will stay happy with your memories. They will last me a lifetime. I think we both can live our entire lives with our memories of each other. Love cannot be measured by time but by being. Distance is immaterial when our souls are never apart. I want you to make our love your strength, and perform your duties as a wife and to the relationships you create after marriage. Your husband deserves your love as his wife, and you deserve marital happiness. As far as our love is concerned, it's like a fragrance that is intangible but very much there. It should only give others pleasure by just being there selflessly.

I have not been able to concentrate on anything ever since I came to know about your father's decision. I wanted to come back to India, but Mr. Wilson, who is my mentor and guardian here and treats me like his son, told me that I would only make things worse. I know that your Ajoo has threatened to kill herself by fasting. Here is another thing I want you to understand. Your family members are not your enemies; they are simply trying to follow the norms of a society they are an integral part of. So please don't stop loving them.

Now I will make another request. I want a letter from you saying that you will do all that I have requested you to do, and also, your letter will be my lifeline. Bua will post it to me. I wish you lots of happiness in the days to come. And remember, I can only live if you are happy.

With abundant and everlasting love,

Kailash

And then, she wrote a letter to him sitting in the same room where Kailash had been staying. Somehow, it had made her feel that he was still there with her and she was talking to him. She had promised to do what he had asked for, but she could not love another person ever. She had also asked him to make her a promise that he would get married and move on with his life.

'It is because I cannot bear the thought of you being lonely and sad. It would keep me going to know that you are being loved and cared for.' She had added in the end.

Those were such sweet dreams, so far away from reality. Though Kailash was intelligent, his love for her had clouded his judgement. Or how could he have thought that he would be able to change age-old traditions and mindsets?

And now she was married to someone else. The time she had spent with Kailash looked like a beautiful dream, but she would have to live a life devoid of hope and happiness now.

She sighed.

She kept her feelings hidden and kept a cheerful countenance when her father came and hugged her. She avoided going to Anuradha's even though she was asked to visit her. But Anuradha came visiting in the evening. She complained of her being indifferent as she was married now, otherwise why hadn't she come to see her? She held her hand and took her home.

'Mishthi, how are you child?' Anuradha asked, the moment she sat down.

That was all that needed to break the dam she had built. She was crying uncontrollably in Anuradha's arms.

'How is he?' she asked after a little while.

'What should I say? He is heartbroken. He has not been eating or sleeping. His performance has gone down. He hasn't even written a letter to us for past two months. Luckily for us, his mentor, Mr. Wilson, is keeping us informed. He treats him like his son and takes care of him,' Anuradha said with a sigh. 'And you know the worst part is that he is blaming us for this. He wrote to his uncle in his last letter that he did not try hard enough. Now how to make him understand that in our country, society plays a very major role and we are governed by its rules. These rules are made by us only but we don't have the power to alter them. Though I respect our culture, yet I feel the need for a change. Two people would have been happy today, had it not been for the rigidity of thoughts and customs. Mishthi! I know what I am about to ask is difficult, but child, you have to let the past go. I know you will never be able to forget Kailash and nor will he, but you both have got your lives ahead of you. It breaks my heart to see you like this. This one month passed very slowly as I waited for you to come. You have always been like a daughter to me and I want you to be happy and move on.'

She felt Anuradha's voice coming from a distance, as she just sat there, reliving the memories that she had made in that very house with Kailash.

CHAPTER 19

1931

Sharmishtha looked at herself in the mirror. The emerald necklace that her father had given her on the occasion of *Gudia*; a festival that was celebrated for daughters, was very becoming on her. Her palms were decorated with henna as was the custom of the festival, and her wrists were adorned with green bangles along with emerald and ruby studded gold bangles, again, part of the gifts.

'It's beautiful, *Baba*. Thank you!' she said beaming when her father gave her the gifts.

'*Arey* Kumari, remind me to ward off the evil eye in the evening,' *Ajoo* said, as usual.

'*Ajoo*, how many kilos of red chillies have you burnt till now? Kumari could have opened a shop with that much,' Sharmishtha said, smiling as Kumari helped her unlatch the necklace, giggling.

'Go ahead, laugh you both. But chillies have protected you and your siblings all these years. And that's why you are becoming more beautiful each day. Your father will have to buy many more sacks of chillies at this rate.'

A year had gone by since Sharmishtha's wedding to Kanti Prasad and this was her second visit to Kanpur. Time had stopped in the same place, like a spinning top. The days and nights revolved around her making innumerable circles on the spot, without moving ahead. She performed the duties of a daughter-in-law. After all, she could not bring a bad name to her family. Fortunately for her, Pt. Shiv Prasad Pandey, her father-in-law had asked Kanti Prasad to sleep in a different room. He felt that they were too young to start a family.

So it would be prudent to wait for a year or so. When Sharmishtha heard of it, she heaved a sigh of relief. She did not feel any love for her husband, only some sort of compassion. She could not bring herself to think of having a conjugal relationship with him. Though, she knew it was not his fault. He was a very decent soul and obeyed his father silently. He was always very cordial towards Sharmishtha. Sharmishtha just blamed the fate that had put three people in this abstruse condition. Little did she know that Kanti Prasad was madly in love with her, and couldn't bear to see her sad even for a minute. So every time he was in the company of his wife, he resolved to keep her happy throughout her life. He was disappointed at the restrictions that his father had put on them, but he was an obedient son, and also felt it was probably right for Sharmishtha to get used to the new environment before they moved towards intimacy. He did not know that his beautiful wife had lost her heart to someone else and her love for some other man was growing stronger each day.

Sharmishtha took to reading as a fish takes to water. There was little else to do at her in-laws' house, as there were many servants to run the household. So she made sure to supervise the chores related to her in-laws, and spent time with her younger sisters and brothers–in-law, yet, she was left with plenty of time for herself. So she devoured books after books and her husband was only too happy to bring a never-ending supply of them to her. She would go out to watch movies with her husband, and to other outings. Once, Kanti found her holding a collection of Wordsworth's poems, and as he watched her from a distance, he noticed a look of wistfulness on her beautiful face. Later that evening he brought up the subject gently; would she like to learn English? It would widen the scope of her reading. She was delighted and agreed immediately. Thus, Miss Margaret Aldrich was brought in and Sharmishtha started learning the language she had wanted to, ever since she had met Kailash.

When her younger brother and *Munim Ji* came to escort her to Kanpur for *Gudia* and *Raksha Bandhan,* an elated Sharmishtha left Lucknow merrily, partly because she always loved to be home in the company of her siblings and her father, and partly because she could visit Anuradha, and there would be some news of Kailash.

'*Kaki*!' Sharmishtha called as she entered Barrister Mathur's house. She was wearing an emerald green Japanese georgette sari with hand embroidered forget-me-not flowers in shades of pink, yellow and light green. The emerald stones shone on her ears and neck. She was told that the Mathur household was leaving for Delhi as Kailash's father had fallen ill.

'*Mishthi*, my child! You look stunning. How have you been?'

'I am fine *Kaki*. How is Kailash's father doing?' She felt a slight tickle in her stomach as she said his name. She used to call his name so many times in her mind but she could only say it aloud in front of Anuradha, because she could not talk about him even in her parents' house. She was expected to have forgotten him since she was married now, and talking about him would have earned disapproval, from not only her mother but her grandmother as well.

'We got a wire last night that he is better than before, but as you must already know, we are leaving in few hours' time,' Anuradha said. 'Come, let's sit and have tea. I will send Gopal for some hot *samosas* and your favourite *jalebis*. It's been so long since we met. But first, you must meet your *Kaka*. He is in his study.'

'*Mishthi*, sweetheart! How are you doing? How is Kanti? Is he coming to Kanpur? I really like to talk to him. He is a sharp boy,' Nandan Mathur said, puffing on his pipe. He had met Kanti over dinner when Kanti had come to fetch Sharmishtha, when she visited last time and had taken an instant liking to him.

'He is fine *Kaka*. Father has invited him over. He will visit after a month,' Sharmishtha said.

'But tell him he must come. We will also extend him an invitation.'

'We are going to have some tea. Would you like some?' Anuradha asked.

'I don't mind a cuppa,' he said.

They exited the study and Sharmishtha breathed. She was somehow not as informal with Nandan Mathur as she was before marriage as he looked imposing and larger than life to her.

'So tell me, how are things in Lucknow? Have you adjusted to your new family?' Anuradha asked as they settled down with tea, hot *samosas* and *jalebis* from her favourite sweet shop. Sharmishtha was dying to talk about Kailash but she waited patiently for Anuradha to bring his name up. She did not want to look too eager. She was married now and had matured in the last year. So she just responded to Anuradha's questions patiently.

'So how is Kailash, *Kaki*?' she asked at last. She used to wait for months to hear a little something about him, and now, here she was, sitting in his house with his aunt who was like a mother to him, and they were making small talk.

'He is fine.' There was a pause as Anuradha looked at her fingers, holding the cup. 'He is reaching India after a week. His father has not been keeping well for some time and he decided to come the moment he came to know,' she said, still gazing at the cup.

Sharmishtha's hand shook a little and she spilled a few drops on her *sari*.

'Oh, let me get you something to wipe it. It's such a beautiful *sari*.' Anuradha stood up.

Sharmishtha did not stop her. She needed a moment to steady herself. The mere thought of Kailash coming to India filled her with elation, and she felt dizzy. There were a thousand flowers blooming in her heart and she breathed deeply to assimilate what she had just heard.

Anuradha was back with a wet towel and was rubbing the part where the tea had spilled. She stole a glance at Sharmishtha and her heart felt the despondence that she had felt when she had left her love behind.

'Why does fate bring two souls together if they are not meant to be together?' she thought bitterly.

Anuradha noticed that the girl was still madly in love with Kailash. There was such a glow on Sharmishtha's face; it would have made the early morning sun pale in comparison. She would never stop loving him. It was the kind of love that stayed fresh for eternity. Her chest constricted because what she was going to tell Sharmishtha would probably rob her of all her happiness. But she had to tell her. She had been dreading meeting her and as much as she had wanted to meet her, she had been delaying it as much as possible. She had debated telling her mother, and therefore letting her break the news to her, but had thought better of it as she knew that her mother had always treated Sharmishtha with insouciance. No, it would have to be her. She would tell her gently and make her understand. She knew that Sharmishtha would only want Kailash's happiness.

'*Mishthi*, Kailash is coming home to see his father and fulfil his wish.'

Sharmishtha looked at her and the warm glow that was there inside her, faded as quickly as it had come. She understood. In fact, she had somehow known for the last few days.

'He wants Kailash and Suchitra to get engaged when he returns to England,' she said gently.

She laid emphasis on his 'father's wish', trying to make it look like his father's decision, not Kailash's, thus trying to soften the blow.

Though Sharmishtha had always known this and had prepared herself for it, yet hearing it in words brought out the reality of it, and it hit her like a deluge. She felt as if she had been pushed from a cliff and was falling into nothingness. How would she bear the thought of Kailash holding someone else in his arms, loving someone else while she craved for a small touch? And then she felt anger filling her like a dark menacing cloud. She wanted to be alone or she would throw something, break something. She managed to get up somehow and left. Anuradha wanted to stop her but then she let her go. She knew that she would have to give her time to absorb the news.

For the remainder of the day, Sharmishtha mostly stayed in her room at the pretext of a migraine. That was not completely untrue, as she felt her head throbbing. She cried till she could no more. But towards the end of the next day, she had calmed down. What was she expecting? She asked herself. Had she expected Kailash to never marry? That he would live his entire life in love with a woman who was never going to be his? And what sort of a wish was that? She loved him more than her life and wanted him to be happy, even if it was by marrying Suchitra.

She chided herself for being so selfish. He had loved her. That was enough for her to live for. Now it was only right that he married and settled down so that she would not worry about him and feel guilty. The love that they shared was the most precious thing and it would always be. She got up, washed her face and donned a pink and turquoise *ghaghra choli* that was one of the dresses that had been made for her, in the generous list of gifts. She looked at herself in the mirror. Her large and beautiful eyes were red but she looked as beautiful as always. She made a resolve. She was going to be happy for Kailash and for herself. She spent the week shopping and meeting relatives.

'I have got jackfruit vegetable made for you, and some *badam halwa*. The Pandeys are not looking after you, it seems. Come and eat. I will see to it that you put on some flesh on your bones. Also I have to ward off the evil eye...' Ajoo said, the moment she came down from her room.

'*Ajoo*, can I go and meet *Kaki*? I will come back fast and then eat everything,' she said, wrapping her arms around her.

'Alright go. But come back fast. I will eat with you not before that.'

She half ran to the next house the moment she heard the Mathurs were back.

'*Kaki*, I am sorry for behaving like that the other day. It's really good news. Kailash would be happy with Suchitra,' she said when they sat down with a cup of tea in Anuradha's room.

'I don't know how happy he would be, but it's best for him to move on. That's what we both want. Don't we?' Anuradha said, taking Sharmishtha's hand in hers. '*Mishthi*, Kailash has sent this for you.' Anuradha took out an envelope from her bag, handing it to her. As much as her heart sang at the sight of the letter, she couldn't help noticing the solemn expression on Anuradha's face. 'Why don't you read it while I go and change into something comfortable?' Anuradha said getting up. 'And *Mishthi* read it carefully and give it a thought before taking any decision. I will be back in some time,' she said exiting the room.

Sharmishtha's elation got eclipsed a bit by Anuradha's tone and words. She opened the letter and started reading it. Her heart soared and her soul sang as she finished reading the letter. Kailash wanted to see her. He wanted them to meet once before he got engaged to Suchitra.

Bua must have informed you about our forthcoming engagement. I want to meet you in person just this once. I need to see you to know that you are happy with this turn of event. There is so much I want to talk about and this is an opportunity we might not get again. Maybe, I want to draw courage by looking at your beautiful face. I will arrange to come to Asanpur after a week. Actually, I will be coming to Shivgarh with my friend and then I will come to Asanpur. Please go to Asanpur and I will send you a message with the date and time once I reach Shivgarh. I have to be with you once before I commit myself to someone else. But if you feel that this request is wrong, which I think might be morally wrong, then please take a decision based on that. I would understand it completely.

Sharmishtha sat holding the letter, feeling tumultuous emotions drowning her in their downpour. Her heart cried out to go and meet him but somewhere her mind shouted caution. She was a married woman now. She belonged to someone else. Would it be right to go and meet another man? But she was only going to see him and talk to him. Kailash was not only her love, but her friend as well. And she would go and meet him in the capacity of a friend.

'But would you be able to resist falling into his arms?' her mind reasoned.

The tussle went on, and when Anuradha entered the room, she found her crying.

CHAPTER 20

PRESENT DAY

Anand found me in the drawing room. I did not hear him entering the room as I was still dazed with the discovery of the photograph.

'Sorry I kept you waiting. How long have you been here?'

I turned back to him with a start.

'Not very long.'

'Are you alright? You look a little peaky,' he added.

'I am fine.'

I was tempted to ask him about the photograph but thought better of it. We were very new in our relationship. In fact, I wasn't even sure whether it was a relationship, because nothing that would have confirmed its status had been exchanged between us. So it would have looked odd that I was snooping around his house looking at his family photographs.

Though I felt happy and content in Anand's company during lunch, I could not shake off the image of the photograph.

'Aparna, would it be too much to request you for dinner tonight? I know I am asking a lot of your company but there is something I want to talk about, and I have to go to Delhi for a couple of days, so I want to talk to you before I leave. Would you come?' Anand asked, looking at me with a hopeful expression.

'Yes of course! Though, *Chachi* is again going to be disappointed that I am not eating the food she painstakingly cooks for me,' I said smiling.

'Just for tonight, then I would not keep you from *Chachi's* sumptuous cooking.'

After lunch, he dropped me home. I went and sat with *Amma* and *Chachi*. I was thinking of a way to tell them that I was going to the Haveli for dinner again. I always found mother looking troubled whenever I mentioned going to the Haveli, which was a bit ironic. I expected her to be happy to see that I was enjoying some one's company and that was at least a start towards something more substantial. Instead she looked resigned and nervous. Though I had not reached that stage with Anand yet, this should have been a good sign for mother.

We made small talk and I had to keep my urge in check to ask mother about the photograph. Did the resemblance between me and the woman in the photograph mean something? I somehow had a hunch that she knew something about the Haveli, but she kept it to herself. After some time when she decided to take a nap, I went to my room and lay down. The image of the stunning woman kept dancing in my mind. I felt my eyes heavy with sleep and dozed off.

Kamla came and woke me up with a cup of tea. It was only when I started sipping the tea that I remembered having a dream. The dream was fading fast but the remnants were there, and as I concentrated to recall them, they came to my mind like a fogged memory. I'd dreamt of her and the gentleman sitting next to the mistress. In my dream, the stunning woman and the man were related. They seemed to be husband and the wife. How did my mind conjure this up? Was it really like that or had my subconscious mind just made a connection? But then, most of the time, our subconscious minds display information that is buried deep in the labyrinths of the mind. I must have somehow heard it somewhere. Maybe it was just instincts. As I got up to decide on the clothes I was going to wear for the evening, I was determined to find out about the woman in the photograph. I felt I would not be at peace till I knew who she was.

I went downstairs and told mother that I was going to the Haveli, and they should not wait up for me for dinner. There was this look on her face that I had begun to understand well so I turned before she could say anything. I knew I was being a little brusque with her but I could not help it. Besides the attraction that I felt for Anand, I wanted to go to the Haveli as many times as possible. But where the thought of being with Anand filled me with pure joy, the pull towards the Haveli felt ominous. My curiosity for the Haveli was mixed with something that was not pleasant. My attraction towards it felt like being lured by an attractive but poisonous fruit.

The car stopped in the porch. I stepped out before Mahesh could open the door. It was a moonlit night. The moon was not full but still the moonlight on the trees made their leaves shimmer as the breeze blew, and the trees swayed. It was still early so the moon was not very high. Suddenly, I had this impulse to go to the garden to the east side of the Haveli, which received the greatest advantage of the rising moon, and see the Haveli in moonlight. I looked up and saw the master bedroom and the bedroom next to it. These were not lit as Anand did not use them. He slept in one of the twin bedrooms in the West wing. The ground floor was well lit, and like always, there were lanterns hanging from the trees and a few glowing on the cemented circular seats around the trees. I walked through the side gardens and went to the narrow lawns on the rear side of the Haveli, from where I could see both the terraces. I could see the candles lit on the terrace of the West wing and their lights quivering in the soft breeze. I could hear the soft splash of the river flowing silently yet making its presence known. I tried to peer at the river, ready to see a boat floating on its bosom, but the cover of trees was too thick for me to see anything clearly. I turned my gaze towards the terrace and was mesmerised by the ambience that had a touch of mystery. I must have stood there for some time, feeling like I had seen the Haveli like this before. It was a sort of déjà vu that came like a flash. An owl hooted somewhere and I was brought back to the present. I decided to go inside, thinking that Anand must be wondering what I was doing standing in the rear lawns. As I tore my gaze from the terrace, and started walking, I had this sudden and strong urge to turn and look back. And as my eyes fell on the spot on the terrace where I'd stood the other day, I froze and my heart missed several beats. In the exact spot where I had stood and heard the rustle of the silk cloth, standing and looking down at me, was the mistress of the Haveli.

She was enveloped in a white gossamer light or cloth. She looked exactly like she had looked in the painting. But it was her eyes that seemed to be boring into me. I felt my whole body going rigid. My mind was not able to process what my eyes were witnessing. I wanted to tear my gaze, run from the spot, but my body refused to move. And then she was gone. Just like that. She vanished into thin air.

When I opened my eyes I saw Anand sitting on the chair. He had a worried look on his face. I looked around to see where I was and realised I was on the bed of the guest room, that was next to Anand's room, as I could see Anand's room through the open connecting door.

I tried to sit up.

'Aparna, please stay in bed. How are you feeling now?' Anand got up and hurried to my side.

'I am... fine. What happened?' I asked.

'I think you just blacked out for some time. I found you in the rear lawns. You were rooted to the spot, not responding as I called out your name. When I took your arm you just collapsed. I have sent for the doctor but it would take some time because he will be coming from Lalgarh,' he said.

'Oh! You shouldn't have. I am feeling much better.'

'No! I must get you checked. There has to be a reason for you... blacking out like that,' he said with worry etched on his handsome face.

'I am feeling much better... really. I think more than the doctor I need a drink.'

'Of course! What should I get you? Your favourite?' he asked looking a little relieved.

'Yes! My favourite!' I said smiling.

He got up to ring the bell, probably to summon Ramesh. I needed some time to gather my nerves. A shiver ran down my spine as I remembered the scene that I had witnessed in the rear lawns. Every fibre in my body screamed to leave and go home in the sanctuary of my mother's house. But at the same time I wanted Anand to be with me. There was an insane urge to throw myself into his arms and hide my face in his chest. I just needed to feel safe and secure with him.

Ramesh pushed in a trolley and Anand poured me some wine. I sipped it gratefully.

'Anand, please call the driver and tell him to come back. I really don't need to see the doctor. Moreover, I cannot stay late as I promised *Amma* that I would be back as early as possible,' I pleaded.

'I will try calling him but the coverage here is always sketchy.'

Luckily, he got through to the driver.

'I will get you something to eat here only. You must eat and then I will drop you home. I don't want you to go alone.'

'I am not very hungry but will have a bite. I am really sorry Anand, I spoiled the evening.'

'Please Aparna! I am feeling bad that I coerced you into having dinner here with me without realising that you might have been tired. After all, you have been coming here every day for the last three days.'

'Ok! Let's not get into the guilt game. I love to spend time with you.'

The moment the words were out of my mouth I realised the weight of them. Anand looked at me with such a tender expression that I blushed. But before he could say anything, Ramesh and Peter came pushing another trolley in, with dinner.

'I thought this room was not in use and was always kept locked,' I asked.

'Oh! It was prepared for the buyers who came visiting the other day, and also, I thought many other people may visit during the selling process,' Anand replied.

I tried to keep my face and conversation light but my mind was still numb. When I sat in the car I kept my eyes fixed on my hands, not daring to look anywhere till the car was out of the Haveli. Anand asked me again whether I was feeling better. I told him I was. When we reached home, Mahesh opened the door for me to get out.

'Thank you Mahesh! But we will take a few minutes,' Anand said.

Mahesh nodded reverently and walked a little away.

'Aparna, I am leaving early morning tomorrow for a couple of days. I have to go to Delhi to be with my lawyer as he is preparing the papers for the sale of the Haveli. I... I will miss you. In the last few days that we have known each other I have really started enjoying your company. Aparna, hope you don't mind my telling you this but I have grown very fond of you,' he said, taking my hands in his.

'The feeling is mutual. I too have grown fond of you,' I said, feeling my cheeks getting warm. My heart was singing with joy and I just wanted to drown myself in the sweet music of his words. We sat in the car for some time, revelling in each other's company. Each wanting to prolong the moment, ensconced together in the confines of the car, but resisting the impulse to give in to the moment. And then, before we both could surrender to temptation, Anand got down and opened the door of the car for me.

'I can't wait to finish this business and come back. We have so much to talk. I probably wouldn't be able to concentrate much there,' he said with a captivating smile.

'It's just two days. I'm sure you will be back before you realise it. I will be waiting here for you.'

He came forward and hugged me. I wished him luck and he sat in the car and waved at me before Mahesh drove him away. I stood there for some time looking at the receding car and feeling blissfully happy. It was only when I saw *Amma* looking at me peculiarly, that I came back to the present. And then I realised that the door was ajar and *Amma* was sitting in the *angan* right in front of the door, and she had seen Anand hugging me.

'Why are you sitting out? It's nippy,' I asked, ignoring her expression.

'I have been telling *Jiji* the same but she said she wanted to sit here till the time you came back,' *Chachi* said, looking at me with a look that told me that something was not right.

'Ok! I am home now. Let me take you inside.'

'*Amma*! What is it?' I asked her once we were inside her room. I wanted her to be candid with me. I was getting tired of her evasiveness.

'It's nothing. I just worry about you,' she said not looking at me. I sat down on the chair next to her bed.

'But why *Amma*? I am not young and immature. I am a grown, responsible woman and I can take care of myself.'

'It's nothing with you being a mature woman, Parni. Remember, your heart is like a clear and pristine lake. It reflects the image in its purity, but a slight ripple can distort the very same image.'

'I can assure you of one thing, that I would not do any such thing that might become the cause of your worry. Have faith in me *Amma*.'

She nodded, and I got up to go to my room. I suddenly felt very tired and the euphoria that I had felt moments back lost some of its sheen. I could not understand mother's reluctance in being happy for me. What was it that troubled her? She had clearly started behaving like this since I'd started going to the Haveli. *Chachi* had also dropped some hints relating to the same. Why didn't she want me to go there? Why wasn't she happy to see me with Anand? All these questions assaulted me again. I had to find the answers to these questions. I could not go on like this.

Tomorrow... tomorrow I would ask *Amma* what was going on in her mind. It was time she opened up to me. Things were moving forward with me and Anand. I felt a very deep connection with him.

CHAPTER 21

I opened my eyes and saw Anand looking concerned. I managed a weak smile.

'How are you feeling now?' He asked me.

'I am fine, really,' I said trying to sit up.

'No, please stay in bed,' he said.

I closed my eyes feeling safe and secure in his presence. But when I opened my eyes again, there was no one else in the room and I was not in the bed, but sitting on the chair of a writing table. I had a note in my hand and I was reading it. It said something about a meeting and then I got up from the chair in haste to reach the place, and found myself in a place that was like a garden. I was feeling a bit distraught and there was this urgency to meet someone. I was looking for the person but was unable to find him. I panicked. My heartbeat increased and I was calling a name.

I woke up with a start. It took me few minutes to realise that it was a dream. But only that it didn't feel like a dream. It was so real. It was still dark outside and the time on my watch was three o'clock.

I tried to replay the dream in my mind. Why did I dream of that room? And what about the note I was reading?

Being a psychiatrist, I fully understood that dreams were products of our subconscious mind. Most of the time, we feel we have never seen the places and people we dream about before, but that is not the case. We only dream of people and places we have seen at some stage in our lives, but do not remember them. We might have seen them fleetingly, not even noticing them, but they get stored in our subconscious mind and in order to free itself from unnecessary data, our brain plays these images in the form of the dreams. But there was another theory too. At times, dreams are manifestations of our long forgotten memories... memories that might have taken place in a past life. Did I have some connection with the Haveli? There were so many signs and they felt like pieces of a puzzle; waiting to be solved. I was getting more and more convinced about my connection with the Haveli and mother knowing about it. There were signs that were just not coincidences, for example, mother's reluctance about my visiting the Haveli and meeting Anand, my resemblance to the woman in the photograph, and above all, my sighting of the mistress of the Haveli. Something was going on, and all these things were connected. My dreams were becoming more and more vivid. And the dreams had started only after I'd come to the village.

I felt agitated. I had to find the answers. I could not leave this place before finding out about the Haveli and its previous occupants and my connection to them. Mother had to tell me what she knew about them. But first I had to go to the Haveli. I wanted to go to that room once again. I didn't know why, but there was this compelling feeling ever since the dream. I had to see that writing table closely. After that I would confront my mother. I felt a calm descend upon me. I was going to find the answers at the cost of angering mother. But I had to do this for my mental peace, my sanity.

After breakfast, I told them that I was going for a stroll and might call Cathy from the phone at the post office. I declined Kamla's offer to accompany me. I walked towards the Haveli. It was pleasantly cool as it was August and it had rained at some point in the night.

I decided to call Jason on my way back from the Haveli. It had been more than two weeks since I had called either him or Cathy, and I felt guilty. But there was another reason; I wanted to discuss the incident in the Haveli and my dreams, but first I wanted to analyse the situation myself.

I went straight to the main door and banged the knocker. Ramesh might have gone with Anand, but Peter, the cook, must be there. Or if he was not inside then he must be in his quarters. I waited for some time and was about to turn back when the door opened.

'Good morning madam! Please come inside.'

'Peter, I think I dropped one of my ear studs in the guest room yesterday. I was wondering if I could go look for it.'

I had thought of the ruse on my way here. I had to have a reason. I couldn't just barge into the private quarters of the Haveli, especially when Anand was not there.

'Yes of course madam! This way please.'

'That's alright Peter! I know the way. Please do whatever you were doing. I will see myself out later.'

'Should I get something for you? Tea or coffee?' He asked.

'I just had a big breakfast. I am quite full. Thank you for asking though.'

'Madam,' he said respectfully and went back to the kitchen where I was sure he must be preparing for the upcoming dinner once Anand was back with the buyers. He had said that there was a chance they would come again as they were bringing a team of professionals with them. I made my way straight to the room. The doors were shut, so I pushed them, and I was inside. In spite of the day light, it was dark inside because of the heavy curtains on the windows. Somehow I had this urge of throwing the curtains back and letting the sunlight in. I still had last night's incident fresh on my mind, and I shivered a little. The sunlight filled the room and I noticed that the windows overlooked the West side gardens that were not in a very good state now, but must have been beautiful in the heydays.

I turned my attention to the writing table. I had had just a fleeting look at it yesterday but as I stood near it, I was surprised to see the accuracy of my dream. I could recall the carving and the rich mahogany colour of the table from my dream. I looked at the small and elegant chair that was meant for a lady and I again stood frozen at the likeness of it from my dream. I slowly lowered myself and sat on the chair. I touched the cool mahogany wood of the table and instantly thought of the note. I opened the drawer. There was nothing inside, and my hand came out coated with dust. I tried the second drawer. It was also empty. I felt disappointed. I did not know why I was hoping to find the note in the drawers. I sat there for some time feeling a bit lost. And then on an impulse, I let my hand trace the wood underneath the table. There was a small knob. I pulled it, and it moved to one side making way for a small cavity. I put my hand inside and my heart almost stopped as I felt a piece of paper.

I pulled my hand out holding the note. It was a single sheet of heavy paper folded into a square. It had turned yellow with time but was still shiny and smooth. I unfolded it with my heart thudding. It read;

I have to talk to you. Things are getting more complicated between me and S. Also we have to discuss Shivani. Come to the usual place on the river bank. And please don't let your sense of morality stop you because I don't know whether we will be able to meet once we go back to the city. Rest I will discuss when we meet.

There was a curling K on the corner of the sheet, denoting that the name of the writer started with the letter K.

I sat there reading and re-reading the note. There were three questions that sprang up in my head. Who were K and S? Who was the recipient of the note? And where was this usual place? And just then an image popped in my mind; a beautiful garden with flowers, trees and birds all around. I didn't know how but I had this feeling that I knew this place. I had to go there and see this place. But as I came down I stopped at the entrance of the drawing room. There was no one around. As if on an impulse I crossed the big hall and reached the door of the small store room where I had seen the photograph of the Barrister's family and friends. I had this mad urge to look at the woman whom I resembled. I removed the photograph from the frame. I knew what I was doing was not ethical but then I was sure the photograph was long forgotten by the people whom it belonged to, and it wouldn't be missed. I wondered if Anand even knew about its existence. Another reason for taking the photograph was that I wanted to show it to mother and ask her if she knew about the people in it. Then suddenly I had another idea. I went towards the quarters of Chandu *Kaka*. I saw *Kaki* sitting and shelling peas.

'*Arey Bitia*! When did you come?' she asked.

'*Kaki*, is *Kaka* there? I have to ask him something.'

'He has gone to Lalgarh, *Bitia*. He had to get certain things from there. He will come back by evening.'

'Ok *Kaki*, I will come again some time.'

'Let me get you something to eat.'

'Some other time *Kaki*! I have to go somewhere,' I said and turned before *Kaki* could insist.

I have to go to this place. I thought to myself. An image of it kept flashing in my mind. But I had to find out where this place was.

'*Kaki*, is there a *bageecha* here somewhere that has a whole lot of flowers and trees?' I asked.

'As far as I know *Bitia*, there is no *bageechaa* in this village. Well Mukhia does have a small patch where he grows seasonal flowers, but I wouldn't call it a *bageechaa*.'

'Thank you *Kaki*.' I was disappointed. I had walked a few paces when she called.

'*Arey Bitia*! There is this *Phulwari* that is very beautiful and has numerous flowers and trees, but it's in Asanpur, across the river.'

I froze in my tracks. The word *Phulwari* sounded so familiar, as if it had been lying buried in the labyrinths of my mind. Yes, of course, it was *Phulwari* that I had to visit.

'Thank you so much *Kaki*,' I said beaming.

Kaki smiled but she looked a little bemused, probably finding my mannerism a bit brusque. But I couldn't worry about that. There was this intense desire to see this *Phulwari*.

I had seen a bridge connecting both the villages while coming from Lucknow. Before I went home, I went to *Mukhia Chacha's* house. He was very pleased to see me and called out for his daughter to get some refreshments which I politely refused.

'*Chacha,* I have heard of this place called *Phulwari*. Where is it? Is it in the village across the river?'

'Yes *Bitia*! It is in Asanpur. Though I was told by my father that it used to be like a garden in the heavens in the olden times, but it's still very beautiful.'

'*Chacha*, can a boat be organised for me? I want to go there.'

'But *Bitia*, there is a bridge now connecting both the villages.'

'I know! But I want to go by a boat,' I said smiling.

'I will organise a boat for you. When do you want to go?'

'Now, if it is possible. You see *Chacha*, I might get some friends from Delhi and I am planning to take them around. So I want to explore a few places. I have a request though. Please don't tell *Amma*. She gets unnecessarily worried.'

I hurried back home and told *Amma* that I had to discuss an important case with my colleagues. I had come home to collect my notes and was going to make a call from the post office. It might take a while but I would be back before lunch. So now I had sufficient time to go across the river and be back for lunch.

The river was not as broad as was in the olden days, the rower told me. He was a middle-aged man with a pleasant demeanour.

'In the olden days one could not see the other side across the river *Bitia ji*, my grandfather used to tell me, and during the monsoon *Nadi Maiya* used to expand and swell so much that even the very accomplished swimmers couldn't swim across it. Even the big barrage would be tossed by the waves.'

'So did your grandfather tell you anything about the Haveli?' I asked.

'I do not know much except that the owners of the Haveli used to visit when they wanted to take a break from the humdrum of city life. You know how rich people are. They like to seek peace in natural surroundings. Baby *Saheb, Baba Saheb's* mother, used to come every now and then. And now *Baba Saheb* has been coming here once in a while. But now there is word that he is selling the Haveli. It's only good that he does. The Haveli has seen some bad times. It might regain some life when new people come to stay here,' he paused.

'Bad times you said?'

'Yes *Bitia* Ji! *Mem Saheb* fell very seriously ill. There was some problem between Barrister *Saheb* and *Mem Saheb*, so my grandfather said. There was some other woman. Now all these big people have different kind of problems than us poor people. But I am sure *Bhauji*, your mother, must have told you about that time, as your grandmother was like a family member to the Barrister clan,' he said smiling.

'My grandmother?' My voice sounded louder than I'd intended because of the strangeness of the words he'd spoken.

He looked a little troubled. He took a little time and then cleared his throat.

'Yes, *Bitia* Ji! I also have been told by my father only. I do not know much,' he added and before I could ask him again he just pointed towards the approaching bank.

'That is Asanpur. We would reach the bank in ten minutes.'

There were too many things churning in my mind at that moment. My grandmother had an association with the Barrister's family and I'd never heard a word about it. Why was it kept a secret? How many secrets was my mother trying to keep from me? And then he'd mentioned something about the other woman. I wanted to ask him more but as I laid my eyes on the approaching bank, I went very still. I had a very strong sense of déjà vu again. And it was as if I had entered another time, another dimension. The questions in my head forgotten, I stood there staring at the elegant marble steps that were slowly coming closer. I did not remember disembarking from the boat. I only vaguely heard the boatman saying something. I climbed the steps, that somehow I knew, were leading to this beautiful place that was called *Phulwari*. I entered *Phulwari* through an arbour that had climbing roses over it, with the scent of roses hanging in the air. I stood frozen on the spot. It was exactly the same as the image in my mind. I had been here before. The gulmohar and neem trees swayed gently as the cool breeze went through, stirring them. I was only aware of two things at the time; the mingled scent of flowers and the gentle sound of the lapping of the water. I had come to this place, not once but quite a few times. Did I come with my parents when I was little? But how come my memory was so fresh and vivid as if I had come here just yesterday? My senses were sharp, drinking and inhaling the sweet scents. The *Phulwari* was a riot of colour. Birds were singing and bumblebees were hovering over flowers. I felt as if I were in a place that was far away from the earth. It was very serene and peaceful, yet lively with the chirping of the birds. I moved forward and slowly started walking. I touched the trees, the flowers, as I moved in a trance and then I noticed the hut. I had an overwhelming sense of joy and sorrow. It was a feeling I couldn't explain. Suddenly my nostrils were filled with a heady scent I was so familiar with. I inhaled it deeply, filling my lungs with it.

Chapter 22

She wraps her shawl around her shoulders and walks. She is walking a little briskly. The moonlight feels cool. The weather is heavenly. It is the time of monsoons, and there is a kiss of a breeze that is heavy with the sweet scent of raat ki rani. Her anklets make a lilting sound and she walks even more carefully in order to mute the sound. There is music filling her heart. She is happy with a slight hint of disquietude. She doesn't know the reason of this mental state and she doesn't know her destination. She is just walking for something, towards something. But she sees the scenery around her very clearly. She is walking through a path that is flanked by dense trees. But the full moon overhead is casting its cool moonlight, illuminating the path. She finds no difficulty seeing the path she is walking on. She has to hurry. Time is of the essence here. She shouldn't make him wait. She wants to run but she has to walk as quietly as possible. Her anklets and bangles would make music enough to wake the entire village if she runs. No, no... she should just walk cautiously. She hears the soft splash of water... Almost there... And then she is calling him, pleading him not to go...

'*Bitia* has opened her eyes,' someone said and I heard *Amma* exclaim, 'Thank you God!'

'What happened?' I asked.

'Please *Didi*, don't get up. The doctor should be here any time,' Kamla said.

'But what happened?' I asked getting a bit agitated.

'Kamla, it's better you tell her what happened. We all will wait outside. *Bitia* looks better now.' The owner of the voice was an old gentleman.

'*Jiji*! *Bitia* is fine now. Let me take you to my room. You don't look very good.' I heard *Chachi* saying.

'What happened to *Amma*?' I asked getting up.

'*Jiji* is fine. Just needs little rest. Kamla, shut the door and be with *Didi*.'

Kamla propped up the pillows and I sat up. I felt physically and mentally tired as if I had run a marathon and gone through huge emotional strain. But all I wanted was to know what had happened.

'*Didi*, you had gone to *Phulwari*. *Navik Chacha* dropped you at the banks of the river and told you that he would wait there for you. He then sat down and waited for you. When you did not return for an hour, he got a little concerned but he decided to wait. Two hours went by, and he got worried as he remembered you telling him that you would like to be back by lunch time. After some debating he got up and went to the *Phulwari*. You were not there. Now he was puzzled. He thought that you had probably gone to the village but that was not very likely as you'd never mentioned that. He called out your name and started walking alongside the river bank. After walking for about half a kilometre he saw a commotion at the far end. He started running and then he saw two people dragging someone out of the river. To his worst fears, he saw it was you. You were not fully conscious and kept murmuring something. Luckily those two people were a father and son who had come to take a dip in the river. They wrapped you in a dhoti that they had brought with them and the son ran to the village asking for help. In no time he came back with blankets and people from the village. They borrowed their *Mukhia's* jeep and brought you home through the bridge. *Dadi* almost fainted after seeing you like that. She has been very quiet ever since. We sent Mahesh to Lalgarh to fetch the doctor.'

'Fainted?'

'Actually *Didi*, *Dadi* kept saying that you shouldn't have gone there. And then she kept saying it was all her fault. She should never have brought you here.'

And then I remembered that I had not told *Amma* about going to *Phulwari*. I felt guilty and a little ashamed.

'You said they dragged me out of the water? What does that mean? Had I fallen into the river?'

'We don't know *Didi*. Don't you remember anything?'

I closed my eyes and tried remembering. I had gone to *Phulwari*. I was in *Phulwari*. And then what had happened? I tried harder and but couldn't recall anything. I felt a headache coming.

'How long was I unconscious for?'

'I think more than half an hour. Are you feeling better now?'

'I think I am going to have a bad headache,' I said pressing my forehead.

'*Vaidya Kaka* asked me to make you drink this.' Kamla brought a glass to my lips.

'What is it?'

'Medicine I guess. He made you sniff some herbs and then only you came around.'

'That old gentleman who was here is *Vaidya Kaka*? I asked.

'Yes, he is the one.'

There was a knock on the door and Kamla opened it to find the doctor standing outside.

'Hello! How are you feeling now?' He asked, checking my pulse.

'I am feeling alright except for a headache.'

'Do you mind if I examine you, Dr. Chaturvedi?' he asked. Apparently he was briefed by Mahesh about me en-route.

'Of course not,' I replied.

The doctor did not find anything abnormal except the headache and he attributed it to the shock I must have got when I fell. His theory was that I was probably taking a stroll along the river bank and had slipped and fallen into the river. The loss of memory was the after effect of the shock, and I would regain memory of the incident gradually.

'But the good news is that no harm is done. Your vitals are alright. You need to get a good night's sleep and some rest for a couple of days. You will be alright in no time.' With that he had left.

Amma and *Chachi* came in the room.

'*Amma*! I am really sorry I did not tell you that I was going to *Phulwari*. I am sorry I caused this trouble for everyone.'

Mother sat on the chair that was kept next to the bed and put her hand on my forehead.

'Promise me *Bitia*, that you will never go to that place again. And I have decided that we should go back to Lucknow.'

'Lucknow? But we have to sell the house!'

'I will tell Ramnath *Bhaiya* to sell it. I will give him the power of attorney. But I want us to go back to Lucknow.'

'*Jiji*, we can talk about it tomorrow. Let *Bitia* take rest now,' *Chachi* said gently.

'Yes of course! Get some rest *Bitia*! But we have to go back to Lucknow.'

'But *Amma* this is your bed. I will go upstairs,' I said, getting up.

'No! I will rest in Urmila's room. I want you to be close to me.'

I was disturbed by my mother's decision to go to Lucknow. I just could not leave yet. I could not just leave Anand and go back. He had expressed his feelings for me... in an indirect way, though. Besides, I had to finalise the sale of the house. I could not leave things midway. Something was not quite right. There was a strained atmosphere in the house after my accident. There was something that was being kept under wraps by my mother, *Chachi*, and even Kamla. I had to find out what was going on. But for now, I just closed my eyes and drifted off to sleep.

I woke up in the middle of the night. Everything was quiet. I lay there for some time thinking about the dreams that I had had. But I could only catch fragments, and they too, were fast disappearing from my memory. Suddenly I felt restless, and I knew that sleep wouldn't come. I quietly got up and went to my room upstairs. I threw open the windows of my room and inhaled the heady fragrance of *raat ki rani*. The air had a delicious nip and I just stood enjoying it. I needed to clear my mind. Ideally, I would have gone for a run in England but I couldn't do that in the village in the dead of night. I wanted to sort things out in my mind. What had actually happened? I remembered going to *Phulwari* in the boat, walking across it, seeing the small old hut there, but after that it was just a blank. Why was my mind blocking the memory? Was the trauma of falling in the river that great or was it connected with some other memory? And then suddenly, I thought of Anand. I wanted him to be here with me. I could have talked to him about all this. I missed him. He had said that he was going for a couple of days. He should be back tomorrow.

I needed a cup of tea. I switched on the electric kettle that I had brought from Lucknow. Making tea on the *chulha* was not my cup of tea. So I had brought my own supply of tea leaves and milk powder pouches, and they were all set up on a small stool in my room. Having tea more than twice was a habit that I had formed in England. There was nothing more soothing than a pretty kettle of tea with a slice of my favourite lemon cake.

I sat in bed with the hot beverage. I felt comforted with the solitude and tea. And then, as I was bringing the cup to my lips my hand suddenly stopped mid-air. I set the cup down, rushed to the cupboard and rummaged through the pocket of my jeans that I'd worn earlier that day. I found the note. I re-read it. The writer of the note had talked about meeting in the usual place on the river bank. Was *Phulwari* the meeting place that the note mentioned? One thing was sure that I had been to *Phulwari* before, because it had felt as if I had known that place all my life, even though I had never heard about it from anyone. Was it again a memory that had surfaced? Was I remembering things from my childhood? Why did mother look so grave? I had a feeling it was more than concern over my accident. I had to speak to mother and ask her the reason behind her decision to go back to Lucknow. Why did the woman in the photograph resemble me? Why did I feel the presence of the mistress of the house in the Haveli? Surely these were not just coincidences, and I had definitely felt some strange and weird things. I had delved deep into the psyche of people's minds and brought out their hidden fears and traumas. That was how I made a living. And now my own mind was playing tricks on me, and I had to get to the bottom of it. There was something buried deep in the recesses of my mind and it was being stirred by some stimuli. And the stimuli were the Haveli and the village.

Finally, in the wee hours of the morning, I felt my eyelids getting heavy with sleep and as I closed my eyes I remembered Kamla telling me that I was murmuring something when I was dragged out of the river.

The moon was in its full glory. The stars looked dull against the brightness of the moon.

Just like my love! She thought, smiling. The moon was like her lover, shining in its glory, fading away the darkness and bathing the scenery in its soft, cool glow.

'Why are you smiling?' he asked, tracing her lips with his finger. She lay with her head on his lap.

'I was just comparing you to the moon.'

'Why the moon?'

'You want to hear your praise now?' she said smiling.

'Yes, I want to.'

She raised her hand to touch his face. Her bangles jingled, breaking the quiet of the night.

'You are the moon of my life; beautiful, calm and cool. Everything

looks so dreamlike when you are with me, like the moonlight casting a spell over things.'

'That's a wrong metaphor,' he said smiling.

'Why?'

'You know a moon is not full on all nights. So if I am the moon then you will only get a little of me every day, and there will be a day when you will not see me at all.'

She got up in an instant, and hugged him with such force that he was taken aback. He held her tightly.

'Don't ever say that.' A muffled sob escaped her.

'Hey! Come on! Look at me. I will always be there with you. I am not the moon, remember?'

She lifted her head from his shoulder and looked into his eyes. His face was very close to her. She felt his breath on her face. Her lips quivered.

He bent a little and kissed her lips lightly. She closed her eyes and her body tensed up but she didn't move. And then it happened.

He started kissing her.

I woke up, aroused and shivering in anticipation of something more intimate. I lay there with my eyes closed, relishing the feeling till some moments passed. And when my mind became clearer, I no longer wondered about the clarity and vividness of my dreams. I was in some place that looked very familiar, but it was not in the village. We were on a roof top terrace somewhere and it felt like home. But though the man in my dream resembled Anand, he looked like the master of the Haveli and I felt my heart filling with a kind of longing that was difficult to explain. Once again my body felt this delicious wave of pleasure that was absolutely primal. I wanted to surrender myself to this man and drown in the pleasures that he would bring by caressing me, loving me.

I got up slowly and tried to analyse the dream. It was clear that

I missed Anand more than I would have liked to admit. I had not felt like this for a long time for any man. But why did he look like his grandfather? Was it because of the resemblance? But in my dream I was very sure that the man was not Anand. And then like a flash it came to me; I was not calling him Anand, I had called him Kailash. I wrapped my gown around myself and ran down the stairs. Kamla and *Chachi* were in the kitchen and mother was sitting close by.

'Kamla! Could you spare a moment please?' I called.

'*Didi*, you are up? I was about to bring tea,' she said.

'Did you sleep well *Bitia*?' *Amma* asked.

'Yes! How are you feeling now?'

'I am fine. You have tea first and then we will talk,' she said, sounding ominous.

I knew what she wanted to talk about, but I went back to the room. After a while Kamla came with a cup of ginger tea that I had every morning.

'Kamla, come sit here. Tell me something. You said yesterday that I was murmuring something when they pulled me out. Do you know what it was?'

Kamla looked at me. She seemed to be deciding whether to tell me or not.

'Kamla please tell me if you know. It's important for me.'

'*Didi*, I believe you were calling out for someone? Those people asked us whether he was someone close to you.'

'Who was I calling out to?' My heart thudded waiting for the answer.

'It seemed you were calling out to someone by the name of 'Kailash'. You were saying 'please don't go' repeatedly. *Dadi* was very upset. She made *Amma* and me promise not to tell you. But I have broken the promise,' she said with tears in her eyes.

'I am sorry I made you break your promise Kamla. But trust me, I will not tell mother what you told me. It was really important for me to know. Look, I have to find out why I did what I did yesterday. Come here. Don't worry. As I said this would stay between us.' I hugged her and she looked little better. I hated myself for making her go against her promise but I knew no one else was going to tell me.

I stood next to the window when she left. What was happening? Why was I having these flashes? If these memories had something to do with my childhood, why was I dreaming of myself as an adult? Did I see the portrait of the Barrister and his wife when I was a kid? Was it possible for a three-four year old child to develop a crush for a man so many years older? Had I heard stories about him and thus, hero-worshipped him? Why did I feel the presence of his wife, and why and how did I resemble the woman in the photograph? Only one person knew the answers to these questions; my mother. I was going to have a talk with my mother. But I would have to do that very carefully. I did not want her to get upset and fall sick. She had looked quite disturbed as it is, and I did not want to add to her consternation. I would have to think of a way. Also, the biggest secret that I was dying to unravel was about my grandmother. Why was she never mentioned and why didn't mother disclose her connection to the Barrister family?

Another person I could ask was Anand, but I wondered whether it was a good idea to ask him. Surely he would know things about his grandfather. But what would I ask? I certainly couldn't tell him that I was dreaming of his grandfather and throwing myself into the river calling out his name. How would that look? I knew he liked me to a certain extent, but he liked a confident, successful psychiatrist who cured the mental ailments of other people, not a loony herself. I rejected the idea of telling him anything. I decided to go to the post office and call Jason. If anyone could help me solve this riddle, it was him.

After a breakfast that was somewhat a strained affair, as mother was unusually quiet, and I'd caught her staring into nothing, I sat with her, checked her pulse and took her blood pressure. It was still on the higher side. *Chachi* told me later that mother had not slept well and kept muttering something in her disturbed sleep. Even *Chachi* looked tired. The gay and carefree atmosphere that had prevailed in the house had now vanished. It seemed as if everyone was tired, speculative and worried. Even Kamla was quiet and the house looked dull without her cheerful chatter. I went to the post office and called Jason. He was happy to hear my voice. We chatted easily about the cases, and he told me that everyone was missing me. My patients wanted me to return as soon as possible. Cathy came to the phone and enquired about mother's health. We talked of this and that for a while and then I asked her to put Jason on the phone.

'Jason! Do you remember a seminar that I had attended related to past lives' memories?'

'Yes I do! I remember that there were two sets of views; 'for and against', and you were in favour of it.'

'Yes! Could you please email me the details? I am sure it must be in the office archives on my official laptop. I will see if I can get it here because the net is sketchy with the dongle.'

'Yes, I can do that. But would you like to tell me what it's about? Have you met someone in India with past life memories? Because I remember most of the cases were from Asia and quite a few from India.'

I could hear the excitement in his voice. That was typically Jason, always enthusiastic about exploring new horizons when it came to knowledge.

'Would you believe me if I were to tell you that I might be one of those Indians?'

There was a pause, as if he was trying to digest this and then his voice came. 'I would believe anything that comes from you.'

'And why is that?' I asked.

'Because I have never seen anyone more level-headed and pragmatic than you.'

'But you do know that I am a romantic and have this acute love for the past and past lives.'

'I know, but then your romanticism also has a shade of credibility.'

I laughed. 'Thank you for your faith in me, Jason! I really don't know how right or wrong I am but certain things have happened, and till I reach the bottom of them, I would not feel comfortable. It's important for my mental peace.'

'Could I ask you a favour?' He asked. 'You know I have been planning to visit India for a long time. Can I come and help you figuring out whatever it is?'

'Oh! That would be wonderful! But only on one condition.'

'And what would that be?'

'You would bill your ticket expenses to the office. After all, it would make an interesting case study for us to follow in the future. And guess what would make this more interesting; me being the subject of it!'

'But Aparna, I would take it as a holiday. I have not taken one for quite some time.'

'I am sorry Jason. The condition stands.'

'Alright! I will book my tickets straight away. I should be in India in the next four days. My God! I can't believe it!'

'Book the flight to Delhi and then take a connecting flight to Lucknow. I will send the car to pick you up from Lucknow, and then you will take approximately two and a half hours to reach here. I am so excited and relieved to know that you will be here. Can't wait to see you! I will call you again tomorrow, and give me the flight details then.'

'Roger! You take care then.'

'And Jason, don't forget the file.'

I felt happy knowing that Jason was coming. I could share every detail with him and together we would figure this whole thing out.

When I reached home, I saw Peter waiting for me.

'Madam, Anand *Saheb* called to say that he would like to invite you for lunch today as he would be reaching around one o'clock.'

I felt even happier. Anand was coming and I would meet him. The thought was joyful and comforting. But as I thought of the Haveli and my previous experiences, a shiver ran down my spine. The enigma that the Haveli had held for me now had a streak of foreboding. But as I went inside to tell mother, I had not anticipated this reaction from her.

When I told her that I would be going to the Haveli for lunch, she almost became overwrought. She caught my hand and asked me to promise her that I would not go to the Haveli or *Phulwari* till we left for Lucknow. She called *Chachi* and Kamla and told them to start packing. She said she did not want to stay another day in the village. I was quite taken aback by her reaction, and in order to calm her down, I promised her that I would not go to either the Haveli or *Phulwari*, but told her that we could not leave for Lucknow as my colleague was coming for a holiday. I sat with her, holding her hand, and gave her a small sleeping draught. I had numerous questions churning in my mind but I decided not to ask her anything. Truth be told, I became a little scared by watching her getting hysterical, and now I was sure that there was something that she had kept from me. And whatever it was that she knew was definitely not pleasant. The more I thought about it, the more restless I felt.

The fact that I had still not gained any memory of falling into the river was also very unsettling. I wanted to go to the Haveli to look for some more clues. I had found the note there. Maybe there were other things that lay hidden, that might give some insight into this whole thing. And then I thought of Chandu *Kaka*. Surely he must know something more about the Barrister *Saheb* and his wife. Though he'd said that he was very young then, but it was possible that he had heard something from his father. I wanted to see him. But I had promised mother that I would not go to the Haveli, though I knew I had done that just to calm her down. I had to go to the Haveli sooner or later. And how could I not see Anand?

All these thoughts made me a little despondent. I wanted to talk to someone desperately. When she dozed off, I wrote a note to Anand and explained that I would not be able to join him for lunch as mother had taken slightly ill. I felt disappointed and forlorn. I was looking forward to seeing Anand, and if anything was making sense in all this confusion, it was his warm smile and pleasant personality. As I sat brooding, I heard a car stop, and my heart did a somersault as there was a knock on the door. I got up as quietly as I could and by the time I reached the door, Kamla had already opened it. There he was, looking so dashing in a white shirt and blue jeans.

'I came to check how *Chachi* is doing. What happened? And how is she feeling now?'

'She is sleeping at the moment. Why don't you come inside?'

'I would rather that you come out for a walk. You look as if you could use some air.'

I realised that I really needed to get out of the house. I'd promised not to go to the Haveli or *Phulwari* but I could definitely take a stroll. *Chachi* was resting in her room, so I told Kamla that I was going out for a walk. She was already beaming as Anand had greeted her and conversed with her. I donned my trainers and went out. Anand's car was parked outside but we walked in the direction where we had bumped into each other the first time.

'I am so glad to see you Aparna! I missed you,' he said looking at me with warmth in his eyes.

'I missed you too,' I said smiling.

'So how was *Chachi* taken ill? Has a doctor seen her?'

'Something happened while you were away.'

And then I narrated the incident of the river to him but omitted the part where I had felt a presence in the Haveli and found the note.

I also did not tell him that I was calling out his grandfather's name. I was not yet ready to tell him all that. I wanted a logical explanation before I told him any of that. And that was only possible once Jason was here. I would probably be able to figure things out with him. So I just told him that mother had got concerned about my safety and that had caused her blood pressure to rise.

'Oh my God! I am so glad that you are alright.' He stopped and held my hand. We looked at each other for some time and a lot got conveyed. He let my hand go as a passer-by gave us a look.

'It's possible that you don't remember the incident. I am no expert, but at times the mind does block unpleasant experiences. So what is the last thing that you remember?' He asked as we resumed our walk.

'I just remember walking in the Phulwari and then came across this small hut and stood looking at it. I felt that I had been there before, but I think that must have been an old memory that just surfaced. I might have gone there with my parents when I was small.'

'So did you ask your mother? I mean surely she would remember taking you there?'

'I could not. She became so distraught that I did not want to ask her anything, but I will surely ask her once she is feeling a little better.' I have to ask her a great deal, I thought to myself.

'Yes, of course! So the next thing you remember is being pulled out of the river?'

'Not that time. I must have passed out because when I opened my eyes I found myself at home.'

'And what did the doctor say?'

'Well, he thought that I must have slipped and I was still in shock, so I could not remember, but gradually it might come back, the same thing that I would have told any of my patients in a similar situation. He checked me for injuries but except for some bruises on my arms he did not find anything, which made me wonder. I have tried thinking about it many times. I could not have fallen into the river from *Phulwari* because there is this five foot high wall all around it. In order to have fallen from there I would have had to climb the wall. Secondly, I was found about half a kilometre away from *Phulwari*. It's not likely that I was carried by the current there because the water around the *Phulwari* is shallow.'

'So how do you think you reached there?'

'I think I walked that distance and then walked into the river.'

'Aparna, that's not a very good sign.' He stopped again and looked at me with concern written all over his face. 'I mean, why would you do that? Forgive my asking, but has it ever happened before?'

'Have I thrown myself into a river before? Not that I remember,' I said smiling.

'I am sorry. I know I am being unreasonable.'

'No you are not. Anyone would ask that. But no, I have a perfectly sane mind. I have never had any reason to believe otherwise. Well... not until now.'

Suddenly, Anand took me in his arms. It was so sudden that I took a few moments to wrap my head around it. But then, I just stayed in his arms and felt such joy that I forgot my troubles for a while.

'Aparna, I know this is not the place where I would have liked to tell you this, but ever since I have met you, I have thought of little else but you. These two days in Delhi were difficult being away from you. I am sorry if I am being forward but I think I am in love with you.'

I felt as if I had waited a lifetime to hear those words.

'I am glad you told me while there was still time. Who knows when I would decide to throw myself in the river again?' I said smiling.

'Please don't joke about it. In any case, I think under the circumstances I would have to chaperone you everywhere,' he said smiling.

'And I would love that very much.'

'And why would you love that?'

'Umm… let's just say that I like you.' I smiled and looked at him with a mischievous glint in my eyes.

'Well, that's a positive start,' he said looking into my eyes.

I threw myself in his arms and whispered to him: 'I have loved you from the moment I saw you.'

'You have no idea how happy you have made me,' he said, embracing me tightly and kissing my forehead.

'I think it's late, we should head home. Mother might have woken up,' I said.

As we turned to go home, I told him about Jason coming to India.

'But though I invited him, I have an issue now.'

'And what is that?' he asked.

'My biggest worry is that we don't have a western style toilet. I don't know what to do about that. Secondly, Jason is not used to spicy food and I can't cook over an earthen stove even if my life depended upon it,' I said.

'Well, I have an easy solution for both your problems. Let Jason stay in the Haveli. All the toilets have been western style since the time this Haveli was bought, because the previous owner entertained lot of British friends. And since my grandparents were also into the western style of living, it was a welcome thing. I am told that the toilets had seats brought from abroad. But of course, the old ones were replaced by my mother when she got some more changes done in the washrooms. So that problem is solved. And as far as food is concerned, you know I myself am not used to eating spicy and heavy food, and Peter is a good cook. So your colleague should not have any problem.'

'But I don't want to impose,' I said.

'Be rest assured, it's no imposition... The guest rooms are lying vacant, and moreover, I will get a chance to discuss you with him,' he said giving me a smile.

'So have you finalised the deal?'

'Yes I have! In fact, I wanted to sit with you and discuss things. That's why I wanted to see you as soon as possible. Wish there was a place to sit somewhere so we could talk,' he said, looking a bit serious, and that worried me a bit.

'Is it something important?' I asked.

'Yes it is... for me,' he replied.

'Why don't you come home? I will offer you some tea and we can talk,' I said.

'Are you sure? I mean, wouldn't it look odd or something? I don't want to give your mother and relatives a bad impression about myself,' he said smiling.

'Oh! I am not exactly a sixteen-year-old and you twenty. We are two adults who can sit together and talk.'

Thankfully mother was still asleep. Despite my courageous act I was weary of facing mother and making some excuse. I knew I had all the right to befriend anyone I wanted. After all, I was a modern, independent woman. But I still had side-effects of the upbringing I was given. I could do as I pleased in England but here I fell into the old ways of living.

I escorted Anand to my room. *Chachi* and Kamla were in their rooms too. I switched the kettle on and we sat down to talk.

'Aparna, I will come straight to the point. I have sold the Haveli and I will move only the antiques and some other items that my mother was fond of, to Delhi. Otherwise, I have sold everything else with it. My plan was to move to the States and carry on with my life there. But now things have changed. I know I am moving fast but if

I have learned one thing in life; that is to do as the heart wishes. Life is too short to be wasted on indecisions and procrastination. So here is what I want to ask you; can we both have a future together?' He asked looking at me earnestly.

I was thrown a bit off balance because it was all very sudden. I wanted nothing more than to have a future with him, but there were other things that were related to this big decision.

'I know what you are thinking.' He sensed the hesitation. 'I would not ask you to move to the States. We can sort things out gradually and there is no rush. If need be, then I would move to UK,' he said.

When I was alone that night, I found that sleep was miles away from me. Anand's words kept reverberating in my mind. I was very happy. I had found love and this time it was for real, and that's what mattered. As far as the other things were concerned, we would figure them out. I was again standing at my favourite spot next to the window when I thought of the photograph that I had brought from the Haveli. I took it out from the armoire and looked at it. I brought it as close to the reading lamp as I could. But this time, I only wanted to look at the mystery woman and the little girl, who I noticed, was as beautiful as the woman. There was a strong resemblance between the two and there was no doubt that they were mother and daughter. I found myself glued to the images and a wave of melancholy took over me. I moved my hand over the image of the child and felt a strong maternal affection.

'Who are you?' I asked the mute images.

I felt a chill as it was late in the night. I pulled the duvet and looked at the photograph before switching off the light.

She was dressing her. It was a beautiful, peach, organza frock, with pearl work on the hem and neck. She looked like an angel. Her heart filled with so much love as if it would burst. She drank in her beauty, inhaled her scent. She was the luckiest mother alive.

'I don't want to go back without you,' she said, pouting.

'It's just a matter of a few days, sweetheart! You would not even come to know. Your father has made whole lot of plans for you, moreover, you could invite your friends home and show them your new dolls, she said, though her heart was breaking.

'I will not trouble you I promise. Please let me stay with you,' she looked at her with those big beautiful eyes.

'I know you would never trouble me, darling. But I have to do some 'grown up' things here and you would get bored. Nanny would be with you and before you know it, I will come back.'

She hugged her as tight as she could. 'I will come back for you darling. That's a promise.'

CHAPTER 23

1935

'Come here sweetheart! It's time for a bath!' Sharmishtha said, scooping her daughter in her arms, carrying her to the *ghusal khana*.

'Will you give a bath to my doll too?' Shivani asked, looking at her mother with her large beautiful eyes.

'Of course I will! But first, it's your turn,' Sharmishtha said, taking her daughter's clothes off and making her sit on the wooden stool. She touched the water in the bucket to check the temperature. The maid had already heated the water and mixed it with the cold water in the bucket. Sharmishtha's heart filled with pure affection as she bathed her daughter. Shivani had inherited the best features of her parents; therefore, she was a very pretty child. Sharmishtha knew that she was going to grow up into a great beauty, and it made her feel very proud, but she wanted her daughter to own more, than just her beauty. She wanted her to gain higher education and have a career. She had big plans for her and she had discussed them with her husband. Kanti Prasad adored his daughter. She was the apple of his eye. He loved Sharmishtha more each day for giving him such a beautiful and cheerful child. Shivani was already showing signs of intelligence. She was a sweet child and a fast learner.

Sharmishtha's world revolved around her daughter. She was enjoying motherhood. She had ensconced herself in the roles of a doting mother and dutiful wife. Though she could not love Kanti Prasad in a romantic way, she felt protective towards him. His unconditional love for her, and now for their daughter, made her feel a little guilty at times. She knew that she could never love him the way a wife should, but she vowed to look after him and his needs, and keep his home happy.

They had shifted to the bungalow that was allotted to Kanti Prasad by the university. It was big for their small family, but then, it had big lawns where Shivani could play. It was also very convenient to host guests and organise a get-together.

There was an atmosphere of gaiety as Shivani's birthday was being celebrated. Sharmishtha's brothers and her younger sister had come as well, bearing gifts sent by her grandparents and great grandmother. And there was a special gift sent by Anuradha. Sharmishtha did not find time to sit and chat with her siblings throughout the day. So when dinner was finally over, the friends and relatives left, and an excited but tired Shivani put to bed, she sat down with her sister. Her brothers were sitting with the male family members and Sharmishtha and her sister found some time to chat.

'*Didi*, should we open *Kaki's* gift?' She asked.

'Oh yes! How could I forget? It's rather big. Looks like a painting of *Kaki's*,' Sharmishtha said.

They unwrapped the package and let out an exclamation as they looked at the life-like portrait of Shivani. Anuradha had insisted on taking a photograph of Shivani when Sharmishtha had visited Kanpur a few months back. Now she understood the reason behind it.

'It's beautiful,' they both exclaimed together.

'*Didi*, *Kaki* has also sent this letter for you.' Her sister gave her a letter.

Sharmishtha took the letter from her but saw something on her sister's face that gave a sign of misgiving. Though Anushtha was three years younger than her, she was mature beyond her age. Anushtha was not blessed with the ravishing beauty of her sister's, but possessed the same amount of intellect. That was the reason; Sharmishtha had insisted that Anushtha be allowed to study more. And her father had yielded to her request, and thus, Anushtha had just joined college and was engaged to a boy from a well-to-do family. Sharmishtha was instrumental in finding the match for her sister. Anushtha had known about her sister and Kailash's love, and had cried her heart out when her sister was married to Kanti Prasad. But now she really respected and liked her brother-in-law for his gentlemanliness.

Sharmishtha opened the letter.

'*Didi*, I will fetch something for you to eat. You haven't eaten anything after the meagre lunch.'

'*My Dear Mishthi*!' The letter read.

Heartiest congratulation's on Shivani's birthday! May she live a long and happy life! I hope you like the portrait. Though I tried to make it as close as possible to Shivani's appearance, I could not do justice to her sparkling beauty. She is a wonderful child and I am eagerly waiting to see her again.

There is news that I wanted to give to you. Kailash and Suchitra's wedding date has been fixed and they are starting their voyage back to India at the end of this month. I don't know whether it's asking too much, but I really want you to attend the wedding with Kanti and Shivani. I just want to spend some time with you and Shivani and this is a suitable opportunity to steal you from Lucknow. Mishthi, I have always seen you as my daughter and you and Kailash are like my children. I could not get you as my daughter–in–law, but please be my daughter. I know that this news would be disquieting for you, but I thought it best for you to have heard it from me, rather than anyone else. If you feel what I am asking of you is too much, then you must not pay any heed to it. I would completely understand. Waiting to hear from you. Please convey my love and blessings to Kanti and Shivani.

Yours ever affectionate,

Anuradha

Sharmishtha sat dazed. She felt as if she had been punched in her guts, and she couldn't breathe. She had played and replayed this scene a hundred times in her mind and had put in lot of hard work convincing herself that she would not get affected by the news of Kailash and Suchitra's wedding. But all her belief and conviction in herself deserted her, and she felt herself plummeting. How was she going to survive? She had known all along that this day would come and had been preparing herself for it, but now that it was here, all she felt was a searing pain in her heart. Finally, it was going to happen. Kailash was going to be someone else's. Would he fall in love with her? Was he already in love with her? Would he ever think of her? Such questions deluged her. She sat there fixed to the spot.

'Mishthi!'

She came out of her reverie. Kanti Prasad was standing in front of her.

'Come, let's eat something. Anushtha and Kishan are waiting for us.'

She nodded.

'Are you all right? You look a little peaky,' he noticed.

'Yes! I am fine, just tired.'

CHAPTER 24

Kailash stood next to the French windows, and looked at the sun setting in the sky. It was late August and the remnants of the retreating English summers were still there. He looked at the trees, green and thick, the flowers still in bloom, making the place look postcard picture perfect. The squirrels were running to and fro and the sky was a brilliant blue. He looked at the surroundings with a tinge of nostalgia. This had been his home for the last five years. He had lots of memories attached to this place. His memories had different colours. Some bright and cheerful, when he had woven dreams of a life with Sharmishtha, some black and colourless when he had come to know about her wedding to someone else. That bleak period had lasted long. He had lost interest in his life. Had it not been for his mentor and teacher, Mr Wilson, he probably would have never come out of it.

And then there was another memory that had the most brilliant colours of a rainbow, and it was that memory that made him whole again. He was ready to go back and live the life he was expected to by his parents, his adoptive parents and his fiancé. He would sail with Suchitra tomorrow, and once back home; they were going to start a new life as husband and wife. He had waited for this moment mainly for two reasons; he would be closer to Sharmishtha and he would start his career as a lawyer, something he had dreamt of and worked hard for. As far as Suchitra was concerned, he would try to be a good husband to her. That was a promise he had made to Sharmishtha and himself, though Sharmishtha would always remain his one and only love. The last five years had not been able to dull her memory in his heart even for a moment. His first thought in the morning was still her beautiful face, as well as the last thing before drifting off to sleep. This was not only love, but a connection that was too deep and strong. He was lucky to have found her and luckier to have been rewarded with her love. That was enough for him. Moreover, his love was sacred and mature, and for the sake of that love, he would fulfil his responsibilities. The time had come to embark on the journey called life and he was quite prepared for that.

Chapter 25

Suchitra sat on the ottoman in front of her dressing mirror and started combing her hair. Her companion, Chanda, had taken the bags to the foyer with the help of the butler. Suchitra looked at her bedroom where she had slept for five years. Today was her last night on a bed where she had spent many sleepless nights. The journey over the last five years had been tumultuous and had changed her a lot. But she had found the gift of love, and that had given her the courage and will to go through everything. She had instantly fallen in love with the handsome youth who was mature and intelligent beyond his age. His eyes had cast such a spell on her that she had felt herself losing in them. And later when he had held her hand after the 'episode', and had soothed her mother's worries, she knew that she had fallen in love with him, a love that would grow stronger with time.

But later, much to her chagrin, Kailash did not give any signs of reciprocating her feelings. He regarded her as a close and dear friend and was deeply concerned about her, but that was all. Suchitra's parents took his friendship and caring attitude towards their daughter as a form of affection, and were overjoyed at the prospect of making him their son-in-law. Suchitra had thought of telling her mother of her apprehensions a couple of times, but had refrained from doing so. She knew that she would love Kailash despite anything. She had already decided not to get married to anyone else. She knew that this was something she could not tell her parents just yet. They were already worried about her 'episodes' and she did not want to disappoint them further. So she just waited, and in the end, her luck smiled and she was going to spend her life with the man whose mere thought brought a surge of happiness in her heart. Chanda had been absolutely right when she had said that her patience and austerity had borne fruit, and now she had got her love.

She looked at her reflection in the mirror. She saw a petite and delicate girl who looked pretty like a china doll. She had taken the best features from her parents. She had arresting eyes and a sharp nose with a well defined mouth. Her complexion was fair bordering on pale and that gave her a little vulnerable look. Her hair was dark and styled in elegant waves. Was her beauty enough to make Kailash fall in love with her? She had asked herself this question many a time. She remembered the girl she had met in Kanpur who had accompanied Kailash and his aunt to a wedding reception. She was their neighbour. Her beauty was exotic. She had never seen anyone so beautiful. Almost everyone at that gathering had seemed mesmerised by her beauty. And Suchitra had felt a jolt of envy. She had tried to gauge Kailash's expression, but he only came off as polite and modest, as he was with anyone else. Was he also affected by that girl's beauty? She could not tell. Mishthi was like an exotic rose that bloomed only once in years. She had tried reasoning out later that she was unnecessarily imagining Mishthi to be her competition. True, that she was very beautiful, but she belonged to a traditional Brahmin family. She probably wouldn't be allowed to continue her education and would be married off to someone from her own caste, whereas Suchitra belonged to the upper class, with exemplary education. She had the sense and means to become a high society wife who would suit Kailash and his family. And with both set of parents wanting this match, there was nothing to worry about.

Yet she had heaved a big sigh of relief when she had come to know that Mishthi was married to someone and had gone to live in Lucknow at her husband's home.

She knew that Kailash had not yet fallen in love with her. Initially, she had mistaken his caring attitude as love but as time went by, she realised with a sinking feeling that that was not the case. She had tried finding out whether there was someone else, but he had never given any such indication. She had once asked his aunt indirectly if Kailash had any close friends in Delhi, because she knew he did not know anyone in Kanpur. He had studied in Delhi and that was the only place where he had his friends. But his aunt had laughed and said that Kailash was too engrossed in his studies and working towards a future, and he was only twenty. When she came to England, she had noticed that though Kailash was cordial to female friends, he mostly kept to himself. She never saw him look at any girl with even the slightest of interest. She knew that the girls, whether his classmates or Suchitra's friends had a crush on him, and that made Suchitra feel very proud, and she considered herself extremely lucky. But there were times when a nagging doubt would creep and cast its shadow on her radiant world. What if Kailash never found her worthy enough to give his love? He had been with her all the time when she was going through therapy, and when settling down in a new atmosphere away from family and friends in England, yet there was an imperceptible distance that she had felt when she was with him.

She was determined to win his heart, but she knew that love was not something that could be imposed. Was it always going to be one-sided? Whenever these thoughts troubled her, she would brush them aside, because she knew that she would not be able to live without him. She loved him and he was going to be with her in her journey of life, and that was enough. She could not ask for more. There must have been some fondness in his heart otherwise he wouldn't have agreed to get engaged to her.

'*Missi Baba*! Dinner is ready. Would you like to dine downstairs or should I bring a tray?' Chanda was asking.

'I think a tray would be a good idea as I am feeling a bit tired. Also, we have to retire early as we have an early start tomorrow,' she said smiling at Chanda. Chanda was such a boon to her. She would not be able to think of a life without her. She was her friend and confidante.

Chanda was the daughter of a sepoy who had been in her father's battalion, and had died during the war, but not before saving her father. Her parents decided to shelter his wife and infant daughter. Chanda was a few years older to Suchitra and she developed such deep affection for her that her parents decided to make her Suchitra's companion. And Chanda had proved. to be a worthy one. She was totally devoted to her charge. Suchitra was exceedingly fond of her and there was nothing that she kept from her. Though she had had some staff in the cottage, thanks to her grandfather, it was Chanda who was like her shadow. Her grandfather had raised an eyebrow when he first saw Chanda, when Suchitra went visiting to his Manor, Chanda by her side. But seeing her devotion to Suchitra, he had given the situation an imperceptible nod.

There was a knock at the door.

'Come in,' Suchitra said.

'Miss Langley, Mr Mathur's bearer has brought a letter for you. Should he wait for the reply?' the butler asked.

'Yes! If he would be kind enough to wait for ten minutes, I will quickly write a reply,' Suchitra said as Chanda took the letter from the butler and handed it to her. A word from Kailash always brought a warm glow to her heart. She walked towards the writing table and opened the letter.

My dear Sue,

Hope the preparations of the travel have not tired you much. You must take adequate rest and do not tire yourself physically and mentally. I will reach at 8 am to escort you to Hamilton cottage. As you are aware, our friends are coming to bid us farewell and I have organised a little refreshment for them. We will leave for the harbour at 10 am. I have sent my butler to collect your cases in order to save time in the morning. All the preparations are done and everything is in order. Wishing you a restful sleep. I shall see you in the morning.

Till then,

Yours affectionately,

Kailash

His letters were always simple but denoted care for her. He

was always concerned about her health, and under the given circumstances, he was not wrong. But Suchitra yearned to hear a few words of love from him. She knew that he cared for her well-being but that was that. He had not ever said anything even remotely bordering on romance. No matter how much she tried telling herself that he was not a very demonstrative person, and it was enough that he cared for her, she still felt a little dismayed. Maybe one day the care would turn into something more and she would wait for that day.

She penned a reply and gave it to Chanda to give to his butler with the instructions to hand all the cases over to him, except her vanity case.

In spite of Kailash's instructions to sleep well, she couldn't. The idea of being close to him for the next six weeks on the vessel left her with butterflies in her stomach. She did not allow herself to think of life with him after marriage, because that excited her to the limit that put her in a restless state. She tried to calm herself and finally fell asleep in the wee hours of the morning.

Kailash reached at the appointed hour and found Suchitra looking very English in a dusty rose skirt suit and a hat resting on her head. The colour added a rosy hue to her pale cheeks and she looked like a delicate flower. Suchitra cast one last glance at the house that had been her abode for the last five years. She bid farewell to the staff that consisted of a butler, cook and a gardener who also doubled as her driver. She gave them each a generous amount of money as a parting gift. Being the daughter of a rich Englishman, and granddaughter of a very rich baron had its advantages. She had lived in England amidst all the comforts that money could buy. Yet, she felt grateful to these people who did their best to make her feel comfortable all the time. She could not repay the care and kindness they had shown to her, and had never given her a chance for any woes, so this was the least she could do.

They were greeted warmly by friends when they reached the cottage Kailash had stayed in. An hour went by, and they took their leave reluctantly, for these were the friends who had become like family in the last years. Promises were made to keep in touch and invitations were extended to them to visit India.

And when Kailash opened the door for her to sit in the car, Suchitra realised that she was finally starting her journey with Kailash and that sent a shiver down her spine. She was going to cross oceans to be by his side throughout the journey that was life. From now on, they were together through thick and thin, rough and smooth, whatever life would present them with, in the path that lay ahead.

CHAPTER 26

'Sue! The jeweller is coming at noon, followed by the tailor, and the vendors are coming from Banaras with the *saris*. I hope you don't have any other programme scheduled for today.' Her soon to be mother–in–law, Kailash's mother, had joined her for a day to see to the selection of the bridal finery. Her parents were arriving in Delhi along with Kailash's aunt and uncle, Anuradha and Mr Mathur after a week, and she wanted to spend some time with them.

Suchitra, along with Chanda, had moved to the bungalow that was one of the wedding gifts from her parents. She was fond of Kailash's aunt Anuradha, and had always felt comfortable around her. But then, they were like extended family for her as her father and Mr Mathur were bosom friends. She felt intimidated by Kailash's mother and wished Anuradha had come sooner. After their honeymoon, they would go to Kanpur for some time, and then move in with Kailash's parents in their villa in Delhi. But Suchitra wanted to live in her own bungalow after the wedding and hoped that Kailash would not resent the idea.

'No Mummy *Ji*! I am home throughout the day,' she replied.

Once in her room, she sighed. The circus of seeing the ornaments and *saris* would start and she would have to go through the painful process of selecting everything. Suchitra was, in many ways, an ardent follower of the European culture. She liked the fuss-free western dresses made with beautiful chiffon and fine silks. She had already bought a huge collection of them along with dozen pairs of shoes during her stay in Europe. Some of the orders were still being sent from France as part of her trousseau. She felt suffocated in the five and a half meter *sari* with heavy embellishment and jewellery she had to wear on her formal engagement, her petite figure disappearing inside the folds of the *sari*. Though Kailash had proposed to her in London with an engagement ring but his mother had insisted on a formal one in Delhi. She had confided in her mother about her reluctance to wear *saris* after marriage and hoped that her in-laws, who were quite open-minded, would allow her to wear western clothes after the wedding. Though her own mother had kept on wearing *saris* after being married to her father, but then, she was an Indian by birth, and Suchitra, being an Anglo-Indian, liked the western culture more, ever since she was a child.

But as she selected *saris* and jewellery dutifully, along with Kailash's mother, her mind kept going back to the six weeks that she had spent with Kailash on the vessel. After the initial few days she had settled down and had taken the voyage well. Those six weeks were the most delightful time she had spent with Kailash, as from the morning up till dinner time, they were together, and she'd loved to spend time with him alone on the deck under the stars. He had seemed happy during that period, though she had caught him standing alone on the deck, gazing at nothing, quite a few times. He had seemed lost in his thoughts and seeing him like that always cast a shadow on her happiness. She had tried asking him whether there was something that was bothering him, but he always deflected and assured her that it was nothing important.

Kailash had thrown himself into his new job, and except for a couple of times when they dined together, he had made himself scarce. As the wedding day approached, they were not supposed to see each other frequently, and that was easy to do as he was staying with his parents.

She had often wondered how their married life was going to be. Would Kailash stay as formal as he had been in the past years, or would he eventually loosen up a bit and they would have a normal married life? There were times when she felt a little exasperated with his excessively formal nature and his overly careful treatment of her. He treated her like a fragile doll which had been endearing in the beginning, but as she fell more deeply in love with him, she wanted him to treat her like a normal person. True, she had gone through an affliction that had left all her near and dear ones in a state of being overly protective, and Kailash was no exception, but she craved to be treated normally by him. His careful treatment of her never let her forget what she so wanted to forget. He did not realise that she wanted him to understand her predicament. That night in Mr. Mathur's country lodge, she had felt safe and secure in his company, and she knew that she could go through any situation if he was beside her. But now she felt as if she was wrong to think that. Though Kailash would always be there to pick her up when she stumbled, he probably would never fall with her. So in the end it was her plunge only, and she had to accept that. She would never be able to get a glimpse into the part of his heart he kept locked. She had often wondered if there was someone else who was residing in that locked chamber, but he had laughed out loud when she had asked him one night on the deck, her mood light with wine. Whatever had made her think that, he had asked and had put her fears to rest by looking into her eyes and telling her that she should never feel that way, ever. His eyes were, later she remembered, full of kindness, not love.

But she loved him beyond any such doubts that could take permanent shape in her heart. Just being with him and sharing his life was all she wanted, and here she was. She was soon going to be his wife, his life partner and she would make it her life's mission to make him happy and never make him regret his decision of marrying her.

Chapter 27

Sharmishtha kept the novel on the night stand and cast a glance at her daughter. She bent down and kissed her, as she stirred in her sleep. 'I probably love you more than anyone I have ever loved, even that one person who has been the core of my existence,' she whispered in her ear. And then, the very thought that she had been avoiding by immersing herself in household work and reading away till her eyes refused to remain open, came like a wave washing her over.

Ever since she had come to know about Kailash's wedding, she had an agonising time making a decision. She kept swinging like a pendulum between two choices; to go and attend his wedding with a big smile on her face or to make an excuse and save herself the heartache of witnessing him putting vermillion on someone else's forehead instead of hers. Hot tears rolled down her cheeks. Every time she envisioned Kailash being with Suchitra, she felt crushed. But she had to decide soon or the agony would drive her crazy. She had come to know that they were back from England. She had received another letter from Kaki, who had again beseeched her to attend the wedding.

'Probably, it will be easier for you to see them getting married than you think. Also, it would help you to get on with your life. Reality, though harsh, is the only antidote for a false hope that is nothing but sweet and slow poison,' she had written.

'Thank you so much Kanti *Ji* for coming to the wedding,' Anuradha said, folding her hands and welcoming Kanti Prasad.

'The pleasure is entirely ours Mrs Mathur,' Kanti Prasad replied smiling.

'Mishthi! You can't imagine how happy I am to see you.' Anuradha embraced Sharmishtha. 'And here is my little angel. My God! She is so beautiful,' Anuradha said looking at Shivani, who gave her a smile as if understanding everything.

There was a pause as Anuradha looked at the child with pure joy. And then she realised that she was keeping them waiting.

'Oh! You must be tired after the journey. I must show you to your room.'

She called Hari *Chacha*, who was as pleased to see Sharmishtha and greeted Kanti Prasad cordially, and told him to show Sharmishtha and her family to their room.

'I am really sorry that Nandan is not here to greet you Kanti *Ji*. He had to attend to certain tasks but he will meet you at dinner,' Anuradha said.

Kanti, in his impeccable manners, said that it was perfectly alright and he would be delighted of Mr Mathur's company at dinner time.

They were given a suite in the sprawling villa, which comprised of a big bedroom with a king-sized bed, two armoires, a dresser, with an attached bathroom. There was a small sitting room for guests, and a small study with a mahogany writing table. Anuradha had assigned Sharmishtha a maid to help her with her clothes and hair. Hari *Chacha* asked Kanti Prasad to ask him for anything that was to be done. Thus, they settled down in their quarters, but there was an unsettling feeling that Sharmishtha couldn't shake off. She was nervous of meeting Kailash. She was afraid that her feelings might betray her and give some indication of the raging storm in her heart. After much debating she had decided to take Anuradha's advice and attend the wedding but now she was a little unsure of her decision. But then she did not want Kailash to think that she was not happy. And by not attending his wedding, it would have definitely made him feel that way. So here they were, to attend a wedding that was going to last three days.

They descended the stairs and were escorted to the dining room by Hari *Chacha*. They could hear voices that indicated that there were more people in the dining room. Nandan Mathur came forward to greet them.

'I am really sorry that I was not here to receive you,' he said shaking hands with Kanti Prasad. 'Welcome Mishthi! It's really nice to see you,' he said embracing Sharmishtha.

'Allow me to introduce you to Anil and Sumitra; Kailash's parents.'

Sharmishtha felt their gaze lingering on her and the silence was broken by Sumitra.

'Anuradha, you were right. I have never seen anyone so beautiful,' she said smiling, and holding Sharmishtha's hands. 'Thank you for joining us in the celebrations,' she said looking at Sharmishtha and her husband. 'I believe you have an adorable daughter,' Sumitra said as they moved towards the dining table.

'Thank you! She is asleep upstairs,' Sharmishtha said.

Sharmishtha was grateful once again that she had listened to her husband and let him employ Mrs Margaret Aldrich to teach her English and etiquettes of the colonial culture. Kanti Prasad knew her passion for reading, and being a voracious reader himself, he did not want her to be found lacking in a language that would have opened more doors for her. This was one of the many reasons Sharmishtha respected her husband. She knew that he loved her immensely and was always trying to make her happy.

As soup was served, there was a commotion as someone entered the dining room.

'Sorry! I got late.'

Sharmishtha's heart skipped few beats as she heard the familiar deep voice. She almost dropped the cutlery.

'It's alright Kailash. Come meet the guests,' his father said.

Sharmishtha saw him coming to shake hands with her husband

and then folding his hands to her and saying something. But she couldn't hear him, as if she was watching the scene from outside her body. It was only when Anuradha, who was sitting next to her, nudged her that she stammered something and her face flushed. She knew that she had made a fool of herself and couldn't meet anyone's gaze for some time. But Kailash saved the situation from becoming more awkward by talking to Kanti Prasad, as if he had known him all his life. Luckily for her, all the men got pulled into the conversation as Kanti Prasad talked about the political situation of the country. The women talked about the ceremonies that were going to take place in the next three days, and Sharmishtha responded politely when they directed any query towards her. But she was feeling a little vexed. Seeing Kailash after so many years had had an unnerving effect on her that she could not shake off. She had thought of him every single day and night, and here he was, sitting just a few meters away from her.

The proximity of having him so close to her was so distressing that her hands shook. She tried keeping her gaze at the women and tried very hard not to look at him, but she couldn't help but steal a glance at him when she thought everyone was busy talking, and her heart missed a beat when she saw him looking at her at the same time. And in that moment they communicated, his eyes intense and mesmerising. She dropped her gaze because she thought she would faint with the emotions churning in her heart. Her heart thudded so loudly that she feared everyone might hear it. She swayed a bit, and as if on cue, Anuradha asked her if she was feeling alright.

After dinner was over, Nandan Mathur invited Kanti Prasad for a night cap in the library and she was asked to sit with the ladies in the drawing room. But before she could gather her wits around her, Anuradha came to her rescue and told her that it was quite alright if she was tired and wanted to retire. Sharmishtha thanked her and bid good night to the ladies. She was escorted by Hari *Chacha* to her room. She went to check on her daughter in the adjoining room. She was sleeping peacefully. Sharmishtha still reeled with the effect of seeing Kailash. She felt tears rolling down her cheeks. The heartache that she thought she had tucked away in a corner of her heart, was back.

'Oh Shivani! How I am going to get through this?' She whispered in her daughter's ears.

'*Bibi ji*, is everything alright?' Shivani's nanny woke up.

'Everything is fine. Please go back to sleep,' Sharmishtha replied, turning away in order to hide her tears.

During the ceremonies the next day, Sharmishtha avoided any direct eye contact with Kailash. Though she felt his eyes on her, she tried keeping a normal expression on her face, even though she was fighting a battle inside. Her husband smiled affectionately at her all the time, thinking that she was happy to be with her people. Her parents had arrived later that day with Anushtha, and Sharmishtha was happy to be in their company. They had taken charge of Shivani and Sharmishtha got a breather for a couple of hours, and excused herself saying that she had a headache. She lay down on her bed in her room and tried sorting her feelings. Suchitra had looked like a delicate doll, draped in a yellow georgette *sari* for her *Haldi* ceremony. She looked sophisticated with her wavy bob and slender figure. But it was Kailash who had taken her breath away again. He was dressed in a white *kurta* and *pyjama*, his sleeves rolled up to show his muscular arms. Sharmishtha averted her eyes when the turmeric paste was being put on his broad forehead. She was trying to be brave for his sake, trying to send a message to him that she was happy for him, but she knew that he was aware of the ruse. Kailash could see through her soul and she could not hide anything from him. She had learned that in the very beginning, when they had been together. She had to go through one more day and then she would walk out of Kailash's sight forever, she told herself. She had to muster a little bit more courage and then she would live her life with the memories they had made together.

There was a soft knock on the door.

'Come in please!' She said, not opening her eyes. It must be her sister or nanny, she thought.

'Are you feeling alright?' Startled, she jumped to her feet, and in an instant was standing next to the bed.

Kailash was standing at the door. She was still in the Banarasi organza she had worn for the ceremony, her long hair that she had undone in order to soothe her headache, fell cascading below her hips. Kailash was riveted to the spot.

'I am fine. But how come you are here?' She finally found her voice.

'My friends are throwing a bachelor party for me tonight. I thought I would ask Kanti to come along. Moreover, I had some work with *Bua*. I did not find you with your folks so thought I would say Hello, as I could not talk to you earlier. Hope I am not being a bother,' he said.

'*Always a gentleman*!' Sharmishtha thought and a smile played on her lips.

'No! It's always a pleasure to see you.' She regretted the words as soon as they were out of her mouth. He was someone else's fiancé, and soon-to-be a married man. She shouldn't talk in a way that was not appropriate.

'Mishthi, thank you so much for accepting the invitation and coming to attend the wedding, it really means a lot to me,' he said.

'I wouldn't have missed your wedding for anything, though you missed mine,' she said with a twinkle in her eyes.

And then they both laughed. The distance of the years melted away in seconds. They were standing there, revelling in each other's company and nothing else mattered. Just looking at each other was enough. It was as if they were two bodies, one soul.

'I haven't seen your daughter. She is Shivani. Right?' he asked.

'She must be with *Amma* and Anushtha. They have taken charge of her. I will go and see.'

But then she stopped.

'Why don't you go ahead and I will follow.'

She did not want anyone to see him with her. He had come to see her, which in itself was a bold thing to do. But she knew that her parents would not like to see them together.

'Alright! I will go find your husband.'

He turned to go and stopped.

'Mishthi, it's easy for me to go through this with you being present here. Thank you so much once again.'

And with that he was gone.

Sharmishtha stood rooted to the spot. He had said so much by saying so little. Her heart ached and tears threatened to roll down. It would always be like this with them. The sweet and gratifying pain; the pain she would nurture and relish. The pain of longing was what she lived for.

The wedding day arrived. Sharmishtha watched Kailash put vermillion on Suchitra's forehead. She watched it with a calmness she did not know she was capable of. But then, she knew that this was how they were meant to live their lives; away from each other, yet in each other's heart till eternity. The day Sharmishtha and Kanti had to leave; Kailash and Suchitra came to meet them. Suchitra came to Sharmishtha's room. She took her hands in her own, and thanked her for attending the wedding.

'It was really nice to see you after all these years. I must say that you are more beautiful than I remembered,' Suchitra said.

'Look who is talking... you looked so radiant in your bridal finery,' Sharmishtha said.

'And yet it was you who stole everyone's attention,' Suchitra said.

They both laughed. There was an ease between them. Sharmishtha felt a big burden lifting from her heart. She felt a wave of warmth for Suchitra and she knew that instant that she was no longer jealous of her. They both loved the same man and that was a bond that she would always respect. Suchitra cooed over Shivani when the nanny brought her into the room after dressing her up, and Shivani gave her brightest smile to Suchitra.

'What a lovely baby!' She looked quite taken with Shivani.

Promises were made to keep in touch.

Kailash held the door open for Sharmishtha when she sat in the car and there was the same tender look in his eyes that Sharmishtha so loved. But she did not look for long at him, as she felt that it would have been morally wrong.

CHAPTER 28

Kailash had rehearsed for the day he would see Mishthi again. He must have replayed the scene hundreds of times. And every time he told himself that he would keep his feelings and emotions in control, as he was going to belong to someone else, and it would not be fair to feel the way he was still feeling for her. The distance of thousands of miles had not been able to dim the memory of her even a little bit. In fact, each day had brought her closer to him. But he had not anticipated the effect it would have when he saw her descending the staircase. She was wearing a midnight blue *sari* with silver embellishments. Her porcelain skin shone against the colour. She looked like a nymph who had draped the colour of the sky with the stars shining. The red vermillion on her forehead and the kohl in her eyes made her look divine. Her figure draped in the transparent material of the *sari* looked like a statue carved out of marble. Her long and lustrous hair was arranged in a bun, with ornaments put in deftly. She looked a little different from the Mishthi he remembered. He then realised that she was even more beautiful now. Gone was the skittishness and feisty charm of adolescence. Instead, there was a mysterious calm and dignity about her. He stopped at the entrance of the dining room when he saw her coming down the stairs. He wanted to look at her without being seen by anyone. He wanted to drink in her beauty. In fact, He was frozen to the spot, forgetting the world around him. He had deliberately taken some more time to calm himself and then finally joined everyone at the table. She avoided looking at him for most of the evening, but once when their eyes met, he found that she had let her guard slip and there was the same intensity he had seen five years back.

His preparation had flown out of the window, though he tried maintaining control over his feelings. And then he gave up; he gave up the effort to convince himself that he could somehow suppress his love for her. It was useless to try. He accepted the fact that he would never be able to stop feeling the way he felt for her. His love was like a fierce river that could not be stopped no matter how many dams were built around it. He could live more peacefully if he lived with the love that he had for her. It was not his fault that he had fallen in love with her. He had every right to love her. If anyone was to be blamed, it was her parents and society. Why should he even try to dim his love for his Mishthi, just to justify some stupid and illogical man-made norms? She had been, and would be his only love. He would try to be a good husband to Sue, but it would be just that. He will breathe and live only for Mishthi.

Chapter 29

Sharmishtha had settled in her life. Her days were full as a mother and wife. There were times when she thought of Kailash and felt a void, but it was soon filled with Shivani's cheerful disposition. Shivani was like a gem spreading colourful rays everywhere. As far as Kanti was concerned, she tried her best to fulfil her duties as his wife, yet she knew she was not being fair to him by not giving him the love he expected from her. Though she felt it was wrong of her not to feel happiness in her husband's gentle and caring love; he was the most selfless man she had ever come across. But she had a feeling he had relented to the fact that he was only going to get this much from her. His greatness lay in him never demanding anything that she couldn't give. He had stood with her when she was chastised for not conceiving a second time. Shivani was four now, Sharmishtha had not conceived again, and it was considered a blasphemy that she had not been able to give Shivani a sibling. Her mother–in–law took her to the best gynaecologist in town but they had to come back with a whole lot of medicines, and an advice to have faith in God. Though why she couldn't conceive was only known to her and her gynaecologist. She had found a good friend in her, and when the gynaecologist had told her that there was nothing wrong with her, and she was going to ask Kanti to go for a check up, Sharmishtha had literally begged her not to say anything. She could not do this to her husband. Though there was little doubt in her gynaecologist's mind that there could hardly be anything wrong with him, as they had had a daughter together. Kanti himself had suggested seeing a doctor but then Sharmishtha had told him that there was nothing wrong with either of them. They had a beautiful daughter and she was more than enough for them. Kanti was a very literate and progressive man. He never believed in age-old traditions. And one such day when she was being reprimanded for her inability to produce another child, he told everyone that he was fed up of the rebuke his wife was being subjected to, and they were happy with their daughter. He did not want to hear anything related to this. He had younger brothers who could add more to the Pandey progenies. So this should end there and then. Her respect for him had increased manifold since then.

And then one day, when Kanti came back from the university, he brought news and an invitation. He had a big smile on his face.

'You cannot guess what news I have brought,' he said, untying his shoes.

'Do I have to go to Kanpur? Have you heard from *Baba*?' she asked.

'No! Someone is coming to Lucknow,' he said, still grinning.

She looked at him questioningly, thinking that her brothers were probably visiting her. But they visited often, so there was no reason for it to be special news. And then he gave her a letter which was addressed to him on his university address.

Her hands shook as she looked at the familiar handwriting. She opened the letter and went through the contents. As she had already guessed, the letter was from Kailash. He was shifting to Lucknow from Bombay. He was coming to join as a senior advocate in the Lucknow bench of the Allahabad High Court. There was a surge of emotions carousing through her body as she read the letter. She was elated at the prospect of seeing him again. It seemed to her that her life had taken an unexpected but very pleasant turn. But along with the euphoria she felt something else. When the rush of adrenalin subsided she realised that the situation was going to become more hopeless than she'd expected. It was easy to go through life, on a day to day basis without a promise of the future. She had become used to living without expectations, but with Kailash coming to Lucknow, was like a storm coming, that would bring a lot of disturbance along with it. She would not be able to carry on with her life as she was doing until now. She knew that once she saw him, it would become very difficult to lead a normal life; that she would crave to see him again and again and it would become a vicious circle. Was the destiny posing some kind of a challenge to them? It would indeed be a very tough one.

She went about doing her chores in a haze as the complexity of the situation unsettled her. Kanti asked her a couple of times whether she was feeling alright. She told him that it was that time of the month for her, and luckily it was. Her periods were the most unpleasant thing, as she had terrible cramps and bled like an animal slaughtered.

As Kailash's arrival came closer, she left things to providence, and the euphoria of seeing him was back once again. And finally, the day came. A bearer came with a dinner invitation and a handwritten note addressed to Kanti. They were invited to Barrister Kailash Mathur's house for dinner, two days from then. He was sending his car and had requested to bring Shivani, and of course, the nanny could accompany. She decided to wear her turquoise blue Japanese georgette *sari* with silver and pearl embellishments, a gift from Kanti on her birthday, with her Basra pearls. A baby pink frock with fine lace was chosen for Shivani and Kanti wore dark trousers with a white shirt and a dark jacket with a tie, looking every inch the dignified English professor that he was.

The car stopped at the massive wrought iron gates of 'The Retreat', as Kailash's bungalow was called, for the sentries to open the gate. The drive-in was flanked by tall bottle palms making a vista, and she caught a glimpse of the manicured lawns through gaps between the palms. The car stopped at the porch and a uniformed Durban opened the door for her. It was a beautiful house made in colonial style. The steps and veranda were done in the finest marble. The house was circular with thick marble pillars running around the veranda. There were big bay windows that overlooked the massive garden. They were escorted to the drawing room that had been done up very tastefully. The furniture was mostly European. There was a big fireplace, and a mantelpiece with big candelabra at both ends. The carpets were Oriental, done in rich colours and the drapes were matching silk. There were Edwardian consoles with fresh flowers and photographs of the family in silver frames. The walls were adorned with beautiful, rich paintings. Kailash and Suchitra's wealth was visible in everything.

Wealth was not new to Sharmishtha as she had been raised in a rich household, and though Kanti's family was not filthy rich, they were financially very comfortable. But while her parents and her husband's family lived in a simple way that reflected a traditional Indian household, Kailash and Suchitra's house looked like a miniature version of European villa. But then, they were both used to that kind of lifestyle and half of Suchitra's parentage added to that. Kailash entered the drawing room and greeted Kanti with a handshake and a charming smile. Her heart skipped a beat. Would she never be able to look at him without feeling like a sixteen-year-old? Probably never, she thought.

'Hello Mishthi! How have you been?' he asked, hugging her lightly. And before she could recover from the sensation of his touch, he kneeled in front of Shivani, who was looking at him with large eyes. 'And look at you... you are such a darling,' he said, picking Shivani up in his arms. He looked at her with such affection that it showed on his face. There was a fluttering in her heart that seemed to be very loud. Seeing Shivani in Kailash's arms had an inexplicable effect on her. Probably it was a reminder of those dreams that she had woven with him... being married to him and bearing his offspring. She looked at him, beaming with undulated joy as he talked to Shivani. Kailash was not only beautiful physically; he possessed an equally beautiful heart. He had no malice, no guise and no arrogance.

Shivani gave him a beaming smile. She also couldn't remain untouched by Kailash's magnetic charm.

'She is such an angel.' They all turned back to the melodious and anglicised voice of Suchitra. She had not changed a bit. Her slim and delicate figure defied her age and she looked like the girl from all those years ago. But the girlish innocence was replaced by a calm serenity and she looked much in control. Her happiness was evident and Sharmishtha felt something akin to jealousy. She wore a smile that seemed to light up her heart-shaped face. Her grey eyes shone like gems and there was an air of contentment and happiness around her. She was dressed in a white frock with small blue flowers; a string of pearls and matching pearl studs completed her ensemble.

'She is going to be a great beauty like her mother,' she added. 'It's so nice to see you Sharmishtha. I am so glad that we have come to Lucknow. We hope that we get to see you all often,' Suchitra said graciously.

The evening went on and they talked and laughed like old friends. Kanti kept them amused with his superb sense of humour. Dinner was served in the big dining room, in translucent china, crystal and silver cutlery, by the liveried waiters. After dinner, the men had a night cap and the ladies had coffee. Shivani was with the nanny in the guest room, and was fast asleep.

'So how is married life, Mishthi?' Suchitra had taken to call her by her nick name. 'Do you miss Kanpur and your family?'

Though it was a simple question, yet Sharmishtha felt something more hidden in it. Or maybe it was just her imagination, she thought.

'I think all daughters, no matter how happy they are with their husbands and children; do miss their parents, siblings and their first home. But in my case the good thing is that I keep going to Kanpur and my siblings keep visiting me. But that is true in your case too. You are closer to your parents now,' Sharmishtha replied.

'Yes! Indeed! But my parents are planning to move to England. My father has to look after the estate my grandfather has left to him, and Sam has to go to Oxford for his education,' she said and Sharmishtha noticed a trace of dismay in her voice.

'Oh! But surely they would visit you,' she said in order to say something soothing.

'They would, but it wouldn't be often, seeing the travel time and my mother's delicate disposition. But it's alright. They were a bit hesitant in the beginning on my account, but now they know that I am in safe hands. They know that Kailash will take good care of me,' she said looking at Sharmishtha. Was there an underlying meaning to what she'd said or was it just her imagination again? And when she looked at her, she thought it was the latter because there was no hint of rancour on her face.

'And there is Chanda. She is the sister I never had. She is only a few years older but she treats me like her child,' she said, smiling warmly. 'Her mother was not feeling too well so I sent her to look after her. Did I tell you that she got married and has a daughter now?'

'Yes, I know. I met her at your wedding.'

'Of course!'

Anuradha had told Sharmishtha about Chanda and her connection with the Langley family. She had got married after coming back from England and conceived in the first month itself. Her husband was a nice young man who had a good farmland and a big house in the village. But she liked to stay with Suchitra. Apparently this was the condition she had kept before getting married. So her husband visited her often and she went to visit him once in a while. Sharmishtha had noticed her dedication towards Suchitra during the wedding, and at that time she had found it a bit obsessive. But then, she hardly knew her and her equation with the family.

The days were flying as Sharmishtha felt a new energy filling her core. She was happy and it was showing. Everyone told her that she was glowing and Kanti seemed to be very pleased with her newfound happiness, though if he wondered about the reason, he neither showed it, nor asked. And then there was another invitation from Kailash. He had planned a picnic and a night's stay in the Chinhat forest, and Sharmishtha and her family were invited again. Kanti borrowed the family car and together they drove down to Chinhat. Kailash's friend had a cottage there and they stayed overnight. It was an enjoyable experience.

Sharmishtha kept looking forward to such invitations from

Kailash and she was never disappointed. They went out for films and theatre and drove to Malihabad to eat fresh mangoes out of the orchard. They took Suchitra to Imambara, Dilkusha kothis and other such historical monuments. Kanti was a born storyteller and his knowledge about such places was deep, so his stories were loved by everyone. Suchitra always complimented him on his knowledge and asked numerous questions. So they made an interesting coterie of like-minded people.

All this while Sharmishtha tried keeping her feelings for Kailash in check but her heart was always thudding. And then there were occasions when she felt he was struggling with the same. She knew that he invited them again and again so that he could see her. But in spite of their feelings for each other, they did not try to get in a situation where they were alone with each other. They were both content spending time with each other and that was more than they had ever hoped for. They had made a promise to each other to move on with their lives and they had to keep it. Moreover their spouses were caring and affectionate people and they deserved all that and more. So Sharmishtha was blissfully happy as the void in her life was filled. Kailash was like the very air she breathed and her love for Kailash was not ephemeral, it was everlasting. But as the days passed Kailash's attachment to Shivani grew and that gave Sharmishtha a cause for worry. She wondered whether they were planning to start a family. It would do well to both of them. She had noticed Suchitra looking at Kailash and Shivani with an affectionate smile, probably thinking that he would make such a good father.

During one such outing, when they were sitting in the lush gardens of the Prince of Wales zoo, an excursion planned for Shivani's amusement, Kailash invited them to Shivgarh, where he had just bought a Haveli. The Haveli belonged to his friend who was moving to England for good. Sharmishtha was happy for the invitation for two reasons; one, that she would get to see Kailash for two-three days continuously; second, she would be able to spend some time with her *Nanoo*. Asanpur was just across the river. Her grandmother had been inviting her to visit her with Kanti and Shivani. She had not seen

Shivani for quite some time and her letters were full of such requests.

They were to go to Shivgarh after two weeks. Kailash offered them a ride but Kanti declined and booked his family in the first class carriage of the Raebareli bound train. Sharmishtha agreed with the idea, as she did not want to smother them with their company all the time.

After two weeks they boarded the train for Raebareli. Kailash's car was waiting to pick them up from the station and as they started for Shivgarh it started raining. Sharmishtha inhaled the rich petrichor, that reminded her of carefree days in the village as a child.

The Haveli was beautiful. It was built by Kailash's friend's father who used to host his friends, including the highly placed British, *Taluqdars*, and other important dignitaries of the princely states. It was built in Victorian architecture and had huge manicured lawns on all sides. But the most striking feature of the Haveli was its terraces that overlooked the river, a short distance away. The rear lawns were narrow, and if one, sitting in a chair, looked over the parapet, could only see the flowing water of the river. It gave a feeling of being suspended in the air, over the river. It was an exhilarating feeling. Kailash escorted them to the terrace after giving them a tour of the Haveli.

'Isn't it beautiful?' he asked as he looked at Sharmishtha. She looked at him and they held each other's gaze.

'So how do you like the view Mishthi?' They tore their gaze hurriedly and looked at Suchitra who had joined them after showing Kanti the other part of the terrace.

Her gaze was steady as she looked at Sharmishtha. Sharmishtha's heart missed a beat, probably because of her guilty conscience.

'It's... beautiful indeed,' she said.

'I keep telling Kailash the same.' She looked at him lovingly and linked her arms into his.

'Shall we proceed for tea?' Suchitra asked and they followed her.

There was something that had left Sharmishtha a little disturbed; call it a woman's intuition. She had always been on her guard lest her feelings betray her, but now she felt a little worried and there were ripples on the calm waters of her mind.

'*Bibi Ji*!' Saroja, Shivani's nanny was standing at the door.

'Come in Saroja! Is Shivani still asleep?' she asked.

She came inside and stood with her head bent.

'What is it? Is everything alright? Are you comfortable in your quarters?' Sharmishtha asked.

'I am fine *Bibi Ji*. But I have to tell you something,' she said hesitatingly.

'Yes, please go on.'

'Please forgive me if I am speaking out of turn but I think Chanda does not like Shivani baby.'

'But why? And how do you know?' Sharmishtha was perplexed.

'I don't know. But many a time I have seen her looking at the baby with a lot of contempt. I am not saying that I am very intuitive or wise but she makes it very obvious. The other day, I went into the kitchen to heat up some milk for baby, and she told me to wait as that stove was being used for dinner. Though the cook offered to take off the pot so I could warm the milk but she scolded him and said the soup would get spoilt and *Missi Baba* would not like it. The cook looked at me apologetically but couldn't do anything. Similarly when her daughter came to play with baby, she shooed her away.'

Sharmishtha did not know what to make of this whole thing. She had noticed that Chanda was a little smug around them and she had caught her staring at her a couple of times, but she had not made much of it. She knew that Chanda was very dedicated to Suchitra, but why would she dislike Shivani? Unless she had noticed Kailash's fondness for Shivani, but why would she feel jealous? Unless there was another reason; the thought left her more worried.

In the next couple of days, Sharmishtha paid more attention to when Chanda was around and though she did not give much indication of any doubtful behaviour, Sharmishtha caught her looking at her and Shivani with a coldness that put her ill at ease.

The day they were to leave, Suchitra took ill. She had vomited in the morning and was resting in her room. Kailash escorted Sharmishtha to her room and left her with Suchitra.

'How are you feeling now?' Sharmishtha asked her. She looked a little pale. Chanda was hovering and helped Suchitra sit in the bed.

'I am much better. It's nothing really. They are just making a fuss. I am sorry I couldn't have breakfast with you all,' she said.

'No, please don't be. I just want to thank you for the wonderful time that we have had here. You are such a gracious hostess.'

'You are always welcome here or in Lucknow,' she said holding Sharmishtha's hand. 'Chanda, be a darling and get me some coconut water please!' Suchitra said.

Chanda looked at Sharmishtha and hesitated but left to fetch coconut water.

'Mishthi, is it possible to get morning sickness in the second month itself?' she asked.

'Morning sickness as in... Oh! Really? Are you expecting?' Sharmishtha asked her.

'I think so,' she said smiling.

'That's wonderful news. Heartiest congratulations!'

'I haven't told Kailash yet. I will get the check up done in Lucknow and then tell him.'

'Well! That's your privilege to give him the news. I am very happy for you both. Do let me know if I can be of any help,' Sharmishtha said holding her hand.

But later she had a mixed reaction on getting the news of

Suchitra's pregnancy. She was happy for her of course; but somewhere a senseless notion had raised its head, denoting that once Kailash became the father of his own progeny, he probably wouldn't love Shivani as much. She snubbed the thought though; Shivani had the most loving and doting father. She didn't need someone else's love.

Suchitra's pregnancy turned out to be a difficult one. Her parents visited her and decided to postpone their move to England till she'd delivered. And one day Kanti came from university and told Sharmishtha that Suchitra had had a problem and they should go and look her up. They left Shivani with the nanny and went to Kailash's residence. Kanti, of course, sat with the men in the drawing room and Sharmishtha was pleasantly surprised to see Anuradha and Nandan Mathur there. Apparently they had also come from Kanpur to look Suchitra up. Anuradha hugged Sharmishtha the moment she saw her.

'My Mishthi! I miss you so much.'

'I miss you too, *Kaki*, every day,' Sharmishtha said hugging her tightly.

'How is Suchitra doing? What happened?' Sharmishtha asked Anuradha as she was escorted to the master bedroom. Suchitra's mother was sitting with her and Chanda was rubbing Suchitra's forehead.

'It's nice to see you Mishthi. You look so radiant,' Mrs Langley said holding Sharmishtha's hand.

Suchitra opened her eyes and gave a weak smile.

'Come here,' she motioned to her on the bed.

'What happened?' Sharmishtha asked her.

'She started bleeding in the night. So we called the doctor. She came and checked her. Thankfully the baby is safe but Suchitra will have to be on bed rest throughout her confinement,' Anuradha said.

'I am sure everything will be alright. And don't worry; we will keep you entertained all the time,' Sharmishtha pressed her hand reassuringly.

She met Kailash while leaving for home. He looked as if he hadn't slept the whole night.

'Thank you so much Mishthi for coming. It always means a lot to me. Why didn't you bring Shivani?' he asked. How she loved this man; he missed Shivani even though he had problems of his own.

'I will bring her next time. Don't worry Kailash, all will be well,' she said taking his hand in hers. It was an involuntary gesture but her hands trembled a little with his touch. He clasped his hands on hers and they stood there for some time. A rustling behind the curtains brought them out of the moment.

'Thank you for your good wishes Mishthi. I hope Sue and the baby remain fine,' he said.

'They will... have faith.'

Sharmishtha went to visit Suchitra as many times as was possible. Suchitra was bored being on bed rest, and had become a little cranky. But they all tried to humour her in their own ways. Kailash was getting busier with his work but he made time for her. But her constant companion Chanda bore the brunt of it, and Sharmishtha was amazed at her dedication towards Suchitra.

And finally, a message that Suchitra had gone into labour sometime in the night, came. Sharmishtha had made two baby sets for the newborn; one in pink and one in blue. She had embroidered and stitched them. She, along with Kanti, hurried to the nursing home, and after being in labour for eight hours, Suchitra gave birth to a baby girl. They named her Shailja Mathur. But she was called Shelly. She was a very pretty child. Sharmishtha, along with Shivani, kept going to 'The Retreat' often to keep Suchitra company.

But gradually, visits to 'The Retreat' reduced. Kailash had become busy with his work and Kanti was doing a doctorate in linguistics. Shivani had started school and Sharmishtha had to go to Kanpur frequently as her father needed help in his business ventures. He was building his second hotel, the first of its kind in the city. Shivani was growing into a beautiful and intelligent girl and Shelly looked adorable. Both the girls had taken a liking to each other and Shivani treated Shelly like her younger sibling. Many a time, Sharmishtha caught Kailash beaming with pride looking at them whenever the families got to meet.

CHAPTER 30

Sharmishtha had come to Kanpur to see the furnishings for her father's newly built hotel, when she was summoned by Anuradha and was surprised to see Kailash there.

'Kailash! When did you come?' she asked, unable to keep the excitement out of her voice.

'Last night and was so happy to know that you are also here.'

'But have you come alone?' she asked.

'I have come for some work. I am going back tomorrow.'

'How are Sue and Shelly doing?'

'They both are fine. I am really happy to see you here. I have been missing our get-togethers. But my work has kept me busy. And Sue being busy with the baby, it's been difficult to meet up. But tell me, how is Shivani? I have missed her.'

'Shivani is fine. She has come with me. I will bring her tomorrow to meet you.'

'That would be really nice. Mishthi! Let's all go to the Haveli for a few days. I will try to take some time out. I hope Kanti would find some free time to come. I really want to spend some time with you and Shivani.'

Her heart again filled with the same warmth, by the way he said 'you and Shivani'. She wanted to forget that she was someone else's wife and he was someone else's husband just for a moment. She wanted to jump to the other side of the chasm that lay gaping between them.

Kailash must have read something on her face because he walked towards her and held her shoulders.

'So, let me speak to Kanti and Sue and let's go to the village. Also I have to ask you something. Can I...'

'The tea is on the table.' Anuradha entered the room at that moment and Kailash let his hands drop. If she noticed the emotional tension between them, she pretended she didn't. But she did not leave them alone thereafter. Sharmishtha wanted to ask Kailash what it was that he wanted to ask. But she never got the chance. She had to leave for Lucknow the next morning as Kanti called to say that his mother had taken ill. Also, she couldn't take Shivani to meet Kailash.

They could not go to the village either as Suchitra was not feeling very bright. That was the message that they received from Kailash. Sharmishtha was a little disappointed, but did not have time to think about it, as she got busy looking after her mother-in-law and supervising two households. A few months went by and then one day Kanti came and told her to get dressed. They were going to watch a new film that had released recently, and was becoming very popular. He had also invited Kailash and Suchitra and they were reaching the theatre directly. She again felt the same nervous excitement at the prospect of seeing Kailash.

She wore a light mauve georgette *sari* with a purple border, with her new amethyst set which her father had gifted her on the inauguration of the hotel. Suchitra was wearing a pale blue frock with a pearl string and studs, and though she looked pretty as always, there were shadows under her eyes.

They bid farewell after the film, and as Sharmishtha advanced to hug Suchitra she felt her body stiffen. She had looked a little distanced and was not her chirpy old self. Sharmishtha attributed it to her ailment, whatever it was that she suffered from. She asked whether she was feeling alright, but Suchitra's responses were lukewarm and she did not press.

Exactly two weeks after the cinema outing, Sharmishtha's

brother came from Kanpur to inform them that *Nanoo* had suffered a mild heart attack. Sharmishtha was distressed. She had not gone to Asanpur for about two years and when she met her grandmother briefly in Kanpur few months back, she had looked tired. When Sharmishtha had expressed her concern over her health, she had assured her that she had had a bout of fever and had almost recovered now. So this news left her feeling remorseful. The responsibilities of married life and motherhood had claimed her mind and time, and she had drifted away from another person she loved so much.

A day prior to her departure, Kailash's bearer came bringing a dinner invitation. And as he handed her a letter, he said that his master awaited a reply and he would wait. Sharmishtha opened the letter. It was rare for Kailash to send her a letter. He had respected her marriage and had never done anything inappropriate. The letter read….

My dear Mishthi,

It's becoming very difficult for me to go on smoothly with my life as I need to ask you about Shivani. Every time I look at her I feel a connection that is difficult to explain. Also I have calculated the time of Shivani's birth. Is what I am thinking possible? Please tell me the truth. I cannot take this agony any longer. I am inviting you all for dinner and hope to steal a few moments alone with you.

Also, Sue has started having those episodes again. They started after Shelly's birth. They are not very frequent but it's a matter of worry. I have contacted her doctor in the UK, and he has very graciously agreed to come to India. He said that he wanted to visit the country and see the Taj Mahal as well. I hope she recovers fast because Shelly needs her mother hale and hearty.

Can't wait to see you and Shivani tomorrow. And I hope with all my heart that you tell me the truth and put me out of my misery.

Much love,

Kailash

CHAPTER 31

She sat down heavily on the chair. She had kept the truth locked in her heart for nine years. It was a burden she was carrying alone. There had been moments of weakness but she had fought them. It was in everyone's best interest that no one ever came to know about Shivani. How could she ever explain that Shivani was not the outcome of some lustful frenzy, but the result of a love that was pure and pious? She never felt any guilt about that night when she conceived her, because it was a gift she had given herself to go through life without the man she loved. She did not know then that she would get her as a gift out of their union. Maybe it was a gift bestowed upon her by the universe as compensation. And then, just as providence was playing a role in everything, her marriage was not yet consummated, as they were both kept apart for a year, honouring the wish of her father-in-law. The 'appropriate date' for the consummation of the marriage was the last day before she left for Kanpur. Kanti behaved like a thorough gentleman and she had come to Kanpur still a virgin, not knowing that she was going to meet Kailash in Asanpur. She had missed her period when Kanti came to take her back to Lucknow. They had started their married life and it was just natural for everyone to think that she had conceived Shivani during the first few unions with her husband. But when she tried to conceive two years after Shivani was born, she couldn't. Shivani turned four and she still couldn't. Kanti came to her rescue to the constant bickering of her mother-in-law and the matter was put to rest. She did feel guilty for keeping Kanti in the dark, but the truth was that it had become easy for her to go through life after that night.

The time had come to tell Kailash. She could not keep it from him any longer. She could never make him sad for anything no matter what the cost was. The father in him had already come to know. It would unburden her soul and it would be easier to live thereafter.

She penned a reply to Kailash's letter. She declined the dinner invitation telling him about her grandmother's condition and her decision to go to Asanpur to look after her. But she made a promise to him, that as soon as she came back she would tell him what he wanted to know.

She went to bed that night, holding Shivani in her arms, as she decided to take Shivani with her to Asanpur. Her nanny would be with her so it would be easier to focus on *Nanoo* and at least she wouldn't miss Shivani. Also, *Nanoo* doted on her, and it would be nice for her to see Shivani. It might put her in good spirits.

Shivani was joyous. Sharmishtha helped her nanny pack Shivani's clothes and her favourite dolls. As she was closing the suitcase, Tara, the household help, came to inform that Kailash *Babu* had come and was waiting in the *Baithak*. Sharmishtha quickly checked her appearance in the tall mirror of her dresser and rushed to receive him. Kanti had left early for the university to complete some work and give in his application for leave.

'Kailash! Is everything alright?' she asked as soon as she saw him. He looked very handsome in dark slacks and a white shirt with a blazer on.

'Mishthi!' He held her hands. 'How is *Nanoo*? I mean, what has happened?'

'She had a mild heart attack and was taken to a hospital in Lalgarh. She is much better now and has been discharged. I am going to Asanpur to take care of her till she fully recovers.'

'I am sorry to learn that. Are you leaving today itself?' he asked.

'Yes! By the afternoon train. Kanti is escorting us and then after a couple of days he will come back as exams are around the corner,' she said.

She was debating whether to tell him what he wanted to know.

Had he come to ask her that? She thought. But somehow, the time and place felt inappropriate to talk about something so delicate, so she just waited for him to say something.

'I came to tell you that I will come to Shivgarh and then to Asanpur to see you, if that is alright with you,' he said looking at her expectantly.

Maybe it would be easier for us to meet in the same place that had given us ultimate happiness for a lifetime. And it would be easier for him to embrace his daughter and spend time with her, away from prying eyes, she thought.

'Mishthi, I would like to spend some time with you. I just want to talk to you. I know I am not making this easy for you but I just need a little time with you, that's all,' he said again.

'There is nothing more I want than to spend time with you. When will you come?' she asked.

He looked relieved and his eyes shone.

'I will come after a week. You will be there for some time I presume?'

'I will stay for as long as it takes *Nanoo* to recover.'

'Then it is settled. I will see you after a week. Oh Mishthi! You have made me so happy.'

He probably wanted to embrace her but just looked at her and went out and sat in the car. She noticed that he had not brought the chauffeur. He smiled and waved at her as the car lurched forward. Despite the worry for her grandmother, she felt happy. Kailash always brought sunshine whenever dark clouds threatened her. She went inside and hugged and tickled Shivani, and they both laughed.

CHAPTER 32

Sharmishtha nursed her grandmother, even though her grandmother kept telling her that she needed to go back to Lucknow. Shivani was missing her school and Kanti was eating food made by the cook, she said.

'I am feeling much better now. My sickness has gone ever since I have seen you and Shivani. Now don't be rigid and go home. I promise I will send for you if I am feeling even a little unwell. Moreover, I have got so many people here and Kishan and Kamal keep coming.'

Out of all of Sharmishtha's siblings, Kishan and Kamal, who were twins, were very fond of their grandmother and kept coming to Asanpur to look her up. Sharmishtha agreed reluctantly on her insistence, and sent a wire to Kanti to take them back to Lucknow. Sharmishtha had not heard from Kailash and thought that he must have got caught up with work. Though she felt disappointed, because somewhere deep down she had been wishing every day for him to come. So her surprise was evident when she was informed that *Jamai Bhaiya* had come with Barrister *Saheb*. She ran through the courtyard and saw them both smiling indulgently.

'You look surprised to see us both together,' Kanti said smiling.

'That means we succeeded. That was the very idea,' Kailash said joining Kanti.

After a little while Kailash left after meeting *Nanoo* and asking about her health. But before he left he told her that he had requested Kanti to come and stay for a couple of days in the Haveli, and Kanti had agreed. Suchitra and Shelly were coming down to the village the following day. So Sharmishtha bid farewell to *Nanoo*, albeit a bit reluctantly, and they all went to the Haveli. Their stay in the Haveli was enjoyable except for the fact that Suchitra looked a tad too formal. Even Kanti noticed the change, but then, they both, knowing her delicate disposition, shrugged it off.

And the day before they were to leave for Lucknow, Kailash caught hold of her as she was going to the kitchen to prepare some authentic Kanauj delicacies.

'Mishthi, please come to the grove on the river bank for five minutes,' he said and walked away, towards the rear door of the Haveli.

The grove he mentioned was next to the eastern side of the rear lawns. Kanti was upstairs with both the girls, teaching them chess. She hurried after Kailash to the grove and found Kailash waiting for her.

'Mishthi, please just say yes or no to what I am going to ask you. Is Shivani my daughter?' he asked, looking into her eyes.

She knew that sooner or later he was going to ask her that, but the directness of his question startled her a bit. But as she gazed into those honest eyes she did not hesitate. After all, he had all the right to know.

'Yes!' she said looking at him with her eyes brimming. He looked so happy and there were tears in his eyes.

'Thank you!' He took her hand and kissed it.

'You have no idea how happy you have made me today.' With that he walked towards the front side of the Haveli, and Sharmishtha turned to go to the kitchen, suddenly feeling very light.

They came back to Lucknow and fell into the routine. Sharmishtha was feeling relieved, light and happy, as she had seen Kailash looking at Shivani with utmost love. She did not know how right it was on a moral compass, but it was a secret she was happy to share with Kailash. They did not go to 'The Retreat' very often now, and she was, in a way, relieved. It was best this way. The less they saw each other the better it was. She did not want Kailash to see Shivani very often as he had a daughter who deserved his love more than Shivani.

And then suddenly, a huge crack appeared in her placid life. Her grandmother suffered another heart attack and passed away. She rushed to the village with Kanti and Shivani. She had always pushed away the thought of her grandmother leaving one day as she could not imagine a life without her *Nanoo*. She was devastated. Kanti stayed for a week. Her parents and brothers came from Kanpur. And when Kailash came to offer his condolences, she could not stop herself and cried her heart out. He knew how close she was to her. He told her and Kanti that he would be in the Haveli for a few days, and they should let him know if they needed anything.

Kanti left for Lucknow. Sharmishtha wanted him to take Shivani with him but Shivani requested to let her stay for a few more days. Sharmishtha's parents left for Kanpur and were supposed to come back after a week. Kanti wanted her to go to Lucknow and come back again, but there were some matters related to the lands and the house that she had to see to, as her grandmother had left most of her money and assets to Shivani and her. Her mother was a little miffed, because though *Nanoo* had left some of her jewellery to her, she did not leave her any other assets. She had also left the *Phulwari* to Sharmishtha.

After a couple of days, Sharmishtha was surprised to see Kailash when he suddenly came to Asanpur.

'I thought you had left for Lucknow?' she asked him.

'I was about to when Suchitra said she was coming to the Haveli for some time. In any case, I will leave after a day or two as I have some very important cases to attend. I have come to take you to the Haveli. It would do you good to have a change of scene for some time. You can come back when your parents arrive from Kanpur. It's only a matter of three-four days. Please don't refuse.'

On his insistence, Sharmishtha agreed to go to the Haveli. But she decided to send Shivani with Kailash first, as the atmosphere in the house was not very conducive for her. Sharmishtha had to stay back for a day before she could go to the Haveli. The next day she stopped at the post office en route to send a wire to Kanti to come and take Shivani back to Lucknow.

Upon reaching the Haveli, Sharmishtha found Suchitra detached when she went to meet her. Suchitra was resting in her bed and her companion Chanda was fussing over her as always. She enquired about Sharmishtha's grandmother but sounded very formal and distant. Sharmishtha did not get very positive vibes from Chanda too. She immediately regretted coming to the Haveli. There was definitely something off about Suchitra. She looked paler and thinner than before. But Sharmishtha was relieved that Kanti was coming to take Shivani back. She decided to make an excuse and go back to Asanpur, once Shivani left with Kanti for Lucknow as she found the atmosphere in the Haveli strained.

Kanti arrived and Sharmishtha cajoled and persuaded Shivani to go back with her father as it was not a good thing to miss her studies. Moreover, she could go for some excursion with her friends and invite them home, to show them her new books and dolls. She warmed up to the idea, her little girl, her lifeline, and agreed to go back on the condition that Sharmishtha would come back home at the earliest.

Kanti had to leave the same day he'd arrived, as there was a meeting with the Vice Chancellor of the university. Sharmishtha felt heartbroken when they left, but at the same time, relieved, thinking Shivani would be more comfortable in her own house, and she did not want anyone to notice that Kailash was extra attentive to her. She was feeling some animosity coming from Chanda, who she'd always found to be shrewd and interfering. She never let a moment pass without showing her proprietary rights over Suchitra.

Sharmishtha came to her room after seeing them off and tried distracting herself with a book. It was then that Rani, Chanda's daughter came to the room bearing a note from Kailash. Sharmishtha was a little worried. She did not want an already uncomfortable atmosphere to get worse. She opened the envelope taking a short note out. It read that Kailash wanted to meet her at their usual place. But why did Kailash want to meet her? He did not give any such indication when he was seeing Shivani and Kanti off. In fact, he had gone straight to his study to prepare for his case as he had said, excusing himself.

'I guess I will have to go and find out what is so urgent that he wants to see me about,' she thought and walked to the writing table. She did not want the note to land in the wrong hands. Somehow, she had a feeling that Chanda came to her room sometimes, when she was not there. She had seen her coming out of her room once but had let it go. She had accidentally discovered a secret nook in the writing table during her last stay in the room. She hid the note there, hoping no one else knew about the hiding place and waited for some time. The clouds were building up and it looked like a storm was on its way. She picked up her shawl and went down the stairs towards the front door, making sure no one was looking.

CHAPTER 33

PRESENT DAY

I got up with a start. In spite of the chill in the room I found myself perspiring. But it was the deep pain in my heart that made me immobile. I had never felt such strong emotions. The dream was as vivid as the previous one. Were these dreams? They did not feel like dreams. After some time, I got up to close the window. I felt heaviness; as if I had left someone behind, left that small girl somewhere and she needed me. And when my mind became clearer, I remembered the face of the girl. It was the same girl I had seen in the photograph. Why was my mind conjuring up these scenes? What was my connection to them? I decided not to wait any longer. It was time I asked mother.

When I woke up, the sun was high in the sky and the rays were filtering through the gaps in the shutters. I lay there for some time and then the dream came back to me. I looked at my nightstand for the photograph that I had kept the previous night, before falling asleep. I did not find it. I pulled back the duvet and looked on the bed and under the bed lest it had fallen off. It was not there. I checked the armoire, though I was certain that I did not keep it there. After searching my room for five minutes I charged downstairs. Someone had taken it. I was sure of it. I was suddenly filled with anger. I did not know why but I felt that no one had the right to take it. Kamla saw me and hurried towards me.

'*Didi*! I was coming to wake you up. *Dadi* is running fever and I think it's very high.'

'But she was alright last night. Since when has she been running a fever?' I asked, my anger replaced with concern.

'Probably, since last night,' she said.

Mother was running a fever. I checked her. Her blood pressure was on the higher side again.

'Get me some water. I will have to make her take her blood pressure pill and then administer a cold compress. Send Mahesh to Lalgarh to fetch the doctor.'

I lifted her gently and tried waking her up. She nodded feebly and swallowed the pill. By the time the doctor came, her fever had come down a bit due to the cold compress. He prescribed some tests and told me that he would send someone to collect the samples. We took turns sitting by her side. And after a bath and some breakfast that *Chachi* insisted on, I sent a note to Anand telling him about mother's sickness. Mahesh went to drop the doctor and brought his nursing assistant who collected the samples. I told him to drop the note at the Haveli.

Anand came to look mother up. He offered to get a nurse from Lucknow which I declined. I was sure that she would feel better in a day or two. He left after some time, but before he left he told me that he would send his car to fetch Jason the next day. In the course of the events, I had almost forgotten that Jason was reaching the next day. I thanked him and he left, promising me he would drop in again.

It was sometime in the evening. I had made mother eat some vegetable soup, given her the meds, and she had dozed off. I was sitting next to her reading a book when she jerked and mumbled something. I got a start, and kept a hand on hers to calm her down. Her mumbling grew a little louder and she kept thrashing her head. I gently called her name and tried waking her up. She opened her eyes, and when she looked at me, she shrank and started mumbling again. She tried getting up from her bed. Kamla and *Chachi* came to the room hearing the commotion. *Chachi* sat next to her and cradled her head and said some soothing words. After some time, mother stopped mumbling and thrashing and dozed off again.

'*Chachi*, why did she look at me as if she was scared? And what was she mumbling? Could you make out anything?' I asked.

Chachi looked at Kamla and a look passed between them.

'I think she was dreaming of her mother. She was calling out for her,' *Chachi* said.

'Her mother? But why did she look at me that way?'

'I think her mind was foggy with sleep. It must have been the effect of the dream *Bitia*. It has got nothing to do with you,' she said.

I was not convinced with her response. The look that had passed between the mother and daughter indicated that they were not telling me everything. I felt a little angry and frustrated but I decided not to press them. *Chachi* insisted on sleeping in mother's room that night.

'I know how to keep her calm and comfortable. You get a good night's sleep and if there is something I will wake you up,' she insisted.

Chachi and Kamla had been looking after mother for a long time, and I did not want them to think that I had a bigger right over her, by the virtue of being her daughter. I told her that I would relieve her in the early hours of the morning so she could get some sleep.

It was only when I switched off the light in the room that I thought of the photograph. I had completely forgotten to ask Kamla if she had taken it and kept it somewhere. Maybe it was the emotional fatigue, but I slept instantly, and this time my dreams were pleasant. I was with Anand, laughing because he had said something funny, or drowning in his kisses. When the alarm went off, I woke up, still feeling the sensations of the delicious dreams. I went down and found mother and *Chachi* sleeping soundly.

When mother got up, she was feeling much better. Her fever was gone but she looked very tired. She smiled at me and asked if I had got some rest. By afternoon, she could eat a little *khichdi* and talk a little. The tests were still awaited and I decided to take a call on whether she needed to go to Lucknow immediately or we could wait a little, after I saw the test results. I had to stay in the village a little longer as Jason was coming, and I had to find out the cause for my dreams and experiences.

When Anand came in the late afternoon, he asked if I could join him and Jason over a glass of wine and a quick bite.

'You have to meet Jason as it is,' he reasoned.

I told *Chachi* that I had to go to Haveli to meet my colleague and would be back by ten or so. He was not only my colleague but my guest also and it would be rude if I did not receive him, when he arrived at the Haveli. She told me not to worry. She would make mother understand.

'By the way Kamla, did you take an old photograph from my room?' I asked.

She exchanged a quick glance with her mother. 'No *Didi*, I didn't,' she clearly looked uncomfortable.

I was a little flummoxed. Kamla was a very sincere and sweet girl. She loved me a lot and looked up to me. She had no reason to lie to me, yet I knew that she had. I decided not to press her and went to my room to dress up. It was already seven and Jason would be arriving at the Haveli in the next half an hour. The thought of meeting Jason filled me with relief. At last I could talk to him about all this. But I was upset for losing the photograph. A lot had depended upon it. I'd wanted to show it to mother and hoped that she would be able to tell me something about the people in it. But now with the photograph gone, I had no way of finding out. I had to find the photograph. I had started believing that I definitely had some connection with the people in it. I dressed in a black skirt and a V-necked shell-pink blouse. I slipped the pearl studs in my ears and wore black suede stilettos. I applied some make-up and sat in the car that was already waiting for me.

Anand came out to receive me. He kissed me on my cheek. 'You look stunning,' he said. 'Jason is about to reach. He gave me a call before he started. I have made arrangements for drinks on the terrace, though we will shift to the dining room for dinner because it will get chilly outside.'

I felt the same perturbation at the mention of the terrace. The terrace had lost some of its charm and tranquillity for me because of my earlier experiences. In fact, the Haveli had lost some of the romanticism that I had felt for it in the beginning, but it still had a pull strong enough to drag me towards it. Or maybe it was the effect of Anand's presence that made the visits to the Haveli more attractive. But I was definitely not a fan of being on the terrace all by myself. Though, of course, I didn't say anything and just smiled.

'Should we wait for Jason in the drawing room? You said he would be reaching anytime,' I asked.

'Of course! In fact, we hardly used the drawing room, as I always thought you liked to sit on the terrace because of its view. Let me show you some things in the drawing room that are quite old.'

He escorted me inside, and as he took me around the room explaining the furniture and other artefacts, I waited for him to come to the portrait of his grandparents.

'And this of course, is the portrait of my grandparents. It was painted by an artist who earned quite a name for himself in the later years,' he said smiling.

'You resemble him a lot,' I said, staring at the portrait again. I had this feeling that the man in my dreams, though I thought looked like Anand; did not feel like Anand. He felt like him, the man in the portrait.

'Yes I do! Even my mother used to tell me that all the time. I guess I am lucky to have taken after him. My mother always felt happy that I looked like him. She was very attached to her father,' he added.

'So tell me something about your grandmother,' I probed.

'Well! She was in a way a blue blood. Her grandfather was a Baron and had a sizable wealth in the form of money and land. Her father was an officer in British army and he was posted in India. He had participated in the First World War with his battalion. But he had to take premature retirement as he had suffered an injury. He fell in love with this Indian girl who was the daughter of a *Taluqdar* and had studied in Oxford. It was love at first sight. So you see, my grandmother was an 'Anglo-Indian' as the mixed breeds were called then. And then, as history would repeat itself, my grandmother fell in love with this dashing and handsome man, who was the adoptive son of Nandan Mathur, a close friend of her father's. All the three sets of parents loved this match. Now you would ask why my grandfather was adopted when his real parents were alive and kicking. So, my great grandfather who was again a successful businessman, doted on his sister. And when he came to know that she could not conceive, he asked her to adopt his son, thinking that they would get many more children as was the custom in those days. But as luck would have it, my great grandmother could not conceive for some reason, and both the families ended up having my grandfather as the only child between them.

'So there you are. Now you know about my grandparents,' he said, flashing his beautiful smile.

'So your grandparents fell in love and it was a love marriage?' I asked.

'Yes! It was something like that. Though, my mother always said that it was my grandmother, who had fallen head over heels in love with my grandfather. And when they happened to go to England for studies at the same time, they bonded. And when the family came to know, they wanted them to get married. So you see, I have my roots in the country you live.' His smile spoke volumes but I wanted to ask him more. As I was about to ask him another question, there was a knock at the door and Peter came informing that the guest *Saheb* had arrived. We both hurried to receive Jason and my questions were left unanswered.

I hugged Jason the moment he got off the car and introduced him to Anand.

'You look good. The village air suits you,' he said in his good-naturedly way.

'I am so glad you could come to India,' I said.

'Would you like to see your room first and freshen up?' Anand asked him.

'That would be wonderful,' he said looking at me. He was probably wondering about Anand and the Haveli.

'I would leave you two to it and send Peter to assist Mr Buckley.'

'Please call me Jason.'

'Jason! You will be staying here in the Haveli with Anand. My house in the village is not... let's say, suitable for your accommodation. Anand has insisted that you should stay with him. Moreover, I thought you would like to experience a stay in an old Haveli. I hope you don't mind,' I said.

'I would have stayed anywhere with you and loved it. But this is absolutely fine. All that matters is that I am here and I already love your country,' he said.

'Alright! Then see your room and we will catch up in a little while.'

'Oh my God! This is absolutely breathtaking!' Jason exclaimed as he looked down the river from the terrace. 'What an amazing place you have here Anand!'

Both the men took to each other and Jason sat listening as Anand narrated the origin of the Haveli. Though I kept a keen ear to what they were talking, and participated in the conversation, my nerves were a little frayed, and in order to feel at ease I kept sipping wine. My gaze kept going to the spot where I had had that experience. We shifted to the dining room for dinner and I felt quite relieved. There was a chill in the air because it kept drizzling intermittently, or probably because of the river being so close, but I felt a different kind of a chill down my spine. So I felt better in the cosy warmth of the dining room. The cook had excelled himself, having prepared a four course dinner. I was feeling a bit tipsy after having four glasses of wine. So when we went to the drawing room for a night cap, I excused myself to go to the powder room. Anand offered to walk me, which I declined feeling a bit embarrassed that my inebriated state was that obvious. Jason too looked at me with slight concern, but I moved with confidence and made an exit as swiftly as I could.

Since all the bedrooms and bathrooms were on the first floor, there was a powder room at the end of the lobby, on the ground floor, which I was aware of. I freshened up and looked at myself in the mirror. My cheeks were a little flushed and my locks had come loose. I smiled as I remembered Anand's admiring gaze at me throughout the evening.

I exited the powder room and closed the door behind me and started to walk towards the drawing room. There was no one in the lobby as the staff was probably busy winding up in the kitchen and preparing the beds. There was a beautiful flower arrangement on the console table, made with fresh flowers from the garden. I took a moment to admire its beauty but when I looked ahead I went numb. My whole body went rigid. I felt as if I had no life left in my limbs. About five meters from where I was standing, was the mistress of the house looking at me directly. She was dressed in the same attire as in the portrait. There was a haze around her but I could see her face clearly. I did not know how long the vision lasted; as far as I was concerned it was probably an eternity. But as I looked at her I noticed a sadness in her eyes and I felt it in my heart, and then my heart was filled with a sense of regret. I was experiencing all these emotions without knowing the reason behind them. And then it was over. In an instant she was gone. I was rooted to the spot but gradually I felt my body loosening up and my senses coming back to me. There was a feeling of detached calm that descended upon me. Suddenly, I no longer felt fear or unease. It was as if I had just woken up from a dream. I quietly walked back to the drawing room.

'Anand, I am not feeling too well. Sorry Jason, I need to go home.'

'You look pale. What happened?' Both the men were alarmed.

'Nothing! I think I am coming down with something. I will see you in the morning Jason!' I managed a feeble smile.

'Don't worry about it. Have a good rest,' he said looking concerned.

'Jason! Please excuse me. I will drop Aparna home,' Anand said.

'No! Please don't. Mahesh is here and it's not that I have to travel miles. Please be with Jason.'

'Are you sure?'

'Yes! I am sure.'

'Take good rest sweetheart. I will be worried about you. Can I drop in the morning to check on you?' Anand asked while opening the door for me.

'I will send you a message. Don't worry. I will be alright after a good night's rest.'

I bid both of them good night and sat in the car. As the car moved forward I looked back at the bay windows of the bedrooms on the first floor. But there was nothing there but darkness.

Upon reaching home, I asked about mother, and *Chachi* told me that she had felt restless when she was told that I had gone to the Haveli, so *Chachi* had made her take a sleeping pill that the doctor had prescribed and now she was asleep.

'You look a little pale *Bitia*. Is everything alright?'

'I am fine *Chachi*. Just a little tired.'

'I will get you some hot milk. That will make you sleep better. Don't worry about *Jiji*. I will sleep in her room,' she said.

'No thank you *Chachi*. I will just carry some water and go to bed.'

Back in my room, all by myself, brought back the vivid memory of the encounter that I had with the mistress of the Haveli. On previous occasions, I had felt her presence and seen her fleetingly, but today, she had been right in front of me, looking at me. Why was I experiencing her presence? What was my connection to her? Was she making her presence felt only to me or had other people also seen her? Whom could I ask?

I did not think that Anand had gone through any such experience. He had talked about her very normally, as anyone would do about their grandparents. And then, there were the dreams and the photograph with the mysterious woman and the girl child. What was this all about? Why and how did I fall in the river? And why was I calling the name of Anand's grandfather when they'd dragged me out? Why did I feel that I had to go to the *Phulwari* after reading the note?

All these questions whirred in my mind and I felt a headache coming. I washed my face with cold water, changed into my pyjamas, and went downstairs to take a sleeping pill from mother's prescription. Everyone was asleep, so I tiptoed to the nightstand and brought the whole packet of meds to my room. I took one pill and popped it in with water. I needed to sleep so I could have a clear mind the next day. I had never taken a pill after wine, but the buzz of the wine was long gone, and I desperately needed to dull my mind. I threw the window open for some fresh air and lay down, waiting for the pill to take its effect.

She read the note and put it in the small cavity of the drawer that she had found accidently during her previous visit. Much as she wanted to meet him, she felt apprehensive about it. What if someone saw them meeting clandestinely? She did not want to destroy their marriages as they both had responsibilities towards their families. Though she desperately wanted him to hold her because if there was anyone who could fill the void in her heart at this time, it was him, only him. But she would tell him that they should not meet like this anymore. She would also ask him to make her travel arrangements and she should go back home, to be with her family, who needed her. She knew he was upset ever since he had come to know about his daughter. She understood that he could not accept the fact that his daughter was carrying someone else's name, not his. But this was how it was going to be. They could not do anything but follow the path destiny had devised for them. The hour was drawing close. She wrapped the shawl around her shoulders and slipped out of the house from the front door. Even if someone saw her, it would be thought that she was going out for some fresh air. She hurried around the Haveli through the side lawns towards the grove on the river bank, where they had met earlier. The sky was getting darker with clouds and it wouldn't be long before the rains started. She quickened her steps. The path was slippery and wet because of last night's rain. She walked carefully, avoiding the parapet because the soil had become loose and anyone could slip from there, plunging directly into the foaming river. The wind picked up and the clouds burst. She stood under the neem tree to save herself from the rain. He should be here any minute, and as the thought crossed her mind, she felt hands on her shoulders. Finally he was here. She let out a sigh of relief.

She plunged into the darkness that was getting denser by the minute. She closed her eyes. It was better this way. It was best to give in to this nothingness. Her mind felt at peace. The journey had to end here. It was a tiring one. And then a voice came from afar through the darkness calling her name. She just has to ignore it. She has to rest. She is tired.

The first thing I saw was Anand sitting in the chair with his eyes upon me.

'You are awake!' he said taking my hand in his and looking at me with such pure love that my heart swelled.

'You gave us all such a scare.' I followed the voice and saw Jason at the other side of the bed. For a few moments I felt happy and relieved to see them smiling and looking at me with relief apparent on their faces, but then I slowly realised that I was in my room.

'What happened? What are you both doing here?'

'You need to rest now. We will fill you in later,' Anand said.'Here, let me give you some sweetened milk. It would make you feel better.'

'Anand please tell me what happened. I can't rest till you both tell me. Don't treat me like a child.' I was getting impatient and it showed in my tone.

'Told you! She does breathe fire at times,' Jason said smiling.

'Alright! Just start sipping this and we will tell you everything.' Anand offered me a mug of hot milk.

'What time is it?'

'It's four thirty in the morning.'

'Where is *Amma*? Is she alright?' My mind filled with dread.

'She is fine. Everyone is fine. Just stay calm. It is you we are here for. Apparently when you came back from the Haveli, you went to sleep in your room. *Chachi* said that she offered you a glass of milk but you declined and she saw you going to your room. She secured the bolts on the main door and went to bed. It was around one thirty that she got up to go to the washroom and found the main door ajar. First she thought that some thief had entered the house, then fearing he might have gone to your room, she took a *lathi* and went to check on you. But on reaching there she found the room empty. She ran down and checked the washroom. You were not there either. She woke Kamla and your mother up and went on to wake Mahesh up. Your mother became hysterical and kept crying throughout. Their first bet was to go to the Haveli assuming you had gone there. They all piled up in the car and came to the Haveli. And we started looking for you. Then as we were still trying to figure out where you could have gone, your mother told us to check the river bank. We all started looking frantically for you up and down the river bank and we found you there, lying unconscious.' Anand was quiet as he finished the narrative.

'God! What is the fascination of going to the river and drowning myself?' I muttered. I always had a fear of water bodies. I could never learn swimming in spite of everyone's best efforts. All this while, Jason was looking at me intently. I felt very tired and just wanted to close my eyes. Anand, as if sensing my mood, held my hand gently.

'I think you should sleep for some time. You have gone through a shock and I think it would be best that you rest. We will figure this whole thing out together. Now that Jason is here we can always find out what had happened and why it happened. Your mother has been given a pill and she is asleep. By the way, did you take a sleeping pill? We found your mother's meds here.'

'Yes! I think I took one,' I said.

He looked at me with a silent question in his eyes.

'It's just that I have not been sleeping very well for the last couple of nights. You know, with mother being unwell and all. So I decided to pop one to get some sleep. It was probably not a good idea, especially after four glasses of wine.'

'It's ok, happens at times. You have been stressed with your mother's illness. We are glad that you are safe and sound. Now go to sleep. We will be here only.'

'No please! Go home and get some rest. You both have not slept for almost the entire night. I wouldn't be able to rest knowing that you are sitting and watching over me. You can bolt the door from outside if you feel I would wander off again,' I protested.

They both looked at each other and then Anand nodded.

'Ok! We will go and get some rest. But we will come to check on you after a few hours. Now close your eyes.'

The knocking at the door jerked me out of my slumber. I lay there confused for a few moments, trying to get my bearings, and then called out for the person to enter.

'*Didi*! It's *Dadi*. She is... I think you better come down.'

I threw the covers and ran downstairs. Mother was running a fever and was thrashing on the bed. She seemed to be murmuring something.

'This started about an hour ago. Initially I thought that she was having a nightmare. But when she did not calm down despite my best efforts, I sent Kamla to inform you,' *Chachi* said.

'I will never forgive you. Never! You took advantage of me... of your own daughter. You will rot in hell.' Mother was muttering.

I looked at *Chachi*. She had this expression on her face as if she knew what this was about.

'*Amma*!' I called out but she kept tossing her head on the pillow.

The fever was not very high but her blood pressure had risen. I had to somehow make her take the medicine for her blood pressure before I could take her to the hospital. I held her hand firmly and called out to her softly. To my surprise she clutched my hand tightly. When a person is having a bad dream it is important to make physical contact and call out their name. It helps most of the time.

'*Amma*! I am here. Don't worry. It's just a dream. Wake up and it will go away.'

I repeated it a few times and then I felt her hand slacken. Her breathing started becoming normal and after several moments she opened her eyes. She looked at me as if she was trying to recognise me.

'Parni! You are alright?' she asked me.

'I am absolutely fine *Amma*. How are you feeling?'

'Parni *Bitia*, we should go from here. It's not safe for you to stay here. I never wanted you to come here. I always kept it that way. But this time I made this mistake of bringing you here but it's still not late. Let us leave this place before any harm comes to you. Please *Bitia* let us go back to Lucknow and you go to England, far away from all this. You will be safe there.'

'*Amma*, I promise we will go back. But first you have to eat something and have your medication.'

After giving her some breakfast and medicine, I had a hot water bath and changed into a shirt and a pair of denims. I wanted to discuss all this with Jason. I was sure that all these incidents had a connection and mother knew what this was all about. Now I realised why I was never brought to the village. Even my father had come up with some excuse when I had asked to accompany him once or twice. Even this time, mother was reluctant but I had insisted. Clearly she was repenting now, and holding herself responsible for whatever was happening to me. Anand and Jason came and were quite relieved to see me up and about and looking my normal self. I told them about mother's frenzied state.

'I think you must discuss everything with Jason. I have to meet with my lawyer who is arriving in the afternoon. I will see you guys in the evening,' Anand said.

I had a feeling he wanted to give me privacy when I talked to Jason about my episodes. He did not want to impose. He knew that seeing the delicate nature of our relationship I probably wouldn't be comfortable discussing my problems in front of him. Moreover, Jason was a professional. He would dig deep and might ask some blunt questions.

When Anand left, we went to our room. I switched the kettle on and started narrating everything to him. He listened to everything without interrupting me. It was only when I'd finished that he started asking.

'Alright, let's start and analyse the incidents in a chronological order as we always do. You said that when you saw the Haveli you felt as if you had already been here. You even remembered the layout. Right?' he asked.

'Yes! But I always attributed it to my childhood memory.'

'And the dreams or the flashes started coming only when you visited the Haveli. You had never dreamt about the Haveli ever before?'

His question made me think. I couldn't recall whether I had dreamt about it before or not. With my mind so replete with the images of the Haveli, it was difficult to think that I had never dreamt about it. And I told him so.

'Okay! Let's just assume for the time being that you didn't dream of any of this before. Now we come to 'the sightings' or 'the presence' that you encountered. Do you think that your mind had conjured this up because you had been thinking of the people in the portrait?'

'I knew you would ask this question. I would have done the same. But there is always a difference between conjuring and experiencing. It's difficult to explain the 'feeling' at the face of logic but I was sure of it. The mind can imagine a particular visual for a few seconds possibly, but to be able to engage all the senses at the same time in creating that experience is difficult. And as for your logic that I was thinking a lot about the people in the portrait, it was actually the man I thought about a lot and then of late my mind has been obsessed with the images of the other woman and the girl in the photograph I told you about. Even my dreams or flashes have been of the man, the woman and the child. I never dreamt of the mistress of the house. Yet, it was her I felt the presence of, and saw in plain sight. And there was this note that I found in the hidden drawer and the image of the *Phulwari* popped into my mind. Another question here, Jason, is why do I keep going to the river? I had always been scared of water bodies but why am I drawn to it now? And there has been a shift in my emotions. Like when I went to the *Phulwari*, I felt happy, as if there were happy memories associated with that place, but when I think about going to the river, my mind is filled with dark and sinister images, that I can't bring clearly to my conscious mind. Also, I am sure that my mother knows something about all this. We left the village and moved to the city when I was three. And after that I was never brought here. Now I know it was intentional. There were excuses all the time. I did not pay much attention to it then but now as I think of it, it sounds significant. Do you think that I have some suppressed memories that are surfacing now?' I asked him.

'As you know, it's possible, but for the memories to be suppressed to the deep unconscious, takes some sort of trauma, and who knows that better than you. But I am having trouble understanding the presence and the sighting of this woman.'

'Jason! You know we have always discussed the possibility of rebirth. What's your take on it now?'

'I have always liked the idea in theory but am a bit skeptical when it comes to believing it.'

'But we discussed it many a time, especially during some of the cases. Remember?'

'Yes I remember the cases and our discussions. Cathy was cheesed off for having to make numerous cups of tea,' he said smiling. 'So you think you have been reborn? But then, as a rebirth of whom?' he asked.

'Certainly not of the woman I saw.'

'Then of the woman in the photograph who resembles you?'

'I really don't know; it could be a coincidence. That's what we have to find out and I need your help with that.' I looked at him steadily.

'I am here to help... wait you don't mean what I think you mean?'

'Yes! Exactly!' I said.

'No! You know I have not done that and don't think I am ready for that.'

'Jason listen, you are ready. You have helped me out many a time and I saw you absorb everything. You can do it.'

'I don't know. I certainly don't want you to be my guinea pig,' he said emphatically.

'You promised to help and this is the only way to find out.'

'There is one more way,' he said.

'And that is?'

'You have to ask your mother. As you said, she seems to know something about this whole thing. I think it's time you asked her.'

'And if I still want to go through regression would you help me?'

He looked at me with a defeated expression. 'Okay! I will.'

I was thoughtful. I did not know whether mother would tell me whatever I wanted to know without getting agitated. I had to tread carefully. I did not want to cause a situation that would be bad for her health.

'When should I talk to her then?' I asked Jason.

'In my opinion, as soon as possible, because I think even she is suffering from some sort of worry and she needs closure too. That would at least put her mind to rest. Secrets are not easy to carry. And who knows for how long she has been carrying this one.'

I agreed with him. It was important for her to share whatever burden she was carrying. At least once I knew what was troubling her; I would be able to help her. I took a deep breath and decided to do that.

'I would have liked you to be with me but I don't know whether she would feel comfortable,' I said to Jason.

'I can wait here in the room or can go to the Haveli. I think it's a family matter and no outsider should be there. It's up to you how much you would like to share with me later.'

I nodded. 'I think you go to the Haveli then. I will tell Mahesh to drop you.'

'Thank you! But I would like to take a stroll. I have been eating a lot and want to breathe some fresh air. Send for me and Anand whenever you are ready to talk.'

The clouds were building and I once again offered Jason the car, but he was adamant on walking. So I gave him an old umbrella that Kamla found in the store.

293

CHAPTER 34

I saw Jason off. I went to mother's room and was relieved to see her sitting and looking better.

'Come Parni! Sit with me. Will you?' she said smiling faintly.

I touched her forehead. There was no fever and her blood pressure was alright. I looked at her, deciding how to start when she surprised me.

'*Bitia*, there is something that I have to tell you. All these years I kept it buried in my heart. I thought I was saving you from the curse that I had to live with. I kept you away from this place because I had this fear that you will remember things that were long forgotten. We thought we had put an end to it all when we moved to Lucknow. And it worked. But as they say, things always come back full circle. I was very apprehensive when you decided to come here. But then I thought that I had always refused to bring you here and it would be for the last time that you would see your father's ancestral house. Now I realise that I was not thinking straight. How could I keep you from the lure of the Haveli? It was beckoning you since the day you arrived here. I could not keep you away from it no matter how hard I tried.'

She paused as if organising her thoughts. *Chachi* and Kamla had come and sat down quietly.

'The dreams started when Chandu told me about the Haveli being sold. It was like someone had thrown a pebble in the still waters. I had never liked to talk about it and had buried it somewhere deep in my mind. So when Chandu told me that it was about to be sold at the same time I was going to the village, I thought about postponing my visit to the village. But Ram Charan had already taken the token amount from the buyers and had given his word, so I was left with no other choice but to go. So the Haveli and everything else that was connected with it, started crowding my mind and then the dreams began. Urmila and Kamla knew that I had been having some dreams of late, but I had told them not to tell you anything. You used to ask me about your grandmother, my mother. But I did not tell you much about her except that she had passed away when I was young, and it was mainly my father and grandmother who'd brought me up.

'Chanda, my mother and your grandmother, was the companion of Suchitra, Barrister *Saheb's* wife. But she was much more than that. She was like a sister and a bosom friend of hers, who she fondly called *Missi Baba*. Suchitra depended completely on my mother for everything. My grandfather was a Sepoy in the same battalion where Suchitra's father, Capt Alcott Langley was an officer. During the First World War, their battalion was sent to France and it was there, that my grandfather saved the life of Capt Langley, during one of the battles. They were outnumbered by the enemy and hiding in a trench where a grenade exploded and Capt Langley got badly injured. My grandfather carried him on his shoulders for two miles to a hospital, ignoring his own injuries. Capt Langley recovered but my grandfather succumbed to his injuries. Capt Langley's leg could not come back to its proper shape and he took an early retirement on the behest of his father. His father was a baron and wanted him to come back to England and look after the estate. Capt *Saheb* brought my grandfather's wife and ten-year-old daughter to his house as my grandfather's family refused to keep them in the village. My grandmother and my mother were not only given shelter, but also treated as family by Capt *Saheb* and his wife. Suchitra was four years younger than my mother, but she found a companion in her, and Capt *Saheb* and his wife thought it only best that their daughter had someone as loyal and doting as my mother, as her companion. So my mother spent all her time looking after Suchitra. She picked up the language as she was young and had a sharp mind. So it became even easier for Suchitra to depend more and more on my mother.

'Though my mother devoted lot of her time to Suchitra, she did love my father and me in the beginning. She divided her time between her family and her charge. But things changed drastically when Suchitra conceived. She had a weak disposition so she had a difficult pregnancy, and when her daughter was born my mother almost became her foster mother. Initially, my father accepted things the way they were because he had huge respect for Barrister *Saheb* and his wife, but as the months rolled by and my mother became more and more occupied with Suchitra's pregnancy, totally ignoring me, his patience started wearing thin. He could see that no matter how much love or attention he gave me, I still needed my mother. He suffered major losses with his crops when he stayed in the city during the first few years, because he had this doubt that my mother would not look after me properly and I would be neglected. But it was becoming more and more difficult as he was a farmer at heart and he loved his land. To spend his time sitting at home doing nothing, while he had a responsibility towards his land and house, made him very restless. I stayed with my mother at Barrister *Saheb's* house and only visited the village when they came to stay in the Haveli. My father stayed in the village and he kept coming to the city often to meet me.

'So, when after few months, my mother became excessively busy with her, she asked my father to take me to the village. Though I was very young at that time, but I must have missed her a lot because no child is ever happy without a mother. But as I was young and my father and grandmother doted on me, I soon got used to living with them. But this incident created a big chasm between my parents. Once I fell sick and my father sent a letter to my mother asking her to come to the village as I needed her. But she sent a letter saying that she could not leave Suchitra as she was on bed rest. That upset my father a lot, and when they met he told her that she did not deserve to have a child or even a family. She should not have got married. She had not only ruined his life but was depriving their child from motherly love and care.

'So thereafter, I got to see my mother mostly when she came to the village with the Mathur clan. My father tried taking me to the city as often as he could, but gradually visits to the city reduced as he got busy looking after his land, and I think, he only thought it best that I not be subjected to mother's uncaring and detached attitude towards us.

'Though I loved my father immensely as he was always there for me, I craved for my mother's love. The more distant she became, the more my craving intensified. Love is the most important emotion, almost a primary need. It's like a vine; it needs a little water and sun to prosper, as long as it gets a tree trunk or any support to wrap itself around. But it withers fast if it's taken off support and thrown on the ground.

'But my father's attempts at making her see reason were in vain. My mother found an easy way to avoid the conflict and she totally stopped coming to the house whenever they came to the Haveli, which, in any case, was not very often. She would justify her devotion by saying that she owed her and her mother's lives to Suchitra's parents. Moreover, Suchitra was like her sister and she couldn't ditch her in her hour of need.

'So time went by, and when I turned six, the Mathur family came to the Haveli, on one of their visits. My happiness knew no bounds when mother called me to the Haveli and gave me new clothes and a doll. Also, she started calling me to the Haveli often, and though after a few hours she would send me back home, I found this new arrangement exhilarating. During such visits to the Haveli I picked fragments of whispered conversation of the servants, that there was some tension between Barrister *Saheb* and *Mem Saheb*. One such day, my mother took me upstairs and asked me to wait in the sitting room while she went to the bedroom to attend to Suchitra. I was sitting when this small girl came and smiled shyly at me. She was a very pretty girl with an alabaster complexion and dark brown eyes. Later I understood that she had taken her mother's complexion and her father's intense eyes. She was wearing a pale pink frock with lace, and her hair was gathered in a ponytail. She looked like the doll my mother had got me from Lucknow.

'My name is Shailja. But I am called Shelly. What's your name?' she asked me in English. I was not very fluent in English but my mother had taught me some basic sentences. I was going to a school in the village where even the English alphabets were taught much later. But I knew who she was because my mother talked about little else but Suchitra and her daughter.'

'My name is Rani,' I replied in English, feeling proud of myself.

'Soon we were chatting. Her Hindi was not as fluent as her English, but language is never a barrier between two people who want to understand each other. Though she was two years younger than me, she talked perfectly well. She had a colourful storybook which was in English and I only knew the English alphabets that my father was teaching me. I could not read anything but it had lots of colourful pictures of beautiful princess and fairies and we both were soon absorbed in the book. Our blissful vocation was broken by some hysterical sobbing. Shelly looked at me with her beautiful dark eyes and I noticed a sadness there. I was a bit shaken as I did not know who was sobbing; my mother or Suchitra. But it subsided as soon as it had arisen.

And then Shelly said, 'That's mummy.'

'I was a little intrigued. It was not that I had not heard a woman crying before. I had often heard my mother cry whenever there was a fight between my parents. But then I'd always associated the occupants of the Haveli with a fairytale-like existence. They were not normal people, but from another world. They were beautiful and rich and led a dream-like existence. They were as beautiful and out of reach as were the glossy pictures in Shelly's book. At least that was the impression I had gathered from my mother's description, and had found it accurate after seeing Suchitra and Barrister *Saheb*. They were so beautiful and different from the people of the village, as if they had walked out of another world.

'So the sobbing cast a shadow on the perfect picture that was in my mind. As far as I was concerned, they had all the happiness in the world. Their world was made of laughter and gaiety. There was no place for sorrow. Before I could think more about it, my mother came out and picked Shelly up and asked me to follow her downstairs. She took us both to the garden and gave some sweets to Shelly and me.

'Why is mum crying?' Shelly asked

'It's nothing sweetheart. She is not feeling very bright. She will be alright soon. Now let's get you some flowers to make a posy for your mum,' my mother replied in perfect English.

'I noticed that my mother was trying to keep a cheerful face but she was upset from within. At that time I could not understand emotions, but in later years, I realised that she could never bear the tiniest wrinkle on Suchitra's perfect life. But things don't work the way we mortals want them to work. There are so many different outcomes of a given situation that one does not have any control over. And when it comes to matters of the heart, nothing can be predicted or controlled. The yearning of the soul is irreplaceable.'

Mother stopped, and there was a silence that hung heavily. It seemed like she was trying to piece the story together. It was not only the story of Kailash and Suchitra, it was her story too. She had become a vital part of it without directly being a part of it. It's so strange how one becomes entangled in someone else's story without ever playing an active role in it. And just when I thought of letting her rest, she spoke.

'After that day, my mother started calling me to the Haveli almost every day. I soon came to know that Shelly had taken a liking to me, and had asked about me repeatedly. Her mother then requested mother to bring me to the Haveli so I could keep Shelly company. I didn't mind it at all. I too liked Shelly a lot. She was a kind hearted and sweet girl. And thus we became very good friends. She shared her chocolates and her picture books with me. We played hide and seek in the garden and any such games which are so typical of childhood.

'Those were happy days for me. Not only was my mother with

me but I had also found a good friend in Shelly. I felt protective and responsible towards her, thinking that it was my duty to act like that since I was a couple of years older. At times I felt that though Shelly's parents doted on her, she must have felt a bit lonely because whenever the Mathurs visited the Haveli, it was basically to entertain their friends. There would be hunting trips, picnics, boating and soirees in the gardens. The staff of the Haveli would get busy, right from preparing the rooms and cooking English and Indian delicacies. The tea, along with refreshment would be laid in the gardens and the gentlemen and ladies would play Croquet. On such occasions, my mother would ask me to wait in the kitchen till Shelly was ready to come and play with me. But I slipped out twice or thrice to take a look at all those good looking people who dressed very nicely and fashionably, and looked from another world.

'On one such occasion as I was trying to peek at the guests from behind a tree in the garden, I felt someone walk on me from behind. I turned and saw Barrister *Saheb* standing there. Though I was a child and it would be a long time before I would be able to define masculine beauty, I was awestruck by his persona. In the later years, as I would grow into a young woman I would understand that no woman could have helped falling in love with him. He had something beyond good looks. He had this solidity about himself, this promise that once he took you under his wing he would not let any harm come to you. My young mind probably could not decipher this impression about him that time, but instead of being frightened I felt secure with him. He was wearing his riding suit, and then I remembered mother mentioning that he and his friends had gone riding for *shikar*. I felt as comfortable as I would have felt with my father, yet I felt some sort of awe.

'So you are Chanda's daughter? Aren't you?' he asked in Hindi.

'I nodded, not finding my voice.

'Where is Shelly? She is not with you? She is very fond of you,' he said smiling. His smile was genuine and full of warmth.

'I was again tongue-tied.

'Do you like to watch this game? Come and watch it properly. I will send for Shelly and you both can watch and play too if you want.'

'And though I was a bit scared that my mother would scold me for being there, I was quite happy to get a chance to see those people and Suchitra up-close. She was sitting under the shade of a huge neem tree. She was wearing a white frock with light blue and baby pink motifs. Her hair was tied in a Chignon and she looked as fragile as a doll. I had heard my mother complaining that she was a poor eater and she was worried that she had lost more weight recently. Barrister *Saheb* kissed his wife on the cheek. She smiled at me when he said something to her. And then I noticed that there was a kind of detached air about her. She was there, but not really there. Of course, I could not understand the feeling at that time, but later as events unfolded and I thought of them in the later years, I could define and understand the sentiment or feeling I had felt looking at her.

'Her detached expression and somewhat sad smile had stayed with me. It probably remained etched in my memory because her demeanour that day was in sharp contrast to what I had conjured her to be; a person with infinite happiness. As I was looking at the well-dressed, pretty ladies, laughing musically, sipping their lemonade and conversing with their husbands and each other, Barrister *Saheb* walked past me ruffling my hair.

'I will ask your mother to bring Shelly down and then you both can have a go at Croquet.' And with that he was gone.

'An excited Shelly with my mother with a somewhat apprehensive look, joined me soon. We were both given lemonade by Gopal *Kaka*, Chandu's father, who used to double as a waiter. One of the gentlemen walked towards us and offered to teach us Croquet. We both were soon absorbed in the game but I would steal a glance in Suchitra's direction intermittently. She seemed in a kind of trance. After a while, Barrister *Saheb* joined the gathering. He looked like a prince from the glossy pages of the book Shelly had shown to me. He was wearing a white shirt that brought out his milk chocolate complexion. His thick and wavy hair was combed back showing his broad forehead. He was wearing a pair of beige trousers, and camel coloured shoes. He looked strong and solid, whereas his wife looked delicate and fragile. Looking at him I suddenly had this notion that I would marry a man who looked like him. I guess girls mature faster than boys, and they start dreaming of their prince charming at an early age, thanks to all those stories of brave princes who always saved the day and their lady love with their bravery and valour. Also, in our day, girls matured faster as they were given more responsibilities at an early age.

'So few months went by and I looked forward to the Mathur clan visiting the Haveli and getting a chance to meet Shelly. And then, I got the news that they were coming to the Haveli. I was in a blissful state when the car came to pick me up and thus Shelly and I were reunited once again.

'One such day when I went to the Haveli, Shelly asked me to play hide and seek inside the Haveli as it had started raining and we were not allowed to play outside. In this entire duration, I had rarely seen Barrister *Saheb* or Suchitra. I guess they kept themselves busy with their interests. Whatever it was that kept Suchitra busy, I did not know but she kept my mother very busy and most of the time, I would go back home without having spent any time with her. But, I did not mind my mother's absence much, because now I had a friend and I looked forward to be with her. So as I was saying, we decided to play hide and seek inside the Haveli and I was going looking around in the obvious places where Shelly could hide. I couldn't find her. My mother had designated the areas we were supposed to use for playing hide and seek and we always stuck to that, but this time I couldn't find Shelly and I started getting a bit cross with her. And then it struck me that she might have gone to her mother's room because at times, Shelly defied everyone and did what she wanted to do. She probably knew that she could break rules as she was the daughter and heiress of the family. So with much trepidation, I started climbing the staircase that led to the first floor where the master bedroom and Shelly's bedroom were situated. All this while I was worried that my mother would not like me to break rules and she would be angry if she saw me going towards the master bedroom. But I continued moving and entered the sitting room, and softly called out for Shelly. I checked behind the curtains, the elegant love seats and Queen Ann chairs but Shelly was not there. I did not have a choice but to return because as much as I wanted to enter the bedroom and then go to the big terrace to look for Shelly, I couldn't dare to, because that part of the Haveli was forbidden for me and I knew that my mother would be furious if I were to be found there. I accepted defeat inwardly and made up my mind of giving a mouthful to Shelly as she had cheated in order to win the game. As I turned to exit the sitting room, I heard raised voices and they seemed closer. I quickly hid behind the curtains and stood there motionless.

'Why are you doing this to me?' I heard Suchitra's voice.

'I am doing nothing to you. I don't know what's come over you. I thought you liked Mishthi and her family. At least that is what it looked like whenever they came home to visit us in Lucknow. But if you don't want them to come here, I will inform them today itself.'

'With that, the door opened and I could hear heavy footsteps going towards the staircase. But as the door opened I heard Suchitra sobbing and someone whispering, I knew that it was my mother who was saying something to her in a soothing voice. I thought it best to come out of hiding and go downstairs and wait in the kitchen for my father to come fetch me. Thomas *Kaka* offered me a piece of cake and soon I forgot about Shelly. The kitchen was the most cheerful and cosy place and I loved being there. Thomas *Kaka*, who was the cook, pampered me and always gave me something nice to eat. There were two more people to help him and he always said something funny about them that made me laugh. Anyway, after a little while Shelly came and all my anger evaporated as it looked like she had been crying. My mother soon entered the kitchen and asked me to go to Shelly's room till she brought her lunch.

'I soon forgot about the incident and went about enjoying my time with Shelly and the proximity of my mother, no matter how distant it was. But the blissful state of my mother's congeniality was short-lived. She looked edgy and short tempered. And then I learned that some guests were coming and she was going to be even busier. Next day, when I went to the Haveli, I found that the guests my mother had talked about had arrived as Shelly was sitting with a girl in the garden, whose back was towards me and the girl was reading a story to her from a book. I stopped in my tracks. I felt a wave of envy as I did not want to share Shelly with anyone else. As if on cue, Shelly looked up from the book and in her most sweet and innocent manner, called out for me. The girl whose back was towards me turned her head and I saw that she was at least four years older than me, but it was her face that captivated me. She was probably the prettiest girl I had ever seen. She had a beautiful face with big watery eyes that made you forget everything. But it was her smile that made her look angelic. As Shelly introduced me to her, she smiled and asked me to join them. Her name was Shivani. Shelly told me that Shivani was the daughter of Sharmishtha aunt and Kanti uncle, who were family friends and lived in Lucknow. The envy that I had felt for her, evaporated, as she took to me as if she had known me all her life. She was more mature than her age and had the most easy manner.

'Soon, we were running around chasing butterflies and laughing, and I was having the time of my life when I heard someone call Shivani. When I looked back to see the caller, I was going to be awestruck for the second time that day. There was this woman who was walking towards us smiling, and for a moment I felt that some goddess from one of those pictures in our *Pooja* room had materialised. I tell you; never ever had I seen such beauty in all of my life. Her beauty was pure, yet ravishing at the same time. Now I knew where her daughter had got her good looks from, but there was something else about the mother that kept one enchanted.

'Now you can understand that the two most perfect people who had been brought together by destiny, had to fall in love with each other. It's not every day that God makes such fine specimens. When in the later years, I started understanding love; I knew that theirs was a love that was not just for one life, but for eternity.

'But then, the universe works in a different manner. These two people were not going to get the bliss of togetherness. Their destiny had put them on different paths and though they tried their best to follow it, they were not able to do so because there were other forces involved.

'But these were not the only two people who were being played by destiny, but there were others whose destinies were also interwoven. Suchitra, who had fallen in love with Barrister *Saheb*, the first time she laid eyes on him, was never going to get the love she wanted, because he had already lost his heart to someone else. Kanti, who was crazily and wholeheartedly in love with his wife, had understood at some point that though she was a good wife and mother, she would never love him the way he did, and he made himself content with what he had.

'But I felt heartbroken for Shivani. She did not deserve what she had to endure. She was a goodhearted and sweet girl. I could feel her pain as I had gone through the same pain. We had both lost our mothers. But while she always had a sweet and loving memory of her mother, mine was tainted with something ugly and sinister. Worse of it all, it made me feel somewhat responsible for the loss of both our mothers.

'The photograph that you found in the Haveli, which I removed from your side table the other night, is of the people whose story I am narrating to you. You must have guessed by now that the other couple, besides Barrister *Saheb* and his wife, are Sharmishtha, and her husband Kanti Prasad, and the little girl, sitting on Barrister *Saheb's* lap, is Shivani, their little daughter. But the photograph was taken during happier times when Suchitra was expecting Shelly. I had stumbled upon this photo in Barrister *Saheb's* bedroom on the night stand, on another day, when I had entered the forbidden territory for the second time, looking for Shelly. I knew Shelly had gone to hide there in order to irk me. I was angry with her for breaching the rule. So my impulsiveness got the better of me and I entered the master bedroom. I forgot about Shelly as I got mesmerised by the beauty of the room. Luckily for me, there was no one in the room. And when I was touching the silk canopy my eyes fell on the photograph that was kept on the night stand. I had forgotten about it till we found it in your room. I was shocked to have found it in your possession. I knew that all my efforts of keeping it all hidden from you were in vain, as you already knew the existence of these people. I hid it, hoping that by hiding the photograph I would probably be able to stop you from delving into the past, as I never wanted you to know the story of these people. Their story was not just their own, it crossed the barriers of time and became a part of the present too.

'But there was a bigger reason for not wanting you to see it. That photograph bore witness of a diabolic catastrophe that was going to tear three families apart. But providence works in its own way, and in spite of all my efforts, you came here and got involved with the past I so wanted to leave behind.

'Anyway, I had made good friends with Shivani and I felt a little heartbroken when they left, but she made me promise that I would come to Lucknow with my mother when she accompanied the Mathur family. And I danced with joy when my mother decided to take me to Lucknow, albeit for a few days. The plan was that I would go along with my mother and my father would fetch me after a few days. I did not feel as dejected this time when she would leave me behind, because once again I was going to be with Shelly and Shivani.

'I was always awed to see the big bungalow belonging to Barrister *Saheb* and Suchitra. It was called 'The Retreat'. I stayed with my mother in her nice and spacious room as she was always considered part of the family. Food was in abundance and Shelly and I played in the big gardens. That was the most beautiful time of my childhood. I was with my mother and Shelly and the world looked just perfect. After a few days, I asked Shelly about Shivani. She promised to ask her mother to invite her over. In the evening, when I met Shelly after her classes with her governess, she looked a bit sad. She told me that her mother had got cross with her when she'd asked to invite Shivani and that had left Shelly in a dejected mood. Later that evening, my mother told me not to fill Shelly's head with ideas. She looked annoyed but unlike Shelly, I was used to my mother's annoyance. She told me that I should not ask Shelly to invite Shivani. It was neither my house nor my place to voice an opinion about anything.

That night I went to bed with a shadow in my perfect sunshine. But it did not end there. The next day my father was sent a telegram to come and collect me. I felt heartbroken and cried. When I begged my mother to let me stay for some more time, she said that it was not a good time as *Missi Baba* was feeling indisposed and she had to devote all her time to her. 'But I would not disturb her, Shelly and I would play quietly', I reasoned, to which she answered that Shelly was becoming a bit disobedient and not concentrating on her lessons.

'It would be best to go back now darling. You can play with Shelly when we come to the village.' My mother had displayed a rare show of love. I left after two days with my father.

'After a couple of months, suddenly they came to the Haveli. We were not expecting them. When my father told me that they would be coming the next day I was ecstatic. I ran all the way to the Haveli to meet my mother and Shelly. The atmosphere in the Haveli was charged, as it was always, when the family came to stay. The staff was busy and once again the Haveli was breathing life. But there was something different, something lacking in the upstairs quarters. The atmosphere felt heavy and even my seven year old instincts told me that things were different this time. I was not allowed to go to the upstairs quarters on my own, so I went to the kitchen hoping to meet mother or Shelly.

'Hello Rani! Are you looking for your mother?' Thomas *Chacha* asked.

'Yes *Chacha*, and Shelly.'

'I am afraid you will have to wait as Shelly is still asleep and your mother... err... is busy with *Mem Saheb*. Come and sit here and I will give you something to eat.'

'I was disappointed. The urgency of seeing mother and Shelly had turned into a lugubrious mood. I hung around in the kitchen just to be polite to Thomas *Chacha* and as soon as I'd finished the slice of cake, I thanked him, excused myself and went to the garden. I moved around looking at the flowers aimlessly as nothing looked bright when Shelly was not with me. Then as I was debating to turn back and go home, I heard some raised voices.

'I don't want her to come here,' Suchitra was almost shouting. 'Why are you making my life more miserable than it already is? How can you do this to me especially now when I know everything.'

'I cannot leave her there to go through this alone. She will come here. It's only a matter of a few days. Please don't be cruel.' It was the voice of Barrister *Saheb*.

'I looked up. I was directly under the side window of the master bedroom. I looked up and saw Suchitra sobbing and my mother putting her arm around her and taking her away from the window, and at that exact moment my mother looked down and our eyes locked, then she moved away from the window. I was expecting to see a glimmer of joy or affection or anything in her eyes, but she looked down at me as if I was someone else at that moment, not her daughter. I felt a deep dejection and walked back home.

'Next day mother sent for me and as I reached the garden my spirits lifted even more as I saw Shelly and Shivani sitting on the garden chairs. I ran to them and though Shelly ran and hugged me Shivani smiled and looked a little subdued.

'Hello Rani! How are you?' she asked. I saw there was a shadow on her beautiful face.

'I am fine and so happy to see you both,' I said.

'Shivani's great grandmother has gone to heaven. That's why she is sad. Daddy brought her here and her mother would come tomorrow,' Shelly said.

'Oh! I am so sorry,' I said holding her hand.

'She smiled but her beautiful eyes brimmed with tears. I did not know what to say so I kept quiet. I sat down with them not knowing what to do. And then we heard footsteps and saw Barrister *Saheb* coming.

'Oh good! Rani is also here. So girls, I have organised an outing for you all. There is an excellent puppet show in Lalgarh and I am sending you all there with a picnic basket. So go and have a good time but listen to Gopal *Kaka* and do as he bids.'

'Then he kissed Shelly on the forehead and walked to Shivani and hugged her.

'Don't worry sweetheart! Everything will be fine.'

'He held her for some time and I saw such intense love in his eyes, the kind I had seen in my father's eyes for me. After a while he disengaged himself and ruffled my hair with the most enigmatic smile. We were bundled into the car and as we started moving towards Lalgarh, the mood lifted and we laughed and chatted. That outing was the most enjoyable experience of my entire childhood. We had a lovely time and when we came back to the Haveli, I stayed till dinner and felt very happy in a long time, oblivious to the storm that was building up and was going to wreck the lives of the people who were staying in the Haveli at that time.'

Mother was quiet. We waited patiently absorbing everything and giving her time to collect her thoughts. She had gone quite pale and looked miserable.

'Do you want to rest a little?' I asked her.

'Just hand me that glass of water.'

I gave her the glass and propped the pillows to support her back, once she'd finished sipping the water.

'Next day Sharmishtha came to the Haveli. She looked pale and those beautiful eyes of hers looked sad. We children were playing in the garden when Barrister *Saheb's* motor stopped in front of the porch. Shivani ran to greet her. It was evident that she had been missing her. She hugged her daughter and they went inside. After a little while Shivani came and sat down heavily on the chair.

'What's the matter?' Shelly asked.

'I am going back tomorrow with papa. He is coming to take me back to Lucknow. Mummy has to stay back for a few more days,' she said a little sullenly.

'But why don't you stay here? Please do,' entreated Shelly in her sweet innocence that was her wont.

'My quarterly exams are starting from next week and papa has to be back at his work. It's alright. I don't want to insist and make mummy sadder. You know she adored her granny. Even I loved her a lot. It's only a matter of a few days,' she said, displaying the maturity of an adult.

'We just sat there feeling bad for her and us. We had grown very fond of each other. And then suddenly, the rain came and we had to run to the safety of the indoors. I was dropped home after a hot dinner that was served to us in the kitchen, as it was still raining heavily. Somehow the weather matched my grim mood and I, who'd always loved the rains, was for once not happy with it. It was as if a cloud of unease had settled on the Haveli and its inhabitants.

'It poured the next day as well, and I waited expectantly for the car to come and take me to the Haveli. I did not want to go to school that day and told my father so. He smiled and pecked me on the forehead. He was always willing to do what gave me joy. By the afternoon the car came and I ran towards it. Upon reaching the Haveli, I saw Shivani all dressed and ready to leave with her father.

'I was waiting for you. I will miss you. Please do come to Lucknow and stay with us,' she said and hugged me.

'I will miss you too. I will ask father to take me to Lucknow,' I said, my voice trembling a bit.

'Shivani hugged Shelly and they made the same promises.

'Alright sweetheart! All set?' A voice interrupted us.

'And then I saw her parents coming into the room. Every time I looked at her mother I couldn't tear my eyes off her. She was smiling as she hugged Shivani and there was such tenderness and affection in her eyes that my heart lurched. I had never seen anything close to this emotion in my mother for me ever. Shivani is so lucky. I remember thinking to myself with a small pang of jealousy. And then Barrister *Saheb* came and he hugged Shivani.

'Don't worry sweetheart! I will make sure your mother reaches Lucknow safe and sound.'

'The staff came to bid farewell to Shivani. They were all fond of her. She was like that. She had a loving heart and she respected everyone alike. But Suchitra and my mother made themselves conspicuous by their absence.

'Shelly and I felt a little bereft when Shivani left. And since it was pouring outside and we couldn't go out in the garden, Shelly took me to her room. As soon as we had settled with some storybooks that were new to her collection, we heard a shout and the clattering of something. We both looked at each other. Every time there were guests in the house, Shelly was shifted to the room next to the master bedroom, which was her mother's room. So it was an easy guess where the shout had come from. The guests were put up in the rooms in the other wing of the Haveli, so it was unlikely that Sharmishtha had heard it. We saw Barrister *Saheb* hurrying down the corridor through the open door of Shelly's room.

'I looked at Shelly's face and saw a shadow of sorrow and then at that moment I realised that her predicament was so like mine. Though her parents loved her, they were not there for her all the time. They did not realise that their daughter needed to be loved and cared for. Their issues were not more important than her. And a nanny, no matter how good she was, could never take the place of parents. But then, the rich lived by their own rules.

'After a little while, we both sneaked out of the room to the garden, as her nanny went to the kitchen, which she often did when Shelly had company. We were walking around on the wet grass, when I instinctively looked up and saw Suchitra standing next to the window. She was always frail but now she looked like a shadow of her former self. Even to my young eyes she looked deathly pale. She was staring into nothingness. I did not know why but I felt something ominous just by looking at her and then I noticed that her wrist was bandaged.

'Mummy was not feeling well last night. Doctor Uncle had to be called from Lalgarh,' Shelly informed. 'Don't tell nanny because I am not supposed to know. I was asleep when I heard the commotion. Nanny was fast asleep and I sneaked out of the room. No one saw me though. I went to look mum up in the morning but she was asleep and your mother told me that I should not disturb her,' she added.

'Oh! No wonder she looked sickly,' I thought to myself.

'I was allowed to stay in the Haveli after lunch. And then my mother found me when Shelly was taken to her mother's room. Apparently her mother had sent for her.

'Rani, I have a small errand for you,' my mother said smiling.

'I looked at her questioningly.

'Can you go to the guest room and give this to Shivani's mother?' she asked, handing over an envelope to me.

'I nodded.

'But I want one more small favour from you. I know you might feel odd with what I am going to ask you to do. But trust me that it is in the interest of everyone. You know that Shivani's mother is feeling sad because of her grandmother's demise. So we decided to give her a small surprise that I will tell you later. But for now you take this letter and tell her it is from Barrister *Saheb*. She is his childhood friend so she will not have any suspicion, but if you say it is from me or *Missi Baba* she might guess. Do you understand?'

'I again nodded a bit dumbly. My mother was entrusting me with something that she made seem important and I suddenly felt all grown up and responsible. I took the envelope from her that felt shiny and smooth, and went to the other wing of the Haveli that housed the guest rooms. I knocked gently at the door and then heard a soft voice saying come in.

'She was wearing a light sea green sari and her long and heavy hair was coiled in a heavy bun that rested on her nape. Her diamond nose ring sparkled when light fell on it. Her eyes were lined with kohl and there was a mesmerising scent in the room which was either her perfume or the scented soap she must have used for her bath. Her studded glass and gold bangles made a musical sound as she kept the book she was reading on the night stand. Her movements were so graceful that I forgot my assignment and kept staring at her.

'Rani! Come darling! It's so nice to see you,' she said smiling through her beautiful eyes. And I thought that no one could ever be like her.

'I have brought this for you,' I said, stammering slightly.

'What is it sweetheart?' she said.

'This is sent by Barrister *Saheb*,' I told the lie, feeling uneasy.

'She looked so pure that I felt I was committing a crime by lying to her. I handed her the envelope. She opened it and at first there was a faint smile on her face but soon it vanished and she looked a bit troubled. I decided to scoot and mumbled something.

'Thank you darling!' she said a little distractedly and I ran back to the sitting room. My mother was lurking there and she asked me whether I had done what I had been asked to. And when I nodded, she left.

'It was sometime late in the night when I was woken up by a sharp knocking at the courtyard gate. My father went to answer it and I heard him talking to people, and then he came inside and said something to granny who had also gotten up hearing the banging, and then he left hurriedly.

'What is it *Ajia?* Where has *Baba* gone?' I asked.

'Mukhia *Chacha* has sent for him. Don't worry. You go to sleep. He will come back soon.'

'I could not sleep for quite some time. But then, it was not unusual for my father to go in the middle of the night, as he had good knowledge of herbs, and many a time when someone would fall sick he would go to attend to them. It was only in the morning when I was eating hot poories that Ajia had made, that father returned looking very grim and tired. I instantly knew that something was wrong but I was never prepared for what he told us.

'When he told us that Sharmishtha had fallen and drowned in the river, my heart sank. I knew that it was something to do with my mother. I had noticed her dislike towards Shivani and her mother many a time. I had caught her staring at Shivani with naked scorn, which I could never understand. Shivani was the most affable and likeable girl. Also, images started coming to my mind and I remembered her being sullen all the time when Shivani and her parents came visiting. I always found her behaviour a little strange, but then my mother behaved strangely most of the time, and there was no knowing what was going on in her mind. But why would she do this to Sharmishtha? Why would she take such a drastic step just because she did not like her? People did not kill people because they did not like them. There was more to this whole thing than was meeting the eye. But I could not put a finger on it. Moreover, I was heartbroken for Shivani. No one deserved the ordeal that she was going to be put through.

'Everyone was puzzled. No one knew why Sharmishtha had gone to the river when it was pouring. Also, there was a rumour that she had probably taken her own life. And then, as if to substantiate the theory, more rumours started doing the rounds. As they say that the walls have ears, it was difficult to keep the things that went on in the upstairs quarters from the staff. The loyal ones heard everything but kept their mouths shut, but the ones who were of a more frivolous nature, shared stories of frequent fights that took place between Barrister *Saheb* and *Mem Saheb*. It's difficult to keep such things hidden with so many servants around. So it was said that Barrister *Saheb* and Sharmishtha were caught having an affair and that was the reason Sharmishtha chose to take this drastic step. Some said that it was nothing more than malicious gossip and she was probably missing her grandmother and taking a walk and slipped. But you know the tendency of human minds is to believe in the theory that is more tantalising, than in something that is banal and insipid.

'The days passed slowly. The atmosphere of the house was heavy and everyone was quiet. My mother did not come home. I overheard conversation that the body was found some five kilometres away. Barrister *Saheb* had shut himself in the room and had only come out when Kanti came. He had come alone after receiving the news. Barrister *Saheb* and Kanti left for Lucknow with Sharmishtha's body. I was in a way relieved that Shivani was left in Lucknow by her father. I had no courage to face her. Suchitra and my mother stayed in the Haveli. Word was that Suchitra had become hysterical and had started having her episodes, as her hallucinations were called. I often overheard village women coming and talking to my grandmother, saying that Suchitra was seeing Sharmishtha. A number of times she had tried jumping into the river from her terrace. It was all very bleak and depressing. I stayed at home but had lost my appetite and felt miserable. Barrister *Saheb's* foster parents and his mother came to the Haveli and it was decided to take Suchitra and Shelly to Delhi.

'Time after that night hung in limbo. It was as if everyone was just going through days mechanically. I came down with a high fever that led me to hallucinate. The horrors of that night were beyond the capabilities of my seven year old self, to forget and move on. My mind was taken over by nightmares and I screamed and thrashed in my sleep. My father and grandmother looked after me day and night, taking turns to get some rest. My father took me to Lalgarh to consult doctors and my grandmother did whatever anyone told her to do. Some said that I was touched by something and therefore cleansing was required. You know how superstitious people in the village are. But amidst all this chaos my mother did not come to see me even once. When my grandmother asked my father to send for her, he refused resolutely and said that she was not required. She was needed more by the mistress of the Haveli as she was distraught and had fallen sick.

'I didn't know what happened to Shivani and her father at that point of time. But later, in the years to come, I came to know that it was her father who was with her at every step and he tried filling the void that was created by Sharmishtha's demise. If there was any consolation for Shivani and her father, it was that her nanny was attached to her, and she stayed on with Shivani till she moved to America. She was a widow and did not have a family of her own.

'But the incident ended the lives of Barrister *Saheb*, Suchitra and my mother. My mother's impulsive and fiendish action made her pay a heavy price. Barrister *Saheb* went almost crazy with grief and shut himself off from everyone. Suchitra's mental condition deteriorated further and she started hallucinating even more. She said that she was seeing Sharmishtha and she would scream and run out of the house. The Haveli reverberated with her screams. She stopped eating. But the worst thing that happened was that she started shouting at my mother. She kept telling her that she was the root cause of everything. The woman who had been such an integral part of her life became the object of her hatred. She blamed my mother for taking Barrister *Saheb* from her. Till date, I do not know whether my mother had confided in her about that night or she'd just guessed everything, but she had started hating my mother from that night onwards.

'My mother was heartbroken, so we were told by the people who worked in the Haveli. She stopped eating and kept crying. And one night, I woke up as I felt a cool palm on my forehead. I opened my eyes and though it was dark yet I knew it was my mother. But before I could shake the cobwebs of sleep from my mind, as I was still under the effect of a sedative, she was gone. It was late in the afternoon the next day, when someone from the Haveli came looking for my mother. We were told that she was not in the Haveli and they had looked everywhere, and thought that she had come down to her house. It was assumed that she had probably gone to Lalgarh to take a break. But when some time passed and there was still no sign of her, panic set in. My father, along with the other staff from the Haveli, searched for her high and low but she couldn't be found. It was as if she had vanished into thin air. I told my father that I had felt my mother's presence, the night before she disappeared, but I did not think I was taken seriously as I was not in a very good mental state and under the effect of sedatives.

'Suchitra's parents came down from England and took her and Shelly to England. We came to know through the servants in the Haveli that Suchitra never recovered from her mental disorder and she kept talking about Sharmishtha and the Haveli. Four years passed and most of the staff was let go. Only Gopal *Kaka* and the old gardener stayed. No one came visiting and people moved on with their lives, and gradually the rumours and the stories dulled.

'And one day, when I came back from school, I saw Gopal *Kaka* sitting with my father. He had brought news that Suchitra had committed suicide. The thought, which came to my mind instantly, was how my mother would have dealt with the news, had she been with Suchitra. I looked at my father and found him looking at me. He was thinking of the same, it seemed.

'It was then that Barrister *Saheb* went to England and brought his daughter back. Barrister *Saheb*'s parents and foster parents took turns looking after Shelly and when she turned fifteen, she went to England again and stayed with her grandparents and completed her studies from there.

'After almost a decade, someone from our village came and told us that he had seen my mother in Kashi but when he called out for her, she ran and got lost in the crowd. My father, upon learning this, decided to go to Kashi and look for her. Your father offered to accompany, but he refused, saying he wanted to do that himself. He stayed in Kashi for a month but couldn't find her. When he came back, he had aged even more and I knew that he still loved her and missed her.

'I did not learn anything about Shivani and often wondered about her. Many years later I bumped into her nanny in Aminabad in Lucknow. I was overjoyed to see her. She had become very old and frail. We sat down on the steps of a temple and I asked her about Shivani. She told me that Kanti and his daughter had shifted to Delhi, a couple of years after Sharmishtha's demise. Kanti had asked for a transfer to Delhi where he was heading the department of English.

Shivani pursued a medical degree from Lady Harding Medical College of Delhi. Kanti had sold the property that was his share and bought a house in Delhi. Then later he shifted to America with Shivani.

'Now you would wonder why I never tried to meet Shivani or at least tried finding about her once we shifted to Lucknow. I actually did not have the guts to face her. In my heart, I knew that I was the daughter of her mother's killer, and I had kept this secret from everyone as I had this mad urge to save my mother. I did not want her to be taken away from me, but in the end she only abandoned me and my father. So I felt happy for Shivani and relieved that I would never have to face her as she had left the country.'

Mother stopped. But I had questions that were burning in my mind.

'*Amma*, you did not tell me, what made you think that it was granny who was responsible for Sharmishtha's death?' I asked her. She looked at me and my heart sank looking at the pained expression on her face.

Mother was silent. We waited and when she spoke her voice seemed to be coming from afar.

'As I grew up, I had to live with the horrors of that evening. I tried to obliterate the memory telling myself that I was very young and it was raining and very dark, so I had probably imagined the whole thing. But I had known throughout that I was just trying to block the truth from my memory because that was the only way I could move on with my life. As much as I wanted to believe that my mother was a normal person, she was not a monster, not capable of doing something like this, I couldn't convince myself.

'After giving the note to Sharmishtha I came back to Shelly's room only to find Shelly sitting with her governess for her lessons. I knew that she would not be free for another couple of hours. My father was supposed to come and take me home. I was told by my mother to always leave the room when Shelly was taking lessons because apparently she was distracted by my presence and the governess did not like that. I sensed a slight disapproval in the manner of the governess, so I left the room reluctantly and went down to kill time as I waited for my father. I roamed around aimlessly in the front gardens and as the clouds were gathering and the wind picked up, I decided to go indoors. But instead of coming through the main entrance I walked to the rear lawns, where I saw a figure walking towards the river bank. As I tried focusing to get a clear view, I saw the purple and black sari of my mother. The light was fading fast and just then, fat droplets of water started falling, and in no time it was pouring. Though my mother had never cared much for me, my love for her was as deep as any child's. I ran inside and grabbed an umbrella from the stand and ran towards the bank. The dirt path where the lawns ended had become slushy so I had to slow down. I could hardly see anything because it had become pitch dark and the rain was falling heavily, creating a curtain. When I reached a little closer to the grove on the river bank, I saw two figures entangled. There was thick foliage of the shrubs. They disappeared behind it. I felt my whole body going tense. And I felt a deep sense of foreboding of something dreadful happening. The rain was blinding me but gathering my courage I kept moving forward. But my progress was slow because the path was very slippery and the river that was just a few feet away, was in full spate and roaring. I knew that if I slipped I would lose my footing and fall into the river.

'Suddenly someone came in front of me and I almost screamed, only to see that it was mother.

'What are you doing here?' she shouted and looked very angry.

'I... I brought this for you,' I tried showing her the umbrella but she caught my hand and dragged me towards the Haveli.

'You are such a troublemaker. Why couldn't you stay in the Haveli? Do you want to die? You know this place is off limits for children. Now listen carefully. Go back at the front gate of the Haveli and wait for your father. Don't go inside the Haveli. I do not want to get a scolding from the mistress which she would surely give when she sees you like this. She as it is thinks that I don't give you enough time. Open the umbrella; it would save you from the rains, though you are drenched already. Go home and change into fresh clothes. And Rani!' she said holding my hand tightly.

'Yes *Amma*!' I said preparing myself for another scolding.

'Don't tell anyone about this episode. I had gone to get some herbs for *Missi Baba*'s headache. Barrister *Saheb* doesn't like it when I use the herbs. He doesn't believe in these kinds of remedies. He would get angry. Do you understand?' she asked me.

'Yes I do.'

'Good girl! It's a secret between the two of us then. Don't even tell your father,' she said smiling at me, and I felt very responsible and swore to myself never to utter a single word about this. I walked back as fast as the muddy path would let me and went to the front gate. I did not have to wait for long as my father came in his cart and was astonished to see me all drenched and waiting outside the wrought iron gate.

'What are you doing here all by yourself? Why didn't you wait inside?' He looked upset.

'Shelly was having her lessons and I was getting bored so I came out to wait for you,' I lied keeping my promise.

'But no one stopped you coming like this... in the rains? Your mother... she might not even know where you are, as usual,' he said, not hiding his annoyance.

'It's ok *Baba*! I enjoy getting wet in the rain. Now let's go home as I am cold and hungry,' I said.

Mother stopped and looked very tired. I had finally learnt the truth about my mother's aversion to the Haveli. It was all so very sad and dark. I was trying to fight the shock that I felt upon learning about my grandmother being a murderess. But there was something else that I felt and it was growing stronger with every moment. There was a nagging feeling of something that I could not put my finger on.

'I finished high school and the proposal for my marriage came from your father's family.' Mother was speaking again.

'We got married as I turned seventeen. I became blissfully happy as your father was a very loving and caring husband. He came from a good and well-to-do family and having lost his mother at an early age, only had his father with him. Though he was from Lalgarh and had a considerable amount of land, yet after his father's demise, he agreed to shift to my father's house as I wanted to take care of my father. And my father had given the full responsibility of his land to him too. After a couple of years of my marriage, *Ajia* also passed away. My father and I felt bereft because she was more a mother to me than my biological mother. But the responsibility of running the household and your father's love and care helped me move on. So life was blissful. If there was a speck in my contended life, it was that I was not able to conceive even after three years of our marriage. And then I started visiting doctors, first in Lalgarh and then in Lucknow. We both went through various tests and medications and did every possible thing that we were asked to do. But I simply could not conceive and that was making me more and more worried. At times, I thought that the universe was punishing me for being a part of my mother's conspiracy. I would have lost my sanity but it was your father who showered his love and did everything to keep me happy and sane.

'And it was at that time that we decided to buy a house in Lucknow. We had to go to Lucknow frequently for my check ups and my father was also getting old and required good medical help every now and then. So your father sold the house and a big portion of the land in Lalgarh, as it was becoming a bit difficult to manage the property and the land. Also he did not have any family in Lalgarh, so it looked only prudent to sell the house.

'A few years passed. We did not get to hear much about Barrister *Saheb* and Shelly except an occasional bit of news that Barrister *Saheb* had gone to Delhi and was becoming known in his profession. Then, after some years, we came to know that Shelly had got married in England and had settled down there only, and Barrister *Saheb* had become the Chief Justice. I was happy for Shelly. But six months or so after Shelly's wedding, we came to know that Barrister *Saheb* had passed away in his sleep. I did not take the news well. I felt sad. His handsome face and beautiful compassionate eyes swam in front of me. I knew that he was heartbroken. When I started understanding the meaning of love, I understood how I had seen him looking at Sharmishtha. She was probably the only love of his life, and to lose her like that must have been the end of him.

'I felt profoundly sad for the man who must have had such a turbulent life after he lost Sharmishtha, and lived a life devoid of any hope. I felt as if he was just waiting to see Shelly find love and settle down, and then he ended the long wait that he had to endure. I wished and prayed for him to find his love in his next life. But little did I know that my wish was going to come true in a very different manner.

'I would admit that after two years of Barrister *Saheb's* demise, when I came to know through Gopal *Kaka*, that Shelly was blessed with a baby boy, I felt sad. Not because of her becoming a mother, but because of my inability to conceive. Motherhood is every woman's most intense desire and I was no exception. And then as if the universe had finally taken pity on me, and when we had given up all hope of ever becoming parents, I found out that I was pregnant with you. I was thirty years old and your father was thirty five.

'When you were born our lives revolved around you. You were the most beautiful child and every time people looked at you, I was told to ward off the evil eye. You brought such happiness to us. Your grandfather doted on you. Everything was fine and then you started speaking. We were very happy when you called me *Amma* and your father *Baba*.

'You were about to turn three when we got a message that Shelly was coming to the Haveli with her family. There was quite a commotion in the village. It had been years since any family member had visited the Haveli. I was torn between meeting her and avoiding going to the Haveli as it would have stirred so many memories. But I was summoned to the Haveli a day after Shelly arrived. She wanted to meet me and see you. The moment we reached the Haveli, you became agitated and you wrestled to be free from my arms. I tried soothing you but you became even more agitated and started crying. You had always been a very cheerful child, so this sudden tantrum was unusual. I tried distracting you by showing you the flowers. You calmed down a bit, but your big eyes were brimming with tears.

'It was the month of January and we found Shelly sitting in the front gardens. The moment she saw us she came hurriedly towards us. We embraced each other and we both were a bit emotional. She looked very pretty and elegant in her light mauve pant suit, pearls adorning her neck and ears. She was taller than me and had a slim figure. Her dark and shiny hair fell over her shoulders. She looked every bit a well bred and sophisticated lady that she was.

'Oh Rani, it's so good to see you! I often thought of you and the lovely time we spent together. You look good. Marriage and motherhood suit you.' She smiled and she was the Shelly I had known years back. The kindness in her eyes was the same, but the spark was replaced with a touch of solemnity.

'And is this your daughter?' she said taking you from my arms.

'She is… so beautiful,' she said looking at you intently. I knew what she meant. It was hard for people to accept that I, with my plain features and ordinary looks, could give birth to such a beautiful daughter. You looked at her and smiled.

'I am so happy that you came here. There is so much to talk about,' I said as we moved towards the chairs.

'Yes I know! But unfortunately I am leaving tomorrow. I had come to Lucknow to sell the house. You remember the house, 'The Retreat', don't you?' she asked.

'Yes I do,' I said quietly.

'Anyway, I had come down to see the state of the Haveli before selling it too. But I am leaving some funds for some renovations and

I think I will take the call when I come next.'

'You had wriggled down from her arms and started walking, and looking at the flowers. I let you roam around a bit and kept an eye on you.

'I want you to meet my son. He must be somewhere here only,' she said looking around.

'And then when tea was served, we got talking and became totally engrossed sharing all that had taken place in our lives. I carefully avoided any mention of my mother and Shelly said that she missed her father a lot. She did not remember much about her mother, only that she was very ill before she passed away. If she knew about the suicide, she didn't say. Anyway, we soon changed the topic and she told me that her husband was an American citizen and she had moved to America after her marriage, she had lost her maternal grandmother when she was sixteen and her grandfather just recently.

'Some time must have passed and then there was a commotion. We both were startled out of our tête à tête and I, with a jolt realised that you were nowhere to be seen. At that very moment we saw Chandu bringing you and a very good looking boy of some six-seven years of age, accompanying him.

'What happened?' My heart sank looking at you. But you opened your eyes and spread your arms towards me. I almost snatched you from Chandu and held you tightly.

'She had wandered off to the bank. It was very fortunate that Anand *Baba* saw her and ran after her,' Chandu said shaking a little.

'She was about to fall into the river,' Anand said in English. I looked at Chandu and he averted his eyes. He probably did not want to tell me the bit of you almost falling into the river.

'Oh my God! You poor darling. I am so glad you are safe,' Shelly's expression was troubled.

'I was shaken more than I liked to show. And Shelly understood my discomfort. We made some small talk and she promised to come to the village again sometime in the future when she came to India.

'You were quiet once we came home and fell asleep sooner than your usual time. Your father had gone to Lucknow. I was feeling immensely guilty that I had let you wander off. So when I told my father about the incident I broke down. He soothed me like always and said all that mattered was that you were fine and I should not blame myself. That night I woke up as I felt your hand on my cheek and found you sitting on the bed and looking at me.

'Parni! What is it darling? Why are you up?' I asked scooping you up in my arms. I was still troubled by the incident at the Haveli.

'You looked at me, smiled and said, 'My name is Mishthi not Parni'.

'I froze there and then. 'What did you say sweetheart? Your name is Aparna. We call you Parni lovingly.'

'No!' You shook your head. 'My name is Mishthi.'

'After some cajoling I put you to sleep but I couldn't sleep the whole night. I spent the night in a restless state. And then as I looked at you while you were sleeping I felt as if I had been punched by something. There was an unmistakeable resemblance in your features. And thereafter, every time I addressed you by your name you looked at me and told me that your name was Mishthi. I found this strange development too much to handle. So the moment your father came back, I again broke down. Though he knew about the incident in the Haveli and my mother's disappearance, I had not told him anything else. You see, I could not let him think that he had married the daughter of a murderess.

'We had never discussed anything about the occupants of the Haveli. My father and I had left all that in the past. We did not even talk about my mother. How did you know the names of the people you had never heard of? For some strange reason I was scared. What if it was a rebirth? I did not want you, my daughter to remember anything from your past, if you were who we thought you were. My consternation was so acute that I decided to tell him everything right from the start to the end. He was quiet, as if absorbing the macabre tale. I gave him time and sat quietly.

'But Rani, it must have been a dreadful thing, to carry a secret as dark as this one all by yourself,' he said with concern written all over his rugged yet pleasant face.

'It was,' I said sobbing. 'But I feel a bit lighter as I have shared it with you. But we can never let *Baba* know about it. He has suffered a lot already and I do not want him to know that the wife he has loved and missed all these years, was capable of a committing a crime so heinous.'

'And then you started remembering more things. One day you started telling us to take you to *Phulwari* where Kailash was waiting for you. When we tried coming up with excuses you started crying and refused to eat anything. You went to sleep sobbing that day. It was getting very difficult for us to go through this whole thing. There were times when you would be happy and ask us when Kailash was coming home, and at others you would insist that you wanted to go either to Phulwari or the Haveli.

'We both were at our wits end. We did not know what to make of this whole thing. Then things became even more complicated. It was Holi and you insisted on wearing a pink lehnga choli. You owned mostly frocks that your father bought in Lucknow or I'd stitched at home. I promised to stitch a pink lehnga choli for you but that did not stop you from crying and sulking.

'My father suggested that we take the opinion of someone, but your father and I were a bit skeptical. One morning you got up and started telling us to take you to Asanpur as you had to take care of things there. My father suggested that we take you there; probably you would stop getting so distressed if we did what you wanted, and it might stop any more memories from surfacing. My father, by now, was quite convinced that it was a matter of rebirth. Your father and I agreed reluctantly, and we decided to take you there. You looked happy but when we took you to the banks of the river as we had to cross the river on a boat, you started screaming and making choking sounds as if you were drowning. We got so scared that we returned home and I put you to sleep. When I came out of the room, your father said that we needed to do something. All three of us sat down and it was decided that we should move to Lucknow. As it is, we were planning to move to the city for your education after a couple of years. My father decided to stay in the village till matters of selling the lands were settled, but he wanted us to move immediately.

'There is no guarantee that Parni would stop having these… memories, but at least you will be in a big city and can consult a good doctor. There might be a chance that the new environment and surroundings will distract her and she may start forgetting these things. This place might be triggering memories, which is the only plausible reason I can come up with. I know with modern science and all, educated people in the cities do not believe in these things, but it is not something that has not been heard of before. All I can say that there are phenomena beyond the understandings of science, and as a Hindu, I do believe in the theory of rebirth. So taking her away from here might do her good,' my father said.

'The selling of the house and land would take some time *Baba*. Though I would keep coming to settle these things, but are you sure you can manage things alone here?' my husband asked.

'*Baba*, promise me that when matters of the properties are settled, you will come to Lucknow and join us,' I told my father, to which he laughed and said that he would come and meet us but would rather stay in the village because this was where he had lived all his life, and he could not bear the idea of moving to the city. He was too set in his ways in the village and the city air would not do him any good.

'We moved to Lucknow and got busy settling down. So one day, when you started asking to be taken to meet Kailash, I simply told you that we would go later as he is not there at the moment. To my surprise you agreed and went on to play with your dolls.

'Once while playing with your dolls you suddenly said, 'Shivani would like this doll. I should give this one to her.' I stopped wringing the towel that was in my hand, as I was washing clothes along with Padma, the girl who helped in the household chores. I was filled with a deep sense of sorrow and misery. We had moved to the city, hoping you would forget all that, but you were still getting the 'memories.' And then this thought struck me. I asked your father to find out about Shivani and her father. I did not know much except that he taught in some big college.

'I don't know where he was teaching. Moreover do you think it is a good idea?' your father asked.

'He must have seen the disappointment on my face for he added, 'Rani! The best course of action would be to leave things the way they are. There is no point raking old wounds. And don't you think that if we tell them... err... what we think about Aparna, it would be very upsetting for them? They must have moved on and it must have been very difficult for them, so why bring all that back.'

'But our daughter...' I said.

'I am sure it's just a phase. Even if she is remembering things from her past, she would forget in the time to come. Let's have faith in God and give Aparna so much love that she remembers only the present. We have brought her here and we are starting afresh. Let bygones be bygones. Let's concentrate on our future from now on,' your father reasoned.

'I nodded as I felt he was right. What he said made sense. There was no point in raking the past. It was time for new beginnings.

'You are right. I only pray and hope that Aparna forgets about it too, sooner rather than later,' I said.

'We have to make sure we don't take her to the village ever. Whenever there is a need to go to the village, I will go alone. I will not take you there either. You and Aparna should make this place home and that would be the best for all of us,' your father said.

'We tried for another child, thinking that a sibling would do you good but I couldn't conceive. You at times, had some nightmares and often cried in your sleep. But gradually the frequency started reducing and though you still asked about Kailash or Shivani and talked about going to Phulwari and the Haveli, they were not as frequent as in the beginning. But one thing that you could never get over was your fear of water. You became restless around rivers and lakes. You stopped talking about those 'memories' once you turned six. Your father and I became relieved and we were very happy. Your grandfather kept coming to Lucknow and we were all a very happy family. But as you know, when your grandfather passed away, I was miserable. But I got the biggest jolt when your father left me. He was such a pillar of strength for me. He was not only my husband but a friend as well. He was with me at every step. He took such good care of me, you and your grandfather. It was his dream to see you become a doctor. He was a man ahead of his time. Life has not been the same without him but I am so grateful to Urmila and Kamla to have become a part of our family.'

Amma stopped and wiped her eyes.

'A few months back Ramcharan *Bhaiya* came to Lucknow. He told me that it would probably be better if I sold the lands and house in the village. It was becoming difficult to keep an eye on them as he was getting old and his sons were busy with their own things. The contractor we had appointed for the maintenance of the house was repeatedly cheating and the house was falling into disrepair.

'*Bhabhi*! Parni *Bitia* would never go to the village and she would never allow you to go and live there. Then why keep the house and lands there? It is becoming a white elephant. I myself am planning to sell most of the land and buy a small house in Lalgarh,' he said.

'He sat with us and we talked about this and that. And after having light refreshments, he got up to leave and I told him that I was in agreement with him and he could talk to the prospective buyers.

'I will make all the arrangements. You just let me know when you are coming. I will get the house ready so you can stay there for a few days if you want to,' he said and left for the village.

'After a few days, Chandu came to meet me and informed me that the Haveli was being sold. And it was that night that the nightmare that had been pushed into the depths of my mind, came back. I think the mention of the Haveli brought all those painful memories back. And this time your father was not there to comfort me. So that is how Kamla probably heard me crying and shouting in my dreams and wrote to you without telling me. I had already made up my mind to sell everything but your presence here, in the village, was the last thing that I had wanted. Your father and I had kept you away from the Haveli and the village. But I think I failed in the end.'

'*Amma*! Please don't blame yourself. It's not your fault. The past had to catch up in one way or the other. And coming here has done me a lot of good. You know that. But there is one thing that you have to do. You have to stop blaming yourself. Whatever happened that night was not your fault. It was only unfortunate that you had to witness your mother...' As I said that, a thought sprung in my mind. But I did not want to ask my mother anything that would upset her further. We gave her a glass of milk and half a sleeping pill.

I narrated the whole thing to Jason when he came the next day.

'So what do you make of the whole thing?' I asked him as we went for a walk.

'Well! I think you are a case of rebirth. It will make an interesting case study,' he said smiling with a glint in his eyes.

'You know *Amma* said that she had seen two people entangled, but it was very dark and raining, and the figures were partially hidden behind the bushes,' I said.

'So! What are you getting at?'

'I don't know... it's just a thought but... how is she sure that it was her mother and Sharmishtha? I mean one of them was certainly Sharmishtha, but the other figure could have been anyone.'

'Well, your mother saw your grandmother coming back. So

where is the doubt? I mean I would have liked to have some other theory, but these are the only facts that we know,' he said.

'I don't know. There is this nagging feeling...' I stopped in my tracks. 'Jason! I have to find out what happened that night.'

'Find out? How?' he asked.

'You know,' I said looking at him meaningfully. 'Jason! That is the only way to find out. It would put so many doubts to rest. And I would probably get rid of all those dreams. It would be like spring cleaning my head.'

'Aparna! You know it's risky. And I don't want to take any risk with you,' he said firmly.

'And you can take risks with others?' I said, a little miffed. 'Come on Jason! You are my prodigy and I trust you more than I trust myself. Please, you have to help me out here.'

He looked at me and then nodded reluctantly.

CHAPTER 35

The wind has picked up and it is wrenching the shawl from my shoulders. And as I try wrapping the shawl tightly around me, it starts pouring. The rain comes in gusts, making everything invisible in front of me. For some strange reason, I am a little scared. I don't know of what. I just have to keep moving and reach the grove. Is Kailash already there, waiting for me, or is he yet to come? In any case, I have to be there because now it would not make any sense to turn back. The ground is becoming slushier by the minute. I have to move carefully. Many a time the soil gets loose and the earth gives way. I am too close to the river. I can make out the shrubs and the big neem tree. Few more steps and I will be there. Finally, I am under the neem tree where we stood last time. The onslaught of rain feels a little less in the thick shade. My clothes are drenched and I am soaked to the bones. What is it that Kailash wants to speak about? Is it about Suchitra or Shivani?

I feel a presence behind me. I feel hands on my shoulders. I am turning back to see who it is. Is it Kailash? And then suddenly I am pushed to the ground. My face is covered in mud. I am trying to get up but the ground is slippery. Someone is dragging me, by my wrists, towards the banks, and then the realisation strikes. This person is not Kailash. I am desperately trying to free my hands from the grip of this person, so I can wipe the mud from my eyes.

'Let me go!' I am screaming but the grip is too strong. I am suddenly very scared. I don't want to die. My daughter... Shivani. 'No God! Please Nooooo...! Help me!'

And then suddenly, my hands are free and I am falling... falling into the river. There is a flash of lightning and I see Suchitra's face twisted with hatred before I hit the water and there is darkness everywhere...

'Aparna! You have to wake up now. You are listening to my voice as I am asking you to wake up.' I hear Jason's voice coming from afar.

I woke up crying and shaking. Jason was holding my hand, saying something in his soothing voice, with a worried look on his face.

CHAPTER 36

SUCHITRA

I guess I knew from the very beginning. But my heart, that was so full of love, refused to believe what my mind tried telling me. Also, somewhere, my hubris, the awareness of my lineage and my refined education put a veil over my eyes. And all this was made more believable by Kailash's unflinching attention to me which I mistook for love. Yes, it was just 'attention and care' that was probably born out of pity.

I had lost my heart to him the moment I had set eyes on him. I couldn't have envisioned someone as perfect as him even in my dreams. He was everything a girl could dream of. His exceptionally good looks combined with intelligence, his perfect etiquettes, and above all, his kind heart, made him someone as rare, as perfect as a pearl in the belly of a shell, lying on the unreachable bed of a deep ocean.

After that night in the cottage, when he had come to my rescue as my knight in shining armour, I knew that I could never love anyone but him. When I first saw Sharmishtha at the wedding reception, I admit that I was as dazzled by her beauty as everyone else present there. But it never crossed my mind that a girl as beautiful as her could capture anyone's heart, and Kailash was no exception. Especially when she was living in the neighbouring house that even shared a common wall. Now I laugh at my naivety. For anyone who looked at them would have thought that they were made for each other. If there was any girl on this earth, who could make a befitting partner for Kailash, it was her and only her. My lineage, education or delicate looks did not have even half the bewitching appeal that

Sharmishtha's beauty had, and if I had half British blood in my veins, she was the daughter of a prominent and revered businessman of the city.

But all these measures were useless because even if Sharmishtha was born into a pauper's family, her astounding beauty would have captured anyone's heart. So, here were two most perfect and suitable people who were bound to fall in love with each other. Then how could I fit into the picture? What bothered me the most was that Kailash married me out of sheer pity. He would have remained unmarried after Sharmishtha had married someone else. But he took pity on me because of my 'affliction' and decided to look after me for as long as it took. So it was not love but his concern for me that made him my husband. And he did look after me with all his heart. I had seen genuine concern in his eyes right from that night in the cottage.

But it was his love that I wanted, not his pity. Before I left for England, we had met. There was this shine in his eyes that indicated happiness in his heart. I felt pure joy after talking to him. He talked about the future with a zest and I listened to him with rapt attention. Of course, it was not only I he talked to, but to both the families, as the Mathurs were invited for dinner just before I left for England. I could see immense pride in my father's eyes and my mother kept looking at him affectionately. After all, he was going to be their son-in-law after he completed his studies. Everyone had assumed that without even bothering to ask. It is so ironic that we presume what we want for ourselves. We often forget that there is another side too. It was only much later that I realised that Kailash had not included me in his future plans. He had talked about coming back to India to start his practice and make a life here. There was a dreamy look in his eyes and a smile playing on his lips. I came to understand later that it was Sharmishtha he was planning a future with, not me.

Now when I look back, I realise that my parents sent me to England because they wanted me to be close to Kailash as he was going there soon. I didn't know whether there was something that prompted them to do that or they just thought it would be better for us to get to know each other. Though he seemed to be happy to see me and made sure to look after me, but he never gave any indication of any romantic intent. This made me wonder often, but I was content to just love him and be close to him. And then, one day, suddenly he changed. I did not hear from him for two days. I decided to go to his place as I got very concerned. Mr Wilson greeted me and asked me to make myself comfortable as he went to call Kailash. But I could read the concern in his eyes as he walked away slowly, to inform Kailash of my arrival.

My heart sank as I looked at him. He looked very different. His eyes were red and clothes crumpled. He had a two-days old stubble on his face. But what troubled me the most that the shine from his eyes had gone. When he smiled, the smile didn't reach his eyes. I got up and walked to him asking if he was feeling alright.

He said that he had got a stomach bug and that had confined him to his quarters. I requested him to shift to my house as I had staff and it would be easier to look after him there. He declined politely, saying that he was recovering and it would look rude as Mr Wilson had looked after him for the last two days, and would feel that his care was not adequate. I reluctantly agreed and came back with a heavy heart. But I kept visiting him till he recovered. But something had changed in him. He was no longer as happy and enthusiastic as he had been. It felt like he just dragged himself and went through the motions of everything. I tried asking him many times, but he just changed the topic and assured me that he was fine. It was only recently that I came to know the reason behind his sorry state in England all those years back, he had received the news of Sharmishtha's wedding and that had broken his heart.

After about a year of his arrival in England, his father had fallen ill and Kailash had to go to India. I offered to go along with him but he said that there was no point travelling for so many days. He would have to come back after a month and a half as his exams were scheduled around that time, anyway. I again felt miserable with the idea of staying without him for so many days, but my friends made sure that I was never alone, and though I missed Kailash, I kept myself busy with studies and various entertainments. But I kept counting the days to Kailash's return.

There was a marked changed when he came back from India. He had got some of the energy back and looked, if not happy, but at least not gloomy. I attributed it to his father's recovery and well-being, and the company of his loved ones. I was relieved and happy to see him laughing and slowly getting back to his life. He threw himself into his studies and did exceedingly well. And then, one day, he took me out for dinner and proposed to me. I burst into tears much to the chagrin of the maître d', but when he saw Kailash sitting on his knees and slipping a ring on my finger, and the other guests clapping, he smiled broadly.

The months and years just went by. I was in a blissful state and there were times when I noticed him slipping into one of those quiet and withdrawn moods of his, I simply waited patiently for him to regain his usual self. During such periods I always wondered about the nature of the problem that troubled him, but could never get him to talk about it. Thankfully, such moods did not last very long and once he was his usual self, I would forget about them.

And then I met Sharmishtha at our wedding after a little over five years. If the dust of the time had obscured my memory of her beauty, then I was in for a big surprise. She looked even more ravishing than she had looked as an unmarried girl. Gone was the careless exuberance of adolescence; it had been replaced by graceful dignity. There was something else that I noticed immediately. There was a new sophistication around her. Though she was still dressed in a sari, but she had a more fashionable look. I came to know later that her husband, who was a Professor of English in the University, had engaged an English governess to teach Sharmishtha English, colonial etiquettes and graces. She had a three-year-old daughter who was absolutely angelic and her husband was reasonably good looking and a thorough gentleman. I felt happy for her.

When we came to Lucknow, we started meeting often and I was happy to have them as our friends. Though there were many families who became our friends. Some of them were Anglo-Indians like me, some bureaucrats and the others hailed from the royalty of Lucknow.

I was too busy enjoying my blissful life that I failed to see the glaring signs. When Chanda tried pointing those to me I gave her a shut up call. But the seed was sown in my mind and I found myself looking for something that would prove her claims right. And then I was amazed at my gullibility for being so oblivious. It was so obvious. I started understanding why Kailash would insist on spending more time with Sharmishtha and her family, than our other friends. But there were never any innuendoes between the two that would have looked out of the ordinary. They both behaved most normally, but then, now that I recall, they didn't talk much from the beginning only. He would be respectable and polite towards Mishthi and she would be as normal as any girl would be with a friend who she knew before marriage. I admired their capability and will power to exercise such restraint even when both must have been dying to be alone with each other. But as far as my memory goes, they were always around and never tried to sneak off or do any such frivolous things lovers often do.

But then I understood that their love was as special as it comes. It had transcended above the physical and had become something akin to spiritual. It was as if they knew that they would always be together in spirit, today and a thousand years later. I must admit that though I envied their love, I was in awe of it. But I was as human as anyone could be. I would have probably forgiven Kailash, had he told me the truth right from the beginning. My love for him might not have been as great as Mishthi's, but I had loved him enough to forgive and forget. Only if he had told me the truth, I would have dealt with his love for Sharmishtha and Shivani, but I could not deal with pity and the leftover crumbs that he threw at me and my daughter. He was smothering me with his kindness and greatness, accepting and making my mental problem his own. I just could not take his charity.

So finding out about Shivani was the last straw. And from that day onwards I started plummeting. And when this time, I met Lieutenant Edmund, I embraced him. At least there was someone who loved me. How did it matter where he was from? How did it *matter whether he was from this world or the world beyond? At least he was there to give me his shoulder to cry on and wipe my tears. The envy, which must have formed on the very first day I had laid my eyes on Sharmishtha, became bigger than my existence. It was foolish of me to have told myself all those years that Kailash was not affected by her beauty. Who was I trying to fool? How could I have been so naïve? My life probably would have taken a different course, had I not been so blinded by his love.*

I saw him looking at Shivani with such love that it broke my heart for my little girl. She had to compete with Shivani for her father's love. Her father's love should have been hers and hers alone. Last night, I was with Lieutenant Edmund and he told me that I should not allow Sharmishtha and her daughter in my house. And when I told Kailash not to bring them to the Haveli, he got upset. I had never seen him getting angry with me or Shelly ever. But last night he was angry and he told me that I was being self-centred and cruel. Sharmishtha had lost her grandmother and he wanted her to come to the Haveli for a few days, as she had to go back to Asanpur again to settle some property matters. I had loved him with all my heart even though my love was not reciprocated. I never complained when he cancelled plans with other friends in order to spend time with Sharmishtha and her family, and yet he was calling me selfish. Chanda was right; that woman had put some spell on him. She'd cheated on her husband and yet she was the epitome of virtue for him. I had thought of writing a letter to her husband telling him about Shivani, but then Chanda stopped me. She was right. Her husband was too besotted with her. She had put a spell on him as well. What if he'd show the letter to Kailash? Kailash would hate me as long as I would live. So no, I didn't want his hatred. I wanted his love.

And last night was the culmination of my tribulation. Kailash was including Shivani in his will. When I asked him how he could do that, he simply told me that though the major portion of his wealth would go to Shelly, he wanted to leave a substantial amount for Shivani too.

'But Shivani's father is financially well off. They have lands and property,' I reasoned.

'Yes I know! That's why I am giving her only a small share,' he replied calmly.

'But why? What right does she have?

'She is my daughter,' he said looking into my eyes.

Though, of late, it was no longer a secret between us, yet his words sliced me like a sharp knife. There was so much propriety and determination in his eyes that I knew I had lost this battle with him forever.

'She is your bastard child,' I said, grinding my teeth.

He left the room in a huff and I screamed at him and threw a book at him. Later, still seething with anger, I opened the window as I needed some fresh air and then I saw her walking through the garden below the window, towards the grove. She was going to meet him. Why else would she go out in this bad weather? And then this thought struck me. I could catch them red handed just as they would be having their romantic tête-à-tête. I would humiliate them by catching them in their despicable little act.

'Go! This is your chance.' Lieutenant Edmund was standing beside me. I did not want anyone to see me, so I went down the stairs cautiously. There was no one around and I sneaked out through the service door under the stairs. It had started pouring. I went through the path through the bushes that was a shortcut, as I wanted to reach before her and hide. The thorns and the branches cut me and I was bleeding, but I didn't care. And as I reached and hid behind the neem tree, I heard the tinkle of her bangles. It was very dark and the rain was falling in torrents. I stood there for a moment and then something came over me. Here was the woman who had stolen my love, my happiness, and now her daughter was stealing my daughter's rightful legacy. How could I let her do this to me? And then Edmund's voice spoke in my head.

'This is your chance. Don't let it go.'

And then I just did what he kept telling me to do. It was only when she was falling into the river; that lightning flashed and she looked directly into my eyes. And I knew that she was going to haunt me for as long as I lived. I was lying huddled and crying when Chanda found me. I did not remember what happened after that. But she brought me back home and changed my clothes and after that I did not remember anything. I kept hearing her voice, telling me that I had to keep quiet and not tell anyone of what had happened. I had to do that for the sake of my daughter.

'Please, please think of Shelly. Her father has another daughter but Shelly has only you. So you are not going to say anything about it to anyone. Promise me.' And as I drifted into a drug-induced sleep I made a promise, for Shelly's sake.

I have come thousands of miles away from that blasted Haveli, yet she is here with me looking at me with her cold eyes. She torments me. She comes and stands next to me. She has done something to Edmund because he no longer comes to soothe me. I keep calling his name but he has vanished into thin air. I cannot go on like this. There is only one solution left. She cannot torment me if I am with her. Yes, I think she wants that. So be it. I am coming to be with you Mishthi.

CHAPTER 37

Kailash

I had always known, but I needed to hear it from Mishthi. Shivani is my daughter; I knew it the instant I saw her for the first time. There was this magnetic pull that a parent feels towards his offspring. It was the same love that I feel for Shelly. My heart fills up with such love and pride when I look at her. Not only has she taken her mother's looks, but she also has a brilliant mind. And she is the sweetest, most well brought up child I ever came across. I would always have this regret that I would never be able to call her my daughter. How I wish I could do that. But it was best for everyone this way. Kanti is a thorough gentleman, and I could see that he was crazily in love with his wife and adored Shivani. I would never take that from him. He deserves Mishthi's and Shivani's love.

But of late, things have been a little tense in our household. Sue had suddenly started behaving strangely. In the beginning, she used to like to meet Mishthi and her family, but later she started coming up with excuses. Something was going on and I was sure her companion had been whispering some nonsense into her ears. I never liked Chanda. She always tried to show her right over Sue. And I knew she was a bit crafty. I had noticed her looking at Mishthi and Shivani with disdain. Was it she who was filling Sue's ears with poison? I wanted to ask Sue. The time had come to address the elephant in the room. It was important that I told her everything before she heard it from someone else. I hoped fervently that she would understand. I wanted to tell her that I had fallen in love with Mishthi much before I had met her. And had it not been for the rigidity of our parents, I would have married her. But it was all in the past. I wanted to assure her that

I was her husband and the father to our daughter now. And I loved them both a lot.

But before I could find a chance to talk to her, all hell broke loose. Apparently her confidante and companion Chanda had been snooping around, and I had a feeling she had been going through my stuff in the study. I had written a note for Mishthi and locked it in the drawer, as I could not get a suitable opportunity to give it to her. I found the note missing. And then it seemed she probably read the letter I wrote to my solicitors, to make a trust fund for Shelly and Shivani.

Sue started screaming at me when I entered the room. I tried to calm her down but she kept shouting and crying. Under the circumstances, it was only best that I left her alone for some time. But I couldn't contain my anger when she called Shivani my bastard child. So I said certain things I was not supposed to say. She threw a book at me as I walked out of the room.

Mishthi is gone. And the world is over for me. I must end my life and join her because I cannot imagine a life without her. Why did she go to the river bank?

I knew that Mishthi was sad about her grandmother, but then she had accepted it and was recovering from it. She was looking forward to going back to Lucknow. There was no way she would have committed suicide, as some people are suggesting. But something has been nagging at my conscience. I have this feeling that someone or something is responsible for this. I want to scream and tell them that someone is responsible for this. But I have no proof. My uncle tells me that nothing could be achieved out of this. I know he is trying to save the family name and wants this whole thing to blow over.

'You have to think of Shelly and Suchitra,' he said.

'There is nothing left between Suchitra and me,' I said. 'From now on we are on separate paths,' I told him and shut the door on him.

They have interrogated everyone, and as it turns out, no one saw her leaving that day. Sue has been exempted by the police from the interrogation as her doctor has declared her mentally confused at the moment. The case has been closed as an accident, on my uncle's behest.

Bua and uncle have taken control of everything and nothing is making any sense to me. What am I missing? I want to end my life but the innocent and tear-streaked face of Shelly is stopping me from doing that. Sue has almost gone mad. She has lost her mental balance. My parents would soon be here to take her to Delhi. Shelly is clinging to me and doesn't want to be with Sue. I will have to live for Shelly. I can't deprive her of the love of at least one parent. And then there is Shivani. I might be able to live for the sake of both my daughters. But one thing is for sure, the day they both grow up and become independent, I will join Mishthi. Till then, I will only be alive in body, as my soul will be with Mishthi.

Chapter 38

'So *Amma*, now you know that it was not grandmother who was responsible for Sharmishtha's death,' I said.

'How does that absolve her from what she did? Why did she send the note to her? It was she who sent her to the river by sending that note. She must have planned something for her! So how can I believe that she had nothing to do with it? And how can I be sure that she was not planning to murder her by throwing her into the river?' *Amma* asked wearily.

I was quiet. Frankly speaking, there was no answer to that. Was it possible that Chanda wanted to get rid of Sharmishtha, but fate had probably played a different role? Suchitra might have seen Sharmishtha going for the rendezvous, and the hatred and anger that had been building in her mind for some time, drove her to do what she did.

'Do you think Chanda forged the note in Kailash's handwriting? She could speak and write English,' Jason said when we were alone in my room. Anand was coming home and we were waiting for him.

'Or she stole the note. She had easy access to everything,' I said.

'So do you feel any different now that you know that you are a rebirth?'

'I am feeling very light, as if a big burden has been lifted from my soul. Ever since I came here and saw the Haveli and *Phulwari*, I felt tired and emotionally drained, as if I were living in two timelines. But I am glad it's all over. Now I just want us to leave this place and go on with our lives.'

'Did you actually feel the presence and see the apparition in the Haveli?' Jason asked.

'Yes I did! There was no ambiguity there.'

'And what could that mean?' Jason asked.

'I don't know. Maybe her soul never left the Haveli, and when I went there, she probably wanted to apologise to me for her actions. Mind you, she never tried to scare me. In fact, when I saw her in the lobby, I could see sadness and helplessness in her eyes.' I sighed.

'Are you going to tell Anand? He was a bit worried when I told him that you were feeling a little under the weather yesterday, before your regression. He wanted to see you but didn't press. But I think he was not convinced with the excuse I gave him. I thought you should know.'

'I don't know Jason. Do you think he would believe me if I told him?'

'I think he would. It's very clear that he is in love with you. He might find this whole thing a little fantastical, but knowing that you are a successful psychiatrist, he would have no doubt on your sanity,' Jason said, smiling. 'Moreover, I think you should tell him everything and leave it to him to believe or not. Your relationship should not be based on any secrets.'

'I think you are right,' I said.

I narrated the whole thing to Anand. He listened without interrupting.

'So that's why you had gone to *Phulwari* that day and then you just blanked out.'

'Yes! After finding the note, the image of *Phulwari* sprang to my mind, though the note said to meet at the 'usual place'. The only explanation is that my subconscious mind probably thought of *Phulwari*, because that was the place that held very pleasant memories for them. At least now I know it was where she met him after her marriage, and that was the place where Shivani was conceived.'

'And the other day, when you fainted in the Haveli, you saw the apparition of my grandmother?'

'Yes! I know it all must sound quite bewildering to you but it is what it is.'

'You should have told me everything. You went through so much and you did not tell me anything especially when it involved my own family.'

'I wanted to; so many times. But we were getting to know each other and then to tell you about all this... it just felt weird. I mean, I first wanted to make sure that whatever I was feeling had some substance. That's why I went through the regression process, despite Jason's reluctance, because I wanted to make sense of this whole thing. I needed answers.'

'And before coming to the village, you did not have any memory flashes?'

'No! I think it all got triggered once I saw the Haveli.'

'I admit that I always felt an overwhelming sense of sorrow in the Haveli that I could never understand. It's so strange to hear all this about my family from you. My mother never ever talked about anything. I mean, she did talk about my grandfather who had passed away before I was born, and I was told that she had lost her mother when she was very young. This is all so surreal. I mean, there was such history with my grandparents and I didn't know anything.' Anand was lost in his own thoughts.

'Anand, there is one more thing that I have to do.'

'Yeah, tell me,' he said, coming out of his reverie.

'I want to go to the Haveli. And I want to know whether I would still feel the presence,' I said looking at him.

'You are most welcome to come any time. But are you sure you want to do this? I mean, shouldn't you just let it go?' he asked.

'I have to do this just once. It's something I want to do before we all leave this place.'

'Let's all have dinner then. Now you rest. You have gone through a trying experience. Though given a choice, I would like to be with you and not leave you even for a moment,' he said kissing my forehead. 'And Aparna!' He paused. 'I am sorry for what my grandmother did to you,' he said, looking at me with utmost affection.

'I have finally found you for keeps. So I guess it was all worth it,' I said.

'You don't mean that I...,' he asked, not completing the sentence.

'I am sure, to quite an extent. How else do I explain the deep connection I felt with you the moment I saw you for the first time, and not to mention your uncanny resemblance to your grandfather?'

'Then thank you for coming into my life again. I am not going to let you go this time. That's a solemn promise,' he said kissing me, and I felt the same sensation I had felt in my dreams.

We both were still hugging each other when Jason knocked and came inside.

'What did I miss?' he asked, looking at us and smiling.

Jason and I reached the Haveli just after dusk.

'I have made arrangements on the terrace. We will have drinks there and then move to the dining room for dinner. Is that ok?' Anand asked me.

I nodded as there was a kind of nervousness that was unsettling. We went to the terrace. In spite of the grim purpose that was on my mind, the terrace looked beautiful with candles and fairy lights. It almost looked cheerful. We sat down and Anand poured us drinks. The soothing strain of jazz were emitting from the portable Bose and the atmosphere became more romantic. I gulped down my drink in order to settle my nerves. Anand poured me another. If he noticed my nervousness, he didn't comment. All three of us kept making conversation, though there was a slight strain in the atmosphere. And then I smelled the familiar scent. I got up as if a little mesmerised, and walked to the far end of the terrace.

'Suchitra, is it you?' The words came out in a whisper. There was a rustle of silk and the scent became stronger. 'All I want to say is that I forgive you. There is no point keeping any malice in our hearts. I have travelled through the times to be with him again and that's what matters now. So go and find peace.'

Suddenly the scent became overpowering, and I felt as if I would choke, but then it slowly started fading, and after a moment or two, it was gone. I felt as if some sort of weight had lifted from my soul. I walked up to the men sitting and pretending to have a conversation while looking at me worriedly.

'Anand, shouldn't we shift to the dining room now? I think it's time for dinner,' I said smiling.

Jason left for England after visiting the Taj Mahal. I stayed in Lucknow for two weeks, organising passports and visas for *Amma*, *Chachi* and Kamla. The house and the lands in the village, were sold. Rajat sent some people to do the needful and they were very helpful. Anand came to Lucknow with us and then left for Delhi to close the deal for the Haveli.

When I reached Delhi to board my flight that was scheduled for the next day, he came to the airport to receive me. Rajat teased me when I told him that Anand would be receiving me.

And then Anand asked me out for dinner that night, and proposed to me on the rooftop of this five star hotel, under the stars.

There were a lot of things that we had to work out. Anand had planned to move to England in due course but he had to take care of his business in America. Also, he was bringing his son to meet me in few weeks.

Epilogue

I saw a big smile on Kamla's face the moment she spotted me at Heathrow airport. She bent and told *Amma* and *Amma* looked at me, her face brightening. At last I was able to persuade her to come to England for some time. Jason came with me to receive them. I drove with *Amma* and Jason drove Kamla and *Chachi* home.

Amma was beaming as she knew that Anand and I were betrothed. I smiled with pleasure as she talked to me while I drove and told her about the places we were driving through.

I stood at the French window of my office looking at the familiar scenery outside. It was early October and soon the trees would lose their lustre with the oncoming winters. But come spring, they would regain it, bearing fruits and flowers. That was how the universe worked. Every animate being had to follow the cycle; the cycle of birth and decay, endings and beginnings. I too had been a part of the cycle: I had endured the ending and now it was time to enjoy a new beginning. I smiled as the image of Anand leapt into my mind.

'Dr. Chat, here is your tea.' I turned and saw Cathy bringing a steaming cup of tea.

'Thank you, Cathy.'

'By the way,' she stopped at the door, 'There is a...'

My heart missed a beat.

'Are you alright? I was saying there is a delivery scheduled for today, for the new kettle we ordered.'

'Oh, of course, I said quickly and looked at the screen of my laptop, pretending to be busy. I laughed inwardly about my nervous reaction. There would be no letter as *Amma*, Kamla and *Chachi* were with me now and I intended to keep them with me for as long as I could. The phone beeped and I saw Anand's handsome face on the screen. I forgot about everything as I heard his deep voice. I could not have imagined being so in love a few months back. I silently thanked God for the letter that had come three months back and had put me on a path that had ended for me in finding love.

351

GLOSSARY

PROLOGUE

Raat ki Rani – Night blooming jasmine

Neem – Margosa tree

Phulwari – A garden with a variety of flowers

Apsara – Nymph

Kurta – A loose collarless shirt worn by males in South Asia

CHAPTER 1

Mukhia – Village head

Chacha – Uncle

Chachi – Aunt

Didi – Sister

Dadi – Grandmother

Amma – Mother

Kaka – Uncle

Kaki – Aunt

Namaste – A form of greeting in India

CHAPTER 2

Angan – Courtyard

Vadi - Dried lentils with spices

Aloo – Potato

Arhar daal – Yellow lentils

Chapati – Indian flat bread

Ghee – Clarified butter

Chouka – Kitchen

Chulha – An earthen stove used in the villages in India

Bitia – Daughter

Jiji – Elder sister

Bhaiya – Elder brother

CHAPTER 3

Ghonghat – A part of the sari used to cover the face, like a veil

Takht – A big wooden bed

Bhabhi – Sister-in-law

Behen – Sister

Baba Saheb – A form of address for the son of the family

Baba – Father

Kheer – A sweet dish made with rice and milk

Poori - Indian deep fried flat bread

Ghusal khana – Bathroom

Arey – Hey

Ladoo – An orb-shaped sweet

Chiristaan – Slang for England used in the villages of India

Choti Baby Saheb – Younger daughter

Mem Saheb – A colonial form of address for a British lady

Taluqdar – An Indian landhoder in the Mughal Empire and the British

Raj

Khansama – Cook

CHAPTER 4

Rasaje – A curried dish made with gram flour

Saheb – A colonial form of address for a gentleman or master

Firangi – A foreigner, especially a British or white person

Baby Saheb – A form of address for the daughter of the family

CHAPTER 5

Aloo ki sabzi – A dish made by frying potatoes

Khichdi – A dish made with lentils and rice

Dalia – Porridge

CHAPTER 6

Lehenga – A long skirt worn by women in India

Chunni – A long scarf worn with a lehenga or other Indian outfits

Dai Ma – Nanny

Lala Ji – A form of address to the husband's younger brother

Gulal – A dry colour used in the Hindu festival, Holi

Sari – A 5-yard long piece of clothing worn by Indian women

Pooja – A prayer or Hindu ritual in honour of the Gods

CHAPTER 7

Munim Ji – A secretary

Ajoo – A form of address for paternal grandmother

CHAPTER 8

Nanoo – A form of address for maternal grandmother

Halwa – A dessert made with semolina and dry fruits

Bua – Aunt

Malmal Chunni – Muslin scarf

Baithak – Parlour or a lounge

Diwan – A wooden couch

Masnad – A bolster

Bhoj – A feast

Kachori – A kind of flat bread filled with mashed lentils and deep fried

Kulfi – An Indian dessert made by freezing milk

CHAPTER 9

Dussehra – A major Hindu festival

Jhankis – Tableau

CHAPTER 10

Bibi Ji – A form of address for the mistress of the house

Boondi Raita – A preparation of curd with chick pea floor

Gulab Jamun – A sweet dish

Babu Saheb – A form of respectful address for a male

Missi Baba – A colonial form of address for a young girl

CHAPTER 12

Chote Babu – Young master

CHAPTER 13

Karwa Chauth – A Hindu festival, where wives traditionally fast for the health and long lives of their husbands.

Mehendi – Henna

Saleema – Slang for cinema

Bahu ji – A form of respectful address for the mistress of the house

Hukka – Hookah

Shehzada – A royal prince

Thali – A round dish

CHAPTER 14

Phalgun – The name of a month according to the Hindu calender

Tollees – Groups of people

Ghujiya – A pastry made with milk solids

Bhang – A drink of cannabis mixed with milk and dry fruits

Ubtan – Body scrub

CHAPTER 15

Gori – A white girl

CHAPTER 16

Rudraksh Mala – A seed used as a prayer bead in Hinduism

Mausi – Aunt

CHAPTER 17

Sadhu – Hermit

Kaitha – Wood apple

Jaap – A religious chanting

CHAPTER 18

Zardozi – A type of heavy metal embroidery

Barat – Wedding procession

CHAPTER 19

Gudia and Raksha bandhan – Hindu festivals

Jalebis – Deep fried Indian dessert

Samosas – Deep fried pastry filled with potatoes

Ghaghra – A long voluminous skirt worn by Indian women

CHAPTER 21

Bageecha – A garden

Nadi Maiya – The river goddess

Bhauji – Sister-in-law

CHAPTER 22

Navik – Boatman

Vaidya – Ayurvedic doctor

Beta – Child

CHAPTER 28

Haldi – Turmeric

Pheras – Vows taken around the fire in an Indian wedding

CHAPTER 33

Jamai Bhaiya – A form of address for son-in-law

Kannauj – A city in Uttar Pradesh

CHAPTER 34

Lathi – Wooden rod

CHAPTER 35

Shikar - Hunt

Ajia – Paternal grandmother